J.R. VAINEO

Hunt the Dragon Within

The Journals of Ravier, Volume II

Tara Jean Hurst Shewmake
"Do your best, and learn the lessons life has to teach."
December 1983 - January 2016

Death and goodbyes . . . yes, they are always unfair.
Dear sister I longed to get to know,
we miss ya down here!
This story, I had wished to share with you.
But it will never be. And that is finally okay with me.
Rest well, dance lots, and fly above the sorrow.
You've completed this journey called: Life.

Contents

Acknowledgement

Special thanks to some people who made this book possible.

J. VaineoHurst, for always being a listening ear; encouraging the continuation of the story, even when it was hard; and being an all-round good guy. Life is better with a partner. I'm glad it's you.

M. Gray, for being an amazing editor. Ever so patient with all questions and concerns. She's a super editor. Up there, with the greats! I can never thank her enough for being tougher on my writing, making me grow as a writer.

T. Barber, of Dissect Designs, for crafting absolutely stunning book covers. His work is that final, breathtaking detail that brings the story to life before the first page is even read. He really outdid himself, with this second cover. Can't wait to see what the third brings.

Lastly, **Wendy Wahlsten Vaineo**, for becoming one of the most loving, persevering people I know. For being truthful, even when it's hard. You are a beautiful soul, and the world needs more of that.

Here's to living an incredible life. Cheers!

Summation of Volume I:

« Kings of Muraine »

Tyler Malik Ravier grieves the loss of his father, Lance. It has been a year since his death. The new reality has set in, and it's crushing Tyler. He wonders how he'll be able to bear it. Over dinner that night, his mother, Amira, gives him the gift Lance had intended on giving the year before: the black-and-gold diver's watch. Tyler has no sooner set it to the current time, that night of his fourteenth birthday, when he finds himself falling fast asleep. His senses are starting to sharpen.

He startles awake, when a creature screeches in the night. After he spots darting lights passing the forest edge, near his home, he knows he must go investigate what it is. With that one decision everything begins to change for Tyler.

Two strangers have arrived from another world: Muraine. To his shock, Tyler learns that Muraine is where his father was from. The land of Paragon, specifically. Talok and Ryco have brought him LanSoren's dragon-horse, Awngeleik. Still young and brash, she's in grave danger on Muraine. The Vitiosyn King, Zymarc, demands that she be given over. But these Paragonians refuse to do so. Tyler doesn't understand *why* they refuse. At first, he doesn't care much either. He's simply consumed with the anger that his father never confessed the truth to him, while living. And, now, Tyler's given the task of finding his father's hidden belongings, while also tending to Awngeleik. What could go wrong?

Much, it seems. Tyler discovers that his hated classmate *and* nearest neighbor, Gemma Galloway, somehow plays a part in all this. She's desperate for a chance to make up for her unkind actions of the prior year. Gemma wants to change. Tyler doesn't believe that she can. Yet, her knowledge of things he's ignorant of, things to do with Muraine and his father's last words, make Tyler hesitate in pushing her away completely. Then there's the plight of Gemma procuring pictures of Awngeleik, swimming in the lake surrounded by forest, near Tyler's home. He must hide Awngeleik's existence. He must steal those pictures. He must destroy the evidence. No one else must ever know about the dragon-horse.

What started out as a task of stealing and lying and sneaking around, however, leads Tyler into the beginnings of a truce. A friendship with Gemma Galloway. She tells Tyler of a particular person she imagined, when she was a child. His name was Soren. Tyler recalls the two strangers calling his father by the name LanSoren. He thinks his father may have been this *Soren* Gemma's talking about. Then Tyler discovers Soren's full name: Soren of the Monel. There's a painting of him, hidden away in Lance's study. Soren's face is blacked-out in the image, and a phrase—*'Thirteen. You're done.'*—is painted in red over it. Also featured in the painting with Soren is Adair Tomatsu Galloway, Gemma's great-grandfather.

More truth starts unfolding, when two King's Guard of Talok's come to check on Tyler. Musgrae and Ben tell Tyler that the portal's been broken for six months on Muraine. Somehow, only days have passed on Earth. It baffles the lot of them. The two guards also seem distressed over the news that a star creature—a Vardiya, which Tyler and his mother caught at the lake—has died. They also don't much like the fact that a beast was hunting Awngeleik, just moments before their visit. Neither Tyler nor Gemma saw it. But they felt it. Tyler sensed the power coursing in its body too. He craved whatever it had to give, yet he had no idea why. These feelings of his, he keeps to himself long after the incident. The beast had almost happened upon where Tyler and Gemma were hidden. There to distract it was Tyler's unseen—and unknown—protector. The two creatures ran off, leaving Tyler and Gemma free to get Awngeleik to safety. They relay all of that to Musgrae and Ben.

Even after traveling to Muraine, to The Eye of Paragon, still, no one has an answer for Tyler and Gemma. Nor an answer for whom the unseen protector could be. Also in question is the matter to do with his father's sister, Miriam. Tyler's never met her, yet she sends birthday cards every year, without fail. Despite this, he's told by Talok that she died many years ago. And why does no one know the real cause of LanSoren's death? Things just aren't lining up.

It's a whirlwind of events, shortly after they make it to Muraine. Tyler helps to save a Keeper of Memories from dying. But not without consequence. He's able to make a quick recovery, and is then given a special coat his father helped to design with a Vaegon woman named Madeleine. King Talok recognizes the coat's design as the Sleeping Dragon. Gemma, as well, is fitted with new clothes. The two of them are quickly fitting in, with the habitants of Eyo'el; even a sad girl, who's possibly lost both of her parents in the attack earlier that morning, makes fast friends with them.

Both Tyler and Gemma have been cleared to stay for two days by Zepharre, and Talok's other advisers, while the Paragonians celebrate their yearly festival, the Withrasyn-Vaegon Festival. This year's different in Eyo'el, however. With their King ReNovak, Gyronawv and the Onyx Warriors are there to perform in the celebration. The last time they were a part of it was centuries ago. Back when Zymarc was a young Onyx Warrior, the favored one of ReNovak, *before* he became the feared King of Vitiosus. It seems, his power is growing. Yet he honors the Rules of Engagement. He gives the Paragonians one last festival, one last chance to hand over the dragon-horse. But war is brewing.

The first night of the festival concludes, after Siveyra Gyronawv—Warrior of the Nyxane—summons Soren of the Monel. Tyler's quick to regret his taunting request of King ReNovak to have Soren summoned. The Sorsryn of Old is more powerful than most. And he's on the hunt for Gemma Galloway. He's obsessed with her, really, and none are sure as to why. What is so different about the Galloway family? Sure, Adair was Soren's apprentice long ago. But was that all? Is there something different about Gemma? In fact, different about all the Galloways in Gemma's lineage?

Tyler has little time to think on the many questions piling up. In the early-morning hours of the celebration's second day, the Vitiosyns strike. It's chaos, during the mad dash to escape the Castle of Sosha. They wish to escape the city, but it's too late. They're forced to stay, to take shelter in the bunkers below the city.

Before heading to the bunkers, Talok commands his King's Guard to protect Tyler and Gemma. He means to create a ceasefire, by offering himself in place of Awngeleik. Against the others' wishes, Talok abandons them to head for more dangerous ground: the forefront of the attack. An Emerald Sorsryn, by the name of Rozeth, takes the Paragonian King there. Hours pass. Khyra, the City Architect, is wounded badly. But Madeleine suffers a bleaker outcome. She nearly dies from her injuries. Members of the King's Guard, Quall and Kent, relay the awful truth that she will most definitely have to relearn everything. Only Tyler's whispered commands to her—to forget the past, forget the pain—save Madeleine from losing everything. But she loses eight years of her memories. What mystery she had about her aura is gone too. Bright and happy, but confused, it seems that Madeleine will survive the worst. But will Talok? He manages to arrange for the Vitiosyns to call a ceasefire. His consequence is to be marked for death. His death will come slowly. At the end of twenty-two days, King Talok of Paragon will die, unless Awngeleik is relinquished to Zymarc.

Tyler is brave to some, and stupid to others, for breaking the Rules of Engagement. With the Paragonians behind him, and the Vitiosyn line in front, he steps onto the forbidden space of ground and demands that Talok be given over to him. The Paragonians have lost out on being named the Onyx Victor. It is a title the Vitiosyns have won, instead. But there's still time to think of a plan, time to save Talok, and opportunities to keep Awngeleik hidden. It's all because Siveyra Gyron was able to procure the twenty-two days for them.

The Onyx Sorsryns are neutral. Their allegiance must be won. Their prospective ally's worth must be proven. And the Vitiosyns have proven their worth, with the work of a spy placed among the Paragonians. Gyron has no choice, but to side with the Vitiosyns. Though he's fallen for a Greyvon ally of Paragon, Rorka of Pariah, there's nothing he can do but obey a new master. And that new master is Zymarc of Vitiosus, by proxy of King ReNovak, who has mysteriously skipped out on giving the verdict in Eyo'el. No one's seen him since the night of the festival. Where could he have gone?

Tensions rise, when the spy's identity is revealed. Tyler duels this spy, this traitor to his heart, as a means to make Zymarc and his Vitiosyns leave for a time. What starts out as a duel is interrupted by the Greyvon Alpha, Jasper. He missed the festival. Now, the commotion of his arrival in Eyo'el is enough to stop Tyler and the Vitiosyn spy from killing each other. During this pause in the fight, something shocks Tyler. He's taken back through time to see his father. Lance is tending to the Arkivara of Trauvo, a place where memories are kept, when he notices Tyler there with him. He hardly believes it.

There's much conversation. Tyler gets some answers. He also gets to hear his father's goodbye. Against his will, Tyler is thrust back into the present. Someone follows him through. As the city of Eyo'el starts coming back into focus, Tyler sees Talok, still looking defeated. Zymarc gazes on, in victory. Then there's Alpha Jasper appearing fearful, as the intruder behind him fades into focus. It is Soren of the Monel, elated to have found his way to the present time. Seeing the ill intent in Soren's gaze, Tyler is certain he means to kill someone. But whom? Find out, in **Hunt the Dragon Within**.

Prologue: Across the Pages of Time

"What!" I seethe. "You've hidden magic in more than three people?"

Pursing his lips in a guilty manner, he answers with one word: "Maybe."

Sounding like Jed, I complain, "You've got to be joking. That's messed up."

"It's hard, Tyler," he defends. "Outsmarting a Sorsryn of Old, among others. It requires being more crafty. Let's hope I was successful, in outsmarting him."

I sigh. "What do I have to do?"

"For now? Wake up and remember a piece of what I made you forget."

"And that would be?"

"When you wake up," he states, half-chuckling, "you will know."

Indignant, I cross my arms. "Then I'm ready."

He smirks. "You're ready? Ready to trust all that I've laid out for your journey to truth?"

"Yes. But one *last* question, before I go? Will I like the end?"

"I've made many preparations, to ensure the best for you, but no one can be sure of your end. Ultimately, it's up to you to forge your fate. Goodbye, Tyler."

I whisper, "I don't want to say goodbye."

In good humor, he replies, "Then don't. But be sure to tell that cousin of yours, he'll be a mighty King of Muraine one day. As was his father, Sosha. Especially with you at his side."

"I will." I grin. But the sight of dim light withering into the blackened canvas tears away my joy. Like a ghost, my father's fingers start slipping away.

Tears pour down his face like rain. Yet he stands tall and proud, while watching me fade away. Between us, the distance widens to a black ocean. Reaching out to me, he echoes across the expanse: *Think of this moment we share, as both of us reaching out across the pages of time.*

Cherishing every moment, I echo.

He continues, *Hoping for brighter days to come.*

Love is lost in the sea of time, I echo. Readying myself, I wave goodbye.

But reason and resolve can mend it all, he finishes.

"Wake up, Tyler," he commands, and I'm summoned to close my eyes. When they open, only the misty black greets me. Then faces start emerging.

On my right is Talok, his face etched with brokenness.

In front of me is Jasper of Pariah. No longer in wolf form, he stands as tall as Quall. His garb is likened to the colors of his fur: mostly black, with gray and some white. Two leather belts are crossed over his chest in an *X*. Dark fur accentuates in all the right places, giving way to the truth that he's still a beast. He stands as a simple warrior, with a single weapon upon his belt. Yet his short hair of pepper-gray is frazzled. His gaze has lost that confidence too. His eyes now dance with fear.

But what fear? I wonder. *For Paragon, me, or* of *me? Who can know?*

On the left is Zymarc, reappearing, as he adjusts his coat. He then leisurely stuffs his hands in his pockets. Victory is in his gaze, fixed on me. And it unsettles me.

More unsettling, however, is a fourth face emerging one step behind Jasper. Shifting from the back of Jasper's head to my face is his murderous gaze. There he stands like a demon. The feared-four-words made flesh. Soren of the Monel. He has hold of my father's daggers, as he leans over Jasper's shoulder. Maliciously, he speaks two words: "Thirteen. Done."

I

Shut the Way Home

"We're always doing something, Tyler," he says.
"You were walking just now.
Then you stopped. Most likely,
you sensed me sleeping . . .
My presence. Did it make you uneasy?"

1

The Face of Terror

Bleak colors gone, the shamrock-grass of Paragon comes into focus. The scene before me brightens. Passed out in the field of Midnight Anemones, with her wrists still bleeding, is Caleiso. At her side, I sit crumpled. The tall flowers partially hide me from him.

Soren, clothed in a coat of white and black, takes hold of Jasper's shoulders. Whirling round, he tosses the Greyvon Alpha into a circular prison-box appearing out of nowhere.

Stunned into a trance of terror, Paragonians and Vitiosyns stare at the commotion. Only Zymarc looks on, unfazed, as though Soren is one of his misbehaving Vitiosyns, such as Belzara.

When Jasper scrambles up to take hold of the iron bars, they seem to melt into the next bar. He pulls away. The prison flashes a solid black. It then goes clear. Jasper presses his palms against the invisible prison then smashes his fists on it before thrashing his body against it.

The prison refuses to crack.

Breaths ragged, Jasper calls out, "What is this? Another dimension?"

Reverberating, Soren laughs maniacally like the demon he is. "How does it feel? With no Great LanSoren to save any of you?"

"Jasper!" Rorka shouts, about to dash out from the frontline of Paragon.

Paragonian onlookers lose their trance of terror. They're ready to follow Rorka onto the expanse of bloodstained grass.

Soren's murderous grin ends. He rushes for the Paragonian line. "Not one step forward, little sunset." He points my father's sleeping-dagger at Rorka. "For the first to step is the first to die by my hands."

One bound away from the formation, Soren slashes into the empty distance. Save for Talok and his guards standing strong, the Paragonians rebound. Behind Talok is Gemma, looking on in fear. She's starting to tremble.

"Who shall it be?" queries Soren. "The first to step, and break *my* Rules of Engagement? Paragonians? I think not. Vitiosyns?" He gasps. Amusement in his eyes, his gaze locks on to Zymarc. "There! Zymarc. King of Vitiosus! It has been too long, little Onyx, since last I saw your face. The face of Vitiosus. Now covered by a special Geldryn mask, I see. Will *he* dare to approach?"

Soren holds the daggers at ease against his sides, and taunts Zymarc. His emerald gaze ridiculing, he beckons the Vitiosyn King to make the first move.

But Zymarc is undaunted. Relaxed, even. He still has his hands deeply buried inside his coat pockets. He takes three steps from his Vitiosyn line, saying, "I don't have to dare, to approach a ghost. You *are* dead." Waving one hand out, he continues, "You are an illusion. Though a good one."

Soren gives a thump of the waking-dagger's pommel to his chest. "After all these years, Zymarc, you think me an illusion? I *am* crushed."

Zymarc's free hand fiddles with his bronze mask. "You got your hands on one of the five unguarded Books of Time, most likely. Threatened a Metimora to teach you of its ways, I'm sure. But all Books of Time have limits. There can be no killing while you are using one. You know that, as well as I. So good ahead, Soren. Do your worst."

A silent chuckle shakes Soren's chest. He takes three long strides toward the Vitiosyn formation, and starts The Count of Despairion: "One, two, three."

"Yes, yes!" Zymarc interrupts. "The count goes. Four, five, then six." Zymarc rolls his free hand. Scoffing under his breath, he commands, "Continue."

A bound away from the Vitiosyns at the front, Soren sings out the words, "Why stop there?"

Talok? Ryco? Can anyone hear me? I echo, but get nothing in return.

"Seven." He strides, then drops the daggers.

When they hit the ground, my breath catches. It's an odd sensation. Almost as if someone's just jabbed me on the back. I look behind to Caleiso. She's barely coming to.

I focus on Soren again, as he's saying, "Eight." He then stops to eye a Vitiosyn woman, from the top of her mud-crusted boots to the crown of her shaved head.

Avoiding his gaze, the Vitiosyn squirms in place.

"But nine," says Soren, curiously lifting an eyebrow.

The woman meets his intent look. Her body quivers.

All curiosity fading, Soren smiles at her, saying the words, "Is best." In an instant, he plunges his now-clawed hand into her chest and out through the other side.

He tears his bloodied hand free of her.

She falls dead.

Horrified surprise takes hold of the Paragonians. Noise erupts from EquiNeins and BlacKaidyns. Even Vitiosyns and Vitasadyns cannot hold back their cries of alarm.

Ripping his other hand free of the pocket, Zymarc bolts forward a few steps. His escaping yell resonates out through the mask. His chest heaves up and down.

Talok and his guards draw their weapons. But they hesitate to advance, when Siveyra Gyronawv quickly signals a warning.

As Soren's occupied with studying his hand covered in dark Vitiosyn blood, Zymarc presses his palms together. One foot stepping forward, he briefly lowers his head. Then he waves his splayed-out hand toward his Vitiosyns, Gyron, and the Onyx Warriors. Wind rushes in front of them, tossing them to the safety of an expanse away from him. Away from the crazed Soren of the Monel, now licking blood off his fingertips.

He relishes the fear in Zymarc's eyes, while admitting, "Never did prefer the taste of Vitiosyn blood. Oh, but those Geldryn were quite the delicacy. Regardless, I'll take whatever I can get this day." Soren sighs. Then laughs. Then yells, practically snarling, "Amazing what illusions can do these days, isn't it? Zymarc of Vitiosus! Do you believe I'm here now?"

Zymarc rips his coat away, even as Soren is talking. It bursts into black-and-gray flames, shifting to frantic black doves trying to escape. They transform into a standing, lifeless, and dark figure.

Ignoring everything around him, Soren takes a white cloth from one of his coat pockets. He begins wiping the remaining blood off his hand.

Gyron rushes forward.

The Paragonians follow suit.

But Soren throws the bloodied cloth on the ground. Fire races from it, taking a vast, circular path. A wall of flames flares up, trapping Zymarc, Caleiso, and me. Jasper in his prison-box too. We're stuck within this makeshift arena created by the crazed Soren. It all happens in an instant. There are shouts; sounds of magic and weapons hitting the wall of flames too. Then the sounds cease.

Zymarc's now garbed as simply as an Onyx, with only two weapons strapped on his back—long-blades crossed in an X pattern. He casts a spell on the barrier, and it turns translucent. He then begins a tentative saunter toward Soren. Side-glancing at the Paragonian frontline, Zymarc speaks out: "King Talok of Paragon. Permission to hold the Rules of Engagement." He pauses. "So that I may subdue, one Soren of the Monel?" He grips the hilts next to his head. Slowly, he unsheathes the blades, all while he glares at Soren.

Talok, his eyes unblinking and bulging, replies, "You'd be doing us all a favor, if you did."

Ryco says something to Talok.

Then Talok is nodding frantically, shouting, "Yes! I release you of the rules, to subdue, even to kill the Withrasyn, Soren."

Zymarc yells an unknown word, and swiftly lunges for Soren. He swings one of his blades.

Soren shrinks the claws of his killing hand back into something less animalistic, while saying, "Now, Paragon, there must be no interference from you." Snapping his fingers, Soren summons the daggers to his grasp, and clangs one of them against Zymarc's blades.

Prismatic colors dance over the clashing, metallic edges. Some spark out, as would fire and liquid metal. Bright and loud, it's altogether powerful. The sounds travel in the air, before stopping to rattle inside my chest.

Zymarc's footfalls are quick and dodging. Soren's steps are smooth and planned. Rhythmic and sure, his forceful strikes push Zymarc back. It's apparent that Soren is all confidence and technique. At first, Zymarc merely defends against Soren's attacks. Then he begins his offense.

Soren doesn't try dodging. He takes the blows on his arms, chest, and legs. His coat and pants are cut with each slash, and his blood splatters across the ground. Yet he refuses to lessen his violent swings at Zymarc. As they go on, Soren's clothing weaves itself back together. Still, he bleeds. The fabric is thoroughly soaked with his blood, more adding to it by the minute.

With each scrape of their metal on metal, or Zymarc's magic absorbed into my father's daggers, my heart pounds harder in my chest. So hard, I barely hear anything but its beat. It seems to want to burst from my chest. It burns, then turns ice-cold.

Together, the Vitiosyn and Sorshrynak dance what appears to be a fight to the death. Slicing, stabbing, and kicking, they then burn or freeze the other.

Neither the victor yet, they heal their wounds in seconds.

More magic, they cast from their hands. They resort to lobbing chunks of the bloodstained ground at each other.

Still, I cannot move. I almost can't think. I'm frozen in place. Only free to watch the horror of Zymarc's stamina wavering at Soren's hand.

Gyron pounds on the barrier. Looking furious, he demands, "Zymarc! Get me in there, before he cuts your head off."

The lifeless form still stands where it was created.

Soren kicks Zymarc square on the ribs, and sends him hurling back. While Zymarc recovers his footing, Soren rushes for the form. He's about to take a swing at it. Zymarc's quick to sheathe both blades, and summon vines from the ground with magic seeping from his hands. Though Soren's fast, he's not swift enough to escape the entanglement of vines. Satisfied with his handiwork, Zymarc aims his hand, and speaks to the form: "Invitas-Gyronawv-el-Nyxane."

As Gyron replaces the lifeless form within the barrier, Soren cuts himself free of the vines and then burns them away. Outside of the barrier, the lifeless form stands where Gyron once was.

Courage rises with Gyron's presence. I stand up, to brush the loose dirt off my coat.

Zymarc catches sight of me. Alarm sinks into his crimson-red eyes.

Talok screams, "Tyler, what are you doing? Stay back! Let them handle it."

Soren sees Zymarc's distraction. He takes the opening, to swing the sleeping-dagger up toward Zymarc's face.

Gyron's too late, in knocking the King Vitiosyn out of the way.

The sleeping-dagger scrapes across Zymarc's metal mask, slightly damaging it, before it finds skin. It rips open flesh. The skin of Zymarc's forehead, to be exact.

Soren's laughter is cut short by Gyron coming at him, commencing a duel.

Facedown, Zymarc writhes on the ground. He presses on the mask, and it releases its hold on him. Gasping in several breaths, he holds his hands to his face. His forehead heals, and black hair grows to cover the tattoos etched upon Zymarc's scalp. Standing up, now taller than before, he turns around. His pale skin's gone. Darkened to match Soren's tone, he's still some shades lighter than I am. Lastly, his gaze of crimson turns green.

Aside from their clothes, the two stand identical.

That's when I think, *What's worse than seeing* one *Soren of the Monel? Zymarc of Vitiosus wearing his face.*

Soren ends his sneer at Gyron, caught in his stranglehold, to gawk at Zymarc now resembling him.

"Zymarc!" Soren laughs, in surprise. "Your gifts astound even me. I must thank you. I've wondered a long time, what it would be like . . . to watch the light go out of my eyes as I die. Now I will know, when I snuff the life from you." Soren throws Gyron down. Sprinting forward, he raises the sleeping-dagger above his shoulder. Menacing psychopath doesn't begin to describe the mad figure of Soren running, in this moment.

Gyron scrambles out of the way, coughing. He tries to catch his breath. Zymarc, calm and calculated, curls his body forward. Head bowed, he crosses his arms in an *X*. Uncrossing them, he holds his hands slightly up, as if preparing to brace for impact.

Soren is five strides from him, when he slams into an invisible wall. Dazed, the Sorshrynak stumbles back but quickly regains composure. His rhythm matching the Arkivara's rattling chorus of leaves, Soren begins stabbing Zymarc's barrier one dagger at a time. Holes are left behind, looking like broken, untempered glass.

Glancing up at the Arkivara, I can't help but wonder what I was supposed to remember. I look to Ryco, next to Talok, pummeling the wall with magic. Both Paragonians and Vitiosyns are attacking it, desperate to save those trapped within. I smile at their disregard for Soren's command not to interfere. That's when Ryco's words start surfacing. *Trust those daggers, Tyler. They were your father's, after all.*

Trust the daggers? I muse. *How can I, when they're in Soren's grasp?*

I snap my fingers, then hold out my left hand, trying to summon even one of the daggers into my grip. Nothing happens. Only more words come to mind. Zymarc's words, regarding Awngeleik. *What did LanSoren do to her? That she will not come to the call of her master?*

Could it be that she can only have one master at a time? What if it's the same way with the daggers?

I start walking forward, even though sweat runs down my back and sinks into the fabric of my diving armor. Probably my Sleeping Dragon coat too. My body's telling me to turn and run. But I can't. There's nowhere to run to. Nowhere is safe.

Zymarc keeps his barrier in place with one hand, as his other draws four symbols in the air. The first lights to red. The second to blue. Then they are wrapping themselves around Zymarc and disappearing to nothing.

Soren momentarily stops his berating of the wall, to say, "Clever Zymarc. Fortifying yourself with Gendras. It won't do. But go on. You've got time to finish."

The third symbol lights to green. The last to bronze. Then they, too, fortify Zymarc.

Soren takes both daggers in one hand. He looks over to me, still tentatively making my way forward.

For a moment, time stills as I stare into his green eyes that look exactly like mine.

My wicked grin flickers across Soren's face. But it's gone, as he plunges the twin-daggers into the barrier at the same time.

No! It cannot be, I scream inside. *He is not me.*

Fighting my panic, I rush to help Gyron as he struggles back to his feet. Still kneeling, he grips one of my shoulders. "Tyler, I know you were gone from here for a moment. Don't deny it. Just tell me what you saw."

"I saw my dad."

"And what did he tell you?" Gyron presses.

When his barrier shatters, Zymarc's hand keeping it up is jerked back. Something slices down his arm. Then his other. Yet Soren's still five strides from him.

"Many things." I sigh.

"Was anything said that could help us now?" queries Gyron.

"I was supposed to remember something. Maybe something to do with the daggers. But I'm not sure what."

Zymarc and Soren's dance of death begins again. Zymarc, however, isn't healing anymore.

Gyron's gaze flits around. He's obviously distressed. He keeps trying to speak, but decides against it.

"You're magically bound not to say." I smile weakly.

Gyron grins back. "I'm trying to find the words around it. It seems this is all I'm permitted to say. Stand up, Tyler, and walk toward the real threat of today. One of three."

"One of three?" I'm confused, replying, "I only see two: Zymarc and Soren."

"As I said. One of three. The choice is yours. I'll work on reviving Caleiso. You should get going." Gyron stands, and goes to Caleiso, who's still mostly unconscious.

She should be faring better, given what she is. A Vitiosyn, and apprentice to Zymarc. But maybe Jasper's wailing howl really did some damage to her Mazhrein. I look to where he sits trapped in the prison-box, drawing symbols on the walls, attempting, and failing, to free himself. It's apparent that he's no threat.

Not in his current state, anyway.

At that moment, I feel eyes on me. Menacing eyes. I glance to the frontline of Paragon. There, just outside of the wall, is Awngeleik taking her demon form. Nobody notices her, as she stands staring at me.

The real threat of the day? I muse. *Maybe she is that. All this destruction and death* did *happen because of her being withheld from Zymarc's grasp.*

I decide that she's the one Gyron means. I make my approach. Each of my steps on the shamrock-green is agony, during Zymarc and Soren's pummeling of each other.

The pounding on the anvil of my chest throbs through me. Still, I move forward. To Awngeleik. Perhaps, to my own death.

Think quick! What was I supposed to remember?

Jasper searches around his prison, studying its physiology more. Then he seems to hear my footsteps, as I approach Awngeleik.

"Is someone there?" he queries.

"Can't you hear what's happening?" I ask. "Soren of the Monel is here. But we're not sure what he wants. Except death to anyone who's against him."

"Sounds about right." Pausing, Jasper states, "I don't recognize your voice. But you sound young. What's a boy doing, facing off with a Sorshrynak? A Withrasyn, at that."

"I don't have a choice. I'm trapped in here with him. With Gyronawv and Zymarc too."

"Whoever you are," he says, "you're out of your league. Break me free from this prison, and I'll help."

"I'm Tyler Ravier, if that makes any difference to you. And I would free you, if I could. But I don't know how."

Jasper wards off a smile. "Tyler Ravier? You're far too modest. And you *can* free me. With your father's daggers, that is. Few barriers can withstand their edges. Their points? Even fewer."

"About that . . ." I start.

"You do have them, don't you?" queries Jasper.

"At the moment"—I pause, to watch Soren wearing Zymarc down to exhaustion, then finish saying—"Soren has them."

"Oh." Jasper's expression sinks. "Well . . . that's unfortunate."

"I have an idea of how to get them back, though."

"Well, get to it," Jasper encourages, "before Soren starts creating real havoc."

"I think we're well past that," I state, turning to face Awngeleik.

"Then he's already cut symbols into his skin, and set himself on fire?" Jasper hides another grin.

Slowly, I reply, "No."

Nodding, Jasper says, "Then you should hurry your idea along, before he reaches that point of fury."

Taking a calming breath, which feels more like a choking wheeze, I face Awngeleik again. She's disappeared. I whirl around, searching. I stop at the sight of her standing next to Azabahk, while he's striking the wall with a great big war hammer. It has veins of glowing ruby forged into it. I shudder to imagine what it does to a body it hits.

My mind races, thinking, *What's she doing, standing there, of all places?*

In my rush toward her, I trip and fall. Finding my footing again, I race forward. But she's gone. My breaths strangle me further. I glance at Gyron, finishing up his healing of Caleiso. Just as I'm about to Mensa-div with him, an arrow whizzes past my ear. It continues on, and plunges straight through Gyron's heart.

I shy to the side, almost falling.

Caleiso screams, and scrambles away on all fours.

Gyron's body within the barrier wall lights on fire. Then that fire passes through the wall and seeps into the lifeless form outside. Awngeleik approaches the form, as Gyron's body completes its transition. He gales in a giant breath, before sinking to his knees. Looking to me, he then glances up at Awngeleik standing beside him.

"You should hurry it along, Ravier," he says.

"But I don't know what to do," I complain. "Can't you tell me anything else?"

Sighing, Gyron says, "Your father commanded me not to tell you the words, but to let you feel them, instead. Forget the daggers, for a moment, and face the *real* threat of today. One of three."

Frustrated, I scream, "I don't know what that means!"

"Fine!" Gyron yells back, standing up. "Just remember the two!" His voice thick with sadness, he says, "No forgetting."

Excitedly, I remember my father speaking those same words, before we said goodbye. "Despairing Marion," I ask, "who is she? Do you know? Is she here?"

Looking away, Gyron whispers, "There's nothing left I can say."

It seems like days ago that I saw my father fading away. Yet here I am, not even an hour later, trying to remember his answer to my question about despairion. Then the two come to me.

Words for riches.

Kindling for thought.

Instead of giving me a third answer, he said, *Forget it. It won't do. Just remember the two. No forgetting. You'll figure it out.*

What do they mean? Kindling could be fire. Fire for thought? That makes no sense. Startling me from my thoughts, right then, are chunks of molten rocks headed straight for me.

Tired, Zymarc still manages to scramble between Soren and me, in time to block the molten rocks with vines growing up from the ground. The vines wrap around the metal in motion, then begin to burn. Rather than being reduced to ashes, they cool and harden into silver-like veins that pin the smoking rocks to the mangled ground.

Zymarc draws Soren away from me, with new attacks of ice spikes.

Calming slightly, I'm still desperate to remember. "Fire of the mind," I muse out loud. "Maybe memory?"

Blue-fire contained in her hands, Caleiso pauses in aiming at Soren. Looking to me, she says, "That's an allusion to Fire of the Soul. Fire of the mind? Same thing. It's a metaphor for a specific Law of Magic. One of six. Although, here, it won't help us much." With that, she begins attacking Soren with the blue-fire.

Instead of expressing gratitude, Zymarc glares at her, then shouts, "Free the alpha from his prison, Caleiso!"

"You want me to do what?" she shrieks. "I just got done healing from his wailing howl."

"Does it look like I can subdue Soren by myself?" queries Zymarc. "Do what I say, if you want out of here."

Something about her mention of metaphor makes me remember the poem, while Soren—glancing every so often toward Jasper—is focused on the two making their exchange.

I take out the letter Rozeth gave me. My father's last words, given to her in a dream. The complete despairion poem. Slipping the paper out, I start unfolding it.

"You're not really reading a letter right now, are you?" Caleiso glowers.

"I'm trying to remember something. Now stand guard, and hush!"

She scoffs. "You think I can take a hit from that . . . thing? I don't even know what to call him, except for a beast."

"What? You're afraid?" I mock. "But you're the apprentice to Zymarc of Vitiosus, aren't you?"

"Everyone here is afraid," she replies. "Except for you, it seems, because you're too dumb to feel fear. Only concerned with reading some stupid letter. If I didn't think it might hold the answer to our way out, I'd burn it this very second."

I sigh, pushing away the slight sting of her words. "I need to focus."

Smirking again, she turns around to stand as my temporary guard.

I startle at the sound of Soren screaming out laughter. The letter crinkles in my grasp. I look up, and I'm sickened by the sight. His coat has disappeared, his vest too. He's now carving symbols on his bare arms.

Zymarc collapses, in fatigue. Propping himself up, he watches Soren preparing his body for something. An act of terror, most likely.

I skim over the words of the letter.

LanSoren's Last:

You will find her, at dusk: my Despairing Marion. The miller of the woods. The tamer of the dyns. The first and last of her kind. Who is she? A foreigner or a warrior? A stranger or a friend?

Into the future, you must reverse the clock. Acknowledge the ever-present danger. The fading light of death's gaze. You cannot escape them. Death and time. They wait. Then turn. And shift. Only at the solar-eclipse, will they flee.

Dance with Gendras. Race to the place of Mirrors. Only then can reflection tell all, but no more. —Rozeth, forever your friend and ally

Something about death and time resonate.

Waiting. Turning. Shifting, I muse. *They perfectly describe Awngeleik in this moment. But what about fire of the mind? Caleiso said it's an allusion to a metaphor.*

I whisper, "Allusion? Sounds like illusion. Could Awngeleik be an illusion?" I fold the note. As I'm tucking it away, the face of my diver's watch flickers to a solid mirror finish. Then it returns to normal.

Excitement rises. Quickly, it's taken away.

Zymarc wearily watches, as additional symbols are cut into Soren's bleeding arms. The Sorshrynak takes that moment to glance toward me. His creepy smile makes another appearance.

Trying to force down the fear creeping up, it sticks like a lump in my throat. I glance back to Awngeleik, looking like death in her demon form. Then I tap the watch face, the representation of time.

Do I have to pick only one? I wonder, before speaking more words. "She's an illusion, but of which one? Quick. Pick one!"

The watch shifts to the mirror finish again, then back to its face ticking away time.

As I'm making my decision, the symbols on Soren's arms ignite. Black marks are left behind. No more wounds. Just twisted tattoos. Twisted like the one wearing them. Although Zymarc wears the same face as Soren, in this moment, his is not a face of terror. Soren's, and his alone, holds that description.

The razor strokes from a night ago are nothing compared to what I'm feeling now. Utter terror. A cold sweat sends me to trembling. I cannot speak even one word. Let alone the phrase I've chosen: illusion of time.

I spot Awngeleik, still in her demon form, waiting outside the wall near where Jasper's held prisoner. I instinctually bolt, hoping to regain my voice along the way.

Soren is thirteen steps from me, when he snaps his fingers. Caleiso's restrained. He then reaches out toward me. Seconds later, my legs are swept out from under me, and I'm dragged toward Soren. I dig my fingers into the grit of the ground, but I don't stop sliding until Soren releases his invisible hold.

Five small steps separate us.

Grinning, Soren leisurely slips his bloodied white vest and coat back on. "I like games with my prey, Ravier," he says, "So, here's how it's going to be. I command you to tell the truth, three times. Three times, you must answer with what you believe to be true deep down in your heart. Are you ready?"

I answer, "Why not?" But it's not what I wanted to say. Then I shrug while still on the ground, even though this really doesn't feel like a shrugging moment. If nothing else, it might throw Soren off his 'prey' game.

After Soren buckles his vest closed, he crouches down, and speaks words of, "What do you see, when you look at me?"

Instantly, I reply, "Death, disobedience, and destruction."

"Oh, that was too quick." Soren sneers, standing up. "A second time. But the *actual* truth this time. The one you feel deep in your heart. What do you see, Tyler Ravier, when you look at me?"

Refusing to answer, because what's rising disturbs me, I clench my jaw tight. Almost to the point where my teeth feel as if they're about to crack.

But I can't stop the thought from finishing its rise to my consciousness. "Me," is my quiet, unsettled reply.

"Again, in case someone missed your quiet, little answer." Soren smiles. "What do you see, Son of LanSoren, when you look at me?"

Unable to stop myself, I reply, "Me." It's just one word. Two letters. But it's my horror turned into reality. Deep down, I think Soren and I are one and the same.

It cannot be. What if it's true? If it is, he can't kill me. Not in this moment where I'm the present one, living. And he's the past, long dead. But how to get him back into his time?

With my right hand, I claw at the side of my face. Desperately, I try to force the phrase out.

Soren starts reaching for me.

I cannot move. I cannot speak. Nothing comes from me, except a few bitter tears. Staring at Soren, I might be looking right at my father's killer. But I think he is me.

Did I kill him? Is it my fault my father's dead? I just don't remember doing the deed.

The last of my thoughts isn't even a question. But, rather, a statement. And it kills me. My eyes sting more.

Breaking me from the torment of my thoughts is a crashing sound all around. Dozens of BlacKaidyns are flying up, breathing fire. They swirl around the barrier, flying among each other's flames. Some claw at the clear obstruction. Others batter themselves against it.

Rising into view beyond the Paragonian's frontline is Reign, lifting his head up high. Too weak to fly, probably too weak to roar too, he looks across the wide expanse to the Vitiosyn line, to the King Vitasadyn meeting his gaze.

The King Vitasadyn bows his head to Reign, as if in agreement on something. Then he lifts his bloodstained snout up to the sky, and begins a roar twice the volume of Reign's.

Sound ripples through the barrier.

The ground trembles.

All fall to their knees, covering their ears.

Even the dragons, swirling above, scatter. Screeching, they land hard on the ground.

Only Soren remains standing, though he *is* struggling.

Then there's Jasper, still in the prison-box, oblivious of all sound around him. Except for my voice, it seems.

"Tyler," he says, "is everything all right? What's happening? I hear some kind of odd buzzing."

Soren, frozen in place, has his hand extended toward me. But he's starting to shake. At last, he collapses to the ground on his hands and knees. Fresh blood stains his coat sleeves, and he cries out.

Whatever was paralyzing me to inaction fades away.

Lifting the watch up toward Muraine's star, Rentwaramein, I center it on the watch face and speak the phrase: "Illusion of time."

The watch crystal shifts to a mirror-finish, shining bright.

I hear the sound of cracking glass.

The watch face turns to an unreflecting black.

I only have to wait a moment, before something starts happening.

2

Until the Next Time

olors around are stripped of their vibrancy. The world seems so gray. Neither dark nor light. It is both. Nor is it loud or silent. Just muted. Lukewarm. A place of in-between. Time appears to stop, with all shifting to look frozen in place. Except for me, alone, standing and then taking a step back.

Like the air at the lake that day the Vardiya died, it's thick and muggy. It's hard to get in a full breath. Still, I sense that something's missing. Words unspoken. Once said in this moment, there's no going back.

Inhaling deeply, I speak out, "I'm here, at twelve and thirteen. Beginning, end, and everything in-between. Now, show me the real enemy of today. One of three."

"I know you," replies the words of my unfinished poem. Yet it isn't my voice continuing the dialogue. Sounding more ghostly and metallic, it says, "But I have never spoken to you. With how much I know about you, though, you seem as familiar as my own face staring back at me. I've often wondered, how can that be? Then I remember that I am a Vardiya, greater than any before me."

"A Vardiya?" I ask, in disbelief. Searching around, I don't see him. "The one back home? Who shocked me, stained my hand black? You are him?"

"The very one," he answers. "I was tasked with accompanying you, on your journey to truth. As I know many things—things others are bound not to say, histories fading into legends and then to forgottenness—he thought I would be a good choice."

"My dad chose you to help me?"

"Among others," replies the Vardiya.

"Others to help, or others chose you too?"

"Both," he says.

"So many seem bound," I state. "But I need names. Names of those I can rely on. And others deemed untrustworthy. Can you give them to me?"

"Yes. However, that would be a waste of Aysivak's short, but valuable time."

"Aysivak?" I hesitate, before asking, "Who's that?"

"Me, Son of LanSoren." He laughs, then turns serious. "There's not enough time. I could have lived a few more hours that day you and your mother pulled me from a trap Soren had set many years ago. But I thought it better to project myself to this moment, and have a talk with you after you had learned a little more of the truth. See, you're asking better questions this time. Less focused on your father's death, and more on the journey ahead. It shows that I made the right choice. Although, it was hard."

I nod. "I get it. I wasn't ready to hear everything. But I don't know what I'm going to do, once I leave this place. How am I supposed to break Jasper free of Soren's prison, when I can't summon the daggers to my grasp? How will I help save Talok and Paragon? I won't give up searching for my father's killer. But I understand that it may have to wait."

"Yes, waiting," says Aysivak. "That's hard, as well as knowing I was supposed to journey with you through four years' time. By your side. Sadly, it wasn't meant to be. Instead, I've left trinkets of the message I was to relay. There are phrases, spells, and . . . some creative means to trigger the pieces I've left for you. It wasn't ideal, and the timing may not always be right. But I had to sift through four years, in the three hours of life I had left. It was . . ." Aysivak trails off.

"Exhausting," I finish.

"Yes! Literally took my breath away."

I chuckle a bit, until my chest tightens. A sudden pang of regret comes over me.

Aysivak seems to sense this, as his humor has faded. "Oh, Ravier! We and your friends would've had fun together. Especially I with that Gemma. Always talking, thinking, and moving, that one. Even in her sleep."

Smiling in agreement, I then ask, "What does Soren want with her?"

"He wants her to free him," replies Aysivak.

"Free him of what?"

"One day, Gemma will discover what that means on her own. Just wait, and worry about your part. And, for Vardiyas' sake, try acting a little more fragile. Your survival is not a guarantee. Those around you? Even less so."

"In other words, stop rushing into the fray?"

"Oh no! By all means, rush out. But think about what comes after the rushing, before you go."

I sigh. "Noted. Anything else?"

"For now, what's left is for you to know more about the daggers and that timepiece. Do *not* lose that watch. Nor let it be broken. It is my only connection to you, from here on."

"Well, why didn't you pick something more resilient than a watch as our link?" I ask.

"Because it was the only piece on you, of a magical capacity. And since your Mazhrein has been dormant for so long, you could not hold all I had to leave behind. Besides, that watch *is* resilient. Not even the jaws of dragons can crack it. Some spells hitting it, however, will wear it down over time."

"Like water rushing over stones?" I ask.

"Exactly," replies Aysivak. "Now, listen closely. Those daggers are old. Their cores filled with remembrance of their previous masters. Though there were others, whom I shall not bother naming, just know this: Soren and your father have been two of several masters. LanSoren was their last. As you are his son, they answer to you. RotaSyn and NeiSator. One is day, the other is night. Together, they are—"

I interrupt, saying, "Dusk and dawn."

"Yes!" Aysivak exclaims. "As such, they are more powerful when used at those times. If used by themselves, they revert to preferring their symbolic time of day or night."

"Is there any particular order to summon them by?" I ask.

"It all depends on the time of day you are in. Now I must hurry," Aysivak says. "You're facing Soren, if I'm not mistaken?"

"You're not," I reply.

"What do you need to defeat him, Tyler?"

"Resistance to death," I reply, shaking my head. "Memories of what my dad made me forget? Powerful magic? I'm not really sure."

"Then this I will give you now," says Aysivak. "The power you will hold, in four years' time, is yours today. You will still look a boy to all. But your power, perhaps even your memory, will be from four years in the future. Will that suffice, do you think?"

I laugh bitterly. "You can do that?"

"Only once, but yes. Are you sure you want it now, rather than when you find more of what I left for you?"

"I don't know. Maybe," is my hesitant reply. "What if worse things are coming?"

"It won't matter, if Soren gets what he is after today."

"Do I even want to know?"

"He wants to switch places with you, Ravier. To make you the past, long dead. And him? The present and future."

In shock, I choke on my next words. "How's that possible? Wouldn't that break some laws of time?"

"It would," Aysivak agrees. "But Soren's been waiting a long time to play his part. Then it was stolen from him, with one devastating blow. It drove him mad. He wants it back. And he can take it back today, if you're not meticulous in your execution of everything. Strikes, dodges, magic, words . . . accusations."

"In other words, I must be perfect? Or I'll be sent to the past?"

"For today, yes. However, with your power of 'age eighteen' to help you, Soren might just come to fear you. Now, Ravier, we've come to our end. In our future meetings, you will see me as a mere projection of my former self. If you've a request, ask it. But know that I may not respond. When the sequences are finished, speak 'Thirteen. Done.' That will begin the transition back into the present. This time, I'll start it. Thirteen. Done!"

"Until the next time, Aysivak."

3

Remember the Fallen

Turning, I face the dismal image of Soren still on his hands and knees.

After the watch face flashes, the watch hands start ticking. Speeding up to a blur of circular motion making several laps, they slow down at noon and then stop at one o'clock.

When a breeze tickles across my face, I take in a breath.

The watch begins the normal rhythm of time.

Soren's the first to regain his complexion and movement. Holding the waking-dagger, he reaches for the other one and tightens his grip on its hilt.

The King Vitasadyn's roar explodes to full volume, and I'm sent sliding and stumbling to the opposite side. Toward the Paragonian side. I slam into the prison-box. Grimacing, I get to my feet.

Colors return to normal as Jasper stands up. Alert, he asks, "Do you have the daggers, Tyler?"

"Not yet, but I will soon." With that, I face Soren.

Though I should be afraid, I'm not. Not anymore. I simply sense that cold heat creeping through. Rather than merely my left hand staining to black, the Prismatic of Magic stains both. I don't know what else to call the ensuing sensations but an ice-cold malice permeating every inch of my chest and arms, my hands and feet too. The rest burns to an ache. A clawing fever, needing to seek some kind of justice. Self-righteous hate and violent justice are what I feel now in my heart.

Will I go too far? I wonder. *Or will I just do what needs doing: to send Soren back to where he belongs?*

Standing confidently, I point at Soren. "Those daggers, they were my father's. Now they're mine. My inheritance!"

Getting up, Soren aims the sleeping-dagger at me. His face flickering with fury, he shouts, "They were mine, long before they were ever his!"

Caleiso manages to free herself of Soren's restraints. She rushes to Zymarc, and begins to heal him.

I shout at Soren, "But you didn't have any children to inherit them! There would have been a record of it. Few even knew who you were, in Paragon, when I came here. If you left some descendants behind, and a legacy of heroics, more would know your name. But hardly any did, until now. So, you have no one. Now, Soren, give me my father's daggers!" I hold out my left hand, visualizing the waking-dagger appearing in it.

"Caleiso, no," Zymarc says weakly, pushing at her hands. "Help free the alpha, so he can stop this madness."

She ignores his command, and continues to heal him with her sparking magic.

Soren throws the waking-dagger back at Caleiso and Zymarc.

She stands, quickly raising her hands. A luminescent wall forms in front of her.

The dagger plunges into her obstruction. When Soren summons the dagger back to his grasp, the barrier shatters.

Caleiso screams in pain, and crumples to the ground. She gasps for breath.

Soren prepares to throw it again.

But I rush forward. Kneeling down on one knee, I cross my arms in an *X* and then speak, "RotaSyn. NeiSator." Closing my eyes fleetingly, I feel the warm hilt of a dagger come into the grasp of my right hand. Nothing is summoned into my left, however. I open my eyes, and see the waking-dagger in my right grip. With colors closer to a sunrise, it must be

RotaSyn. Uncrossing my arms, I look up at Soren.

He stands somewhat closer to me, his feet planted. His eyes, first fearful and wide, narrow with hate, then empty of all but his sick humor. "No, no, Ravier." He taps one of his fingers on the black hilt. "NeiSator is mine!"

"Fine!" I shout. When I stand up, I'm calm. "I'll fight you for it. And I will win." At the word *win*, my voice deepens. Not like a beast or a demon, but like I'm older than my fourteen years. Four years older, most likely. The world is brighter. More colorful too. Each breath taken makes me feel stronger. My body almost weightless, movements are effortless. Invigorating, even.

I smile my wicked grin, knowing that I'll stand a chance. Or better? I'll make Soren regret this day of meeting me face-to-face. Tightening my grip on RotaSyn, I feel the wood and metal hilt mold to my grasp. Suddenly, it truly is mine. An extension of my reach, my magic. A gift of power. All given to me, through time.

Soren stares me down, pacing back and forth. Finally, he stops to say, "You're serious, aren't you? Oh, Ravier, you're priceless!" He laughs. "If you were anyone else, I'd love you for saying that."

Deciding it's the best move, I sprint toward him. In response, Paragonians shout in horror. The voices of Talok, Gemma, and the King's Guard are lost in the chaos of noise. Even some Vitiosyns rush forward in alarm, though they remain silent.

Soren shortens the distance, taking giant steps. He lifts the dagger and swings it at me.

Although he appeared fast before, while fighting Zymarc, his swing slows the closer it gets to my face. I'm able to dodge, then slice across his right side.

Soren yells in pain, whirling around to chase me down.

My steps quick and sure, I make it back to the prison-box. I'm about to plunge the dagger tip into it, but Soren pulls me back with a gale-storm shot from his free hand.

Instead of fighting the storm's pull, I turn and run toward my would-be attacker. Timing my movements precisely, I catch him by surprise and kick him in the chest.

Surprisingly, he falls down.

I want to free Jasper this very second. But I know Soren will just keep coming, stopping me, until I immobilize him. So, I go to stab him in the leg, the part of him closest to me. But he rolls out of the way, and I miss.

He grabs my right arm. When his fingers press into my skin, his hand freezes to frostbitten purple and blue. He pulls away. It goes black, looking frozen stiff.

Startled, he slowly looks to my face. "What did that wretched Aysivak do?"

I shrug, replying, "You tell me." Then I swing at him again.

He stands, and clashes the sleeping-dagger against RotaSyn. Light flashes, seeming to temporarily blind him.

The color of warmth returns to his hand, and he switches NeiSator back into his left grip. When our metal edges clash again, the flash is dimmer. We fight for several minutes, sometimes dodging each other's attacks altogether.

The Paragonian line quiets. I can almost feel their apprehension. It isn't quiet for long over there, however, because someone screams and cries about what's happened to Paragon. I recognize Khyra's voice, frantically saying, "Ryco, you lied to me! It wasn't a drill. Vitiosyns have destroyed *my* city. Killed our people. What are we going to do? And what's Tyler doing in there, fighting by himself? Dragon's Spike! Is that Soren? The one from last night?"

"Khyra," Ryco practically growls. "Quiet! Or you might distract Tyler—you could get him killed!"

"Well, why isn't anyone helping him?"

"Believe me," says Musgrae, "we've tried. No one's getting through this barrier."

There's a pause in their conversation, while I continue fighting Soren. The sweat beading above his brow proves the effort of it all is finally getting to him. I'm starting to tire out, as well, but I just need one good stab to his arm. At least, that's what I'm hoping for.

"Ryco," Khyra says, "I have an idea. Give me one of your supply pouches."

"Khyra, we've tried everything. But here, take it, if it makes you feel better."

"Yes," she says. "This will do perfectly."

"For what?" Eli's tone is smug.

"What are you going to do?" Ben pipes in.

I glance at Khyra, in time to see her effortlessly coming through the obstruction.

Behind her, Ryco claws at the space of barrier she just went through. Dumbfounded, he exclaims, "Khyra, how? What *are* you doing?"

Next to Ryco are Gemma and Talok, looking on fearfully.

Talok's Mensa-div bleeds through, echoing, *Don't miss one step, Tyler. And, please, let Khyra help you. Her Gendras is remarkable. She couldn't be the Architect of Paragon, if it were otherwise.*

"Khyra?" I ask. "Distract him?"

"Of course!" She nods. Fishing out wood and metal chips from Ryco's supply pouch, she tosses it away.

I manage to fend off Soren, while Khyra readies herself. Next thing I know, she's throwing wood chips at him. While in motion, they grow to the size of large evergreens. But when they hit Soren, he just laughs.

"What was that, daughter of Withrasyn?" Soren taunts. "A little puff of air? It tickled a bit. Do it again." He grins, and actually stands still, waiting for her to throw another.

"Khyra!" Ryco shouts, annoyed. "You have to give it its weight back." More quietly, he says to Talok, "Have I taught her nothing?"

Since Soren's thoroughly distracted with watching Khyra, I'm able to saunter over to free Jasper. When I get there, I repeatedly stab the prison-box. Like Zymarc's barrier, the holes left by the dagger appear as broken glass.

"Tyler, stop," Jasper commands. "It will take too long to break it like that. Mark it, right here." He places his long, slender ring finger a ways above my head, then says, "As you pull the dagger out, scrape the tip to the next mark, which is here." He taps on a spot at my hip's height.

Following his instructions, I create a diamond shape made of eight holes, with cut-lines connecting those gaps.

Meanwhile, Khyra seems to be distracting Soren rather well.

Excited, he gasps. Then he proclaims, "Snakes altered from branches! What's a daughter of Withrasyn going to do with snakes? Eat them. Or are they for me? How thoughtful!"

Next comes Khyra's blood-curdling scream.

She rushes over to me, breathlessly asking, "Why are there two Sorens, Tyler? What are we going to do? We're going to die!"

I haven't time to respond, before Jasper says, "Put the dagger away, Tyler."

"Khyra, you've created the lifeless form!" Ryco shouts. "Quick, summon Ben to it. Remember, it's *Invitas* for present; not *Invitios*, which is used for past."

"Ben? Why not you, Ryco?"

Ryco replies, "You're not strong enough to summon someone like me."

I tell Khyra, "That one in the black is Zymarc, wearing Soren's face. For now, he's . . . helping?"

"Helping!" Khyra shrieks. "After destroying our cities, and killing a good portion of us, he's helping?"

"Just don't think about it. Not until Soren's gone."

Livid, she heads back to summon Ben to the lifeless form.

"What is this, now?" queries Jasper. "A Vitiosyn fancies Soren's face attractive enough to wear?"

"So it seems," I reply. "What do I do next?"

"This part requires no interruptions," says Jasper. "Are you safe to start?"

Looking back, I see Soren finishing up his snack of a raw snake. All around, the shamrock-green has been ripped apart, dug up, burned, and flooded, in an attempt to restrain the Sorshrynak. No longer a peaceful place of green, it's a maze with tossed mounds of dirt, mud, grass, and rocks.

From this fresh war zone of Khyra and Soren, Zymarc has dragged Caleiso and himself to a safe distance away.

Now Ben's being commanded rather harshly by Quall, to heal Zymarc enough for him to help Khyra restrain Soren.

One look at Ben's eyes darkening to hate, and I know he's at war with himself.

"How long do I need, Jasper?" I ask.

"One minute. Maybe less, if you're fast and precise. So you say that Zymarc is wearing black? And I assume that Soren is in . . . white?"

"Yes," I reply, turning back to face Jasper. "Well, actually, it's more red now than white."

"That's usually how it went, with him." Jasper nods. "One last note of caution. You're going to need to move away from this prison very quickly, after moving your hand back. You're turning this inside out, essentially. If you're too close, you'll be the one stuck in here. And we'll have to finish breaking it the hard way. Is there someone who can pull you away?"

"Yes," says a familiar voice, from behind me.

Startling, I whirl around. It's Zymarc standing in front of me. His voice this close, and absent of the mask, sounds different somehow.

I wonder, *Is it because he's taken so many hits, and is still injured?*

Shaking the sudden thought away, I nod once at Zymarc and then face Jasper again. "Yes, there's someone to pull me to safety."

Jasper points. "Then, begin here. Follow the motions of my hands, paying particular attention to finger placement. Think of it as if you are playing an instrument. The appropriate beat strung out, in time to the rhythm of whatever symbol's being drawn."

"Tell the alpha you're a fast learner," says Zymarc. "We need this done quickly. For Caleiso's sake, and your friends. They won't last long, against him."

"Draw the symbol faster, Jasper," I state. "I'll keep up."

Jasper and I begin the process. Oddly enough, it's as if I've been drawing strange symbols like some kind of musician my whole life.

I ask Zymarc, "Why aren't you with them?"

"The young guard's healing tonics need a minute to work. That's how long you have, before I abandon you to try to rush away yourself. Be quick."

I continue following Jasper's smooth motions.

Then he's proclaiming, "This is the last one. When you're ready, take your hand off the barrier."

Gripping my sides, Zymarc is ready to pull me to safety.

I lift my hand off the cold prison-box, as Zymarc yanks me back.

Jasper is suddenly thrust out of the prison.

In the background, Soren yells furiously.

Done with my part, I toss Jasper the dagger, RotaSyn, while he runs forward.

Catching it, Jasper draws out his own long-blade of an iridescent icy-blue and pale-green. It glimmers akin to glass, rather than metal. Near its steel guard are three inset stones shining as dull mirrors.

"Winter's Vondaen," remarks Zymarc, letting go of me. "Perhaps the one blade Soren fears. This shouldn't take long."

Adjusting my coat, I side-glance at Zymarc. "Are you admitting to Jasper being superior to yourself?"

"Not at all," replies Zymarc, his grin far less dark than Soren's own of murderous intent. "Jasper has been reserving his magic, since he has been in there. I, on the other hand, have put forth my best effort in restraining the Sorshrynak. Even attempting a mortal blow on him a few times. But it's rather hard to contend with him, when there's frantic prey running about."

Refusing to glance at him, I ask, "Prey such as me?"

"You, Ravier, are not prey," remarks Zymarc.

"What about your *apprentice*?" I ask.

"She isn't, usually. But, growing up, she's heard the legends of Soren. Her fear of him is justified. And your lack of fear toward him is due to your stupidity. How does that Earth saying go?" Zymarc thinks a moment. "Oh yes! Ignorance is bliss. In your case, however, it should be ignorance is brash. Do you ever think about what you are doing?"

I reply, "I'm starting to." Then I decide that this conversation is weary. I saunter over to Ben, as he's attending to Khyra's surface wounds. Along the way, I watch Jasper corner Soren. He makes it look all too easy, threatening the Sorshrynak with wounds incurable for all of his days remaining, from the time that he left behind, until the day he meets his end.

Slashing the Sorshrynak's arm open, Jasper drops RotaSyn. He manages to get one of his hands wrapped around Soren's neck. Then he starts speaking, "Sleep, slumbering deep—"

Soren shouts, "No! You're not going to make me sleep, Alpha Jasper! I've gained resistance to that." Breaking free, Soren moves to attack Jasper with NeiSator.

Jasper's faster, however, only getting nicked a few times on one of his arms. Dropping his own weapon, the alpha positions himself behind Soren to grip his neck again. This time, with both hands, Jasper has Soren in a stranglehold. Softly, he says, "Sleep, slumbering." Slowing his speech more, he adds, "deep in the dark."

"I hate you, Jasper." Soren spits and coughs, viciously struggling.

Halfway grinning, Jasper continues, "Light of the night, bright on the right of the Kyanite asleep."

Soren sighs deeply, calming. He sways a bit, before shaking his head to wake himself.

"To sleep," soothes Jasper, "so deep you'll reap of the keep fast asleep."

Eyes struggling to stay open, Soren fights the inevitable.

On, Jasper continues with, "To summoning a slumbering Rubidyn to sleep."

"Just had to add that part about a Rubidyn, didn't you?" says Soren. When his eyes close, they stay that way.

Jasper, his hold still on the Sorshrynak's neck, turns serious. He then throws Soren's limp body hard.

Soren hits the barrier. Like a dead fish, he flops to the ground.

Jasper sheathes Winter's Vondaen.

Then Zymarc nods, looking around curiously. "Now. How do we get out of here?"

I fasten the daggers back to my belt.

All wait for the Greyvon Alpha to answer him.

Jasper peers about, his features briefly creasing in utter shock. "I, um

. . ." Trailing off, Jasper swallows hard. "Does anyone care to explain what's happened?" More sternly, he says, "Why were two Minor-Pristines in a deadly duel, upon my entrance into the city? Also, why was I not summoned? And where is King ReNovak!" He shouts the last part, his hands temporarily taking on a beastly appearance, before changing into human hands again.

"Please, Jasper," says Gyron. "Let's work on getting Soren out of here, before there's any more talk."

"Yes, you are right." Jasper points toward the Paragonian Sovereignty in attendance. "That spot in front of you, Musgrae, has been weakened. A good beating of it with a strong war hammer should do the trick."

Someone starts making their way over from the Vitiosyn line. About to start the beating on the barrier with his war hammer is Prince-General Azabahk. But Musgrae steps in front of him, holding out his hand.

"Not so fast, Vitiosyn," states Musgrae. "I started this weak point. It's mine to finish off."

"And this is my most prized weapon." Azabahk scowls. "I'm not going to hand—"

"Azabahk, don't argue!" Zymarc raises his voice. "Give it to him. I want out of here."

His scowl deepening, Azabahk thrusts the hammer to Musgrae. "Very well," he says. "But I'm standing here until he, with a touch of Greyvon stench, is through!"

Musgrae roughly takes the war hammer, to inspect it.

"Careful, Azabahk," Zymarc warns. "The alpha is listening. And his Matriarch Candidate is right behind you."

Azabahk turns enough to see Rorka's glare at him. He grins, showing all his sharp teeth. "Greyvon stench refers to mix brood. Not purebloods. For Greyvons are fearsome beasts on the battlefield. Worthy and powerful adversaries. I've had to end several, sadly, and many others, to earn that war hammer of Deezalo's. Be cautious how you hold it, Greyvon mutt." Azabahk looks back to Musgrae, while digging one of his boot heels into the ground.

"I'm not even enough to be a mutt, you idiot," Musgrae fumes. "Now, shut your face. And let me get to work."

"Very well." Azabahk crosses his arms. "I'll quiet down, because it suits me. But I'm not closing my eyes. So, you can forget about that, little dog."

Ignoring him, Musgrae begins pummeling the barrier with Azabahk's hammer, as if he's using a wooden mallet rather than a giant, black war hammer. But the sound gives away how heavy that hammer is. It's a sound of metallic crashing, and glass crunching reminiscent to colliding vehicles.

Jasper approaches the space in front of Rorka, asking, "Please send for Paydinn. We need his book of time."

Rorka looks down in shame. She whispers, "Someone else should send it."

"Whatever for?" queries Jasper.

She glances up, distress showing in her juniper-green eyes. "I've been trying to reach you all night and into this morning. I don't think my letter-birds are working properly."

Jasper stares off toward the broken gates of Paragon, seeming to intentionally avoid a glance at Rorka. "You're sure you sent them to me?"

"Yes. I told each one to find you in Pariah," replies Rorka. "The last dozen or so took longer to send, because I enchanted them to just *find* you, wherever you were."

Jasper slowly nods, about to say something. But he clamps his mouth shut, then proceeds to walk in long, precise strides past the Paragonian Sovereignty. He pauses in front of Ryco, Talok, and Gemma. Brushing his hand along the barrier, he continues on walking. He stops in front of Rozeth.

"Alpha Jasper," she whispers, leaning closer to the barrier. "May I be of service to thee?"

"Perhaps," he replies. "Have you met Paydinn, Father of the Jokryn? More importantly, do you know his physiology well enough to send him an arrow-letter?"

"An arrow-letter!" she exclaims. "I haven't sent one of those in quite a long time, as they're only necessary when someone's in a hurry to get them to their recipient."

"Yes, Rozeth." Ryco briefly clenches his fists. "In a hurry, like we are now. I would send it. But he's probably farther east than I've ever traveled. Unlike you and your kind."

"I suspect," says Jasper, "that he's on his way to his father's homeland of the Metimoras. Will that help with your letter's speed in catching up to him?"

"Oh, yes, that is helpful," says Rozeth, chattering away. "Since I know the general whereabouts of the Metimoras' home, I can most certainly send it by arrow-letter. Should reach him in half an hour or so. What would you like for it to say, Jasper?"

Whipping out a quill and piece of paper from thin air, Rozeth smiles and waits for Jasper's reply.

Looking around, Jasper thinks a moment. Then he meets with Rozeth's quizzical gaze. "Promise not to ask questions about the content?"

After slight hesitation, she nods.

"Very good." Jasper says, "First line: Siveyra Paydinn of the Jokryn, Keeper to The Watchman's Log."

"That's quite the opening," remarks Rozeth, widening her eyes a bit but writing the words down anyway.

"Next line, On the Eye of Paragon. Next, rendered murderer of many. New line, esteemed savior of one." Jasper stops, to sigh in frustration.

Rozeth peers up, to grin tensely. "Is . . . that all? I must say, Alpha Jasper, this is a most unusual letter. Why not simply say, 'Soren of the Monel broke laws of time. We need you and your *book* of time. Immediately. Come to the Eye of Paragon.'"

Jasper faintly chuckles, returning Rozeth's grin with a look of knowing something she does not. Then he says, "If you can write that, Rozeth, by all means, please do. It would save me the trouble of worrying over whether my meaning will be understood or no."

Rozeth's forehead scrunches in confusion, as she makes her attempt to write down the straightforward message but finds that she cannot. Like the same ends of two magnets repelling each other, the quill and paper won't make contact.

"I don't understand!" she exclaims, looking her quill over distastefully.

"Never mind that," says Jasper, clasping his hands behind himself. "Last line, before the closing: named assassin of the three. Closing, and this is important: May you have all the books in the world, right round your neck, if you fail the blue, white, and black. Sign my name to it—Jasper of Vondurheil—circle the word 'books' a few times, and then send it at forty-five, on its way."

Rozeth pauses in her folding of the letter, to ask, "Forty-five?"

"Yes, Rozeth!" Ryco growls. "Land is at zero degrees. Sky is ninety. Things such as arrow-letters are to be shot off at halfway—forty-five degrees—for optimal speed."

"Oh!" Rozeth perks up, completing the letter's folding. "Then it should take less than half an hour. Simply did I always shoot them off, at whatever felt right. Come to think of it, I do vaguely remember Siveyra Dezarin saying something about items and forty-five-degree angles, in one of our training sessions. But it had been a long day, on that *particular* day."

Blushing, Rozeth smiles slightly. The letter, wrung by her hands, is forced to shift into a whitish arrow. She then slips her bow up over her head. In her firm grip, she readies the arrow-letter. After pulling the string back, she whispers a few words, then releases the arrow. It ignites to a fiery, white eagle. As it flies away, without instruction of where to go, it lengthens to appear as an odd type of snaking cloud in the sky. Very quickly, it's gone from sight.

"Musgrae," Ryco commands. "Let the hammer's owner have it back, before you pass out and it smashes down on your head."

The crashing, crunching sound stops. Musgrae pants for air, sweat pouring down his flushed face. "Fine," he says, winded. He holds it out to Azabahk.

But Rorka cuts in front of him, taking his hammer from Musgrae.

"Excuse me, little sunset, Rorka," Azabahk nearly shouts. "But that is *my* hammer."

Jasper turns around, alarm sweeping over his face before he suppresses all signs of emotion. "What did you call her, Prince-General?" he queries.

Stopping his complaints, Azabahk glances at Jasper. Even though a barrier separates them, Azabahk shows respect with a bow of his head, saying, "It was the Withrasyn's nickname for her. Does it offend you, Alpha? Th-that was not my intent." Drawing his mouth into an intense frown, the Prince-General reluctantly steps back away from Rorka. Motioning for her to have a swing at the fractured spot of barrier, his face goes blank.

Inhaling an unsteady breath, Rorka takes up the task of pounding on the barrier. Because the hammer's almost as long as Rorka is tall, it looks unwieldy in her grip. Yet she manages to swing it almost as fast and hard as Musgrae.

"While we are waiting," says Jasper rather impatiently, switching his hands to be clasped in front of himself, "perhaps someone can explain the course of events I mentioned earlier. King Zymarc of Vitiosus, care to start?"

"No, I don't care to start," he calmly replies. "But I will tell all on the matters that I know. Will that suffice? Or would you rather hear it from Gyronawv, as I am a Vitiosyn? Most certainly, untrustworthy."

That last part irritates Jasper more. It's evident in the way he tenses his longish neck, and grips his clasped hands tighter together, turning his knuckles white. Yet his voice is calm, when next he speaks, "Whomever wishes to clarify matters, I'm inclined to believe. In this moment, at any rate."

Voice absent of emotion, Zymarc describes me breaking the Rules of Engagement three times, and the events following that offense.

As he's doing so, Ben, Khyra, and I approach the space in front of Gemma and the Sovereignty.

She stares at me. Her lower lip quivers. No words come. Only concern in her chocolate-brown eyes.

I try reassuring her with, "It won't be long now, before we're out of here."

Bobbing her head up and down, she finally says, "Then what? We go home?"

"I'm not going home. Not for a while. If ever. As for you, it's not my decision." I pause, unsure whether I should voice my next thought or not, then I speak it anyway. "I'd like for you to stay. I mean that."

"Though it is self-centered of me," Ben quietly adds, "I would want for you to stay too."

"Yes, Gigi!" Khyra sniffles. "I'm inclined to agree with them. As is King Talok, though he's too distracted to say it, at the moment."

Talok breaks his fixation on the direction of Zymarc and Jasper, to glance at Gemma. He manages a brief smile at her.

"Then I'll stay," she says, crowding closer to the barrier. "Just please, Tyler, stop being so much of a *hero*."

"What about me being the Hero of Nyrim?" I grin. "I'm just trying to live up to the name."

"No, you're not." Her eyes narrow on me. "You're just high on magic. Must feel good. Maybe too good."

"Possibly," I agree, as the sound of crunching glass unexpectedly reminds me of something.

Glancing over at Rorka, hammering on the barrier, I recall commanding her to crush a glass in her hand. And she did. Come to find out later, that command of mine came after she and I shared the same thought. The words of my unfinished poem started by Mirror Lake, and the words of Aysivak's introduction cut short. I can't help but think now, *Is she more than who she seems, like me, but doesn't know it? Or is she somewhat aware, and just as confused as I am?*

While I'm preoccupied with my thoughts, Khyra presses on the barrier, attempting to go through it again. But, like the rest of us, she's trapped.

"How'd you get through, before?" queries Ryco.

"I didn't perform any spells," Khyra replies. "It merely let me through. I could see gentle light reflecting from it. Then, for the briefest of moments, it was as if the barrier was gone."

Ryco, and even Quall, are perplexed at this bit of news, whispering to one another, while Talok and the others give their opinions on spell combinations for Khyra to try.

Though I want to listen to them, I sense something pulling me toward

Rorka. She's not looking my way; in fact, no one is, not even when I saunter over to the space in front of where she's smashing on the barrier. The closer I get, the louder it is. Painfully loud. Yet, I have to keep going.

Reaching out with my mind, I start a Mensa-div with her. *Vanquished happiness. A love lost. Arising sadness. What do they mean to you, Rorka?*

Startling from her task of hammering, Rorka almost loses her grip. Then she stares at me, looking uneasy.

"Cautious with it!" Azabahk exclaims, taking a few steps forward. "It doesn't like being dropped. Happened to me once. It held a grudge, until I appeased it with dozens of kills. Unless you want a severe disadvantage toward me, when the war between us officially starts, I suggest you be kind in how you treat it, Matriarch Candidate."

While Azabahk continues ranting on about his hammer's temperament, Rorka divs back with, *They mean nothing to me, except that they are what I felt when meeting you. Perhaps I felt what your heart has been preoccupied with for a long while. Think about it. Your happiness was taken. Your loved one, gone. Sadness is what was left.*

Her words hold a mirror of truth, and it stings.

She starts the hammering again. This time, with more fervor.

Suddenly, I realize the words are near identical to the ones my father spoke before I was thrust back to Paragon. The ensuing sensations were of fire and ice: contradictions. Heartbreak, death, hopelessness: constant battles. Then there was utter death, disobedience, and destruction—ruled by fear and hate. That's when I think, *What was next? Number four? Something about pain turning to nirvana, and not remembering again. But what did I feel?*

In the background, Zymarc's emotionless recount is cut short by Jasper. "I've heard quite enough, Vitiosyn. But you've yet to explain why King ReNovak is not here, thereby breaking Onyx Law . . . if I'm not mistaken."

"You are not," replies Gyron.

"Then where is he?" Jasper presses.

Smirking, Zymarc says, "He had an errand to run."

"An errand?" Jasper's eyes narrow in anger. "What errand could surpass the importance of his being here?"

"He refused to say," replies Zymarc calmly. "Gyronawv, and then a little later myself, tried to force it from him. However, he was not legally bound to tell either of us."

His breath settling, Jasper states, "Then I only see four options ReNovak could have chosen. Either this *errand* was of the same importance to his being present, or it was of greater import. Although, I cannot think of anything that exceeds his announcement of the Onyx allegiance. A second choice is that he may have found a functional portal to Earth, and is hiding out. However, he will still face the consequences, upon his return. Gyronawv, you've been oddly quiet. Have you anything to say?"

Staring blankly at the ground in front of Jasper's feet, Gyron looks up to ask, "What are the other two options he had?"

Jasper takes a deep breath. "The third is potentially a coward's way. As I've not seen ReNovak ever act in such a way, it's doubtful he would've chosen it. But it's very possible he was desperate to escape giving the verdict. And all the ensuing chaos. Seeing the way it's starting to turn out, I can't say that I blame him. Then again, he may have had ulterior motives for . . ." Looking away in distress, Jasper trails off.

Zymarc's stance stiffens. His expression turns dark for a moment too, before he says, "You think he might've . . . killed himself? Is he even allowed to do that? I thought the Onyx outlawed it. That it is quite literally *not* an option."

Shock or interest on their faces, sudden murmurs initiate amid the Paragonians. Among the Vitiosyns, as well.

"That is true," Gyron confirms. "However, ReNovak is king. He needs only three signatures, to start the process of changing a simpler law to no longer apply to himself. His own signature, that of a highly regarded Onyx, as well as an Onyx Warrior's. As he has many warriors loyal to a fault, that signature would've been easy to obtain. Also, his brother's widow—former queen to the Onyx—most likely would've granted him hers as well. Though it seems unlikely, he could have done this *deed*. It's also important to mention that when changes to laws are in their beginning stages, the monarch may choose to tell whom he wishes."

"Thank you, Gyronawv," Jasper replies, taking three, aimless strides around. "I was unaware of that last bit, believe it or no. And since we're already on the task of attacking ReNovak's character, why not add more firewood to the blaze? The fourth choice I see is that he *is* here, and has been the entire time, watching while wearing someone else's face. Like you, Zymarc! Will you please make yourself look like anyone but Soren? It's getting on my nerves. And believe me, you don't want me shifting back into a Greyvon beast. It could get quite messy."

"I've a better idea," remarks Zymarc, walking about the area. "Do turn back into that beast, once this barrier is gone, and search among all my Vitiosyns for ReNovak. The Onyx Warriors presently accounted for, too, if you want."

Leaning back against the barrier, I tuck my arms in front of my chest. I can't help but be a little amused imagining what that would look like: Jasper sniffing out a cowardly king.

"A good idea," says Jasper, standing still, but watching Zymarc. "You know what would be another good idea, Vitiosyn?"

I force back a laugh, truly thrilled at Zymarc's complete shift in attitude. Previously domineering, he's now nearly respectful.

"Coming from you?" Zymarc stops in his tracks, before saying, "I've no idea. Your mind is like the frozen ground in winter. Unyielding, vast, and cold."

"You should surrender, while you can," Jasper states. "The last official war Greyvons had, was with Rubidyns. And all who are old know how that ended. The death of two matriarchs—Shena and Fayel—thousands of years ago. Neither race a victor, we both lost that day. The striking of the first ShenawFayel was then. The day before I became the Greyvon Alpha. And Rentwar, the Rubidyn King. Do not deceive yourself in thinking you will be successful."

"Successful?" Zymarc says. "You do not know all of my intentions, because I've not made them clear nor known for all to see. Therefore, how can you infer that I will be unsuccessful? I have many intentions. Even you, Alpha Jasper, do not have enough time to learn them all."

"But he doesn't have to learn them," I interrupt. "Because my father already knew them. Probably left clues for us to find too."

The soft hum of voices stops among the Paragonians and Vitiosyns. And I feel all their gazes on me. That's when Zymarc's face, still wearing the mask of Soren, goes cold. His eyes are scowling, like a frost-covered forest: frigid and harsh. For a second, the green eyes flash back to his crimson-red. He's about to say something.

But Talok cuts in. "Siveyra Gyronawv, I wonder, is there a way to test whether King ReNovak is living or dead? If he truly is gone, who would be the Onyx monarch in his place?"

Apparently, Talok's question resonates enough with Jasper and Zymarc that their focus shifts to Gyron.

"Yes, who would be his replacement, Warrior of the Nyxane?" queries Zymarc, with a devilish smile curling the edges of his lips upward, ever so slightly.

My heart drops to a throbbing and steady pound, as I think, *Please not Zymarc.*

"The oldest living Siveyra," replies Gyronawv, before his face goes deathly pale. He looks past Zymarc and Jasper, to Soren still lying in a heap of unconsciousness.

Even Jasper's unsettled, scrunching his eyes shut, and holding his breath.

Rorka stops swinging the hammer. Resting its head and part of the handle on her shoulder, she looks on at Jasper fearfully. "This hammer isn't working quickly enough, Alpha Jasper. What do you wish for me to do?"

"I don't know," Jasper whispers, squeezing his eyes shut.

"No, no!" Zymarc exclaims. "It cannot be Soren. Onyx Law, regarding their monarchy, only permits Siveyras into a position typically inherited, if they have never died. They can be neither resurrected, nor use the guiles of time, to gain such a position. Soren is dead in the present. Onyx Law perceives him as such."

I push off the barrier, straightening my back. I fear that this was Soren's real intent: to trade bodies with me, and outwit time, to potentially become the current Onyx King. *Is it even possible?* I wonder. *He's not Onyx. Would their laws written with magic sense that? Or has he found a way to bypass it?*

"If it's not Soren," Jasper says, "then it would be Siveyra Dezarin."

"But no one knows where he is," Ryco states.

"Or even if he's still alive," Rozeth adds.

"Then Gyronawv would be the next oldest Siveyra living," remarks Zymarc. "A Siveyra thrice over. A Diveyra, as we call them."

"Is there a test to be done?" queries Talok, excitement rising in his voice. "A way to know if it *is* Siveyra Gyronawv?"

Gyron looks unsure, searching for words, until one of the younger Onyx Warriors behind, comes to tell him something.

"Thank you, Zenzar," Gyron says, to the tall and slender warrior stepping back to the front of the Onyx formation. "It's been a while, and I'd quite forgotten about that."

"Well?" Zymarc says, tapping his foot impatiently a couple of times.

"It is a command of King's Orders," replies Gyron. "I will begin it now, if you wish."

"By all means." Jasper motions for him to proceed.

Then Talok says, "Please do."

Facing the thirteen warriors, Gyron taps two of his fingers on the palm of his opposite hand, then shouts, "King's Orders, Onyx Warriors!" Gripping one of his wrists, he continues more softly, "As many have perished this day, your king commands you to light the skies with fire, in honor of the fallen."

All thirteen warriors take a step away from each other, widening their stances. They gracefully lift their hands up to hip height, fire starting to wisp over their palms.

From the front of the formation, Zenzar shouts, "At the King's Command!"

The twelve behind him stand there, ready and waiting.

Gyron snaps his attention toward the Vitiosyns.

They're all eyeing him with lust and hate and envy, possibly even hunger.

The Siveyra draws out both of his blades from their sheaths. Ready for a coming attack, he says to Zenzar, "Release it."

The flames grow in their palms, as they lift their hands higher.

Everything goes quiet. There's only the crackling, wisping flame of the Onyx Warriors making a sound. That, and a slight rustling of leaves. At least, it seems similar. Yet it's not coming from the Arkivara, which is behind the Onyx Warriors. But, instead, from the opposite end of the barrier. Somewhere near Soren lying in a heap on the torn-up ground.

As quickly as it started, the flames of the Onyx recede to flickering.

The thirteen lower their hands.

"At the King's Command," states Zenzar. "We still wait, Siveyra-lord Gyronawv."

Either relieved or disappointed, though I cannot tell which, Gyron takes in a deep sighing breath. "Well, that answers that. If King ReNovak has perished, I am not the new Onyx monarch."

Talok glances down in disappointment. All Paragonians seem sad, as well. Their love for Gyron is apparent, in their concerned and hurt glances toward him. With a playful look back at Rorka, I smile my wicked grin.

She shakes her head, then shrugs. To me, she divs, *Go on, Ravier! Give the command. See if you're the next Onyx King.*

Walking forward, I align myself with Zenzar. On the way, I copy Gyron's hand-motions, while speaking the command, "King's Orders, Onyx Warriors!" Stopping many strides from Zenzar and Gyron, I softly say, "In their honor, light the sky with fire, and remember the fallen."

The thirteen's flame flares again. And they lift their hands slightly up, readying for another attempt.

"At the King's Command!" Zenzar shouts, a second time.

For a moment, I hesitate, unsure of what will happen if they *do* release their fire. Thinking it's very unlikely, I speak the words, "Do it!"

As the words leave my mouth, I spot the look of horror on Gyron's face. I almost wish I could take the command back. But there's no going back. Only forward, to an unknown outcome . . .

4

Strikes of the Hammer

The thirteen Onyx Warriors lift their hands higher.

Sweat beads on my brow. I'm anxious for what will happen. More than I thought possible.

Crossing arms in their Onyx way, the warriors clench their fists. Fire and smoke gently billow from their hands. They bow their heads, then flash their attention up. Their hands open. Their arms uncross. Birds of bright, wisping fire form in between their palms. Thirteen in all. As the warriors draw out one blade each, they thrust the points into the ground. They take to one knee.

The fiery birds brighten more. Their white eyes shift to brilliant blue. Bursting with a hazy energy, they fly upward to their destination. All thirteen draw together, forming what resembles a fierce, white dragon made of both fire and mist. Its wings are feathered and elegant. It outsizes even the largest living reptiles of Earth. So small are they in its shadow, they would be its fodder. The dragon is as spindly as a snake. Fast like one too, up in the sky.

The Onyx Warriors slowly stand up. Blades are put back in their sheaths. With that clinking sound of weapons being made harmless, the swift dragon fractures in the sky, flooding it with fire; colors of cobalt, ruby, and brass race across the atmosphere, high above us. It's as the rain at night. Only better, for it shifts to flashing scenes of the festival. It ends with me,

45

standing on the ruby-stone stage, saying, "To the people and world I never knew existed. To a love for magic. To the death of Vitiosus."

Fire fading from the atmosphere, pale-blue sky and soft, white clouds replace it.

Everyone stands frozen in place, staring at me. Shock's etched on their faces.

A voice from Talok's direction breaks the silence, scoffing, "That's ridiculous!"

Turning, I see that it is none other than Zepharre.

He continues, "The Son of LanSoren is not Onyx. How could *he* be their new king? It's absurd."

"Not absurd," says Zymarc, to Zepharre. He looks to me. "Caleiso was right. You cheat magic; though, it's undetectable. Even to me. But I recognize its result. One too many impossibles made possible. Something else telling is your voice. It's deeper, as if you are older. I wouldn't have noticed that, if not for hearing your spoken words at the festival, just now."

Zepharre's exasperated, interrupting to ask Zymarc, "What is all this? A parley? Wait! Are you that Soren? And who is this Caleiso you talk of? Also, how long have *you* been here, Jasper?"

"Who is this fool?" Zymarc says, to no one in particular. Quickly, he saunters toward the Paragonian Sovereignty. Once in front of Zepharre, Zymarc asks of him, "Are you a king, that you would address the Greyvon Alpha in such a tone of disrespect?"

"N-no," replies Zepharre, trying to gather his wits. "But I'm head adviser to King Talok."

"You mean the young king I whisked away, marked for death in twenty-two days, and then brought back?" queries Zymarc.

Zepharre just sputters, utterly confused and glancing at Talok.

Zymarc continues, "As you have failed in that duty of advising your king, perhaps you are a high-ranking warrior that you would dare to talk out of turn among leaders."

"I am the City Warrior to the Eye—"

Laughing, Zymarc cuts him off. "Look behind you, fool, and tell me what city you talk of. For if there is, indeed, a city behind you, then I am not Zymarc, King of Vitiosus. And I will take my leave, immediately, once this barrier of Soren's is broken." He points at the slumbering Soren, as if that finalizes something unsaid.

Talok whispers to Zepharre, who then blushes a deep red. He is struck silent.

But the Vitiosyn isn't finished in mocking the adviser, because next thing we know, Zymarc is saying, "Oh! You must be one of the Arkiveis, for only the Arkivara stills stands strong to testify of her keeper. Defiant to destruction, she is an emblem of magnificence for her people. She slaughtered many of mine, who dared to approach her roots. Her branches too. Are you her tender? Her tamer? I will bow, touching my forehead to the ground, in front of you, if *you* are her Arkivy."

Looking down, Zepharre mumbles, "I am not."

"I thought not." Zymarc turns to face the Onyx Warriors. "Now, to show all of you what I mean about cheating magic. That this young Ravier is not the only one here, able to deceive its laws."

Zymarc takes out a small knife that's tucked in at the top of his right boot. With it, he cuts symbols into each of his palms. Putting the knife away, he rubs his palms together. Smoke emits from them. Then he speaks, "Vitio-sev-sous!"

His palms flash with red-and-black fire. Left behind are the black symbols cut into his skin. Approaching the warriors, Zymarc repeats Gyron's hand motions, speaking, "King's Orders, Onyx Warriors. As there has been much loss of life these centuries of my dominion, let the sky split with weeping for the fearless fallen."

Looking quite unhappy, yet joining in this time, is Gyron with the thirteen warriors repeating the motions. Their hands do not ignite with fire. Rather, with a fogging, sparking mist. When they release their magic, the flash is bright then blinding. A crack of thunder booms out, its sound fading up. Dark clouds draw together. Clear rain drizzles down. Then it begins pelting anything in its trajectory. On the barrier, it collects, then runs downward on the vast, iridescent dome of our displeasure.

In seconds, the rain is over.

Zymarc grins briefly. "You see? Cheating." He shows his hands, now starting to heal of the marks.

Behind me, Rorka puffs out a breath of frustration.

I can't help but look. She has one hand pressed on the barrier. In the grasp of her other is the hammer, which rests upon her shoulder. To Jasper, she gazes. He paces around and studies the barrier.

Instinctually, I blurt out, "Well, then, let's put cheating to the test."

I rush to Rorka. Placing my left hand where her right is pressed on the other side, the Prismatic of Magic lets my hand pass through enough that I'm able to intertwine my fingers with Rorka's. I pull her in. When I do, surprise takes hold of her. She stumbles, letting go of the hammer as she does. I catch it by the handle, since that's the part to enter the barrier with her.

But catching hold of his hammer's head, before it too is swallowed up, is Azabahk, shrieking on the other side. "I've had about enough of these creatures abusing my hammer. Will someone please reinitiate the Rules of Engagement? I really want to smash some heads in."

When he yanks hard, I'm lugged toward the barrier. Though I slam against it, I refuse to let go of the hammer. I pull back instead, and tug the handle a little to the left.

The sound of crunching glass startles us.

We both almost let go of the weapon.

Azabahk, meeting my gaze, laughs a bit. "You devil-born tyke!" he exclaims. "Look, Zymarc! Deezalo's hammer-handle cuts the barrier." He focuses on me again. "Hang on to it, boy."

"Oh, I will." I grin. "Like a devil-born tyke."

Gripping the handle tighter with both hands, it shifts to conform to my grip as RotaSyn did.

Azabahk's thin, black eyebrows draw together, and he studies me a moment. He seems confused by something.

Is it the confidence of my tone?

Perhaps it is the fact that his hammer permits the grip of another master so willingly.

Or maybe it is the Deathasyn, turned Vitiosyn, way of showing curiosity.

Whatever he feels, it has the result I desire: his grip loosening on the hammerhead.

One swift pull from me, and the hammer slips the rest of the way in. The weight of it is incredible, making my muscles feel as if they're going to tear at any second. I stumble back a few steps, barely able to keep it lifted to my waist's height.

Azabahk whines and growls, then grates his nails down both cheeks. "The tyke's going to drop it."

Before it can rip itself from my grip, to fall and smash my feet, Jasper is there to catch it.

Frantically, Azabahk claws at the sliver of broken space, desperate to get his prized weapon back.

I pant for breath, winded by the hammer struggle.

Jasper hides a smile, telling me, "Best to leave this last bit, Tyler Ravier, to Greyvons."

"And that," I say, "is why I let you have it."

"Oh no!" says Jasper, in good humor. "Where is that modesty you had earlier?"

"Hmm, modesty? I think Soren took it."

"Yes, he is good at taking," interrupts Zymarc, watching Azabahk intently. "But we shall turn the tide against him, if you are quick, Alpha Jasper."

"Yes, of course," replies Jasper. "First, I must know if there is anyone here knowledgeable in the binding of Sorshrynaks. It is an art similar to magically restraining Siveyras."

Gyron says, "The Onyx were never taught the art. And then it was said to be lost."

Stepping forward in her awkward way, Rozeth replies, "Siveyra Dezarin was quite knowledgeable in the art, Jasper. Therefore, as well, we are. Ryco and myself."

"However," states Ryco, appearing unfazed by anything, even Rozeth's slaughtering of English. "It has been years since we rehearsed the motions together."

"It takes two, for the binding of Sorshrynaks?" queries Gyron curiously.

"A Siveyra could do it alone," replies Ryco, from across the distance. "At least, that was Master Dezarin's claim. I'm surprised he never taught you, seeing as how you were his apprentice a few thousand years ago."

Huffing, Gyron shakes his head. "He didn't teach me everything."

Looking to me, Ryco Mensa-divs with, *And it's a good thing he didn't, seeing where the Onyx now stand in this war. Tyler, would it be too much to ask you to let me and Rozeth handle Soren, after the barrier is broken? I fear Talok's heart is about to explode with worry . . . or rage toward you. Perhaps both.*

I look to Talok, and see what Ryco means. His face glistens, as if he's just been on a good run. Yet, he's pale. Almost sickly looking. But it's his icy-blue eyes, watching me like a tiger to a rival, that tell me what he's really feeling: rage, and a desire to get to me.

I swallow hard, suddenly sensing guilt for what he must be going through. To Ryco, I div, *Yes, I think that's a good idea.*

Making my way back to being nearer to Talok, I glance over my shoulder, right as Jasper tosses Winter's Vondaen to Zymarc. He says, "Make the marks, former warrior to the Onyx. You do still remember the motions, don't you?"

Not responding, the King Vitiosyn begins his precise, well-timed slashes on the barrier. All completed symbols are a variety of colors. The Greyvon Alpha has readied the hammer in his grip. When Zymarc gets to the third one, Jasper starts smashing the center of the first finished symbol.

Like a rock almost going through a windshield, the barrier is fractured in a circular pattern where the hammer hits it.

Across from them, and several strides down the line from Talok and the others, Azabahk is still tearing at the break in the barrier. And he's actually broken off more pieces. Even though his hands are bloodied with his own magic, and a liquid darker red than human blood, he still goes on.

A few steps from Talok, I position myself to watch the activity by the Vitiosyn line.

Jasper has caught up to Zymarc drawing his sixth symbol. The last two, he cuts even faster. Standing back, he lets Jasper hammer on the eighth.

"At last," cries Azabahk, as he thrusts his entire arm through the hole finally made big enough. "My hammer, Alpha Jasper, if you will?" he pleads.

"My word, Azabahk!" Zymarc rants. "You can't wait for us to finish, before you have your hammer back? You know, if you had shown this much fervent dedication in everything you do, you might have overthrown me, and made yourself King of Vitiosus."

"No, no! I'm quite content with you as king," Azabahk states, even as his hands drip with blood and magic.

"Oh, you are?" Zymarc teases. "Quite content, you say? I'll remember that, the next time you ask for a special favor or token of my appreciation."

"Shut up, Zymarc!" Azabahk growls. "Stop teasing me. Did I ever ridicule you, during your early, stupid years, with you running about—always away from Soren—like some little bird in the shadow of a great dragon?"

Not answering him, Zymarc goes to give Jasper back his blade. But he hesitates a moment to take up Deezalo's Hammer from Jasper.

Slowly, he reaches for it, even while Azabahk continues his rant. "I saved you quite a lot of times, even from Soren a time or twice. Me and Belzara. But those beginning years of the breeding, hoping for an Equidyn. Those were the best. No wars. Just roars, blood, hunts, and bets. Those poor dragons, you know, they were so confused over what you wanted them to *do* with the horses. Loads of us had bets going for how long the horses would last before, well, they became a dragon's dinner." Azabahk laughs a tad, then grimaces in remembrance.

Many among the Paragonians look on squeamishly. Some even clutch at their stomachs.

Zymarc continues reaching for the hammer, but it appears to be leaning toward Jasper.

And Jasper seems amused at this, hiding a smirk.

Azabahk must see it too, because he's exclaiming, "Zymarc! Did you do something to the hammer?"

"For fate's sake!" Zymarc manages to forcefully take hold of the hammer.

"At least you had the good fortune of a warning from me not to lose your grip on it. And, what? A drop from the height of six feet, while you were carelessly swinging it around that night you won it? Try mending your connection, after dropping it from the height of one thousand meters, while you're up in the air riding a dragon and trying to escape that crazed beast, Soren."

Azabahk's mouth drops open in shock. He has no words for Zymarc, not even as the Vitiosyn King paces over to the frontline of the Paragonians and shoves the handle through to Azabahk, then proceeds to beat on the head of it with his bare fist. The hammer breaks off more shards of the barrier, before it ends up in the hands of its horrified master, Azabahk.

"Well, no wonder it doesn't like you," says Azabahk coldly, while he pets the hammer tenderly. At the Prince-General's touch, the ruby stones brighten as if a light has suddenly been put in them. Azabahk's injuries are healed.

"Are you quite content, now, Azabahk?" queries Zymarc calmly.

"Yes, we are, thank you," he replies, gripping the handle with both hands.

"Good." Zymarc rubs the side of his face. He feels along his jawline, before saying, "Now, not to insult your abilities, Alpha Jasper, but why is this barrier even still here?"

His features amused, Jasper glances from Zymarc to Azabahk. "The marks need a good smashing from the outside."

"Well, Azabahk, what are you waiting for?" queries Zymarc, with a slight sneer. "You've another chance to help rescue me from Soren. Caleiso, as well, will be in your debt."

"Does that mean I'll get a token of appreciation, without any snide remarks from King Zymarc?" queries Azabahk, in a patronizing tone.

"Let's see how today ends, first," replies Zymarc, stuffing his hands in his coat pockets.

Azabahk's scarlet-red eyes brighten in excitement. He jogs his way back, to join the Vitiosyn line. Stopping at the smashed mark nearest to him, Azabahk states, "Well, these aren't heads, but they'll have to do."

After he's hit seven of them effortlessly, while holding the hammer one-handed, Azabahk pauses at the last.

Jasper and Zymarc have positioned themselves at opposite ends of the barrier. Gyron stands in front of Rorka. The two are separated by the space of fractured barrier. The Siveyra gazes down at her, in sad longing; she simply stares blankly into nothing.

"Khyra," Ryco states, "when the barrier breaks, release Ben of the lifeless form."

"Yes, of course," she says, as the Prince-General lines up to hit the last symbol.

When Azabahk smashes the eighth, a loud thundering erupts.

My legs buckle, and my hearing fades out for several seconds. My sight too. Someone grabs me, pulls me back. I start blacking out.

A voice calls my name. It's Gemma. I feel her grasp on my shoulder.

"Tyler?" she shrieks again. "I don't think he can hear us."

"Let me get a look at his eyes," says Quall.

Large hands grip the sides of my head.

My sight slowly comes back.

"There, Ravier!" Quall smiles, and gives the side of my neck a hard pat. "Welcome back to where you belong."

He moves aside to let Talok help me stand. Even after I'm standing, my cousin refuses to release my arm, though I gently try to pull away.

He holds tight to me. "Until Soren is no longer a threat, Tyler, you are to remain at my side. Or behind me. Understand?"

Blinking away my surprise at the sternness in his voice, I just nod.

Gemma huddles up against my back. She whispers, "We were all so scared for you, Ty. Then Ben and Khyra. Jasper too."

"It's not over yet," says Warren, beside Quall.

Watching the chaos is hard, here at the sidelines. But I remember Ryco's request, and stay planted next to Talok.

On the far side is Zymarc, attending to Caleiso. She's been injured quite badly by the whole ordeal. The twenty-one surrounding them, with Azabahk, I assume are the other Prince-Generals. All merely a head shorter than Azabahk, their skins are various shades of gray, and their eyes are that Vitiosyn-scarlet.

At this point, Ryco and Rozeth have already made it to Soren, who is starting to come to.

Jasper stands near to them. But he becomes distracted by a bird or two fluttering around his head. They refuse to leave him be, though he bats at them as if they're pesky flies. More birds come and begin pelting him with their very own bodies. Then a whole flock approaches. Set on fire, they throw themselves down onto Jasper.

"Rorka, a little help?" Jasper yells. "Your letter-birds have gone mad!"

Blushing to match her hair, Rorka frantically douses the firebirds with water.

Gyron runs past the Sovereignty, right then, divving to me, *I've a favor to ask of you, Ravier. Think you can make me forget what I'm about to see?*

I watch Gyron approach Ryco and Rozeth, as they are still restraining Soren's hands with rope. Currently, the Withrasyn's on his knees and groggy. But that could change at any moment.

You want to know how to restrain a Sorshrynak? I div back.

Yes, but then I must forget how. King ReNovak and Zymarc could otherwise force the information from me. As it is an art strong enough to restrain a Greyvon, perhaps even a Rubidyn, the knowledge of its art is potentially dangerous for me to remember. If, however, I am ever free of the King's Command, or you find a way to put me under your *command, you, and you alone, may make me remember.*

I'm about to ask someone in the Sovereignty for help, but Gyron Mensa-divs again, saying, *You don't need their help, Ravier. If you want something badly enough, right now, you will have it. So long as you are reasonable rather than greedy in your desire.*

He makes it to Dezarin's two apprentices, as Ryco is yelling, "Rozeth, shove the knives into his wrists, and hurry! He's getting his strength back."

Gemma takes the position at my side. She grips my arm tight, but remains quiet.

When Rozeth does as Ryco instructs, the sound of knives cutting into flesh is sickening. Soren screams a tormented cry. Going silent, his face blank too, tears pour from his eyes.

Gemma buries her face against my sleeve, silently sobbing.

Ryco releases his grip on Soren's arm, and trades places with Rozeth. She undoes her coat's belt, to rip the long strip of leather free. Making a loop, she slips it over Soren's head and then cinches it round his neck. Planting one of her boot-clad feet on his backside, she pulls the belt back hard, choking him. Ryco finishes tying the bindings, even while Gyron stands next to Rozeth. Wisping magic is held in the Siveyra's hands, ready to fire at Soren.

"Done!" Ryco proclaims. "Rozeth, check it for weaknesses."

As Rozeth releases the belt, to go check Ryco's work, Soren's tears cease. But then he starts quivering, sweating profusely.

"It's perfect," says Rozeth. "Nothing amiss."

Both apprentices touch a hand to opposite sides of Soren's face. Their eyes close, then begins their soft, haunting chant. The words cannot be made out, but they can be felt through the air. It's like my deepest fear turned into a physical being biting at me, though it cannot be seen. Adrenaline detonates. I want to run. To flee or attack? It doesn't matter. I just don't want to hold still. But I must.

The need to focus is desperate, almost unattainable, until Gyron looks back at me, divving, *Get ready, Ravier.*

When the apprentices stop their chant, Soren shakes violently. Blood oozes from his eyes, running down his pain-stricken face. His showing skin splits and cracks, bleeding him, and he cries out again.

Tears sting my eyes. He no longer looks like a monster, and I pity him. Only the hardening of my heart cuts off that flow of pity.

Closing my eyes, I reach out with my mind. It seems to bump around, searching. I picture Gyron's face. His voice, saying at the festival, *"You are a prized one of Paragon, too, Tyler Ravier . . . you're mine to protect."*

I latch on to that word *protect.* I desperately want to protect Gyron. From what I've learned of the Onyx, they are a prize to be won. A weapon of war. I think, *With any luck, I'll save him from the heartache of being used as such.*

The searching for the Siveyra stops, and I sync with his mind. At least, that's how it feels. He's calm and confident. Altogether, a source of strength. I all of a sudden remember the sensations felt from my father's fourth line: the rising hope after wars, and light after storms.

I wonder, *Could the lines refer to people I can trust, like Gyron?*

The Siveyra pushes back with his mind, taking the feelings away. *Now, Tyler!* he divs.

I'm still not sure what to do, in order to make a Siveyra forget. Not until the fourth line resounds in my mind, in the voice of Aysivak, *Hatred's pain turns to nirvana, never again to remember.*

Opening my eyes, I focus on hate. Hating anything and everything. I hold tight to Gyron's mind, refusing to let go, the same way I held on to Deezalo's Hammer. All fear flees from me, like when I summoned RotaSyn to my grasp, before battling against a Sorshrynak.

I then remember Caleiso's betrayal to my heart, and fury ignites.

My blood seems to boil.

Gemma lets go. Startled by something, she retreats to standing behind me again.

Gyron's cries—only heard in my mind—begin to fill me, blocking out all else.

As I hear a great snap of a whip, Gyron's mind is released.

He staggers back one step, and his magic fades to nothing in his grasp.

"It is done!" Rozeth shouts. "We are safe."

"For now," Ryco adds.

When Gyron makes no returning Mensa-div, I assume that he's been made to forget by my will.

"Now, wherever is that Borrower of Time?" queries Azabahk.

Quite finished with his destroying of the letter-birds gone wild, but still a bit flustered, is Jasper, replying, "Yes, Paydinn should have been here by now."

"Actually," says a voice, beside Azabahk and the Prince-Generals, "I've been here a while."

Walking away from them, and closer to Soren, is a rather odd-looking man dressed in brown-and-black robes. When he steps on a patch of shamrock-grass, his robes take on a textured, green hue. His hair goes past his shoulders, and is patterned as brown, tan, and straw-colored snakeskin. His eyes, too, are reptilian. At first, they're a bright-yellow with black slits. Then the yellow transitions to a golden color and then orange.

Zepharre scowls. Finding his voice, he queries, "And you didn't bother to assist with this, Master Paydinn, until now, because . . . ?"

"Well, how could I, with the barrier in the way?" Paydinn's defensive, as his eyes darken to a rusty-orange. "Besides, I *was* standing among Zymarc's Prince-Generals for several seconds. They noticed nothing. I suspect they were too enthralled by the discussion of ReNovak's whereabouts and fortune. As was everyone. Then Jasper's revelation of him potentially being here the whole time, watching, well, it was too good of an idea not to try for myself. Gave me quite a lot of time to study Soren unhindered, in order to determine what time he's from. But, I must say, I am very thwarted in my efforts."

"Why?" queries Jasper, now less flustered. "Is something wrong? You've never had any prior trouble with doing that."

"Because, as far as I can tell," says Paydinn, lifting his broad shoulders, "he's two Sorens; a younger one from long ago, and a much older and crazier Soren. The one all of us know much too well."

Jasper shakes his head, lost in thought.

"That cannot be," states Gyron.

"And yet, I agree with the Time Borrower," remarks Zymarc, as he helps Caleiso up to her feet. "Last time I dueled with Soren, he had nowhere near this level of strength."

"Well, well, isn't this a day to mark in history? Nothing like it, I dare say. At least, not in my time of being the Keeper to The Watchman's Log. Which reminds me, Jasper," Paydinn says, as he turns to him, "was it *really* necessary to threaten me, with the weight of all the books upon my neck? That wasn't very nice. Is it because of that tedious favor I asked of you?"

"That had nothing to do with it," replies Jasper, as he approaches Gyron. "But seeing how you arrived in a timely fashion, I think the threat *was* necessary. I know how you like to tarry with your time. I fear it's a quality all Borrowers of Time will suffer to eternity."

Slipping Winter's Vondaen from its sheath, Jasper offers Gyron the blade, which the Siveyra does not reach for.

"I do not understand your meaning, Jasper," he says. "What am I to do with that?"

"Split Soren," Jasper replies, "so that we may send each back to his proper time. As my blade transcends planes of existence, it can pierce anything of the ethereal world. Soren must be using the guiles of some unknown magic, to accomplish what none other ever has. But Winter's Vondaen cannot be fooled. It will help to put this right. You are a Siveyra, Gyron. Ask Zymarc, in place of King ReNovak, to release you to your full power, in order to send Soren back."

Zymarc says, "Do as he commands, Siveyra Gyronawv."

"I cannot," Gyron argues. "Not until this business of Onyx command has been cleared up."

"Oh, I can help with that," says Paydinn happily, rubbing his hands together. "A command of the Metimoran-Siveyra, to tell the truth, Onyx Warriors: who is your mighty monarch?" Pleased with himself, Paydinn gives one nod and then turns and strides the rest of the way to Soren. Under his breath, he says, "I love making them do this. Never did it with you around, though, Gyronawv."

Zenzar, at the formations' front, loudly speaks, "Strong and sure, our King ReNovak, of the House of Dovak, leads us!"

The remaining warriors join in for the rest of it, like a chant, saying, "Younger brother to King Jzorrdawv; the sons of Aygawnax; only son to RethnoBane; second son of Divoldane; daughter to Siveyra-lord Novak; only child of Dovak; the daughter of Nyxane, first among the Sorsryns of Onyx."

For a moment, they pause, seeming finished with their recital. And Paydinn, who's been silently counting the Onyx monarchs, now happily sighs. He starts to say something, but the Onyx Warriors cut him off, adding, "Friend to Soren; brothers to Monel, first Withrasyn King."

Paydinn whirls around. His wide eyes shift to the color of lime-green. He exclaims, "That part's new!"

Now finished, the warriors relax their stances, and appear to take in what they've just said.

"Well, how do you like that," says Paydinn, in surprise. "If you go back far enough, the first Onyx and Withrasyn Sorsryns were, indeed, brothers. Three brothers."

"Triple terror, if you ask me and the old legends written of them," says another voice, much deeper, approaching from behind the Vitiosyns.

They clear away, in startled fear of the voice.

Standing taller than anyone present, and on two legs, is some giant of a man dressed in black clothes accentuated by dark fur. He appears to be Rorka's age. Somewhere in his twenties, he strides onto the torn-up battleground as would a gladiator after a recent victory.

I don't have to wonder for long whom the newcomer could be, because Gyron somewhat cringes, saying one name under his breath: "Mekka."

"Took you long enough," states Jasper coldly. "Go stand with the Sovereignty, until this is finished. And I want not one word from you. Understand? You, or Rorka. For if I hear one utterance—from either of you—before the Vitiosyns have taken their leave, I'm liable to lose two of the best candidates ever born. All in one day."

Mekka obeys, though he sends a great scowl in Rorka's direction.

She peers away, to Jasper offering Gyron his blade yet again.

"Please, Gyron," he says, "let us end this now. I feel that Greyvon side of me wanting to be let loose, to gnaw on something."

"Yes, we're all so starving!" Talok practically shouts, sounding quite unlike himself. He's clawing at the Geldryn bangle on his wrist. His blue eyes are wild, darting their focus around every few seconds, to watch anything that moves.

Mekka stoops down, to mutter to Musgrae, "What's gotten into him? Is he about to go into shock, over all that's happened?"

Musgrae lifts a shoulder in answer, before glancing at Talok in concern.

Taking Jasper's offered blade, Gyron shifts into a mortal far greater than any I've seen. He's darker and taller. White, gray, and black flames wisp off his skin. It's as if lit liquid fuel coats his flesh, without burning him. His eyes are pure, glowing white. And his hair is an unreflecting black. But what startles me, then disturbs me, are his hands gripping Winter's Vondaen. They are enhanced with the Prismatic of Magic, though more elegant in appearance to mine. Akin to gauntlets painted on with precision, the black starts at his fingertips. At his wrists, it shifts to intricately woven lines, and then fades away at both elbows, blending in with his dark olive-toned skin. His fingernails glow white too, and the colors of all the magics flare like fire on his hands.

In shock, I think, *Did Aysivak and Awngeleik somehow give me the beginning power of a Siveyra? It would explain a lot. But how's it even possible?*

He saunters to the Sorshrynak, still kneeling as his bound hands tremble. The splits on his skin have stopped bleeding. Soren glares up at the Siveyra facing him, but quickly shifts his focus to me. Utter terror sinks into his eyes, and he manages a Mensa-div, echoing, *Not the beginning power of a Siveyra, Ravier. Today, you are no mere boy. Can't you feel it? The power it gives? An ultimate strength. If you wanted to, you could vanquish the Vitiosyn this very day.*

If Soren had anything else he wished for me to know, it's cut short by Gyron thrusting Winter's Vondaen into the center of Soren's chest.

Crying out, Soren tries to grip the blade with his restrained hands. But the pain must be too great for him to do anything except continuously tremor.

Gyron rotates the blade edge, from vertical to horizontal. While it's still partly in Soren's chest, Winter's Vondaen shifts to looking like the inset jewels of dull mirrors. The jewels are now reminiscent of what the blade previously was—icy-blue, pale-green, and a new color of turquoise. All still resemble colored glass.

Gyron grips Soren's shoulder, and slowly moves the blade to his right with his other hand.

In agony, Soren shuts his eyes. Kneeling and bound, he shouts torturous screams. He then goes silent, seeming to have lost his strength even to cry out.

A figure starts to stand up. Gradually, it separates from Soren, on his knees. It's made of a sort of black energy. Dark, even cold-like, it consumes all light near to it. Likened to a shadow made of fire, it takes on a humanoid appearance. Two legs. Two arms. Five fingers on each hand. But the two eyes are what draw me in. They hold my attention. Uncorrupted, glowing white. It's akin to looking into the sun. I should look away. But I don't want to, for the feelings this gaze gives me. Hope. Light. Life. Happiness. Elation. My life, before losing my dad. A sense of wholeness comes over me, taking the place of the brokenness, confusion, and anger.

"What *is* that?" queries Paydinn, his eyes widening. They change yet again. This time, to a faint color of blue.

The figure's eyes dim, while Winter's Vondaen is still in its chest.

"A command of truth," speaks Gyron, to the figure, as the blade softly glows. "Are you friend or foe, to the laws of time?"

Tilting its head as if curious of something, it peers down at the Greyvon blade. The figure grips the edge in both hands, speaking back, "I am friend to Vardiyas, yes, even to the greatest among many: Aysivak from the Pools of Vosh-Perida."

Posture relaxing, Gyron releases Soren's shoulder. He also slides Winter's Vondaen out of the figure's chest.

That figure then takes confident steps back from the Onyx Siveyra. The black energy becomes a person: Soren of the Monel. Younger and brighter. It's as if years of horror have been wiped away.

Pleasantly, he smiles. His vampire fangs are hardly noticeable, as he looks Gyron up and down in awe. "What an honor to have been summoned to such a moment as this. You look to have descended from my little brother, Nyxane. Or others like him. Though I must say, Sorsryn, you are much mightier than my little Onyx brother could ever hope to be." Holding out his left hand in greeting, Soren takes a step forward.

Cautiously, Gyron is about to grip Soren's hand in a friendly greeting.

But the sound of footsteps rushing toward the two of them startles Soren away.

Azabahk's taken to running at the two, with his hammer raised menacingly. Shock on his face, he exclaims, "I don't know what's happening! I can't stop myself! Best to get out of the way, Gyronawv. Let the hammer end Soren, instead."

"End me?" Soren shrieks, rushing to hide behind Rorka. "What have I ever done to him? And, Shena, what's happened to you? You're so small." Smiling playfully, Soren says to her, "Shall I start calling you Little Sunset?"

In reaction to that last line, all Paragonians at the front—as well as the line behind them—aim unfired arrows and magic at Soren. Yet the present-and-accounted-for Sovereignty aim at Azabahk.

Petrified in place, Rorka simply stares at Azabahk running full speed toward them.

Talok shouts, "Hold fire, Paragonians! King Zymarc, restrain your man!"

Zymarc yells, "Stop this, Azabahk, stand down!"

Even while Zymarc is attempting to command him, Azabahk looks over his shoulder and throws an ice spike back at his king.

Dodging it, Zymarc readies himself. He raises his hand, and tenses it. After he takes aim, he pulls at Azabahk with magic.

"Forgiveness, Zymarc!" Azabahk shouts, in apology. "Deezalo's Hammer demands the blood of this Soren."

Zymarc, lifting up his other hand, pulls on Azabahk's running figure harder.

That's when Azabahk's stride somewhat slows.

"Well, come on, Maetreis Shena." Soren elbows Rorka's back. "Where's that big bad bark of yours?"

Her back to him, all she manages to reply is, "I'm not the former Matriarch, Shena."

Soren startles at this revelation, slinking away from her. Clearly, he's confused. Perhaps, even grieved.

Azabahk is mid-run, when Gyron blocks the path to Soren and, consequently, to Rorka. But the Prince-General veers out of the way, falling to the ground. He scrambles back up, but immediately slams into Mekka, who's made his way out into the fray.

"Forgiveness, Greyvon!" Azabahk cringes. "But I can't seem to control these hands. Nor these feet of mine."

"Oh, that's quite all right, Vitiosyn. No need to apologize," replies Mekka, looking Azabahk over hungrily. Mekka's form starts to smoke as would a fire about to ignite. Then the smoke thickens, and flashes with white sparks.

My mouth goes dry, at the sight of a wolf-like beast beginning to emerge within the smoke. His eyes are as two hot coals looking out from a fire. And his fur is thick and black, and shimmering with mist. His size surpassing that of even the largest of bears, he's recognizably none other than Jack Wayeland's beast. He's larger now, however, than he was in the pictures.

Gemma tenses, seeming to also realize who he is.

Azabahk recovers his wits. His tension shifts to hostility. He takes a swing at Mekka.

Zymarc yells, "Azabahk, drop the hammer!"

"No!" Azabahk shouts back. "It would never forgive me!"

Mekka lunges at the Prince-General, who's occupied with fighting the pull Zymarc has on his arm swinging the hammer.

"Come now," says the younger Soren, chuckling. "Why are there three of me here? Can anyone tell me? And why's that creature not swinging the hammer at you? This fight's not fair at all. Well, best to even my odds."

When Soren snaps his fingers, Zymarc's hold on Azabahk is cut off.

Zymarc falls back, clambering to regain his senses.

The hammer hits Mekka on the snout.

He yelps, then snarls. Next, his shimmering fur changes into a coat of spiked metal. Yet he remains sleek, in appearance.

Breaking from her petrified pose, Rorka rushes to assist Mekka.

Soren giggles a little, then says, "Bet that hurt! Now, will someone explain what's happening? Why are there three of me? It's rather unconventional." He shrugs.

"That's what he said," whispers Warren, more to himself than anyone.

"Not the time, Warren," Quall mutters, watching Paydinn at the sidelines, flipping through The Watchman's Log.

"I just don't know, Jasper!" Paydinn exclaims, closing the book. "I still can't find the truth of what time they're from."

"Ooh! A Borrower of Time?" Soren exclaims. "Yes! Let me see that! I want out of here." Soren rushes toward Paydinn, saying, "Hearing all these thoughts of people wishing me dead, well, it's rather frightening. I don't mean that I'm afraid. Only, rather, disconcerted. Perhaps, a little sad. I've no idea why I'm so hated by both sides of this war you're in."

As Soren gets closer to Paydinn, the Arkivara begins a ruckus of noise. Shaking her leaves like some kind of rattlesnake warning, she fans her branches out to appear alert.

Soren stops. In fright, he slowly looks past Paydinn to the white-and-black bark of the Arkivara. Up, he continues his gaze to her rattling leaves colored of turquoise.

Musgrae queries, "What is she doing, Kent?"

"Readying for a kill strike," he replies, in pride.

Jasper yells across the expanse, "Get down!"

Right then, leaves launch from the Arkivara, shifting to glass-like knives midair. They pelt the ground. A few graze Paydinn and Soren on their necks.

Not crying out, the two manage to stumble away.

"Quick," says Soren breathlessly, holding out his hand. "Your book, Borrower. Though you do not, *I* know what moment I have left behind."

Paydinn gives it to him, lifting his hands in time to shield them from another Arkivara attack. "How is it that you know its art, if I'm permitted to ask?"

Ignoring him, Soren appears to throw the book on the ground in disgust. But then it grows into a blue-bound book of massive proportions. Soren's barely tall enough for his head to be seen from over the top of it. Opening it, he shuffles through the pages, saying, "Oh, The Watchman's Log. Such a slow one. Have you already appeased it with a good viewing today, Keeper?"

His breaths unsteady, Paydinn replies, "Yes," even as he's using magic to knock the Arkivara's lethal leaves aside.

"Very good," states Soren. "Almost there."

Deciding that the leaf-knives must not be enough, the Arkivara's trunk shifts as if it's taking a breath. Its bark then transitions to seem as scuffed mirrors.

"Hurry!" Paydinn shouts.

Soren looks up, peering over the top of the book. He focuses on Azabahk, who's managed to evade Vitiosyns and the three Greyvons, alike. The Prince-General now sprints toward the book, at full speed.

Zymarc runs in front of the Vitiosyn line, commanding them to stop Azabahk. "But do not hit the hammer!" he yells. "Azabahk, let go of it!"

"I can't!" the Prince-General screams in horror.

Face etched with regret, Zymarc stops running. He takes aim at Azabahk, with the bow-and-arrow appearing in his grasp. After the shot is released, the arrow's tail of attached rope-light slides within Zymarc's loose grip.

The arrow tip bursts right through Azabahk's shoulder. Like a grappling hook on a wall, Azabahk is snagged by his king. Screeching and struggling, he's dragged back by him.

The hammer slips from his grip and falls to the ground.

When it thuds onto the battlefield, Azabahk yells out what I take to be angry curses. Though I've no idea what they mean, their sound is hateful and threatening.

Relief sweeps over Soren's face, until he spots me standing steadfast beside Talok. Then it's nothing except curiosity in his eyes.

I look behind for Gemma, to ensure she's not spotted. But I don't see her. Catching Musgrae's gaze, he motions to her form, retreating deeper into the Paragonian crowd.

She's scared, Ravier, Musgrae divs. *Too many Sorens. And she's terrified of Mekka. Ryco told her to go to the castle and wait. Eli and Khyra too.*

Relieved, I look back to Soren, and Mensa-div, *Are you going to claim that we're one and the same, as well?*

Is that *what the bound one did?* he echoes, returning to his viewing of the pages. He flips through more of them. *No, no, young Sorsivyte. You are better. Yes, better. More powerful than any here. Yet you merely watch, while stoic and standing there beside a king. Haven't you told him what you are?*

He knows who I am, is my echoing reply.

What, *not who,* echoes Soren, correcting me. *How interesting. You don't know. Could be attributed to you having a power not meant to be yours yet. Ah! Well, we're out of time. We'll talk again, I'm sure . . . given what you are. Farewell!*

Soon after, Soren announces, "I've found the right moment. But I've one thing to say, before I go." Quickening his voice, and looking right at me, Soren continues, "Life's riches cannot be spent. Nor can they be burned. They soar in memories left behind, long after a life has lost its breath. Yes! That one should do." Second-guessing himself, Soren says, "Or maybe I should've picked the other one. Ah, well! Just remember this: when in doubt, burn it! Farewell, sons and daughters of Withrasyn!"

Kent steps forward, shouting, "He's leaving, Eyo'el! Let him go in peace."

The Arkivara quiets down. But her leaves soon start their rattle again.

"That won't quiet her for long. Go now, Soren." Kent gestures.

"Wait!" Zymarc exclaims, his focus shifting from the injured Azabahk coddling his hammer, to the Soren about to leave.

Ignoring him, Paydinn turns. Swiftly, he closes the book on Soren. Within seconds, it has changed back into being a small-handbook size.

"For fate's sake, Borrower," Zymarc fumes. "You didn't think to ask him about the time frame the other is from, before slamming the book on him?"

"I have had enough!" Jasper yells, in fury.

That's when an erupting, roaring howl sounds out.

All turn and look at Jasper. It's not like we have a choice. His voice commands attention. All who hear it, must heed its sound with respect.

Now back in his Greyvon form is Jasper. The glint in his emerald-green eyes says it all. He's hungry for blood. And I don't think he cares whose it is. But judging by how he's eyeing the bound Soren, he will most certainly be the first victim of Jasper in this beast form.

Rorka sees his intent too, and she screams, "Jasper, don't! Mekka, stop him!"

5

Rabid Beast

In Greyvon form, Mekka trots along in front of the Paragonian formation. Gruffly, he replies to Rorka, "Come guard our allies!"

As she does, I get the urge to help in some way. I'm restless, standing in place. The need to do something grows; it claws up my spine. My foot lifts. I'm about to step forward.

But Talok juts his arm out in front of me. He sends me a look of warning, while Mensa-divving, *Don't you even dare do it! Jasper will tear apart the first to get in his way. Doesn't matter if they're friend or foe.*

"Jasper," Gyron shouts, shifted into his normal Onyx self. "If you kill him, you'll fracture time. Please, try to fight your hunger!"

Zymarc sprints farther along his Vitiosyn line. He slides down, to being bent over. He reaches desperately for something; the Vitiosyn, absent of her heart. Grabbing her body by the ankle, Zymarc flings her out onto the battlefield.

Jasper can't help but focus on that body up in the air.

It gives Gyron time to rush away, and grab the bound Soren. He drags him to safety, amid the field of Midnight Anemones.

When the dead Vitiosyn lands several feet from him, Jasper lunges for it. Hard, he bites into its flesh. I look away, even as sounds of flesh and bone being ripped apart sicken me, making my stomach twist uncomfortably.

"Why aren't there more bodies around?" queries Zymarc frantically.

"Scepter," he shouts at the King Vitasadyn, peering over the scene in amusement. "What are you waiting for? Feed him the bodies we brought with us, for this very sort of scenario."

Looking down at Zymarc, Scepter rumbles rather innocently, "I got hungry, watching all this action."

"You ate them!" Zymarc yells, in a raging fit. "Good-for-nothing dragon! You roar once, then you're done? I should've let your younger brother, Reign, rip your throat out rather than save you."

Deeply, Scepter rumbles, "I brought the Sorshrynak to his knees, with that roar. It's more than any else here hath done, save for the boy across the way. He is as a little bird in the shadow of a great dragon. But this little bird is more than he appears."

"Well, then, be that great dragon, Scepter, and *do* something!" Zymarc commands.

Lifting his head higher, Scepter replies, "As that bird does nothing but stand beside the King of Dragon Tamers, so shall I be. Still, and unmoving. Pity you've kept Soren's looks, up to this point. You're the target, now. And there's no time for a change of face. But if you are unable to withstand a row with a hungry Greyvon, while unassisted, Zymarc, then you are not worthy to be King of Vitiosus. As you've said to Soren, do your worst!"

"What an Onyx way to answer," says Zymarc, with venom edging his voice. Clenching his fists, he rips one of his blades free of its sheath. He then faces Jasper, who's finishing up his impromptu meal of dead Vitiosyn.

Zymarc is the one to rush forward, stopping once he has Jasper's attention.

Jasper snarls at him. The fur on his back stands up, like an angry cat's. Dark-red blood drips from his snout, even from his furry chest of peppered-gray hair.

Zymarc stands his ground, shouting at Paydinn, "Borrower, continue your work. I'll buy you time."

The fight starts. And it's terrifying. Yet beautiful. I smile, ever so slightly.

In one leap, Jasper easily covers thirty feet. He dodges Zymarc's blade, and latches his sharp teeth into Zymarc's swinging arm.

The growls of Jasper and shouts of Zymarc blend into something melodic. Satisfying, even. It's reminiscent of the beast by Mirror Lake, going after Awngeleik. The sound isn't quite right, however.

Flowing words, Zymarc speaks. For a few seconds, Jasper is stunned. He's forced to release Zymarc. But he's even angrier. Tensing his stance on four legs, he roars his wailing howl.

Zymarc holds up a hand, to shield himself. He struggles. His arm begins to shake, as if pushing on something beyond his strength. In pain, he cries out the same way an athlete tearing a muscle would. Yet he holds back Jasper's wail, while managing to keep a grip on his blade.

Jasper's voice ceases its wail. Mere seconds he waits, then charges at Zymarc.

The Vitiosyn King runs full speed, in the opposite direction. Jumping high, he drops his blade to catch the edge of an appearing sheet of glass suspended midair. He pulls himself up, and out of Jasper's reach.

"Please, Jasper!" Zymarc yells. "This is not how I want a duel with you, as some rabid beast. But a duel between kings! See reason, and fight your hunger!"

Jasper circles around the space below Zymarc, looking above at his desired victim. He growls out the words, "Yes, a rabid beast. That is true. But you are wrong of something, Soren. I am not a king. I am Alpha to the Greyvons!"

"I'm not Soren!" Zymarc shouts desperately. He trembles, as he balances atop the small sheet of glass. In fear, he gazes down at Jasper.

"I don't care!" Jasper snarls. "Most likely, you'll taste just as good, as I rip your throat out!" With that, Jasper lunges up and breaks the glass.

Zymarc falls, scrambling to get away.

But Jasper is already on top of him, violently biting and snarling at the Vitiosyn's face.

Zymarc seizes hold of the top and bottom of Jasper's snapping snout, pushing with all his strength. At least, what strength he has left.

Caleiso screams. She's caught mid-run by Azabahk. He wraps his arms around her, keeping her at the front of the Vitiosyn line.

"Azabahk, stop him!" Caleiso cries, thrashing to get away. Tears stream down her face. "He's going to kill Zymarc."

"I know," says Azabahk, in sorrow.

Zymarc struggles out the words, "Please, Jasper, you don't want to see the creature I become, when provoked. There will be nothing left of Paragon, save for us still fighting each other."

Jasper stops the snapping of his teeth, and starts forcing his jaw to close in. He cuts into Zymarc's fingers, which are wrapped over the front rows of teeth.

Cringing, Zymarc pants with the effort of saving his neck from the bite of Jasper.

"Is there no one to calm him?" queries Rozeth, to Ryco.

"Not until he's had his fill," replies Ryco.

As Ryco's talking, someone from the Vitiosyn side confidently steps out onto the battlefield.

It's Belzara, saying, "Vitiosyns behind, bring out the rebels among us, half-dead. Let us see if traitor flesh will satisfy a great and hungry wolf."

Panic erupts among the Vitiosyns. Several scramble away, but are caught. The twenty-one Prince-Generals toss mortally wounded, screaming, and terrified Vitiosyns onto the battlefield.

"There, look, Jasper," Zymarc says, "easy prey for you to have, till you're most content."

Jasper tightens his jaw harder, and Zymarc's arms shake from the struggle against him.

Belzara bravely approaches the two. Holding out her hand, palm facing up, she speaks hissing and soothing words that somewhat calm Jasper.

Zymarc manages to push Jasper hard enough that he's able to sit up. His footing, he readies for standing. But he can't quite get Jasper off him enough to reclaim his feet.

To one of the Prince-Generals, Belzara looks, commanding, "Possess one of them to insult the Greyvon."

A Prince-General grabs an injured Vitiosyn woman, by the back of her head. Then that Vitiosyn woman shouts at Jasper, "Look at you, leading dog of little rats! Bet you couldn't do more than leave teeth marks, with how old you're looking wearing that fur coat of gray. Are you on your deathbed, rabid little dog?" The injured Vitiosyn laughs maniacally.

The Prince-General on the field lets go of her, to make for his retreat.

Uninterested in Zymarc, Jasper now stalks the Vitiosyn as she's shouting insults.

When her laugh cuts out, she whimpers in fear.

Jasper lunges. In one leap, he's reached her. It's a bloodbath, as he tears her apart and then finishes off the other Vitiosyn traitors.

Meanwhile, Zymarc stands up. He saunters over, to join with Azabahk and Caleiso's company. Sheathing his fallen blade along the way, he then picks up Deezalo's Hammer, which rests at Azabahk's feet. He looks it over. When his injured hands grip it tight, it ignites with red-fire and then shape-shifts into something far more menacing than a war hammer. Now in Zymarc's healed grasp is a scuffed war axe, glowing red, made of solid metal. It has inset stones of black, with a curved blade on one side and a chipped hammerhead on the other. A dull spike is at the top of it. Smiling in great satisfaction, Zymarc takes off the sheathed blades from his back, replacing them with the war axe.

The sight disturbs me. I break out sweating again. Somehow, I know Zymarc has just gotten one of the things on his wish list. Perhaps the one nearly at the top.

"Jasper," Rorka calls out, "come to reason, and stop this. You're scaring our allies. Mekka, what are you waiting for?"

"For him to calm down some!" Mekka shouts. "He'll come at me, if I approach right now. I disrupted him once, during one of his binges. I swore, never again!"

While they're conversing, Zymarc picks up his discarded metal mask. Brushing it off, he puts it back on. That's when one of his Vitiosyns hits him with red flames.

Zymarc startles. He's about to attack that Vitiosyn. Then he sees her amused smile.

"It helps with the transition back into being our mighty king," she says.

"Does it not, King Zymarc?"

He nods, then pats at the smoking embers on his heart-armor's scaly fabric.

Azabahk holds up a new coat of black for him, saying, "I brought a spare."

Before Zymarc can put the offered coat on, another Vitiosyn lets water loose from her hand to drench him.

He laughs, even as Jasper kills off his traitors in the background. "Well, where's the wind, Vitiosyns?" calls out Zymarc, holding out his arms.

Taking the invitation, they send gales of wind at him. He is unshaken. Instead, he transitions back into his Vitiosyn self: tattooed scalp, pale skin, crimson eyes, and all.

The gale cuts out, and Zymarc puts on the coat. Adjusting it, he remarks, "See, I am worthy. As is Belzara, once again. You will tolerate her, in your midst."

Unconcerned with the Vitiosyn dialogue, Rorka is still fixed on Jasper. "Mekka! Jasper's never like this. What's happened to him?" she shrieks, while standing in front of Talok.

My cousin's incredibly calm, yet biting at his nails in a nervously bored sort of way.

"He hasn't eaten for three days, Rorka!" Mekka yells, now shifted back to being on two legs. "And I've been meaning to ask you, *why* do you reek of Onyx? The smell is maddening. To both me *and* Alpha Jasper. He caught a whiff of you, then went all bizarre. *What* have you done?" Mekka demands to know.

Jasper's ruckus quiets down, as the two candidates are bickering. Then he's surrounded by black smoke. He changes into human form. A dark, haunting scowl on his face, Jasper slowly stands. He shouts at them, "I said, not *one* word!"

The candidates stop short, instantly focusing on the ground.

Zymarc clears his throat. He calls out, through the marred mask, "Nice to have you back, Alpha Jasper. The Rules of Engagement initiate again, at your word."

Jasper's covered head to boot with blood. Panting, as if catching his breath, the alpha looks around in shame. He advances toward Talok, but someone holding out a wetted, white cloth catches his attention.

It's Ben, forcing a grin. "For your face, Alpha Jasper," he says.

Slightly grinning back, Jasper takes the offered cloth. He thanks Ben, then begins cleaning his face and hands. Motioning toward the Midnight Anemone field, Jasper says, "Bring him back out, Gyron. I am no longer hungry."

Gyron emerges from the field of tall flowers, with the bound Soren in tow. Paydinn emerges, as well, and follows after them, tripping over his robes a little.

Jasper strides forward. His pace quickens. When Soren's almost within reach, he drops the cloth and then lashes out to grip Soren's face. He spits out the words: "Now, you listen to me, White Wretch. We're not going to hear any more words from you, unless it directly relates to your being put back in your time. No rhymes. No counting. No smiling. Just walking. Understand?" Jasper shakes him a bit.

Soren is silent, and unmoving.

"There," says Jasper. "Was that so hard? Ryco, you may remove his bindings."

Gyron pushes Soren toward the Paragonian Sovereignty, where Ryco stands.

But Ryco motions to Talok, saying, "As Talok is King of Paragon, it is his right. This is his land to defend. His people to protect. Soren has slighted him, above all."

"Very well." Jasper beckons for my cousin's approach.

Sighing, Talok stops his nail biting to saunter forward. Roughly, he grabs Soren's wrists and begins to unwind the restraints. Dropping them, he then pulls the knives slowly from Soren's wrists one at a time. He slips the first into one of the many slots on his left bracer. When he removes the second knife, he hesitates. After wiping some of the blood off the metal with his thumb, Talok's stance goes rigid. Then he wipes all the blood on the knife carefully onto his palm. Tucking the knife into the bracer, he clenches his bloodied hand, and fire ignites within it. He wipes this blood-ash onto Soren's face, seething out the words, "I never want to see you again, Withrasyn Taint. Don't ever come back."

As Talok comes to stand near me again, I catch sight of his gaze on anything *except* me. Rather than a shadow of worry, his expression is an unusual one of spiteful fire.

Soren stands, appearing unsteady on his feet. Observing Paydinn opening The Watchman's Log to full-size, he ambles that way.

And when he does, Zymarc ridicules him, saying, "You know, Soren, I've long had a regret from that day you died. Centuries ago, we danced a Dance of Death for you. To celebrate your passing into another place. And I do believe some Vitiosyns who danced then, are here now. *Those Vitiosyns come forward.*"

Even as hundreds of battle-scarred Vitiosyns come to the frontline, joining with Azabahk and the Prince-Generals, Zymarc continues, "I was always a little saddened that you weren't there to see how wonderfully they performed, in your honor. Though *I* am too tired for it, many of my Vitiosyns are restless, and I will permit—No! Rather, command—them to dance again. This time, to celebrate your second death. Vitiosyns, make your quick preparations."

From across the great distance separating us, it's unclear what those Vitiosyns' preparations are. But there's much movement and soft chanting amongst them.

Jasper clasps his hands behind his back, looking to Gyron. Nodding once his way, Jasper then focuses on Zymarc.

The two approach the Greyvon Alpha, while the candidates stand protectively at his sides.

Vitiosyn hums and chants begin.

Magic and symbols explode up.

Then screams ring out.

Much blood is spilled.

Watching the Dance of Death is like just that: death, and the disturbance of seeing it violently played out. Some Vitiosyns fall dead. Then they're brought back to life, screaming and thrashing. Somewhat calming, they stand up to perform the rhythmic flow of drawing symbols in the air, and cutting curving lines into the flesh of their 'dance' partners. It's like imagining a whole fleet of demons being exorcized, then forced back into their victims. Over and over, they dance this act of disturbance. Yet, there's a beauty to it I cannot deny.

So unforgettable is it, I'm both horrified and in awe.

Chills race through me. That sensation of contradiction wants to rise up. But I push it down.

Focusing on the alpha with the others, I see Zymarc hand Jasper a scroll of paper with a red-wax seal upon it. The Vitiosyn King states, "This is the agreement the Onyx King and I signed before dawn. Look it over, you and the young king. I will send King ReNovak, and my man Azabahk, to hear any counteroffers either of you may have. Shall we now reengage the rules?"

"As soon as Paydinn has put Soren back," replies Jasper. "Paydinn, are you ready?"

"I, um . . . don't know. I've never had this much trouble getting a reading."

"A trick for free?" Soren says. "Open the book, until you hear its spine crack."

Hesitating, Paydinn does it. But he still grips the cover.

"Let go of it, all the way, Borrower," Soren instructs. "It will stand on its own."

When Paydinn lets it go, it does what Soren said.

The Sorshrynak approaches The Watchman's Log, expanded to full-size, during the Vitiosyns' frightening dance. He's one step away from the blank pages of parchment, when he pivots around. He holds his arms out, not straight, but all bent and graceful-like. Striding forward with purpose, he gradually lowers his arms.

I can't help but count his steps. He gets to twelve, then turns around. Taking a step back, he glances to Paydinn, who's looking quite embarrassed with his flushed face, and eyes colored to magenta.

Pages of The Watchman's Log rapidly flutter almost all the way to the end of the book. Then the pages slow, in their turning. After thirteen more pages flip, it settles to stillness.

Soren grimaces, and I assume that he's tried to smile yet cannot. Next, he motions toward the steps he's taken, then he moves his hands out as if weighing something in his grasp. He ends with pointing to his path, taken from the book, saying, "Thirteen forward. Thirteen along. Thirteen back. Close the book. Thirteen done. Always in that order, Borrower. Then there's no need to search out the answer. The book does it for you."

Paydinn rocks back and forth on his feet nervously, replying, "Honestly, it's not something any Metimora has ever mentioned. Maybe—"

Soren interrupts, "Here's a *trick* they don't know. And it's also how you know it will work, see. There are four thirteens. Four and one and three is eight. Eight and thirteen is twenty-one. And twenty-one plus one is twenty-two. Then you start it all over again, because two plus two is four. Or you can take the beginning *four* and the end *four* and get eight. A sort of completion of magic, to rise, conquer, and slumber. You do know what those actually are, don't you, Borrower?"

Magical completion, I muse. What is he talking about? And those numbers? They came to mind, with the two paintings. Vision of the Dragon, and the one of Soren with his face blacked-out. Red letters of: Thirteen. You're done. *I still don't know what it all means. But this Paydinn* must *know.*

"Yes, but wait!" Paydinn exclaims. "Where does the one added to twenty-one come from?"

"The book, you fool!" Zymarc shakes his head. "The great number of children you have had, Jokryn, has greatly dampened your wit. Please, do Muraine a favor by having no more."

Ignoring Zymarc, Paydinn mumbles to Soren, "My father never taught me that trick."

"Well," says Soren, glancing at me, "fathers sometimes have bad habits of forgetting to teach little tricks to their offspring."

With one last look around, Soren strides forward. On the thirteenth step, a scene appears on the pages of the book.

But Paydinn closes it too quickly for us to watch, while he speaks words of, "Thirteen. Done."

Soren is gone.

Paydinn shrinks his book down to pendant-size. What previously were metal chains decorating the book's spine, is now a single, simplistic necklace string of silver. Slipping it over his head, Paydinn tucks the string and pendant behind the neck edge of his robes. As he's standing on a patch of grass, rock, and dirt, his many layers of fabric replicate an organic pattern.

Zymarc raises his hand. Looking at his Vitiosyns, he commands them, saying, "He's gone! You may stop."

They obey.

Then Gyron, after cutting his palm and letting blood drip onto the battleground, resonates out the words: "The Rules of Engagement are now recommenced."

"If there is nothing else, Alpha Jasper," remarks Zymarc, "we shall take our leave. We've lingered here far too long. Though you've had your lunch, we have not. And neither have your allies. We're all very hungry. King ReNovak, and Azabahk, will return to hear your counteroffers."

"You, yourself, will not return with them, this dusk?" queries Jasper.

Zymarc replies, "I've *errands* to run, myself. Otherwise, I would."

"You've worked very hard for this moment," states Jasper. "A table of sitting down with kings, and negotiating. This is not something you've ever done. And you're going to be absent of it, for errands? What has gone wrong with the lot of you, Onyx?"

"Plenty, it seems," remarks Zymarc. "And not to worry. I've watched an ample number of negotiations. I know how they're done. As for the errands . . . those traitors you were so kind as to have feasted on, cannot be the only traitorous Deathasyns posing as my possessed ones. However, I'll be here again, to sign the final document." Looking Jasper over briefly, Zymarc gives a slight bow from the waist. Turning, he yells a slew of foreign, harsh-sounding words.

His Vitiosyns clamber onto horses and smaller dragons, to ready themselves for the ride out of Paragon.

As Gyron goes to assist the Onyx Warriors, Caleiso joins Azabahk and Belzara atop the King Vitasadyn's back.

Scepter looks down, curiously eyeing the battleground, before rumbling, "King Zymarc, may I?" Scepter pauses, and parts his mouth, smacking his tongue a bit.

"Yes, Scepter." Zymarc sighs. "You may have Alpha Jasper's leftovers."

Irritated, Jasper shoves the scroll into an interior vest pocket. Turning to Talok, he's about to say something.

But Zepharre immediately vies for attention, voicing, "Good riddance, I say. Now for the reason I came over here to this horrific sight, in the first place. King Talok?"

"Yes, what do you want?" Talok looks at him.

"Grover needs to gather memories of the . . . um . . . fallen." Zepharre clears his throat. "He, and the other Arkiveis, asked that I find you. Bring you to the gravesite that the dragons have helped to prepare. I shall lead the way now, if you are ready."

Though Zepharre tries to soften his voice, he just ends up sounding like an insensitive, small-minded politician.

"Lead on," Talok mumbles.

"Very good!" Zepharre grips Talok's arm. "As we wait for everyone to gather, you'll have time to think of what parting words to say of them—the fallen of Paragon—before you bear their blood."

6

Words with the Castle

All King's Guard have gathered round Talok. Stripped of his coat, he kneels on the ground. He hides his face in his hands, and silently weeps. Behind us, the fountain and pond of waterfowl has been destroyed, along with just about everything. There's nothing left of beauty, save for the castle and Arkivara.

Solemn looks on their faces, the guards gaze out across the cavernous hole made in what was previously a meadow of lush yellow grass, sprinkled with white flowers.

Hundreds upon hundreds of bodies have been wrapped in brilliant white cloth, and are laid out with great care within the mass grave. Many more wait to be added. Some wrapped, others laid down as if they are sleeping. If it weren't for the sight of their wounds, I would think they were pretending. They are at rest, some looking slightly happy. But the wrapped-up ones ... I cannot fathom what lies beneath the cloth. Nor do I wish to.

Gemma's beside me, quiet, not even crying. She must be in shock.

I wonder, *Why am I not afraid? Only sad. Though not enough to cry over it. I should feel so much. Yet there's only peace in me.*

Grover, hobbling over without his staff, has a great sadness upon his face. Managing a speck of a smile, he adjusts his spectacles.

I push thoughts away, before going to tap Talok lightly on the shoulder. He lifts his head and sniffles. "Yes? Is it already that time?"

"I think so, Cousin," I whisper.

Standing, Talok inhales a ragged breath.

While waiting, his stained coat was cleaned by Paydinn and Warren. But it's Khyra now offering it to him, her tears pouring down her cheeks the entire time.

Five Arkiveis stand by, near to Nyrim. The Yharss-Rawshuen Arkivy holds two white-bristled brushes similar to paintbrushes. A tall Arkivy—at least, tall for a Vaegon—hands Grover a large bowl and then takes one brush from Nyrim. He looks oddly familiar, like a much older version of Kent. He must be Lokasi of Dysarda.

To the back and left are Paragonians, dragons, and horses, gathered for the mass funeral.

On the right, Paydinn, Jasper, and the two candidates wait, as well as Talok's advisers and the cloaked Awngeleik. Though we can't see her, we hear her hooves pawing frantically, while dirt is flung away from her digging hooves.

Talok gazes forward. He rubs at the Geldryn bangle on his wrist, while making his way up to a makeshift platform fashioned of Blackwood. After a moment, he begins the eulogy, calling out, "People of Pawv'Ragaen! As I am your king, I bear their blood. The blood of our fallen. It lies with me forever. We will never forget their great courage. Our men and women. Warriors and children. Neins and dyns. No, not even the smaller creatures of land nor of air. We shall miss them. Only seeing them in memory now." Talok pauses.

Turning his head aside, my cousin struggles to control the quivering of his lower lip. Then he looks forward, to start again, his voice stronger than before. "As a war is brewing for tomorrow, take this day, even this very hour to grieve until there's no regret left to spill out onto the land. Our land! It will remain ours, or it will be no one's. Now, mighty warriors and dyns, bury them as I bear their blood upon my king's coat."

While Talok says that last part, Zepharre, Nyrim, Lokasi, and Grover slowly make their way up to the plain, black stage. Nyrim dips his brush into Grover's bowl first. Then he flicks a red liquid onto Talok. It splatters across the back of his clean coat, staining it with bright-red specks.

"Is . . . is that blood?" queries Gemma, stammering.

Next to her is Ben, nodding with a downward glance.

Lokasi not only dips his brush in the bowl, but the fingers of his free hand too. After flicking more stains on the coat, he paints blood along the contours of Talok's face.

Zepharre dips both hands in the blood. Then, using his fingertips, he paints stripes on the sleeves and back of the king's coat. Motioning for Talok to turn, Zepharre continues on the front of the king's coat.

Talok's gaze locks on to me right then. He doesn't look away until it's all over.

My heart breaks for him. And I feel all the held back pain upon my shoulders, while wondering, *My cousin is broken in two, with three weeks to live. Whatever will I do, in order to save him?*

* * *

In silence, the Paragonian Sovereignty—Arkiveis included—started the long walk back to the Castle of Sosha. Heads hanging, feet dragging, they refuse to weep.

Jasper, still covered in blood, more blood than even Talok is splattered with now, leads at the front with my cousin. Behind them are Rorka and Mekka. Like three sentinels, they seem to be guarding the little king. Or, maybe, they are sharing his burden. Regardless, Talok's stride lengthens. He lifts his head, to look at the castle now coming into view.

His breath catching, Talok stops. "I can't believe it. My uncle's work is still whole. Only true damage to the upper floors."

One of the older Arkiveis, leaning on his black staff sprinkled with flecks of gold and silver, proudly says, "Yes, 'tis remarkable. But given LanSoren's abilities as a boy, I cannot say that I'm surprised." The Arkivy, drumming some of his fingers on the staff, looks to the castle, then to Talok, asking him, "Shall I open it back up? The doors got wedged a bit, upon our leave to the gravesite with Awngeleik."

"No, Trauvo's Eishal," Talok replies, "my cousin and I will manage."

Eishal stills his fingers on the staff, gripping it firmly in both hands. He flicks his gaze across the three Greyvon sentinels, who are now stepping away from Talok to give me enough room to walk forward.

Holding out his hand to me—the one with the bangle clasped on it—Talok says, "Come, Cousin. We'll enter together, and be the first to assess the damage of the upper floors."

After a glance at Gemma, hugging herself as she stares at the ground, I stride farther forward to Talok. We walk up the thirteen steps, together. Once at the top, the doors try to open themselves, yet without success.

The castle seems to be grieving, with its creaking and cracking and shifting where it has been marred, slashed, and charred on the outside.

Talok weakly pushes against the castle doors, but they won't budge. His face turns whiter. When his arms tremble from the effort, I move to help him.

Barely do I brush my left hand on the gap between the doors, before they fly open, ripping themselves off their hinges.

A wind sucks us in, to the grand entrance strewn with shattered furnishings and glass. Evidence of the injured carried through this very place remains as dried, smeared blood on the floor.

Others rush up the steps. They don't make it inside, however, because the castle doors are swiftly floating back in front of the doorway. Reattaching themselves, the doors then slam shut to bar us in.

"What's wrong with it?" queries Talok, easing up from where he's landed on the stairs. "Why's it trapped us?"

Pushing away from the stair rail, I brush dust off me, replying, "Maybe it's trying to protect you."

"Or you, from yourself," says Talok, frowning. "Cousin Tyler, there are some things we need to—"

Right then, a frightened voice calls from outside, "Talok, Tyler, are you all right?"

"Yes, Rorka, we are fine," replies Talok.

"Oh good!" says Rorka, in relief.

Talok states, "Tyler thinks the castle is protecting me."

"That very well could be," says Rorka. "And your guardsman, Ryco, wants you to know that I'm the only one you're able to hear. Which is a bit peculiar, if you don't mind my saying so."

Talok glances at me oddly, before commenting, "Yes. *That* is a bit strange." Lowering his voice, he whispers, "How did you get Rorka through Soren's wall?"

Fighting the urge to shrug, I reply, "It was a reaction. Instinct. Nature. I don't know."

"Regardless, whatever you did then," says Talok, "should work here. See if you can convince my father's castle to let them in."

Tearing my gaze from my cousin's exhausted, blood-streaked face, I stare at the twin doors. I want to go over to them, to yank one open. But my feet stay planted. It's almost like when Soren wouldn't let me speak a phrase; the right phrase, leading to greater things.

"Well, Tyler?" Talok urges. "Is there something you're waiting for?"

Taking a quick breath, I reply, "No. I just . . . feel uneasy about something. Why do you still call this castle your father's, when you are now its king? And have been for three years."

Talok hangs his head. His voice thick with emotion, he replies, "Because I am no king. I'm just a boy, in a man's coat." Talok smiles brokenly, correcting himself, "A king's coat I'm not worthy to wear. Not after today."

"But they know you love them, Talok," I argue. "They know you'd do anything for them."

"Look at me, Cousin!" Talok shouts, tightly scrunching the front of his coat in his fists. "I wear their spilled blood! Obviously, love is not enough! Not when you're a monarch. Now I'm going to die in a month's time, or negotiate with the killer of my people. I don't know what your thoughts are of them, but those are two of the most wretched choices I've ever been given."

"I think they're arguing," says Rorka quietly, to someone. "Tyler, Talok, how can we assist in opening the doors? Ryco wants to know what's holding them."

Ignoring her, I state, "Our people, Talok. They're *our* people. And if you don't like those options, then forge a new one. A third choice!" I shout, taking the steps to reach my cousin.

With each footfall of mine, the castle shifts and creaks more. Next, the red vines strewn about us are writhing around on the floor—on the walls and pillars too—before dozens hail down from the ceiling, letting in more light of the midday.

Talok rushes to cover my head, during the raining down of red vines.

The doors crack and then burst open. Awngeleik, uncloaked, comes trotting in, her hooves clattering on the stone floor. If a harness wasn't currently restraining them, I suspect that her wings would be flapping too. Running in after her are Ryco, Khyra, and Zepharre, as the rest of the Sovereignty and sentinels come in behind them. But Gemma, Paydinn, and Rozeth hang back on the topmost step.

No one's able to say a word, before the castle makes its statement of what has been bothering it. All vines shift to hundreds of contorted 'S' shapes. Slowly, they slither to form two names: Sosha and Soren. Then two phrases appear. *Sosha has sacrificed. Soren is coming.*

More phrases form in rapid succession, spelling out:

The Midnight Anemones has sheltered a secret.

Zymarc was here.

The Sorshrynak has come.

A shadow looms, waiting to rise.

When it has finished that last phrase, all vines draw together and form a tangled mass of quivering red at the foot of the stairwell leading up to the second floor.

Khyra approaches them slowly. But, at her movement toward them, they scatter out of sight.

Awngeleik lunges, wanting to chase after them. Ben's quick in blocking her way. He pets her head, and speaks softly to her. She stills, somewhat.

Shoulders slumping, Khyra mutters, "It still doesn't like me. Hasn't mattered how much Gendras I've learned." She turns to Ryco, to ask of him, "How could the castle know all that, Ryco?"

Talok adds, "Yes, and why wait till now to warn us? It's a little late. All are now fairly clear in their meaning, except for the Midnight Anemone part. Whatever important thing could that mean?"

"Midnight Anemones!" Kent exclaims, turning to look intently at Lokasi. "Father. That Caleiso gave me eleven Midnight Anemones, while I was at the infirmary recovering. Why eleven? And how'd she know they're Mother's favorite flower? Have you seen her, prior to these past few days?"

The tall Arkivy, apparently Lokasi, is confused, asking, "Who is Caleiso?"

"Callie of Dysarda," I reply. "But she's actually the Apprentice to Vitiosus. Zymarc's apprentice."

Those absent of witnessing Caleiso's transformation are stunned at this revelation.

Whether their feelings are of pain, anger, or fear, my words just hang in the air.

Coming in, to join the rest of us, are Gemma and the other two with her: Paydinn and Rozeth.

At last, Lokasi nods his head sadly. "Yes, I've seen this *Caleiso*, before. She's been coming to my Arkivara's outer room, since she was of age ten. There was nothing odd of her behavior, nor her questions. Most Paragonian children are very inquisitive, especially when it comes to Arkivaras. And, given that I've seen her with a Paragonian twosome many times in Dysarda, I would have had no reason to be suspicious. In case you were wondering, Zepharre."

Folding his arms defensively, Zepharre clenches his jaw.

"As for the flowers," Lokasi continues, "she asked me why I kept freshly cut ones, in the outer room at all times. Which, in turn, led to a few conversations of your mother and you, Kent. Eleven years is how long your mother has been away from Dysarda. It is also how old Callie was, when LanSoren died two years ago. It was merely symbolic."

Kent, unsatisfied with that answer, queries, "Even knowing her true identity now, you think that?"

"Yes, I still believe that to be the case," replies Lokasi.

"That seems like mockery, on her part," says Kent, thinking a moment.

"You didn't give anything important away to her, did you?"

"I will have to think on it. But, no, I don't believe so." Lokasi strolls about the room a bit. Then he stops, to sweep some of his fingers across his forehead. "The only spot of good news now is that I won't have to tell her of her parents being some of the first to fall in Dysarda. Looking back, they must've been deemed as a 'loose end' that needing trimming away."

Suddenly very angry, I still manage to calmly ask, "Is it possible she led the attack in Dysarda?"

Lokasi replies, "No, I saw her depart with a few young, pre-festival travelers the day before the attack. It might be worth noting, however, those she traveled with were among the dead, here in Eyo'el. Found near the foot of the castle stairs, no less. They've not been buried, as of yet, though they *have* been prepared for it." Ending his talk, Lokasi crosses his arms over his chest.

"Arkivy Grover," says Eishal, turning to him. "Give Talok the vessel, to finish his ritual in private. We should go assist in recovering very specific memories of these young ones Lokasi talks of. See if their memories will bring to light anything useful, for the darker coming days ahead."

Grover starts hobbling over to Talok, while carrying a corked, black bottle. It seems too large for the Arkivy to be carrying by himself. I worry that it's going to slip from his unsteady grasp.

"I've already tried that," says Lokasi, irritated with Eishal. "Thinking they were her friends, I thought their memories would comfort her. Especially since her 'parents' were burned to ash. There's no recovering anything, after that."

"Yes, well," says Eishal, "you are not the oldest of the Arkiveis, Lokasi. As Grover and I are, we have a few tricks in our staffs that you do not as of yet."

Grover stops mid-hobble, looking behind to Eishal with that same scowl he gave Warren, after being thrown down to Musgrae.

Lokasi's Vaegon-eyes narrow on Eishal. He uncrosses his arms. He looks as though he's about to reprimand one of his fellow Arkiveis. But the sound of soft footsteps approaching, from a hallway close by, makes us all turn to look.

Shyly, a bright-eyed woman with short, blonde, fuzzy hair—fuzzy like a newborn's—is peeking around the corner.

"Feeling better, Madeleine?" queries Lokasi, ceasing his irritation immediately.

"Yes." She nods happily. "Though, I am still getting used to the lack of hair upon my head. It is a bit colder, without my long tresses. But I did not come up here to complain. Sosha's Castle and I have had a bit of a conversation. He's been telling me that we're at war. Paragon and the devils currently encroaching upon the land of Vosh-Perida. Then he was quite beside himself, over the arguments ensuing within his entrance. Now that I am here, I see that Paragon is at war with itself. And not only that, but the Arkiveis. Allow me to set things in order."

Lokasi blushes, and adjusts the short collar of his Arkiveis robe. "That's unnecessary, Madeleine," he says. "I was just about to correct Eishal, myself. But it does not matter much, in the end, given our circumstances."

"I insist," Madeleine states, "for you are too modest, Lokasi, to tell of your lineage and past. As is Kent, wherever he's gone off to."

Tensing, Kent slowly edges his way to having Ryco block Madeleine's view of him.

Amused, Lokasi watches his son from the corner of his vision. Then he focuses on Madeleine, while she paces forward to Eishal, and says, "It is true. Arkivy Lokasi is not the oldest Arkivy amongst the seven of you; nor those able to tend Arkivaras, if one of you should fall prey to violence or the completion of age. But he is unlike all other Vaegons, in that he has tended all active Arkivaras, save for Eyo'el. And, as I remember Kent's mother, Leira, conveying to me once, it was by his choice that he did not become head over the Arkiveis."

"Is that true?" queries Nyrim, stepping forward. "That you forfeited the position as Prime Arkivy?"

"I outright refused," says Lokasi. "Tending Eyo'el is a lifetime commitment. As I was born and raised in Dysarda, it is where my loyalty lies. Besides, Patron Grover has a mind for keeping Eyo'el happy. Who am I to stand in the way of a grand friendship of a lifetime. As I am younger than he, it's very likely I'll outlive him and be forced to tend the center-most Arkivara anyway. But, dyns willing, that day is long into the future, waiting. Now, Patron Grover, you had something to tell our King Talok?"

Somewhat startling, Grover hobbles the rest of the way to Talok. Carefully, he gives his young king the black vessel and then grips his arm, instructing him, "Pick two, for assisting you with this last part, young Talok. One to pour its . . . contents out. And another to witness it being done. Then you may wash all this away." Grover motions to the blood on the king's coat.

Swallowing hard, Talok accepts the corked vessel.

Then Grover, with his gnarled and frail hands, smooths the front of Talok's coat. "And remember," he says, pausing to look up at Talok, "you have every right and worth of wearing this coat."

"We'll second that," says Nyrim, briefly glancing at the other Arkiveis.

"Well, well," says Paydinn, looking on proudly, "the oldest and youngest of the Arkiveis have, indeed, spoken. And good words too. I shan't dare to argue with them."

Talok glances from Paydinn and the Arkiveis, up toward the stairwell and then the second floor. Quietly, he says, "I will need a few minutes alone."

"Of course!" Zepharre exclaims, shooing him. "We'll begin carrying out the plans discussed yesterday. Be sure to collect anything useful you find, on the way up to your quarters."

"Yes," Talok replies. "And, Zepharre?"

The head adviser looks back at him, shifting on his feet as if a little anxious.

Talok continues, "Thank you for your service. Arkivy Lokasi has Mensa-divved, telling me that you used your skills in alchemy, to make tonics and more food for our sick and injured. And that you actually took it upon yourself to serve them."

"Oh, that?" Zepharre shakes his head. "'Twas nothing."

"It's something, to me," replies Talok, glancing at Jasper. "And I know that you and Jasper have your differences to settle. But I do hope that you can overlook, possibly even admire, how violent our new ally can be. We need that sort of violence, to protect what we love. Do we not, Zepharre?"

"We do, indeed," mutters Zepharre, before clenching his jaw.

"While I am gathering courage for this last part of the ritual," says Talok, "I want you, the Sovereignty, and Jasper to decide on who's to take the Paragonian throne, in the event that I do not escape the fate given to me."

"Certainly, we shall," says Zepharre quietly. "Before you go, we need to know whom you would prefer. Or, rather, which race. Paragonian or Vaegon?"

"Also," EmiKal pipes in, "would you approve a foreigner being named as a potential heir to your throne?"

Sighing, Talok starts up the stairs, saying, "Pick one, for all three. Whoever survives will be the next King or Queen of Paragon."

Khyra speaks up, asking, "Would you like for me to accompany you, Talok?"

Shaking his head sadly, Talok continues up and out of sight.

Lokasi saunters to Madeleine, and grips her arm. "Shall we go to the infirmary? See what food and supplies are to be found?"

"Oh, yes! That is a good idea," says Khyra, taking hold of Gemma by the hand. "Come, Gigi. We shall help."

"Ben"—Ryco motions to him—"you should go with them. Take Awngeleik too. And you, Rozeth. Tidy up the castle, as you go. It might cheer it a bit."

The six solemnly make their exit with Awngeleik, who's snorting. Stubbornly, she shuffles along behind them, as Ben pulls on the harness strapped on her.

I try catching Gemma's attention with a Mensa-div, to see if she wants me to go with them, but she's unreachable and blank, blindly letting Khyra lead her out.

"Can Talok still hear us?" queries Kent.

Hesitating, Ryco then says, "Now he can't."

Starting to cough, Quall asks, "Eli, have you a spot of water?"

After giving him a small flask, Eli assists Siege, Warren, and a few advisers with clearing the castle entrance of debris.

Jasper quietly says, to Rorka and Mekka, "Start clearing the second floor, making your way to the symposium room. Once there, wait for us."

Musgrae, still appearing exhausted from swinging the hammer earlier, is about to help the other Paragonians with clearing the room.

But Jasper addresses him. "Musgrae of Bethsaide. Would you be so kind as to accompany my candidates? Make sure they don't kill each other, during the spilling out of the argument brewing in their minds?"

Stiffening his neck, Mekka points at Musgrae. "You think that little Paragonian can stop me? Do not insult Greyvons, Jasper."

"I do not," replies Jasper, slowly clasping his hands. "But Greyvons acting as Vonsai? I will most certainly insult them. The two of you will work out your differences. Or suffer the consequences."

"I can take any amount of pain," says Mekka proudly.

"As such," replies Jasper, "what I have planned involves no pain, whatsoever. Well, not physical, that is."

"Fine, Alpha," Mekka says, "I won't argue this time."

Musgrae briefly purses his lips, then says, "Wish me luck."

He follows after the two candidates tensely making their way out of our sight.

Next, Ryco turns to Zepharre. "Why didn't you tell Talok we already agreed on a list of three, as we were waiting for his arrival to the meeting yesterday?"

"Because, Ryco," Zepharre declares, "he needs to feel as if he's initiating the next step forward."

"That may be," replies Ryco, "but Talok dislikes being offered falsehoods. Do not hide the truth from him again. Or, at least, not in my presence. I won't tolerate it."

"Nor I," adds Nyrim. "Now, what's this vote verdict? Who has been chosen?"

Sinking down to sit on the grimy floor, Kent says, "Given my father's lineage as a descendant of Kristos—younger brother to King Kailon—I was voted in as the Vaegon candidate."

Quall, seemingly finished with the water, starts capping the flask.

"A good choice." Nyrim nods. "I will add my vote to the majority. But what of the Paragonian choice?"

"Why, it's Quall," Grover says, with vigor.

Horrified, Quall flushes bright-red. He drops the flask, and what little water is left inside spills out.

Scowling, Eli fetches his flask, and tucks it away in his pocket, then goes back to assisting with clearing away debris.

Oblivious of Quall's reaction, Grover continues, "There is no other sensible choice. He's been serving Paragon for over twenty years. And, for a King's Guard, that is quite a lot of years. They don't usually last that long. Either they retire early, or meet their tragic end at the hand of brutality."

"Yes, our Quall is seemingly made of dragon skin," Eishal adds. "And he was a good friend of LanSoren's. Those two were inseparable, in their youth. Both loved by Paragon. If our young king should fall, our Quall most surely can lead us to brighter days."

Finding his voice, Quall is asking, "Have I no choice in this matter? Can't you pick some other Paragonian?"

I state, "Probably not, Quall. Bet it's why you were sent to fetch us from the portal, rather than Ryco."

Paydinn lets out a laugh, saying, "Smart *and* sharp, this one is. Tyler Ravier, as no one here is polite enough to introduce us, I will, myself. I'm Paydinn of, well . . . many titles. But my favorite is Keeper to The Watchman's Log."

Shaking his offered hand, I'm filled with hope. In that moment, I know he's most likely to be trusted.

I softly reply, "Now I'm the one saying, I wish we were meeting during better times."

Paydinn steps back, grinning sadly. Then his curious snake-eyes change to a dark-violet color. He looks to Jasper, the King's Guard, advisers, and Arkiveis, as they start a dialogue over the foreign candidate for the Paragonian throne.

"We had wanted it to be Siveyra Gyronawv," states Ryco. "But with us losing the title of Onyx Victor, and Vitiosyns winning it, instead, we have to come up with someone else."

"I suppose," EmiKal says, "that you want it to be Siveyra Dezarin, don't you, Ryco?"

"I never once suggested him, EmiKal," Ryco defends.

On and on, several in the room go back and forth. Suggesting many names. Names I do not recognize at all. But a few are Siveyras. Then they start arguing amongst each other, in a foreign language. And I'm lost to it all.

That's when a chill pricks at me. I'm about to panic. But then a calm voice starts talking to me. Like a voice in my head, clear as daylight, someone is saying, *"Don't look my way. Act normal. I know I sound different in Mensa-div than I do aloud. I blame it on being a Borrower of Time. Regardless, you must listen, Ravier."*

"Paydinn?" I ask. *"Aren't you worried someone will hear us?"*

"No, no! It's why I shook hands with you. It makes Mensa-div stronger, if you know what you're doing. Which I do. Anyway, where to start? So many things to tell you. I suppose I'll start here. Sosha's Castle wrote that: Zymarc was here. While this was clearly taken by everyone in this room to mean 'here in Paragon,' he, indeed, meant within these very walls."

Refraining from an outburst, I div back, *"The castle's walls? Are you sure?"*

"I'm sure that it's what the castle meant, yes. Possibly Ryco caught its meaning. Perhaps Rozeth, as well. But they know Paragonian temperaments all too well. They're creatures easily frightened. You would think being able to tame dragons would strike fear out of them, permanently. But, alas, some things still scare them. They'll lose focus, if they think Zymarc walked within this castle, without their knowing it."

I continue the Mensa-div, *"You think they'll be distracted over that, rather than focusing on more important things?"*

"Exactly," he says. *"Now, here's the imperative part. Someone here in Paragon has most likely seen Zymarc in his Onyx form. If I know his face, I might be able to piece some things together, using The Watchman's Log. I need you to*

discreetly ask one of the Arkiveis, to search the Arkivara's heart for any Onyx seen entering and leaving the castle yesterday."

"That one's easy," I tell him. *"All the warriors and ReNovak were put in a room on the second floor, for the night. Meaning, all Onyx who came to Paragon, also entered the castle. But they left very early. Well before the attack started. Come to think of it, Talok did see ReNovak leaving very late last night. Sometime after the festival concluded. I kind of get the feeling he didn't come back."*

"King ReNovak came here, to the castle, then left for the night?" Paydinn's voice sounds troubled, yet his face is only contemplative while he pretends to listen to the continued arguments over whom the last candidate should be.

Then a voice is loudly interrupting our Mensa-div, saying, *"Paydinn, pay attention! Quall's about to name you as the foreign candidate."*

"Over my dead body, will that be so!" Paydinn yells at the other Mensa-divver.

That's when Jasper winces, then scowls at Paydinn.

"Well, what about Master Paydinn?" queries Quall, pointing at the distraught Borrower of Time. "He has a family of great number. He's traveled Muraine extensively. And he's shown himself to be a great warrior, on other occasions. Also, we need never worry over him being bound to Onyx Law, like Gyronawv is."

Several nod or mumble their agreements with Quall.

"Now, now, this need not be a hasty decision," proclaims Paydinn.

"I agree," says Zepharre. "Master Paydinn has never been in a monarch's position. And the head of a family, large in number, is not a very sound qualification."

Indignant over Zepharre's words, Paydinn brims with displeasure. "I beg your pardon? My title as Father of the Jokryn is not a qualification? Do you know how many living children I have, Zepharre? Of course you don't, due to your hardly ever leaving Paragon. Well, I'll tell you. Forty *living* children. I had more. But they passed on, through various causes of death. My family is now in its fourth generation. In another decade or so, it will be at five. While my children, on their own, have not had nearly as many offspring as me, there is certainly no lack of us."

Although Paydinn says more, I've stopped listening. My mind gets stuck on forty *living* children, and who knows how many descendants conceived after them. I start to imagine if they're all warriors, or meddlers of time, as their ancestor Paydinn is.

Then I'm thinking, *What if they could be convinced to join the war? To be an ally to Paragon. To Talok. I should suggest it to him. Especially before Zepharre can interject, and give Talok his opinion of Paydinn. Hopefully, he hasn't already.*

While all are occupied in the conversation, I slip away.

Deciding that Talok needs a bit of food, I quietly wander toward the infirmary. Along the way, the hallways and steps are spotless; a result of Rozeth's tidying, no doubt. Turning a corner, I'm almost there. But then I spot Gemma, alone, in the dim and narrow hallway ahead.

Sitting on the floor, she's leaned up against the wall, and hugging her knees close to herself.

My chest tightens, and I hold my breath. It hurts so much seeing her like that.

Sniffling, she wipes at her eyes and then looks in my direction. "Hey, Ty," she mumbles. "I was just—"

Cutting her off gently, I ask, "Want some company, Gem?"

She shakes her head. "Not *some* company. But yours sounds nice."

Briefly, I smile and then go sit beside her. As soon as my shoulder bumps against her, she's clamping her hands on my arm, and plastering the side of her face against my sleeve. I stare down at her face, and watch as fresh tears roll down her pale cheeks.

"Did they find you any food, in the infirmary?"

Sitting up some, she replies, "Yes, but I couldn't finish it." She pulls a satchel onto her lap, and opens it. "It's just bread, but you're welcome to have it."

"Actually, I wanted to take something to Talok." I stand up, and offer my hand. "Want to come?"

"I'll try," she says. "But I can barely stay awake. Just, go slow?"

"Sure thing." I nod, gripping her hand tightly. I lead the way.

In silence, we walk together. I feel her trying to hold back the trembling of her hand. And the longer we walk, the more her hand resembles something made of ice: stiff and cold.

Traversing through a sea of debris, we've almost made our way to the flight of stairs leading up to the third floor. But I sense that Gemma can't go any farther.

I'm proved right, as she stops to say, "I need to rest, Tyler. I'm falling asleep. To cry and sleep. It's all I want to do today."

On cue, more tears brim in her especially sad brown eyes.

Glancing about, I spot a thin passage adjacent to the stairwell. Only broken sconces and some splintered debris litter the floor. Overall, it looks all right.

Pointing at it, I ask, "Want to see what's down that way?"

"No," she says. "But it looks dark enough for getting a good nap in. Won't someone wonder where we've gone?"

I reply, "If they do, most likely Ryco will be asking the castle."

Satisfied at my answer, Gemma begins the careful walk down the child-size passageway.

Though she's able to walk down it in a normal fashion, I'm forced to contort myself, sometimes sidestepping my way through it. The whole time, Gemma refuses to let go of my hand. Tighter and tighter, she grips my fingers, cutting off my circulation. At last, we get to the end, and it opens up to a dim room. In fact, the very room we slept in, with the King's Guard. It's a mess now. Overturned beds, cracked shelves, and the desk—Ryco's desk—has been obliterated. As has Quall's bed and chest filled with trinkets. Where the window was, is now a wound sealed up with vines and branches of the castle.

Releasing my hand held captive, Gemma takes to Eli's corner bed, as it's the only bed undisturbed by the events of today. She collapses upon it.

I crawl in behind her, but hesitate to wrap my arm around her. The thought of lying in the same bed as Gemma, and napping with her, is almost enough to make me slide out to sit on the floor and let her sleep alone. Yet motionless I remain, as I ask, "Are you sure you don't want to go home, Gemma?"

She rolls over to face me, barely keeping her tears at bay. "It's too late to go home, Tyler. Besides, are *you* thinking of going home, if the way is clear?"

Swallowing hard, I contemplate what she's asking. I don't think for too long, however, before I shake my head. "I can't leave. Not with everything that's happening. Then there's Talok. I think we need each other. Maybe that sounds stupid." Looking away, I wait for her response.

"It's not, Ty," she says. A strange glint has crept into her gaze, as she looks at me.

I can't quite decide what she's thinking about. And I don't want to search her mind for it, either, knowing it wouldn't be fair. Although, I do desperately want to try, with each passing minute of her eyes searching my face or struggling to stay open.

At last, I tell her, "You should sleep, Gem. I'll wake you, if anything exciting starts happening."

Rolling over, she scoots back to press up against me. Deeply sighing, she falls fast asleep.

Timidly, I rest my left hand on her waist, and will myself to sleep. As I drift off beside the ice-cold Gemma, I only hope that I get a chance to have a talk with Talok alone, before King ReNovak and Azabahk are at the broken gates of Paragon, demanding to hear his and Jasper's counteroffers to whatever Zymarc or the Onyx King have requested.

7

Bear Their Blood

I start coming to, at the calling of my name. It's Paydinn, Mensa-divving, *"Ah! Tyler, good, you're awake! The guardsmen and advisers are searching for you. Do you want to be found?"*

When footsteps approach from the doorway of the room, I div back with, *"Someone already has."*

Looking over my shoulder, I spot Talok—still covered in dried blood—gazing curiously at me, then Gemma on the bed.

"It's Talok," I tell Paydinn. *"Talk later."*

Before I can explain, Talok is asking, "On Earth, you're allowed to sleep with the opposite gender, while in your years of youth?"

"Well, not exactly," I reply, cringing. "It's a thing usually frowned on, for minors."

"I won't tell Aunt Amira," Talok says, "if you let me join the two of you, for a minute. We need to have a talk. And Miss Galloway doesn't look as though she's waking anytime soon."

When I shake Gemma gently, and she remains limp with sleep, Talok is proved correct. Grinning, I warn him, saying, "She feels like an ice queen. Still want to cuddle?"

Talok nods. "It beats spending the night in a stall with Awngeleik, to prevent her escaping in the night. A few nights before visiting you, I was stationed as the nightly *watch master.*"

My cousin grabs a tattered blanket from another bed, and slips it over Gemma as he crawls onto the bed with us. Tucking the blanket in around her, he doesn't even pause before pulling her close to himself. He rubs her back, and I feel heat radiate from the blanket where his hands touch it.

Drawing closer, I wrap my arm around Gemma, tucked in. Beneath where my hand rests, her ribs rise and fall with each of her steady breaths.

Gently cupping Gemma's neck, Talok moves her head to rest against the nape of his own neck. It's then that he looks to me with such intensity, I nearly stop breathing. "I will say this once, to you, Cousin Tyler," he states. "She would go to the end of all, for you. Do not take that kind of friendship and loyalty for granted."

"I don't," I whisper. "But I'm scared about what might happen to her."

"As am I," Talok agrees. "This Soren frightens her. Frightens me. Frightens us all."

Next, I suggest, "If the way is clear—"

Cutting me off, Talok says for us, "She will leave."

"Good," I reply, even as a wave of guilt creeps into my stomach, to make me feel sick.

"There's still more to discuss," says Talok, crawling off the bed. "But at least we've agreed on that. Will you help me now, with this last part of the ritual I must do?"

Nodding, I slip off the bed. But, looking back at Gemma, I state, "We shouldn't leave her, though."

"No worries," replies Talok. "With how thin she is, I have strength enough to carry her. My quarters aren't far."

Stooping down, he scoops up Gemma's limp body, still wrapped in the blanket.

Clearing his path, I open the door for Talok. I'm about to tug it closed behind us. But it's slamming itself shut, smashing into my face.

I stumble back, in pained shock.

Talok sighs, in frustration. "Now that the castle's had its spout of grief, it's incredibly angry. Best to avoid the doors, or treat them with the utmost care. Or better? Let them do as they please."

Momentarily rubbing at my nose, I follow him up the stairs to the third floor. Recognizing the hallway, I see that we're about halfway to his quarters, where I recovered from helping Nyrim yesterday.

Talok's arms start shaking, and his face goes pale again.

"Want me to try waking her up?" I ask.

"Yes," he says. "Would it be mean of us, to pinch her?"

Chuckling, I reply, "I'll do it."

I'm about to pinch her arm that's hanging out of the blanket. But she must sense our ill intentions, because her eyes pop wide open. She gazes upon Talok's blood-streaked face.

Immediately, she screams, and hits him square on the nose.

He drops her squirming body. Then he falls to the floor.

Fighting with the blanket that's wrapped around her, Gemma stumbles all over herself.

Then there's Talok, sprawled on the floor, gripping his nose that's gushing blood.

Before I can make it to Talok, Gemma's already there.

Apologizing profusely, she exclaims, "Talok! Talok? Are you all right?"

He sits up, then crawls away to lean his back against a nearby wall.

Whilst he still holds his hands protectively to his nose, Gemma makes her demand of: "Let me see." She pries Talok's hands away. Plopping down to straddle his lap, Gemma resets Talok's broken nose. He hasn't even time to process what she's doing, before it's over and he's yelling and groaning, as his eyes tear up.

Her good deed done, Gemma bolts up, proclaiming, "There! At least your nose won't be disfigured."

"I think they have magic for that, Gem," I state, chuckling a little at her look of horror.

Before I've finished talking, a stampede gallops up the stairwell. It's Zepharre, Nyrim, and six of the King's Guard. Aiming weapons and magic at the two of us, they're confused.

"What's happened?" queries Ryco calmly, lowering his bow.

"King Talok," Zepharre says, sheathing his dagger, "did someone attack you? What's wrong with your nose?"

I help Talok regain his feet, before I pass him the cloth Ben is offering.

My cousin blinks away dissipating tears. "Stand down," he says, waving his people off. He takes the cloth, and presses it to his nose. "Miss Gemma woke up, and I startled her is all. No need to panic. But now that you have found me, Ryco, you and Tyler are to come with me." Burning the cloth to ash, Talok glances from Ryco to Gemma.

Nervously biting her lower lip, she just stares at the top of her boots.

I div, to Talok, *"Ask Gemma if she has some food. It'll cheer her up, sharing with you."*

Talok strides toward Gemma. Crossing his arms, he queries, "Cousin Tyler tells me you have something to share?"

When Gemma meets his gaze, he eyes her hungrily. The glint in his gaze is so brief, I wonder if I imagined it. But Gemma's reaction tells me that I didn't.

She trembles and then yanks the satchel off her shoulder. As soon as Talok accepts it from her, she's running down the hall, then down the stairs, and out of sight.

Ryco, seeming the most startled by the silent altercation, harshly asks Talok, "What did you say to her, Talok?"

He ignores him, addressing Zepharre, instead, with a command of, "Take a team of scouts to the portal, Zepharre. Make sure the way is clear. Then take Gemma Galloway there, if it is. That is all. No arguments. No vote. I will not risk her life, by letting her stay here. Now, go. All of you, except for Ryco."

Nyrim queries, "But, Talok, what of your cousin?"

"He's staying. Tyler has proved that he's able to defend himself. Though we don't know how, it is so. But Gemma . . ." Talok trails off.

"Say no more," states Nyrim. "We will see to what you've asked. Though many of us will be sad to see her go home, your heart is in the right place."

They leave.

Ryco stays.

But he's silent, until we're within Talok's quarters, when his king is asking him, "Where are Quall and Musgrae?"

"Musgrae is still with the Greyvons," says Ryco quietly. "And Quall is organizing makeshift infirmaries and food stations, with Lokasi and Paydinn's help."

"You do not agree that Gemma should go home, Ryco?" Talok says, whilst grabbing the black vessel off the table.

"My instinct tells me that you're right, to want her returned safely home," Ryco replies. "However, Ben's report to me mentioned what he saw in LanSoren's study. Your uncle was adamant that Gemma should not be left behind, under any circumstances. I believe she has a part to play, here on Muraine. Then there's the fact that LanSoren has been playing this game of time longer than we have, Talok. He was a meticulous planner."

Hesitating, Talok queries, "What if something's happened that he hadn't planned for?"

Ryco hides a smile. "Well, you need only look as far as a Borrower of Time, to get some answers on that. And it just so happens we have one here, in Siveyra Paydinn. Some might see it as convenience, but you should not. As I said, LanSoren was meticulous."

"Very well." Talok huffs. "I will make sure that my decision is the best choice. Now, I want this ritual finished. You will be the witness, Ryco. And you, Tyler, will be the one pouring this on my head."

To me, he hands the vessel Grover gave to him earlier. He strides for the corner of his quarters, where there's an L-shaped wall.

Motioning that I go first, Ryco follows me.

Once behind the wall with Talok, we find him kneeling on a white-stone floor. Head bowed, his eyes are closed. His hands are clasped in front of him.

Ryco uncorks the bottle. The smell of blood drifts out of it.

I feel sick. My hands start to shake.

"Please!" Talok shouts. "Get on with it." His lips quiver.

Ryco grips my left arm. But my trembling doesn't stop, until he divs, saying, *"Today, you are no mere boy, Tyler. You've nothing to fear in this moment, except yourself. We'll find a way to save him. Even if it kills me, I will find a way. But come back to this moment. Talok has chosen you, to be with him during his vulnerability. He needs us to be his strength."*

Letting go of me, Ryco takes a step back.

I nod at him and then slowly approach Talok. I begin pouring the blood upon his head. As soon as it has landed on him, he cries out.

I want to stop.

But Ryco shakes his head, motioning that I continue.

Talok's cries turn to silent sobs.

When the blood of his people has been drained from the vessel, I step back.

My breaths hammer out. I want to scream. I'm so torn up inside. Suddenly, I can't bear to be without Gemma. The very thought of her leaving leaves me feeling like a wreck.

"It's finished, King Talok," Ryco states. "Break the vessel, Tyler."

Not needing a second command, I throw it down on the floor, and it shatters.

What blood remains inside, splatters across the tiles of the floor.

Talok's on all fours. Panting, he looks too weak even to stand.

Ryco does the honor of picking him up. Pressing him against the wall, Ryco undoes all the belts, buckles, and laces keeping Talok's coat and vest on. After ripping the bloodied clothing off, Ryco grips Talok's face, saying to him, "It's over, Talok. Let their voices rest. Their faces fade. Today, you've done all you could. And that is enough."

Talok bursts out weeping, and he reaches out to hug Ryco.

Ryco hugs him back, and lets Talok bury his face against his chest.

Though muffled, I hear Talok say, "Please don't leave me."

Ryco looks to me with those yellow, Sylvadyn eyes, now filled with sadness.

Part of me wonders, *Is this a taste of what it was like, the day my dad died? Talok broken. And Ryco holding him, reassuring him.*

I think more of what Ryco has said. And there's something I now agree on. Going to stand by Talok, I tell him, "We won't ever leave you, so long as Gemma stays."

In the moments after I've given him the ultimatum, I wonder if I've overstepped a boundary. Will Talok snap? Will he see it as manipulation? It's agony wondering how he will react. But I've made up my mind.

Gemma *is* staying.

Or I am leaving.

8

Ever-Changing Intentions

The pain slowly fades from Talok's face. He pushes away from Ryco, to study me. Fury creeps into my cousin's expression. He starts to come at me. And not in a friendly sort of way.

I stand stiff, ready for a fight.

Before either of us can do anything we'll later regret, Ryco grabs Talok and holds him back. "You're both drained, letting your emotions lead. No more talk of this right now. Wait until you've both had something to eat."

Nails biting into his palms, Talok states, "I will do as you suggest, Ryco, so long as you keep an eye on Tyler. Stop him from being stupid. *Saying something stupid.*"

"Of course," replies Ryco, adding in Mensa-div to me, *"However, it wouldn't do much to stop you today, would it, Ravier?"*

"Not a chance," I div back.

Someone knocks on the door, interrupting us.

Talok storms out of the blood-splattered bathing quarter.

Ryco and I follow a ways behind. Just as Talok's about to jerk the door open, he steadies his hand. Gently, he turns the knob.

It's Eishal, asking, "It is done, then, King Talok?"

Talok stands aside to let him in. "What do you want, Keeper of Trauvo?"

Eishal enters, carrying a paper-wrapped bundle.

"Is that what I think it is?" queries Ryco, glancing at the parcel.

"Yes, yes, 'tis his coat and vest," replies Eishal, nervously fiddling with the string tied round the brown bundle. "Sosha's Waking Dragon."

Talok goes from being angrily distracted, biting his nails, to appearing troubled. "Absolutely not!" he yells. "I know what you're going to say, Ryco. And I won't have it! I'm not wearing my uncle's coat. Nor his heart-armor."

Ryco says, "Don't be ridiculous, Talok. It's the strongest enchanted clothing we have, here in Eyo'el. You are the king. You *will* wear it. You can choose to put it on, or Tyler, Eishal, and myself will devise a way to get you in it. And don't be thinking that you can just take it off, afterwards, either. Rozeth and I can and *will* cast a spell that prevents your removal of it."

Eishal adds, "Also, don't count on Zepharre coming to your aid, for this matter. He was beside himself with happiness, at the news of LanSoren's coat being given to you . . . well, as much happiness as ever can be seen in Zepharre."

Smirking, Ryco nods his agreement.

"Fine!" Talok shouts, taking the package. He slams it down on the table. "If you wish to treat me as Zymarc did, forcing that mask on my face, I will choose to put this on—of my own accord—for I will not have my own people forcing me into anything. But you'll have a great deal of alterations to do. I'm nowhere near my uncle's stature. And Madeleine's in no state of mind to help."

Talok tears the package open, with a little more fervor than I expect, ripping it into more pieces than is necessary.

Ryco motions to me, saying, "Ravier, go find Paydinn. See what details you can get from him, regarding Talok's concerns."

I head out. Before closing the door, I look back and spot my cousin sitting at the table, devouring a bread roll, and scowling at me. Meanwhile, Eishal holds up a brilliant white vest made of dragon scales. That's when heat creeps across my scalp. I suspect that Talok's trying to Mensa-div with me, but Ryco is blocking him. My judgment's proved accurate, when Talok huffs. He then glowers darkly at Ryco.

Undaunted, Ryco states, "Since this won't take as long as Talok reckons, we'll be down in the council room soon, Ravier. The symposium room, as Jasper calls it."

Talok's glower at Ryco turns lethal, as I close the door.

After a deep breath, I start for the stairs. Galloping down them two at a time, I wonder where to start the conversation with Paydinn. *In Mensa-div? Face-to-face? And what will I say first?*

Wandering my way through the corridors, then to the stairs leading to the second floor, I stop at an unfamiliar presence. It's as if a heaviness has wrapped itself round my feet, making me want to stop and look for something amiss. To my left is an alcove. It overlooks the castle's center gardens of rich, deep colors that have ruby-stone fountains scattered about. Surrounded by the castle itself, the especially stunning beauty remains intact, and creates its own light.

I amble into the alcove, for a closer view. At its core is a long, curved bench made of scuffed silver. On the backside, facing me, are intertwined carvings of Paragon's creatures: dragons, horses, birds, and such. Bookcases line the alcove's left wall, their shelves brimming with bound books and loose scrolls. Lining the opposite wall are dried flowers and herbs in metallic vases. Above them on little shelves are hundreds upon hundreds of tiny bottles and vials, held within wooden trays. Then there's a black table, with many indentations and golden symbols cut into them. To the right of this table, a mini nursery of plants and saplings wait to be picked. All together? It's like Quall's dream for mixing a plethora of herb concoctions.

Unable to help myself, I approach the table.

From somewhere in the room, there's movement.

"It's an alchemist's board," says a sleepy voice, startling me.

Sitting upright on the silver bench in human form is Jasper, watching me with those fierce, green eyes. His clothes have been cleared of the blood. He almost looks unthreatening. Especially as he sighs, relaxing his shoulders, before saying, "Come, sit a moment."

"Shouldn't we be doing something?" I ask.

"We're always doing something, Tyler," he says. "You were walking just now. Then you stopped. Most likely, you sensed me sleeping. Mekka has complained how I sleep with both eyes open. Meaning, he never knew when it was safe to sneak out, during his Vonsai years of night frolicking. My only tell is the change in my aura. My presence. Did it make you uneasy?"

"A little," I reply. "But only because something felt out of place."

Jasper angles his head to the side a moment, stating, "A sleeping Greyvon, lonesome on a bench made of the reflective core of Blackwood trees, within a grieving castle made of those same trees? Yes," he jokes, "it is most definitely out of place. I prefer my warm lodge, during Vondurheil's endless winter, to be sure. Blanketed with furs, and surrounded by the wild Vonsai and my Vons' misbehaving pups."

Quietly, I join Jasper on the bench. "Greyvons are pack-oriented, then?"

"Most definitely," replies Jasper. "We hate being alone for too long. And my Greyvons dislike Vondurheil absent of me. No matter what is decided today, I must be away to my home soon."

"How vast is Vondurheil?" I ask. "And is the journey to get there long?"

Standing up, Jasper approaches the bay window of the alcove, replying after a time, "It depends on how fast the travelers are. A pack of Greyvons can make it in a day. We feed off each other's energy. It makes us faster than if we are alone. But with riders, or accompanied by other races, it can take up to three days' time, as their company is very draining for us."

"Was my dad draining to Greyvons?" I ask.

"He was neither enlivening nor draining. A sort of neutral aura. To Greyvons, that is."

Contemplating on the phantom notes, and the bloodied glass shard still tucked away in one of my pouches, I wonder if I should even bring up Rorka at all. Deciding against it for now, I rise up to go to the window, and stand beside Jasper. Below us, in the garden's courtyard, Quall, Lokasi, and Paydinn have set up tents and tables for the sick, whom they are now healing; Zepharre is amongst them, passing out food and drink. His movements are stiff and hurried, however. It's apparent that he is not enjoying himself. Then he stops mid-step and looks up at the bay window.

Jasper grins, lifting his hand in greeting.

Zepharre looks away, stiffening his neck, then goes back to hurriedly serving the Paragonians.

Frowning, Jasper clasps his hands behind his back.

That's when I ask, "What was the quarrel between the two of you?"

"The first time Zepharre and I met was on a wet and frigid day, when we were all weary. Sosha had just died. And I was asked by LanSoren to come begin negotiations for an alliance with Paragon. Zepharre did not greet Greyvons with the respect we demand. Even Vitiosyns, it seems, know better than to enrage a full-grown Von."

"But he's Zepharre," I point out. "Would we have him any other way than smug?"

"You'd better be careful, Tyler," says Jasper, with some wit in his voice. "Zepharre is stronger than he seems. Did you know that he was only beat out by Ryco, during their youth, to become an Eyo'el nominee for the King's Guard? Should there be an opening?"

I shake my head, trying to imagine Zepharre a warrior. It's contradictory to what I've witnessed.

Jasper continues, "He has a good following, here in Paragon. EmiKal, as well. All three grew up in Eyo'el: Ryco, Zepharre, and EmiKal. Given Ryco's heritage, the other two voices carry more weight in The Eye."

"But Ryco is not his ancestors," I state.

"Nor are you your father," says Jasper. "Yet, you've been given privileges without earning them, because of who he was. You see how privilege can be worked to your advantage, without you doing much of anything?"

After a nod, I counter with, "If you look hard enough, Alpha Jasper, everyone's been given a privilege they did not earn. What is yours, I wonder?"

He's silent a moment. Unclasping his hands, he presses them on the glass.

Spotting Paydinn looking up at me, I Mensa-div, *Talok wants to send Gemma home. And I will be leaving, if that happens. Is there anything I should say, to change his mind? Or give him reassurance that he's making the right choice in letting us stay?"*

"This," says Jasper, with his hands still pressed on the glass, "is the gift I was given at birth."

He looks from me to Paydinn. Colors of blue and then green ice over the glass like frost. Slowly, they make their way toward the space in front of me. They swirl out like mist and show a sort of link between the Time Borrower and myself. Then the colorful mist wisps away, and fades to nothing.

I look to the alpha. "I don't know what that was."

"It's a gift that reveals magical signatures, to put it simply," says Jasper, taking his hands off the glass. "What is unseen by nearly all others, is seen by me. While I can't hear all Mensa-div, I know when it is happening. That is the privilege I was given through no hard work of my own, whatsoever. But I use it to my advantage every day. And I hone the skill, to be more proficient. What was previously a privilege is now all my own, through time and hard work."

Chuckling a little, I state, "I feel a lesson coming on."

"Oh no!" Jasper exclaims playfully. "The lesson's over. Didn't you catch it?"

"Maybe," I reply, as paper rustles behind us.

"Maybe?" Jasper laughs. "My word! He says maybe, Paydinn. What are we going to do with him?"

Turning around, I spot Paydinn eyeing us from the alcove's entryway, his eyes now a light-pink color.

"Before you say anything," I begin, after folding my arms across my chest. "Care to explain what's up with your eyes constantly changing color?"

Paydinn straightens. Startling a little, he replies, "Oh, I quite forget about them. My auratic eyes. They change with my mood. My aura. Metimorans are meant to be of the snake aura. But my mother is Sorsryn. And, it seems, I am of no particular aura. But, rather, all of them. My father, GrawVadian, had eyes swirling with many colors. But they stayed that way—constant and fixed in color. Mine, obviously, do not. Much to my dismay. And my three younger brothers' delight."

"Moody eyes?" I state, "That should be fun."

"Don't you be getting any ideas, now, human half-blood." Paydinn points a long finger at me. "As I taught LanSoren to respect me the hard way, I will most assuredly teach you. Watch yourself."

"Sorry." I shrug. "I don't have any mirrors with me."

"That can be remedied," states Jasper, handing me a small metal disk.

Before I can accept it, however, Paydinn is already in front of me—as if he just *appeared* there—taking the reflective disk, and tucking it away in one of my exterior pockets. Running his hands up to my coat collar, he says, "Yes, yes! This Sleeping Dragon is quite nice. But you know what's better?"

Shaking my head, I reply, "Sosha's Waking Dragon?"

"No," says Paydinn, tapping his fingers on my chest. "The scaled armor beneath. It protects you, in more ways than you know."

I ask, "The diving armor, you mean?"

"Yes, exactly, the diving armor," replies Paydinn, whirling around and striding out of the alcove. "Now, come! Ryco is escorting Talok and Eishal to the symposium room. And we don't want to be late, do we, Ravier? Or Jasper is liable to put all the weight of the books right round our necks."

Jasper and I follow in Paydinn's swift, traversing trail through the castle. As we go, I ask him, "What about what I asked you?"

"Ah! That!" Paydinn says, "Talok must decide, free of my counsel. It will go as it *should* go, if I hold my tongue. Refusing to answer. I don't like it, but there it is. The way it must be. And you, Jasper. You refuse to answer him, as well. If you are patient, Alpha, you will get an answer you don't even know that you want, as of yet."

"Metimoras, Tyler," Jasper whispers, leaning down a moment. "They are the most draining of all the races."

I reply, "With talk like that, who wouldn't be tired from listening?"

Paydinn holds up a defensive hand. "You will thank me later. Now, here we are to the room of chaos and shouting voices. Listen! They've already started."

The Time Borrower is about to press his ear against the door and listen to the muffled, arguing voices inside. But the castle has a fit, throwing the symposium door open with such violence, it cracks a bit as it hits the wall and embeds itself there.

Paydinn is barely able to get out of its way. Now, he just stares at it, his eyes changing to teal.

Silence ensues inside the room.

Jasper and Paydinn enter, then I bravely follow.

My cousin—covered by a black cloak streaked with white and some gray—sits in the same chair he was in yesterday, when Quall brought Gemma and me in. Talok's hands are folded on the table; to his left is Mekka, and at his right sits Rorka. All his advisers are seated at the center table with him. On one side of the room, the Arkiveis have taken to sitting, as well. Positioned between Nyrim and Lokasi is Gemma, refusing to look up. Along the opposite wall, all King's Guard stand at attention.

When Ben briefly looks to the empty space beside him, I take the invitation and go stand with the guards.

Jasper and Paydinn take to the empty seats at the council table.

But it's Talok starting the dialogue, saying, "I do believe Zymarc gave you the contract, Alpha Jasper. Now that we're all gathered, please break its seal."

Zepharre adds, "We're all very anxious to see this over with."

Jasper does as Talok bids, taking out the document from one of his pockets. Breaking its seal, he reads the contract and then passes it along to EmiKal.

"It's as we thought," says EmiKal, passing it on down the line to eager, outstretched hands. "He demands Awngeleik's return, claiming that she is his property. Merely a gift to LanSoren—and *only* to LanSoren—upon his death, she became his once more."

I interrupt, saying, "I'm not suggesting that you do, but if Awngeleik *does* rightfully belong to him, what's stopped you from giving her back?"

"I can answer that," says Jasper. "At LanSoren's request, I altered her genetics. She is now more than she was ever meant to be—a sort of abomination to dyn and horse, alike. Saying she is a weapon of war would not be wrong. And she's not sensible enough to refrain from being used as such."

"What was changed about her?" queries Gemma, sitting up.

"Everything," Mekka replies, fiddling with some rectangular device. When his alpha taps thrice on the table, he puts the device away and then looks up, saying, "Alpha, where would you like that painting you had me fetch yesterday?"

"Did you and Rorka have that talk?" queries Jasper, sounding too calm.

Mekka loudly huffs. "Brewing argument? Now talk? I don't know what you're meaning. Rorka and I are fine. We're perfectly fine. Look! I'll even share this thing I stole from Jack Wayeland. When was that? Three years ago? Four. I don't remember."

Whipping the device back out, Mekka shoves it across the table toward Rorka.

Talok just leans back, his mouth twitching in anger, as the two begin their dialogue.

"See, Rorka," Mekka says. "It even has this little bird game. But unlike some of your fleet of letter-birds *attacking* me, while I was returning from that errand Jasper sent me on, *these* little birds do what you tell them."

"My letter-birds attacked you?" Rorka asks, in disbelief.

"Yes! They were after me. Because you must have been thinking of me," replies Mekka. "Or, rather, how much you hate the idea of me. I think—"

Jasper interrupts, saying, "*I* think you should go hang that painting down in the bunkers below. You *and* Rorka."

"In the bunkers?" queries Mekka, pushing his chair away from the table. "Why there?"

"Because it is safe down there," replies Jasper. "And *not* angry. If you get my meaning."

Grabbing the stolen device and tucking it away, Mekka clicks his tongue. He nods reluctantly. "Yes, Alpha, I get your meaning."

Both candidates stand to leave.

"And be sure," says Jasper, "to have that talk, while down there."

Rorka exits first. Mekka starts to follow.

Then Jasper says, "Don't let the door hit you on the way out."

"What door?" Mekka scoffs. "It's disappeared."

Turning back, he takes a step forward.

Then the door slams itself shut, and smashes into Mekka's face.

Mekka yells in pain. He hits the door with his fist, and it unlatches, creaking open innocently.

"I don't like this castle," says Mekka. "It's misleading."

"Jasper," Rorka queries, "when are we going home?"

Curiously looking about him, Jasper says, "Are those Greyvons talking, Zepharre?"

Hesitating, Zepharre reluctantly replies, "All I hear is the yapping of two Vonsai."

"As do I," says Jasper. "Go now, Vonsai."

"Yes, Alpha," they say.

Jasper rubs his temples, as the two candidates' footsteps and hushed arguments fade away. Next, Jasper looks to Quall, asking, "Where have the other Greyvons gone? The ones sent to assist with the cloaking spell?"

"Once the spell was complete," replies Ryco, "they went about their own business. I imagine they went on a hunt, during the festival, as nighttime is when your prey of choice is running about. Yes?"

"That is true," Jasper agrees.

"But they should have shown themselves, once the attack started," states Quall.

Jasper adds, "I fear something has happened to them." After a pause, he shouts, "Mekka! Come back a moment."

As we wait for Mekka's return, I wonder if he was the one terrorizing Awngeleik, me, and Gemma back home. He's already admitted to stealing Jack Wayeland's phone. He looks like the Bear-Wolf in the still-shot, too, only bigger now, probably because he's older. A full-grown Von in his prime, no doubt.

The council room door opens, and there's Mekka standing in the doorway, saying, "Yes, Alpha?"

"Keep a lookout for the Vons sent to assist with Awngeleik's spell." Jasper says, "They've not been seen for an entire day."

"Do you want that done before or after I hang up the painting and Rorka?" Cringing, Mekka corrects himself, saying, "I mean after hanging up the painting *with* Rorka—after Rorka and I hang up the painting together, while 'talking.' There! Have I said it right?" Mekka's nostrils flare with every breath.

Jasper calmly looks back at him. "I don't care, either way."

Not responding, Mekka leaves again.

Closing the door, then running down the hall outside, Mekka yells, "On the dragon heart of that Scepter I'll slay tomorrow, Rorka, you're not going to make it down there ahead of me!"

The rest is jumbled, as his voice fades out of range.

Zepharre, lounging comfortably in his seat, says, "If you don't mind my saying so, Alpha Jasper, those two don't seem like themselves."

"They're not." Jasper sighs. "But do not worry. I will have made them face their greatest fear, by the end of tonight."

"And that would be?" queries Zepharre, while cupping his face.

"A compromise between two equals," replies Jasper. "It's what Greyvons of equal status fear most: compromising. But they learn to like it, for the sake and sanity of those around them. Now, back to this contract. You've all read it. Are there any counteroffers you wish to give, to end the war before it starts?"

EmiKal states, "He only wants Awngeleik."

"Yes," Jasper replies, "but if you offer him something of equal value, he may be tempted to consider it in place of her."

"No," Talok interrupts. "We're not negotiating. The only one we will even consider offering in her place is me. But Zymarc has made it clear that I'm worth nothing to him alive. He does not care if I die. Hence, the device his apprentice was so kind as to put on me. We've been made fools of, thinking it randomly latched on to me. Now, there will be no more talk of this, until another mattered is cleared up."

Talok abruptly looks to me. "Cousin Tyler, have you anything to say on the other *matter*?"

Though I fear the outcome, I reply, "The decision lies with you."

"Then it's time we make our way for the portal," says Talok, standing up. "My scouts have returned just now. They say the way is clear. You and Gemma are going home."

9

Take Away the Key

Gemma and I were rushed out through the cracked city gate so quickly, we weren't able to bid goodbye to anyone, not even Awngeleik.

Dusk paints its way across the sky, casting shades of red and pink light—orange and yellow too—through the thick of the trees.

Trailing along with us are the scouts, the guards, Talok, Zepharre, and Jasper. We're halfway there, the place where Gemma and I were greeted by Quall and the others only yesterday.

Fear claws at my heart. I don't want to leave. But I don't see how to make my cousin set his mind in a different direction. I remember Paydinn's words. And I hope something good waits for us, at the end of this chosen path.

A stench drifts through the forest, pushing out all thought.

"What is that horrid smell?" queries Zepharre, covering his mouth with the crook of his arm.

"Dead Vitiosyns," replies Ryco. "Quall, this is near where they were dispatched by the warriors, yes?"

Quall nods stiffly, stepping off the path.

Talok and the guards follow Quall's leading. Then the rest of us, after them. The foul scent of corpses fades, while we shove our way through low-hanging branches and silver-leaf bushes.

Partway through, Gemma grabs my hand and holds tight. Her steps are shuffling and forced, and, every few steps, she pulls me back. It's as if she worries over something at this new trail's end.

Regardless, I'm about fed up, ready to make her take the lead. But Quall stops abruptly, saying, "Someone's already drawn the portal waters together, and appears to be waiting."

Zepharre and Ryco make their way to stand beside Quall.

"What in Vardiya's name is he doing here?" queries Zepharre in a whispering outrage.

Ryco states, "It's ReNovak."

Going to the front of the line, Talok whispers, "I hear splashing. What's he doing?"

Zepharre scratches at his temple. "He's . . . stone-skipping? Is that what he's doing? He goes for an errand. And now he's stone-skipping. Pray tell, Alpha Jasper, what is the purpose of that?"

"Practicing," replies Jasper quietly.

"Practicing for what?" queries Zepharre, indignant.

"Opening the portal, using an Enigma Star," Ben mutters, from his place behind me.

"It's very hard to do," Jasper adds. "And only some Enigmas work like that."

"Oh," says Zepharre flatly, clamping his mouth shut.

Before we can assess what to do, Talok marches out from the cover of the trees. Once out in the open, he comes to a standstill.

About to skip another small, plain stone, ReNovak hesitates. Turning his head slightly toward our direction, he drops the stone and then cautiously advances to greet Talok.

"My dear Talok," he says, with some shame in his voice, "before you say anything, I would like for you to know, I would've chosen Paragon, if I could have. But Zymarc is good at playing the game. As he should be. For he was, once, one of us. Onyx. Favored by me. And, now, starting tomorrow, I will answer to him directly. And my Onyx Warriors, to me. In fact, through me, all the Onyx residing in the land of the Nyxane will be under his rule."

"That is not why I'm currently here," Talok proclaims, "to hear stories and histories; no, not even apologies, if that's where you're going with all this talk."

"Quite right." ReNovak nods. "I would ask, however, if you'd allow me to do a last servitude for you and your people, by opening the way for Tyler and his friend to go safely home?"

Talok startles. "I was not aware that you could open the portal."

"Well, I was never given the chance," says ReNovak, "because I didn't know where a functional one was. But then I put together bits of Belzara and Zymarc's recounts, regarding yesterday's events. Pair that with Gyronawv's report and the knowledge that portals need something reflective to work properly. It all led me here. To this spot. A place near a patch of ground ridden with riddles of many hurrying footsteps, winding in very odd patterns. It's clever how you make the water draw away into numerous trickling streams, then force them into this shallow basin only when necessary."

"Not clever enough, it seems," says Talok, through clenched teeth.

"Shall I open the way?" queries ReNovak innocently.

Something about the gleam in his gaze is alarming. I wonder, *Will Talok see it?*

"Yes, that is a good idea," states Talok.

The air is suddenly filled with a stronger scent of pinesap.

Wrinkling his nose, Jasper glances at Ryco, then back to the two kings.

Several in the group are uneasy. Even Ryco appears worried, as sweat glistens on his forehead.

"What's he doing?" queries Quall. "Has he gone mad?"

Zepharre adds, "ReNovak is not neutral today, is he, Alpha Jasper?"

"I do not know," replies Jasper, stepping out into the open.

ReNovak locks on to the alpha, bowing his head respectfully. "Forgive my absence, Jasper, at the announcement. It couldn't be helped."

"Where were you, Onyx King?" queries Jasper.

"I cannot say. But it was . . . of the utmost importance. And now *this* is of the utmost importance. To return those two to their home. But we must hurry. I've told Azabahk to meet me near here, at dusk. It will be simple to explain that I also asked you to meet us, outside of Paragon's gate. He will not suspect that anything is amiss."

"Very well," replies Talok. "Open it."

ReNovak's heterochromian eyes take on a victorious gleam. He reveals a metallic-white Enigma Star and begins preparing it for the throw.

I position myself to get a better view.

Dusk's light hits the rippling waters. The water goes still. As a perfect mirror, it reflects the tree canopy of Paragon. Burnt umber. Rust. Yellow ochre. Ash. And coal. Wispy malachite-colored leaves, red quills, and citrine thorns too. All of it reflects to be a colorful web upon the waters.

After I release Gemma, an icy heat rises within my chest and then up my throat. It's the same sensation as when the beast by Mirror Lake approached. Unlike then, however, I do not crave its warmth. But, rather, I reject it, wanting frigid-cold, instead. Needle-like pain stabs into my arms, and I clench my fists. Closing my eyes, I wish someone here could tell me what to do. What to feel. What to say. In a flash of sadness, my chest stings at the remembrance that Aysivak was supposed to guide me through it all. Four years' time, until the end of something.

That's when I think, *Maybe he is guiding me. Just not in a way that I would suspect. Paydinn's lack of advice, and my refusal to let Gemma go home without me, led here to this moment of me sensing the lurking beast. Whoever he is, he's here. Not on Earth. Is he waiting for me to go? Are we just playing into an adversary's greater plan, by abandoning Talok when he needs us most?*

I open my eyes, in time to watch ReNovak toss the star out toward the still waters.

It starts skipping: one, two, three times.

My fists unclench, and I hold my breath. Unblinking, I stare at the water's center, willing it to explode away into trickling streams. Wanting to provoke it to frenzied, I take a quick step forward, as if daring it to face me, to challenge me. I speak something under my breath. The word's so quiet, like a curse my subconscious doesn't yet want me to know. It's chilling.

The water explodes out, rushing straight for ReNovak. The force knocks him to the ground, seemingly trying to drown him.

Talok and Jasper dash out of the water's way.

It separates, whipping into many snaking streams. As if they are made of solid matter, they twist themselves and then together, like malleable blown glass. The water continues rushing within the strands, but is trapped, unable to flow out onto the ground.

The likeness of a howling wolf is constructed by these glass-like water strands, yet it remains silent. It then shapes itself into a dragon, with its wings outspread. It ends with forming a Vardiya figure that's twice the size of Aysivak. The water strands turn black. It initiates like ink dropping in water. The movement of its eight tentacles slows to a mesmerizing rhythm.

I look around. Everyone's frozen in place, except for Jasper, glancing about apprehensively. He whirls around. Like how my movements were that day at the lake, his glitch and blur together.

He grips the hilt of Winter's Vondaen. "What did you do, Tyler?"

"I'm closing the way to my home," I reply, striding forward.

The air pulls on me, with every step. It's musty and humid, but it is merely an annoyance. Hardly an obstacle, as I make my way to standing at the empty basin's edge, some distance in front of the Vardiya form.

It shifts and shrinks to looking exactly like Aysivak; an Aysivak, possessing all eight tentacles. His bluish-gray scales reflect those dark, iridescent turquoise and burgundy colors.

When his six slanted, black eyes blink at me, I smile.

"Aysivak," I speak in a sharp tone, watching his hovering form. "Close the way home. Only open it back up, when it's safe for Gemma and me to go."

"You are sure, Ravier?" He quickly adds, "For you must *be* sure, as there's no undoing the consequences."

Side-glancing at Jasper, I see him dip his head down.

"I think it is a good idea, Tyler," Jasper says.

"Yes, Aysivak," I reply. "Close the doorway."

"Very well," he says. "Until the next time, Tyler."

The thirteen steps I took to stand before Aysivak, I now look back at and then to the thirteen in front, separating me from him. I swiftly realize he's at the center of thirteen steps in all directions of the empty basin's edge.

Inwardly, I shake my head, while speaking the words, "Thirteen. We're done, for now."

Aysivak's black eyes widen, until only two are staring out. They shift to pure white. His body turns black again. It writhes and shakes. Exploding out, the water strands return. Landing on the ground, each stream searches for its path. They then settle within their designated places, and begin their streaming to wherever they're called to go.

As the waters find their conduits, I pace back to where I stood hidden by the trees.

With a blurred, sweeping gesture of his hand, Jasper erases my tracks. Then he, too, takes the position he was in, when scrambling away from the water.

"Is it always that easy to hide tracks?" I ask.

"Anyone knowing a fair amount of magic can do it," replies Jasper. "But Greyvons are especially gifted in it. You will tell me later, why it is that you asked."

The heavy, humid air fades.

Movement of the others initiates.

ReNovak, completely soaked, hurries back to his feet, searching around. "What's happened?" he exclaims.

"It's refused to open the portal," states Ryco, stepping out.

"Has it ever done that before?" Talok tugs his cloak closed as he speaks, attempting to conceal the new coat threatening to reveal itself.

"Not that I've ever witnessed," says Quall, helping Talok up from where he landed after tripping.

"What have you done, Tyler?" My cousin practically screams the words. He rushes for me, reaching out with a menacing hand.

Ryco protectively blocks the path to me, pressing on Talok's chest.

"Tyler's stood here, through it all, my king. He has done nothing but watch."

Talok calms down a mere fraction, as he lowers his arm. But he refuses to look at me. Picking up ReNovak's white Enigma Star, which was tossed away during the water frenzy, he strides to the Onyx King, and gives it back to him.

ReNovak accepts it, right as Azabahk silently steps out into the clearing.

"What is this, King ReNovak?" queries Azabahk, in disbelief. "You've invited Paragon to our meetup, *and* you've gone for a swim? This morning, it was some unknown, but very vital errand. You are ever busy. What luck it must be, to be the monarch of Onyx, always able to have time for everything and everyone, save for your allies and their would-be foes."

"I've not gone for a swim," replies ReNovak, tucking the Enigma Star away. "I fell into a spout of water, on the way here. And I didn't tell you of Paragon meeting us outside, because they did not answer my letter to them, sent a while ago. I was unsure whether they would come or not. I thought, why tell you? If they didn't show, you'd never know they shirked me. Why add insult to injury?"

Tapping a finger to his lips, Azabahk seems to mull over ReNovak's words. Spotting Jasper, Azabahk straightens his stance. "Very well, Onyx. I will choose to believe you. Have you at least read Zymarc's note, left for you before he went on his own *errand?*"

"Yes, I read its entirety," replies the Onyx King. "Bit dramatic, if you ask me."

Giving a little chortle, Azabahk glances behind. He signals for someone to approach. A party of eight male Vitiosyns does, exiting the forest, to come stand behind Azabahk.

"Shall we go?" queries Azabahk, in good humor. "Be on our way to see these dramatics Zymarc has written of?"

Huffing, ReNovak turns around. He indicates that Talok should lead the way.

We traverse to the path Quall led us on yesterday.

After a short while, the corpse stench drifts from up ahead.

The forest is darkening, as dusk is fading into night.

Scouts light torches, carefully dispersing themselves amongst our group as walking wayfinders. But Ryco touches a hand to the ash-colored bark of the trees near the path, and the citrine thorns begin glowing like lit yellow glass.

"Put out the fire," he commands, and the Scouts of Paragon obey.

We cover our mouths, the closer we get to the foul-smelling corpses. All of us do so, except for Azabahk, his Vitiosyns, Jasper, and . . . Talok.

Confusion fills me, turning my stomach on end. I worry that something is changing in my cousin. Or is he just refusing to show any signs of weakness, in the presence of those currently about him?

Azabahk clears his throat, before asking, "Would you permit me to clear the smell of their flesh from the forest? Whilst it does not ail us, it seems to trouble many of you."

Talok's uninterested, saying, "They're your corpses. Do what you want with them."

Azabahk strides ahead. In the distance, flashes spark and water rushes. Then he's coming back, and the smell dies down to nothing but the pleasant scents of the forest: trees, flowers, and the gentle wind carrying scents of earthy herbs.

As we pass the corpses, I can't help but take a glimpse at them, to see what Azabahk has done.

Still in the same positions as when they were dispatched, they're now encased in a silvery-black metal, looking like cast museum figures within some slaughter scene.

Though the forest continues to be lighted by Ryco, and the citrine thorns that match his glowing eyes, the darkness presses in as a black fog.

We make it back to Paragon's broken gate and stop; rather, ReNovak stops, taking in a sharp breath.

Eyo'el is lighted within, by torch-fire and the artificial light of magic. The city is still gone. Only mounds of mangled ground and piles of rubble around tell of its previous greatness. Replacing its former glory are tents and shacks dotting the area.

"Where is the city?" ReNovak whispers, sounding panicked.

"Did you not believe Zymarc, in his note?" Azabahk answers. "It is gone."

Whirling around in fury, ReNovak shouts at the Prince-General, "I thought he was bragging, Azabahk! This is a war crime, Vitiosyn!"

"No, no," Azabahk corrects, lifting his finger. "If this had been our first or second strike, it would've been. It's true. But this was after they refused to answer our demand, for the third time. They told us 'no' twice. On thrice, they didn't even answer. This was our reply. Now, 'tis wise to have no more words, till we are at Paragon's negotiating table."

"I'm inclined to agree," states Jasper. "King Talok, you are the ruler here. Lead our way."

Exhausted, but determined, we follow my cousin to the castle. Once at its first step, Talok slows his pace and then continues heading for the double doors. As before, they won't budge for him.

"Open the doors, Metsa," says Ryco coldly. "We have important business to attend to."

The doors remain obstinate.

Tensing his body, Talok steps back. Then he kicks the doors with such force, they've no choice but to crack then open from the fury of their king. The wood has split a bit. Confidently, Talok strides in. "You are not welcome here," he says, to ReNovak and the nine, before they enter. "But you are permitted entrance, so long as there's no use of magic amongst yourselves, not even Mensa-div. That is the castle's term. Do you consent?"

"We do," says Azabahk, entering ahead of us all. "Zymarc, in fact, already instructed us to respect your castle, stating that it was prized by LanSoren, himself. Possibly even crafted by him too. We could never destroy something crafted by such gifted hands."

Talok states, "Once we are at the negotiating table, Prince-General, you will clarify your words."

Gemma comes to stand beside me, as Talok and Zepharre start for the stairs. Jasper, the King's Guard, ReNovak, and the Vitiosyns follow behind them.

Unsure if we should go with them, I just look down at Gemma, to say,

"Sorry we plotted against you, Gem. Do you forgive us?"

"It depends," she replies.

"On what?" I ask.

"If you plan on keeping me in the dark about everything, or if you'll actually start including me."

"I'm trying to trust others, Gemma," I reply, in earnest.

"Then try harder, Ty," she says, her voice filled with bitterness.

From above, Ben softly calls down, "Tyler, Gemma, Talok says you are to come. He wants you within his sight."

"Obviously, your cousin has trust issues too," says Gemma, slowly going up the stairs. "At least, trusting you to behave."

Through the dim corridors, we make our way to the symposium room at Ben's leading.

Talok's already at the table, addressing Azabahk. "I find it hard to believe that my uncle was involved with Vitiosyns."

"Why is it that war would never have been waged, if he were still alive?" queries Zepharre, taking his place with the other advisers.

EmiKal adds, "I suppose your King Zymarc would also not be asking for Awngeleik's return."

"Yes, that is how it would be," replies Azabahk politely. "If LanSoren were living."

"Something is missing," says Jasper. "Something you are not telling us."

Azabahk taps a finger to his lips. "That is so, as well."

Jasper points at the Prince-General. "As is the fact that you are in need of a new hammer."

Frowning, Azabahk leans forward. "You leave my hammer out of it. I have a new one being forged, as we speak. The hostages are forced to watch, whilst weapons are made. Weapons to end their brothers and sisters of Paragon. Their noble Von allies too. I had wished for you, Alpha Jasper, not to ally Greyvons with Paragon. I detest killing Vons. But, come tomorrow, I must kill or be killed. That is the way of war."

"There are hostages?" I ask.

Azabahk rests his hands on the table, smugly replying, "You didn't think we killed all those souls, in Yharss and Dysarda, did you? It would've been a war crime. Of course we took hostages. They were going to be for a trade. Twenty-two dyns, of which would include Reign, for them. But Zymarc has thought of something else he wants more."

"Out with it, Vitiosyn," says Ryco. "We are tired."

"Very well," Azabahk replies. "My King Zymarc wishes to see LanSoren's belongings that the tyke has brought with him. Especially, he wants to read the four journals and inspect those twin-daggers."

"Absolutely not," Talok states, in anger.

I interrupt to say, "Actually, he can read three of the journals, *and* inspect the daggers. But he will not see the rest. Will that do?"

"Cousin Tyler," Talok fumes, "what makes you think you have the right to—"

Cutting him off, I reply, "Because they belong to me. And what is done with them is my choice."

Azabahk coughs, then mutters, "I will pass the offer on to Zymarc. You should have his answer in the morning, regarding the release of hostages."

"Alpha Jasper," Talok says, in a dull voice. "Do you trust that I can handle negotiations from here?"

"Yes, I do believe you'll be fine, from here."

"Very good," says Talok. "I want my cousin out of here. And Gemma needs something to eat, before she faints. Will you see to their care?"

"Certainly," Jasper replies, leading us out.

Upon closing the symposium door, Jasper hands Gemma a small stick-looking thing. "Chew a bit of this. It'll help with the faintness and hunger. Though it doesn't work on me too well, my Vonsai are often satisfied by it."

Crunching on the offered gift, Gemma sighs in satisfaction.

"Better?" he asks, and Gemma nods.

Once we're out of earshot from the council room, she says, "See, Tyler, he doesn't trust you to behave."

Jasper chuckles, saying, "I shouldn't find that humorous. But it kind of is. Until I remember my own misbehaving Vons. And, look, there's Mekka now, making his way to Ryco's guardroom."

"But where's Rorka?" I ask.

"You don't think he hung her up with the painting, do you?" queries Gemma, now finished with Jasper's gift.

"We shall find out," he replies.

Entering the room where I napped earlier with Gemma, we see Paydinn conversing with Mekka and the Arkiveis.

"Where is Rorka?" Jasper asks, clasping his hands behind himself.

Facing Jasper, Mekka replies, "She's down with that little Khyra, and the tailor, preparing a bit of food."

Jasper eyes the room curiously, before asking, "If you had that talk, then why are you not in each other's company?"

"We talked, Alpha. Quite a bit too," Mekka defends. "Then we hung up the painting, and went on our way to different tasks. Is that wrong? Have we offended you?"

Jasper motions to the bed, nearest to Mekka. "Arkiveis of Paragon, I ask that you prepare beds for our tired souls. I will start here. See to preparing other rooms, if you please."

"An excellent idea, Alpha Jasper," says Grover, his robes fluttering about during his haste out of the room. "We shall see to it straightaway."

"I speak for Talok," Eishal adds, slowly following Grover, who's already gone from the room. "In saying that he will want to be in this room, rather than up in his personal quarters."

"What sleep-enchantments is he in need of?" queries Jasper, in concern.

"A little of all the renewing ones," replies Eishal. "But especially of mental healing."

"I'll see to it," Jasper reassures.

The Arkiveis leave.

Mekka and Paydinn start roughly straightening the tossed bed frames and bedding. Yet, they leave Ryco's bed untouched.

Gemma hesitates to assist them. Her eyes are wide and frightened.

"Miss Galloway," says Jasper, "would you go to the infirmary, to tell Rorka I summon her?"

Not needing to be asked a second time, Gemma nods, and practically flees the room in terror.

"Tyler, grab a box or crate," Jasper instructs. "Start packing clothes and supplies. I'm going to need your help, in convincing Talok to leave Paragon tomorrow. We might as well have a head start, in preparing for the journey to Vondurheil."

I do as he asks, wading through the room strewn with clutter. It's as if Grover's counter in the Arkivara has replicated its mess upon this room's floor. Opening the wardrobe, I find a box of books. Dumping them out on the floor, in Eli-like fashion, I start packing coats and other such things I think we'll need on the journey.

Jasper begins fixing Ryco's bed, making the frame much longer, and slightly wider. He takes great care in tightening the sheets and a quilt across it. Turning down the bedding, he then sits upon Ryco's desk chair. Crossing one leg over his opposite knee, he patiently waits.

When Mekka and Paydinn have finished, Jasper stands up, saying, "Master Paydinn, you may leave us. Tyler, keep packing."

Paydinn's anxious eyes flash an icy-blue color. He makes for his quick escape, closing the door gently.

"Take off your clothes, Mekka," Jasper commands, "merely keeping on enough to remain modest."

"I will not!" Mekka shouts, crossing his massive arms across his gladiator-sized chest. "That is a ridiculous request."

"You're refusing me?" queries Jasper calmly.

"I'm refusing that, yes." Mekka fumes.

"Very well," states Jasper. "I shall make you."

Shock sends Mekka into sweating profusely, blanketing the room with what must be considered Greyvon stench. It's musky, and I liken it to rain-drenched earth on a damp day. It's not unpleasant. But it's not a smell I want to bask in, either.

Jasper rushes Mekka, and the two wrestle with each other.

In minutes, Jasper has pinned Mekka down on the floor, and has ripped the candidate's boots off violently. Now he's working on the belt and pants, while Mekka's hands claw at him, trying to ward him off. Mekka then hits his alpha. And hard. He gets away, his pants intact. But not his shirt, which Jasper has caught hold of, and shredded in his zeal to de-clothe his candidate.

I keep packing the box, doing as I'm told. It's almost full.

Jasper blocks the door. His stance is relaxed, though he bars the way out.

Mekka shouts in a foreign, growling sort of language.

But Jasper simply queries, "Will you finish the rest, or do you wish for me to keep going?"

Mekka screams and yells more words, unrecognizable, at Jasper. After a minute or two of this, he's silent. Furiously, he takes off his pants. Just a bit of dark cloth covers him for modesty. Mekka holds his arms out. "There! I'm properly stripped of dignity. You might as well have shaved all my fur off, while I was in Von form. Now, where would you like me?"

"In that bed." Jasper points to Ryco's prepared one.

Mekka storms his way to it, then throws himself down upon it. Covering most of himself with the covers, he folds his arms. His eyes hold such fury that I think he's going to start chewing on his own arm, simply to get the anger out.

I start on another box, pretending that I've not just witnessed a battle of Greyvon wills.

In a short while, the King's Guard enter the room with Gemma and Rorka behind them.

Jasper is the first to say anything, telling Rorka, "Get in the bed with Mekka, and do not argue. You may ask Tyler how it will end, if you must."

Rorka glances to me, and I shrug, saying, "Do what you want, Rorka."

She timidly gets in bed with Mekka, then looks up at Jasper in confusion.

Handing Ryco a small hammer, Jasper says, "This is a trick you're going to love, Sylvadyn."

Going to Mekka's side of the bed, Jasper makes eight long metal nails appear in his hand. He bends down, pulling the sheet and quilt taut, and then lines up the nails for the hammer to strike. Ryco pounds them in, three hits on each nail head. Three are at Mekka's bedside. Two, at the foot. And three more, on Rorka's side of the bed.

Straightening, Jasper says, "There's no escaping each other, now. I suggest all of us rest for three hours, then regroup to talk of tomorrow's plans."

"Three hours!" Mekka shouts. "You're going to leave us like this for three hours? I can hardly move."

"What if Paragon is attacked again, during the three hours?" queries Rorka, resentfully kicking at Mekka beneath the covers.

"It won't be, as Zymarc is coming just before dawn," says Quall.

"With the hostages," Siege adds.

"Though we don't know how many there are," is Warren's input.

Eli finishes his thought, with, "We do hope it's a great many he's bringing."

Quall queries, "Do you have a trick I can use to stop these three from stealing the words right from my mouth, Jasper?"

"Even if there was," says Jasper, "I wouldn't teach you, for it would break their hearts. Now, Warren, I've a favor to ask. Will you create a minor time-distortion round the two of them? I don't much care to hear their talk, for these three solid hours."

"Sure thing, Jasper." Warren prepares himself to fulfill the request. "How long do you want it set for?"

Jasper starts to say, "Eight—"

But Mekka cuts him off, saying, "Oh, so now you care? Eight minutes in here, while three hours pass out there. Yes, that is quite generous, Alpha. See! He does love us, Rorka." Mekka grins, in utter elation.

"Hours." Jasper glares. "Set it for eight hours."

Mekka's face shifts to horror, and Rorka mutters, "You just had to cut him off, didn't you, you loudmouth, Mekka."

Warren practices his bit of Blue Magic, to create an iridescent dome round the two candidates on the bed.

Meanwhile, Gemma carries a tray of food and drink to the corner bed, hiding a grin, as she passes me.

I follow her. Then Eli and Ben do, as well. Crashing on the corner bed, I press my back against the wall, and pick food off the tray.

Devouring something textured like meat, yet very sweet, I feel content enough to rest. I fall asleep to the sound of swirling conversations. But the most comforting one is Gemma finding her voice, feeding off of Eli's humor and knowledge in object retrieval.

Before I know it, I'm waking up to a silent, blackened room. I hear someone open the door and quietly slip out. Like the night that I saw Talok and Ryco chasing down Awngeleik, in the woods back home, I feel compelled to follow whoever has slipped out of here. Something in my heart tells me to stay in bed. But, being me, I don't listen. I crawl off the corner bed, and make for my way out.

II

Journey to Discover

"I fear you are a legend made flesh, before my eyes."

10

Two Hearts

The floor has been cleared of all clutter, while I slept. It makes it easier to sneak out. With the faint moonlight streaming through the branches covering the broken window, I can spot at least two upon each bed. None, however, are small enough to be Gemma; nor are any tall enough to be Quall or Jasper. Slight sounds come from the candidates' time-distortion prison. But that's all the sound there is in the room, as I traverse it.

I gently brush my fingertips along the door, hoping it will quietly open. Low light shines through the doorframe's crevices. It fades, and the door silently opens. I go out, trying to shake the eerie feeling that abruptly takes hold. I grip the cold, roundish knob, and close the door. As I do, the castle Mensa-divs, saying, *"They wait in the gardens. Talking, planning, and teaching. Go to them. I will light the way."*

To my right, a torch fastened to the wall lights itself.

I advance in that direction, sticking to the path as more torches light themselves. I follow where they lead, until I pass into a kitchen of sorts, on the first floor, illuminated by dim light. Numerous freestanding counters—fashioned from whitewood—line two parallel walls, as well as fill the kitchen's vast center. The place has been picked bare of food, save for small loaves of rising bread, and others cooking over coals in a stone oven. In the corner, fragrant steam climbs up from a large vat of something. Its scent fills the entirety of the kitchen. And I actually feel a pang of hunger.

I glance around, looking for the tender of the vat and oven. But no one's around. Part of me hopes Zima will come popping in, all unexpectedly. But she doesn't.

Approaching the oven, I squat down to watch eight little loaves cooking on a stone turntable that's hovering above the heat source. Their crusts are golden brown. Surely, they're done.

"Someone obviously forgot about these," I remark.

Standing up, I search for something to use for fishing them out with. There's nothing. No cloth. No utensils. No pans. Just powder ingredients in jars. And liquids in bottles. It's akin to a kitchen robbed of half its things.

I'm about to walk out through the doorway that leads to the castle gardens, to look for someone out there. That's when the baked loaves shift and move about. One by one, they float to one of the center counters. They set themselves down, beside a rising loaf. Then those uncooked loaves are lifted, seemingly by unseen hands, before making their way to the oven to place themselves atop the hot turntable.

A smile escapes, as I whisper, "Enchanted kitchen. Should've known."

Grabbing a loaf that's surprisingly the right kind of warm for eating, I head out into the gardens. Nibbling at the sweet bread filled with seeds, nuts, dried fruits, and such, I wander around the picturesque scene. There's a sense of safeness about it. Pastel-red and magenta-pink light seeps out from the ruby-stone fountains scattered all around. Green, turquoise, and purple light emit from the scattered plants and flowers. They brighten the various stone walkways. Aside from sounds of flowing water, it's quiet. Peaceful, even. Untouched by the horrors of slaughter outside.

In one corner of the gardens, which I've managed to find my way to, there are small groves of fruit trees. Behind them, the castle walls soar up high. Moonlight catches on white veins embedded within the wood; also on the red vines, which are mixed in with the main structure of Blackwood trees.

Grazing among the groves are horses of all sizes, their dull coats splotched with many patterns and colors. Some are merely two feet tall; others, when lifting their heads up, are taller than the fruit trees themselves. All these EquiNeins have wings. A few, however, did not escape the onslaught of earlier. Injured, and missing one wing from their set, are some of them, looking my way. But only one holds my gaze. Though the others have their uninjured wings tucked up like birds, this one of average height—having a dingy coat of dark-gray, flecked with burnt umber and white—lets his battered wings hang down to the ground.

When he lowers his head dejectedly, I approach.

Petting his forehead, I ask, "Are they broken? Can you fly?"

He tries lifting them. Then he grunts and shrieks in pain. Giving up, he starts to turn away.

I reach out. Touching one of his wings, I speak a word. Again, I don't know what it is that I say. It doesn't feel like a curse, however. Hopeful yet sad describe the feelings in my heart.

His wings stir then crack, initially alarming me.

But then his flight feathers grow to full length. Lifting his wings, surprise overcomes the nein. He bolts away to take flight, contentedly flying off to an unknown destination.

Others take interest. They surround me. They won't let me leave, until they're healed of their wounds too. Even those absent of one wing on my arrival, have a complete set by the end. Yet I still have no idea how I'm doing it. Words leave my mouth. But I'm clueless as to what they are, or what they could mean. I only know that they work. Words I must have learned between now and age eighteen.

Healed and happy, the EquiNeins take off in a storm of galloping. Racing each other, they fly up, then over the castle's vine roof.

"You know," says a woman, strolling amongst the grove's shadows. "You are quite gifted, Green Eyes."

Spotting a glimpse of her bright face, I state, "So were you, Madeleine."

"Lokasi told me that you saved two-thirds of my memory." She smiles sadly. "I wish I could remember all of it. But I'm thankful for what you did, Tyler of Ravier. You must take me to your city, one day. For it must be a glorious city, to have produced someone like you. Like your father, LanSoren, too."

"Actually," I state, "Ravier isn't a city. It's just my name. Probably one my dad liked enough to take as his own."

"Not a city?" Madeleine frowns. "How very sad that it's just a name to you. Or is it more?"

Furrowing my brow, I ask, "How could it be more?"

Strolling closer, Madeleine says, "Names can always be more, Ravier. Names can even hold power, but only if you believe in them. Some spell names, were once names of mortals. Over time, they became spells."

"I suppose you have an example for me?" I ask.

Coming even closer, she grabs my hand. Warmth travels up my arm, as she says, "Yes. Nyxane is a good example. He was the first Onyx King. His spell was Nyxavond. The power it held could black out the sky. Not the whole sky of the world. But a portion of darkness, as large as the caster wanted or could manage, would shroud the land."

Letting go of her hand, I nervously fiddle with my watch. "How does that work? A name being turned into a spell? I don't understand."

"I wish I could remember what she told me," replies Madeleine. "My own mother, I mean. Perhaps if I continue, I'll remember more."

Gripping her hand again, hoping my magic will somehow help her lapse in memory, I speak the words, "Go on, Madeleine. I'm listening."

"Another name turned to a spell is Zotekavond," she says. "Zotek was the first Withrasyn King voted in, after King Monel was no more."

I interrupt, asking, "Do you know why the Withrasyn monarchy didn't go to Soren?"

Pulling away gently, Madeleine strolls over to a nearby tree. She leans back against it, gazing up to the stars through the thin canopy of fruit trees. After a while, she says, "I have the feeling that I used to know why. But, now, I cannot remember."

"No matter." I shrug. "You were saying something about Zotekavond?"

Nodding, she continues, "It is the opposite of Nyxavond, in that it whites out the sky. It's especially damaging to Deathasyns and Onyx, whereas

Nyxavond is detrimental to Withrasyns. And, now, Paragonians. But those who remain unhurt by either spell—"

Interrupting again, I confirm, "Are both Onyx and Withrasyn. But, when you say *unhurt*, do you mean they are completely unaffected? Or could it be empowering to them? Those who are both?"

"I don't know, Tyler," Madeleine says, as she plucks a round fruit off the tree she's near. "But one who is both old and wise might know. One such as Jasper. If not him, then Paydinn."

"Or the Rubidyn, King Rentwar?" I ask.

"Rubidyns?" queries Madeleine, scrunching her forehead. "I've not heard of that kind of dyn, though I'm a Dragon Tamer. If Rubidyns are an untamable sort, I wouldn't have learned of them until leaving Dysarda. And I've been told that I didn't come here to Eyo'el, until I was nineteen."

Startling us both right then is Kent, saying, "Madeleine, what are you doing out here alone? The Arkiveis specifically told you to stay inside the castle."

"I got hungry," she says, before chucking the fruit in her hand at Kent, who fumbles to catch it. "And I didn't want more bread. Besides, Tyler of Ravier is here. You should've witnessed what he did with the horses. It was rather beautiful *and* kind. Unlike you letting me fall off that dyn."

"Woman!" Kent exclaims, throwing the fruit on the ground. "It was eight years ago."

"For you, it was," Madeleine fumes. "But for me, it was yesterday."

"Well, what is it you want me to do?" queries Kent, his voice somewhat squeaking.

"I want you to tell me why it is that we don't have a family," Madeleine says. "How we went from a Dragon Ride of Promise, to you being a King Guardsman. And *I* a tailor, when I've not made a single stitch prior to my eighteenth birthday."

"Because you almost died that day," replies Kent quietly, looking heartbroken. "You were physically fragile at eighteen. And my heart was fragile then too. I couldn't bear to lose you that easily. So I cut you off, broke our agreement, and came to Eyo'el for extensive training, to be in the King's Guard. But you followed me here, less than a year later."

Madeleine's speechless, as tears well up.

Feeling awkward and out of place, I prepare to leave.

But Madeleine quickly brushes at her eyes, collecting herself. She strides forward, to grab me by the arm. "You don't need to leave, Tyler, unless you want to."

Glancing briefly at Kent looking sick, I state, "You're wrong, Madeleine. There's a lot you should talk about. Just the two of you. We don't know what today's going to be like. You may not get another chance to talk with Kent. Possibly, you may never see him again. My parents left many things unsaid. Don't do the same."

Looking down, Madeleine slowly nods.

Kent manages a grateful smile. "Gemma's in the center garden," he says, "sharing herbs with Quall and Jasper. Possibly Talok, Ryco, and Paydinn too. We'll be along to join you in a bit."

Lifting a hand goodbye, I turn to take purposeful strides forward. Toward the center garden. After a time, quiet voices fade within earshot. I'm able to make out their group, up ahead, sitting on circular benches around a blazing fire pit.

Gemma's the first I hear, saying, "You're giving me my own spell-book? Before Tyler gets one? Won't he be hurt by that?"

"From what I've seen of my cousin," says Talok, "not much can hurt him. Besides, that's the best I can do as an apology gift for trying to force you to leave, when you didn't want to. Will it do?"

"My own spell-book?" Gemma chuckles. "Definitely, it'll do. Will I get graded on it, like Eli and Ben with theirs?"

"Eventually," says Ryco. "For now, concentrate on learning. Taking notes and such."

"When can she get started?" I ask, striding into the circular space.

"Ah! Good!" exclaims Paydinn, setting his silver teacup down on the bench. "The castle woke you up. Took him long enough."

"Come, sit between us, Tyler," says Jasper, glancing at the teacup then Paydinn.

"What?" Paydinn says. "I was testing it for you, to make sure it'll have the desired effect."

Jasper mutters, "Do you doubt Quall's abilities?"

"Not a bit." Paydinn gently smacks at Jasper's arm. "But I know how you dislike sharing your food. Your drink too. I figure, if I irritate you a little bit throughout the day, you'll have to face your anger in small bits at a time. Then, we won't have to witness another one of your raging binges as the rabid beast, drawn out because you've kept yourself as a hidden storm for too long. You keep your temper at bay too much, Jazzy-von."

Leaning against the bench backrest, Paydinn flashes a wide grin at the Greyvon.

Jasper just picks up the dainty-looking silver cup and looks away into the fire, stating, "I don't like silver. It ruins the flavor. And, call me Jazzy-von again, you'll lose a finger. Possibly two, for good measure."

I've just barely sat down and am about to ask Gemma how she likes her spell-book; she's across from me, on the other side of the fire pit, enraptured with her reading of its pages.

But Paydinn is talking more, saying, "See! Don't you feel better voicing your emotions?"

"No," states Jasper flatly.

Paydinn continues, "I don't know what you're talking about, regarding silver changing the taste. Is that for all Vons? Or just you?"

"All," says Jasper, sipping from the cup and then grimacing.

Sprawled out on a bench by himself, Quall happily sighs, saying, "That explains why Musgrae complains about the food at the banquet dinners every month, served on silver instead of wood. 'Tastes like metal,' he says. 'And metal is for dyns, not the descendants of their tamers.'"

Talok chuckles a little, asking, "Ryco, is that why you always pack the finest silver, for your journeys? To make Musgrae miserable?"

"Not miserable," replies Ryco, whittling away at some small carving. "Just a little less enthusiastic about eating." Looking over to Jasper, Ryco adds, "But I thought it only an oddity of Musgrae's. Not all Vons."

"Someone talking about me, in my absence?" queries Musgrae, stepping off one of the garden pathways, and into everyone's view. His eyes are quite tired, only halfway open. He covers a giant yawn, before he sits between Gemma and Ryco. Instead of remarks on Ryco's carving skills, or Gemma reading her spell-book, however, Musgrae looks over to Jasper, and says, "Thought you should know, Jasper, that Warren's time-distortion has ended."

"Very good," replies Jasper, continuing to sip from his teacup. "I'll go free them, in a—"

Interrupting, Musgrae reluctantly adds, "And that the two upon the bed managed to bribe Eli into setting them free. At least, that's what I was able to find out."

Though Jasper's eyes had been calm, they aren't anymore. Yet, he *seems* calm with his sipping from the silver cup. But then, that cup is melting in Jasper's grasp.

Cringing, Paydinn scoots to the edge of the bench.

I simply smile, and glance at my cousin through the flames flaring up from the pit; though he tries not to, he is also grinning.

Jasper bolts up in a tirade, throwing the deformed cup into the fire. "What do you mean he was bribed? What was said to him?"

"Something about being made to eat Red Demon Berries." Musgrae lifts his shoulders. "I didn't catch any more than that, due to Eli's hysteria. I think Rorka made him feel a ghost sensation of the, um . . . Berry Itch."

Ryco stares at the tired Musgrae, saying, "By bribed, Musgrae, I'm sure you mean threatened."

"Threatened? Bribed?" Musgrae shrugs. "They mean the same thing to Eli. Anyway, as I was about to tell you, Jasper, they've already gone off into the night for hunting. There was no stopping them. They were hungry, before you imprisoned them on the bed. Upon waking, they were ravenous. Mekka even transformed into that black beast, and burst out the covered window. Took Rorka with him. She said they'd be back before dawn. They hope to have those other Vons with them too."

"What are Red Demon Berries?" queries Gemma, pausing from her reading. "Are they poisonous, or something?"

"Raspberries," replies Jasper, practically growling. "Mekka has a patch of them growing somewhere. Often slips them into others' food and drink, thinking the hives and itch they bring upon Murainians to be funny." Huffing, Jasper starts heading for the path Musgrae was on.

But Quall sits up, saying, "It's no use going after them, Jasper. Dawn's not long off, when Zymarc will, hopefully, be bringing hostages with him."

"Come sit back down, Jazzy-von," says Paydinn. "Look over one of those journals of Ravier's, to pass the time."

Relaxing his stance, Jasper comes to sit beside me, saying to no one in particular, "All I wanted was for them to get along better, not make threats in unison. Those two will be my undoing. Never did raise any offspring of my own. Glad of that fact, now. I imagine the love so deep, and hate so great that I have for both Mekka and Rorka is what I would feel for my own." Pausing, Jasper looks at me. "In any case, Grover has told me of a certain journal, with both wolf and dragon upon its cover. Do you trust enough, to show me its contents?"

Thinking briefly of the phantom notes, and Rorka's glass shard, I reply, "Only if you promise to do me a favor, when we get to Vondurheil."

Talok sits up straighter. "Who said we're going to Vondurheil?"

"The castle said there was planning being done in the gardens," I reply. "Isn't that what you were planning? A getaway trip?"

"We're not leaving Paragon, Tyler," Talok says. "We will not abandon the land, nor the Arkivaras, making way for it all to be overrun by Vitiosyns."

"The Arkivaras will protect themselves," I state. "Even Soren fears the one here. You don't have to worry about them. You shouldn't let that keep you from leaving, or asking that others leave with you."

"Possibly." Then Talok argues, "But Paragonians and Vaegons, alike, will not be so easily convinced. This is their home."

I continue, "Then tell them you're going to Vondurheil, to see about getting that Geldryn thing off your wrist. Tell them that Jasper needs the resources available there, since Paragon is ill-equipped in safely removing it from you here. It wouldn't be lying, since we *do* need to find a way of getting it off you."

Leaning back, Talok states, "That's fine. But *you* will be the one telling Zepharre and the others the news. Convincing them, if necessary. You also will be the one hashing it out, over what to do with Awngeleik."

"That's easy," I reply, shrugging. "She's mine. She'll go with me to Vondurheil. As for hashing it out with your advisers, let Paydinn stay and do that. Having forty *living* children? He should have no trouble convincing twelve advisers of anything."

Paydinn snorts, letting out a small laugh, before turning serious.

Talok just blinks at me, his mouth slowly drawing into a thin, tight line.

"You know, Talok," says Ryco, clearing his throat. "I'm not sure which *Tyler* amuses me more. That scared, skinny one, nearly jumping out of his skin when I smiled and waved at him. Or this braver one, in front of us now, telling us how it's going to be. Which do you prefer?" No longer interested in carving, Ryco looks to his king.

But Talok is silent.

Quall's now asleep.

Then there's Musgrae lazily raising his hand, and pointing at me, saying, "I vote this one. Every time."

Gemma says, "I vote any Tyler Ravier who doesn't hate or lie to me." Smirking, she goes back to reading.

Slumping, I state, "I didn't lie to you, Gemma."

She jolts up, slamming her book shut.

"Well," I confess, "maybe I did withhold the truth a bit. But at least you don't owe me that third favor. I'd say we're even, now."

Scoffing, Gemma sits back down. "Even? No, I think you owe me. Twice over, actually." Flipping through her spell-book pages to find her last place, she says, "I caught that slipup of mine. Had lots of time to think about it, while you were recovering." Looking down, she starts reading again.

I hold back a smile. Pulling one of the pouches from my belt, I rummage through it for the dragon-wolf journal. Finding it in its shrunken state, I carefully lift it out. It grows to full-size. I look at Jasper, and say, "A favor given to me in Vondurheil, in exchange for a reading of this. What do you say, Alpha Jasper?"

"I say," he replies, taking the journal from me, but glancing at Gemma, "that you're a con artist, taught by LanSoren—the very best among us. And that your friend thinks you are becoming like Jed Craven, in all his manipulative, arrogant ways. Though I've not met this *Craven*, Gemma's thoughts paint him to be very Vonsai, in nature."

Gemma gawks at Jasper. "I thought I was doing better at blocking Mensa-div, Ryco?"

"You are," replies Ryco. "But Jasper has few to match his tenacity."

"And rightly so," Musgrae adds. "He's an old Von-dog; as in, well over seven thousand years old, if I'm remembering things correctly."

"You are, Musgrae of Bethsaide," Jasper replies, brushing his hand across the journal's cover. "You've come a long way from that unwanted boy, with no other purpose but to get in fights. I would call them dog fights, but your comrades weren't exactly equal to you, in strength, were they?" Opening the journal, Jasper searches for the parts written in his native tongue.

Musgrae folds his hands, looking down uncomfortably.

Gemma sees his discomfort over having his past brought up, and she's about to do something.

But I do something first, saying, "Since you've agreed to do me a favor, Jasper, I wonder . . . would you give it to Gemma, instead? Whatever she wants from you, will you do it?"

Gemma and Jasper's gazes meet, and they're saying in unison, "Within reason."

Gemma grins triumphantly.

Then the alpha laughs. Sweeping a few of his fingers across his lips, he quiets himself. "That will be acceptable," he says.

Talok leans forward, licking his lips. He seems envious of this favor given to Gemma rather than him. Perhaps, I'm wrong.

Gemma starts, by saying, "I don't want a favor in Vondurheil. But I would like to know what Mekka was doing on Earth. Why he terrorized Jack Wayeland. What he's doing with his phone. More importantly, who attacked Awngeleik, after scaring Tyler and me half to death? I thought my heart was going to explode that day."

"Actually," says Musgrae, "it was the mud that exploded all over her."

Gemma flicks Musgrae's arm, asking, "Was I talking to you, Stubbornness On Two Legs?"

Jasper looks up from reading. "'Tis a good name for you, Grae. If it hadn't been for that Greyvon obstinance lingering through your ancestry, we wouldn't have met during your youth. As for your concerns, Miss Galloway, I'm unsure what you're talking of. I've not been informed of anything attacking Awngeleik, while she was away to Earth. And Musgrae has filled me in, on most happenings."

"You've not been told everything," says Ryco, "because the evidence was wiped away, at the lake near LanSoren's home. There was nothing to officially document."

Jasper Mensa-divs, *"Is that why you asked about tracks being hidden, Ravier?"*

Instead of answering him directly, I ask aloud, "Would you know anything about a Greyvon being sent to Earth, around the time Awngeleik was sent there?"

"No," replies Jasper. "I had been hibernating for two months, during the same time Ryco and Talok were dropping her off. Mekka was stationed at the Cave of Ichors Von, to guard me as I recovered. Merlynite of Thedaesiim was one of the Vons left in charge, during my absence. I will question him, when I get back home. Or you can, yourself, Miss Galloway."

Squirming on the bench, Gemma says, "No, I think it's your place to do that. But what is Thedaesiim? Is it another city, close to Vondurheil?"

"They are my personal wolf pack of twelve. Although I'm the Greyvon Alpha, ruling over all Von packs, I'm permitted to have one closer to me than the rest. Mekka is a part of that pack. Rorka used to be, as well, but her gifts outgrew her position in Thedaesiim. Therefore, I gave her, her very own Von pack: Theocktras. A pack of eight. I'm not sure why they stayed home, rather than coming with her."

"It might have had something to do with speed, and compatibility," suggests Musgrae.

"That could be," Jasper agrees. "They've not been together, for very long. But to answer your other questions, Galloway. Mekka and Droediin often—and sometimes Nebukahn—went with me to Earth, when I wished to visit LanSoren."

"Nebukahn?" Paydinn interrupts. "You don't mean that *Nebukahn* always out adventuring with my youngest brother, Craesha, do you?"

"The very one," replies Jasper. "He's half Greyvon, and just so happens to be Mekka's cousin. The two hated each other, while growing up. Naturally, I made them face that hatred, hoping it would ultimately lead to their getting along better. But Nebukahn left Vondurheil, before their relationship could mature into something better. Not to mention, Mekka was perhaps the most stubborn Vonsai that I've ever had to deal with. It's possible that Nebukahn *has* gone to Earth, without my knowing it. He's not under Greyvon rule, since his Von mother has passed. And his sire has no allegiance, whatsoever, with Greyvons."

Gemma states, "But Mekka mentioned Jack Wayeland. And he has his phone. What explanation do you have for that?"

"None," Jasper says, "except for the possibility that Nebukahn and Mekka did, in fact, get along better than I had perceived. They loved games and challenges. Mekka still loves to scare innocent bystanders. He's more bark than bite, though, unless you're a perceived threat. And Nebukahn always loved showing off his gifts in magic. Even Kyanistic spells, like time-distortion."

Gemma asks, "Are you suggesting that the two toyed with Jack Wayeland? Scaring him, and then killing a bear too? Jack's still paranoid to this day, you know?"

"Was he black?" queries Jasper, slightly smiling. "The bear, I mean."

I nod, in answer.

Jasper states, "Given Nebukahn's uncanny abilities in Meta-Morfeis—Transformation Magic—most likely, he made himself the bear. And playing the obvious role of the wolf would've been Mekka."

I start laughing. Then I ask, "And where were you and my dad, during their *game?*"

Jasper replies, "Wherever Nebukahn could've managed a time-distortion without us knowing it, if, in fact, I am correct in my assumptions." Looking to Gemma, Jasper asks, "Does that satisfy your curiosity, for now?"

Gemma nods. "Yes, except for whom the other one could be."

"Other one?" queries Musgrae, life coming back into his tired eyes.

Ryco states, "She means the one they call the Phantom of Muraine."

Paydinn's puzzled eyes change to a muted-green color, and he scratches at his hairline.

Jasper closes the journal. "There were two chasing you, before you came to Muraine?"

"One was hunting us," says Gemma. "The other, the phantom, was protecting us. Possibly, Awngeleik too."

"I wish to see Awngeleik, now," states Jasper, abruptly standing up. "If you don't mind, King Talok, take me to her. Perhaps she can communicate a bit of truth. Any who wish to follow may, of course, come with us."

* * *

Deep in the tunnels below the castle, Metsa, we wander.

Carrying a torch, Talok leads the way at the front.

"Ryco," Musgrae whispers, "won't Quall reprimand us, for abandoning him by the fire?"

"Not a bit. Kent should be getting there about now, to wake him."

Paydinn, trailing beside Jasper, asks the alpha, "Was there anything good in the Greyvon parts of that journal?"

"So far," he says, "it recalls our history; not anything I can repeat. I will finish skimming it over, after having a look at her."

"Almost there," Talok says, taking a sharp turn. "Hopefully, Nyrim and Ben were successful in getting her to sleep peacefully."

I ask, "Why is it not anything you can repeat, Jasper?"

"There are things Greyvons deem as only theirs to know," he says. "Oddly enough, however, LanSoren knew some of these things. I cannot guess how, but he did. It's there on the pages, plainly in his own writing; not any enchanted quill's penmanship."

"Ben," Talok whispers into a wide, shut door. "Is it safe to come in?"

It opens, and Nyrim looks at Talok tiredly, saying, "I thought you'd never send someone to relieve us. The beast is finally asleep. Please, say nothing above a whisper." Stepping aside, Nyrim lets us creep in single file.

Bedded down atop a giant pile of long, cut grass and broken branches, at the small room's center, is Awngeleik, still wearing the harness confining her wings. Ben's seated next to her. He pets her head, as it's resting on his lap. Gently, he feels along the contours of her facial scales.

Glancing up at us, he stops for a moment.

Awngeleik's snake-eyes pop wide open.

Before Ben can react, she bolts up. Grass and branches scatter across the stone floor, as she's lunging at us.

We all recoil, except for Jasper and Ryco.

Exhausted, Nyrim just falls down, in his rush to get away. He moans. "Why can't she be content for even two minutes together?"

Holding a rope tight in his grip, Ryco's ready to use it on her.

Ignoring him, Awngeleik stands in front of Jasper. Her pretty blue eyes turn to a demon's black, and she tenses her neck, making her head shake like a rattlesnake's tail.

"You don't scare me, Equidyn," Jasper says. "If you wish to bite me, then do it rather than making your threats."

Mid-lunge, her teeth turn sharper. Awngeleik latches on to Jasper's arm, and she gnaws on him like a chew toy.

We watch, too shocked or tired to say anything.

Jasper's arm bleeds. And his blood drips down, to splatter both floor and debris.

Talok licks his lips, intently watching that blood stain the stone tiles that Jasper stands upon.

"Are you done, dragon's bane?" queries Jasper mildly.

Releasing Jasper, Awngeleik snarls and growls. Huffing out smoke through her nostrils, she pauses, laboring somewhat.

"My turn," Jasper says, his voice composed. "Deep sleep, to summoning a Ruby dyn's slumbering keep. To sleep. Deep."

Jasper snaps his fingers. A loud shattering sounds out.

Awngeleik falls limp to the ground.

Bending down, Jasper brushes at her scaly face and neck, his touch lightly running down to her shoulder and then ribs.

After a time, he's saying, "There were, indeed, two. One was most definitely a Greyvon. Though her wounds have healed, I still see the remnants of claw marks upon her shoulder. But this wound at the start of her ribs . . . this was made by something else, entirely. Something I've not encountered before. They are claw marks, to be sure. But not of a Von's. It's as if a clawed hand were digging into her flesh, searching for something."

Gemma shivers. "You don't think whatever it was, wanted to rip her heart out, do you?"

"It is a possibility, Miss Galloway," Jasper says, while standing up. "Paydinn, can you think of reasons why someone would want her heart?"

Paydinn replies, "It would be a sure way of killing her. Aside from that, I'm unsure."

"Oh, but it wouldn't kill her," Jasper corrects.

"Not to dampen your faith in our little Awngeleik, Alpha Jasper," says Nyrim, now sitting on a stool in the room's corner, "but nothing can live without its heart for long."

"That is so, for most," Jasper agrees. "But she has two hearts. One of her EquiNein line. The other of her dragon roots. The side previously injured leads to her dragon heart. Are there any spells that specifically use dragon hearts, Ryco?"

"There are two that I know of, but they're not of much use to either side," replies Ryco. "And they're nothing any respectful soul would perform."

"Zymarc is no such soul," Paydinn states. "But what spell of the Dei-Athos-Kree would benefit him, or anyone else with dark intentions? The ancient Deathasyn spells, I mean."

"I do not know of those spells, Jokryn," Ryco says. "I'll wager few Sorsryns do. Deathasyns guard their secrets like Greyvons."

"Unless they see you as one of them," says Paydinn, with a broad grin.

"One such as my mother, RayVora. She was practically raised by them. Even was favored by their king, Vit'Dod, before Zymarc overthrew him, executing him and his entire royal line. Such dark times, those days. My mother's weeping lasted for years. Nothing my father did could console her. If you would like, I can go to her. Or send for her, at the very least."

"Yes," Talok says. "I want to see her again. She and my father were good friends, before his passing. She with my uncle too. Perhaps she can shed some light, on others' intentions toward Awngeleik and her hearts."

Ryco startles right then, striding out into the tunnels.

"What is it, Sylvadyn?" queries Paydinn.

Ryco states, "Siege is reporting that Zymarc's fleet will be here in less than an hour. I'm sure the cloaking of her aura has worn off. We shall leave you to your spells, Jasper. Make sure he cannot sense her, if even he were to come down here, himself, for a look."

"I will see to it," Jasper reassures, while herding us out. "And I will keep this journal safe, Tyler. You have my oath, for what it's worth."

Talok, Ryco, and Paydinn begin a conversation about contacting RayVora, the Queen Mother of the Jokryn.

Then there's Nyrim, Ben, Musgrae, and Gemma trailing behind them, discussing the possibility of journeying to Vondurheil.

Looking to Jasper, I reply, "Just find something to help us now. And don't leave her alone. She doesn't like it."

Jasper smiles sadly. "Believe me, being the Greyvon Alpha, I know how she feels. It's a lonely life, not having an equal to your spirit. She will be at peace while with me. But be sure to keep your own heart at peace, while up there negotiating for hostages. Don't let that Vitiosyn into your head. Not even for a Mensa-div."

As the others are headed back the way we came, I linger by Jasper, asking, "Any particular reason why?"

"Because I searched his mind, while trying to rip into his throat," says Jasper, his voice slightly deepening. "What I saw was a new desire. You, Ravier. Now, he knows you exist. Now, he knows you are strong. Now, he craves your allegiance, more than anything that has come before. I don't know the truth of his relations with your father. But they were neither friend nor foe. They had some kind of understanding. It sickens me, to think about what it could've been. Do not be a fool, thinking Zymarc can be easily read. It took me nearly killing him, to see a glimpse into merely one of his desires."

Suddenly, I'm taking in a sharp inhale. I've been holding my breath, afraid of what Jasper is suggesting: that my father may have had an alliance with a Vitiosyn. The King Vitiosyn! The murderer of an innocent population—Paragonians and Vaegons, and their many creatures too.

Jasper grips my shoulder. "Be ever careful, Tyler. Zymarc is remarkable in his ways of getting you to give him what he wants, all while you think you're resisting or hurting him." Letting go of me, Jasper adds, "Today, I gave him exactly what he wanted."

"You're not the only one, Jasper. It happened the morning Gemma and I came here. He used Gyron and the Onyx Warriors, to slaughter Vitiosyns under Belzara's command. Possessed her, using two black snakes biting into her neck. I'm not sure if anyone told you that, but it could be important for you to know."

"Two black snakes?" queries Jasper. "I will have to think about why that sounds familiar. I will let you know what I come up with. May the dyns' will be with you and Talok. You'd best be off, now, in a hurry. Your voice makes Awngeleik stir out of her slumber quicker than I would like."

Peeking behind Jasper, I get one last look at Awngeleik. Her snake-eyes are struggling to open. Tears are streaming down her face, collecting on the mosaic of feathers woven in with her facial scales. She looks at me desperately.

It takes everything in me to leave her, with only Jasper for company.

As I'm making my way out of the tunnels, I brush my hand along one of the stone-and-dirt walls, starting a div with Metsa, asking, *"What do you know about Jasper of Vondurheil? Can he be trusted?"*

Metsa replies, *"What does the dyn's heart tell you?"*

"I don't understand," I tell him. *"Who's the dyn, and how could it tell me?"*

Metsa is silent. I try a few rephrases of the question. But, still, there is no answer.

I give up, silently trudging the rest of the way to the symposium room.

11

Farewells to an Age

During his entire time in the symposium room, Talok has sat tensely silent in his chair, studying the Geldryn bangle.

The guards are gathered, as are all the Arkiveis. Of the King's Advisers, it's EmiKal present, and poring over maps, ignoring the rest of us.

Gemma and I sit in seats set along the guard's wall. But only Musgrae and Eli stand there, waiting with us. The others restlessly pace about, or talk with Quall in the barest corner of the room.

Catching Kent's attention, I div, *"How'd things go with Madeleine?"*

"Fairly well," he divs back, *"until the end. I made it clear that I would've chosen the same path, even if I could go back and change things. She didn't like that answer."*

Interrupting us is Gemma, as she fidgets with her hands, asking me, "Do you think everyone's going to leave Paragon, and make their way to Vondurheil, Tyler?"

"It possibly depends on how things go with this," I reply.

She timidly looks off toward Talok.

He drums his fingers on the table, asking, after a time, "Where is Zepharre? Is he not coming?"

EmiKal sneaks a look up from the maps. "He's at the gate, feeding our injured, and waiting for our, uh . . . *visitors.*" Hissing that last word, EmiKal goes back to his task, whatever that task is.

Warren sits beside him, adding, "Paydinn has also gone to the gate to wait."

Eli opens his mouth, about to say something.

Ryco, however, stops briefly from conversing with Quall. "Don't even think about adding a rhyme to that, Eli," he says, then resumes talking with Quall.

After a thespian sigh, Eli mutters to Gemma, "At least someone here doesn't mind my rhymes."

Gemma grins. "Do you have any rhymes for helping me to remember all these spells? I'm overwhelmed."

"Of course," replies Eli, thrusting out his hand. "But I'd better write them in for you. Don't want Ryco getting frazzled enough that smoke secretes from his nose. My rookie year, he was very . . . smoldering."

Gemma suppresses a laugh, while giving Eli her spell-book and pen.

"Siege," Talok says, stilling his hand on the table, "what are the dragons saying?"

Mid-sentence, Siege pauses from his talk with Quall and Ryco. "Dragons?" he queries. "What do you mean, what are they saying?"

Talok's fingernails softly claw the table surface, until his hand is made into a fist. He states, "You are the most adept at communicating with them, out of all presently here, no? Has Zymarc arrived yet?"

Siege first bows his head, then answers, "I will ask them. I've need of a moment, though." He approaches the bay window. His shoulders press back. His gaze is steady, as he looks out into the dim light of dawn. Stilling his breath to inaudible, he waits, then announces, "They say that Zymarc is just approaching the gate. He now sees Zepharre, but Zepharre has not presently noticed him." Pausing, Siege inhales deeply. More confidently, he continues, "The sun is rising. They've made eye contact, seeming most displeased with the other. The dragons are smiling at their apparent displeasure. Neither one has said a word."

Warren asks, "Are they in Mensa-div with each other?"

Siege shakes his head. "The dyns don't think so. Zepharre's motioning for Zymarc to follow him."

"Who else is with him?" queries Quall.

"Azabahk, for certain," replies Siege. "The dragons don't recognize the other three. The hostages are still yet too far away to be approximated in number, as well."

"Why hasn't Jasper come up yet?" queries Talok impatiently. "Someone go fetch him."

"Yes," EmiKal agrees. "And take him a bone too. Don't want him getting hungry again."

"I'll go," Musgrae grumbles, abruptly standing up.

No sooner has he left, than Siege startles away from the bay window.

"What's got you worried, Siege?" queries Eli. He looks up from what he's writing in Gemma's spell-book.

"They're stopping," he replies. "Or, rather, Zymarc has stopped on the path. He's gazing at the Arkivara. Taken a couple of steps toward her too."

A dark scowl seeps into Talok's expression. He moves about in his chair. "What's he doing? Etiquette doesn't permit him to approach her."

Hesitating, Siege says, "He's bowing. The dragons are growling. Zepharre doesn't know what to do. Nor Master Paydinn. Surprise has struck them both."

Roars and rumblings of dragons shake the castle, then they settle.

Siege continues, "He's on the path again. Nonetheless, Zepharre's gaze toward him is of malice. The dragons have never seen him so angry. He's trying to hide his white-knuckled hands in the folds of his robes. His face is deathly pale, and he's staring out into nothing. So say the dyns." Siege turns around, his breaths sporadic and loud.

"Can you see them from the window?" queries Talok.

"Not yet," replies Siege. "They're almost halfway."

Talok stands, to hurry to the window. "What is Zepharre thinking? If he hits Zymarc with even one harmless swing, it's all over. Zymarc will have every right to kill the hostages."

Siege relaxes somewhat, gripping the back of a chair. "Paydinn has seen Zepharre's intent, and has touched his arm, snapping him out of it."

Warren booms, "Thank the Vardiyas for that!"

"I wouldn't thank them just yet," says Ryco. "They've not entered the castle. That could be where the real trouble lies. Be ready for anything. In the meantime, we'd best give the ruse that we've lost track of the time, and are unaware that he is here. Warren, have you a deck of cards? Set it up for the endgame, as if you've been playing with Drauggen for a while."

The shortest, stoutest of the Arkiveis goes for the seat across from Warren, at the main table.

With a snap of his fingers, Warren summons cards from one of his pouches. They flutter and sputter out, and then onto the table.

Siege joins in the game.

"Which game shall it be, Arkivy of our Veldar?" queries Warren.

Drauggen clasps his short, thick fingers together. "Capture the Wolf, Free the Dyn," he replies.

The three commence the game. All have four cards in their hand. And four cards are on the table, in front of each player. Nearly the rest of the deck faces up on the table, in a pattern.

"EmiKal"—Ryco points—"put those maps away, back on the wall. We don't want him seeing us looking them over."

EmiKal quickly rolls up the maps, grumbling, "I suppose it's a fortunate thing I decided not to mark the varying paths we could take, just yet."

"A very good thing, yes," says Quall, taking the seat closest to my cousin, who's sat back down. "Are you ready, Talok?"

"It doesn't matter if I am." Talok glances at the reassuring gazes of the Arkiveis. "I only wish Musgrae would hurry up, in bringing Jasper back."

I twist the watch round my wrist, realizing for the first time that it fits me better now.

Unable am I to think more on it, though, because Gemma's asking, "Should Tyler and I stay over here, Talok?"

Nervously, he picks at his nails. "Sit beside Quall. The seats opposite of there are for Zymarc and his man."

Gemma and I quietly take our assigned places—she, by Quall; I, next to her. Ryco's beside me.

"Should I lay out the daggers and journals?" I ask, first looking to Ryco, then my cousin.

"Not yet," says Ryco. "That will tell him we've been expecting him. At least, for a little while."

"But *aren't* we expecting him?" queries Gemma. "What benefit is there in the ruse?"

Ryco replies, "Zymarc believes Paragonians are an inferior race. A young race. And it's true. We are young. But we're not dim-witted. However, if we give him the impression that we are less than intelligent, too single-focused, or that we put off planning—even for war—he may underestimate us. And that is where a portion of power-hungry souls find their downfall: underestimation of their enemies' abilities."

"How can I help?" Gemma asks.

"If you *must* say something," says Quall, "be careful what you may be revealing. As for the rest of you, absolutely no asking about Awngeleik's dragon heart."

They all nod, except for EmiKal. Though he quizzically glances at Ryco, he remains silent.

Minutes tick by. The agony of waiting is almost as bad as it was in the tunnels, while the city was under fire.

EmiKal paces around, adding to our agitation. Finally, he sits beside Ryco.

Ryco's brow furrows. "That is where Zepharre will want to be," he says.

"Doubtful," replies EmiKal, scooting his chair in. "He will want that spot across from Quall, regardless of the usual seating."

"If you say so." Ryco inhales fully, then whispers, "They're here. One Vitiosyn has been left outside the castle. Four are now entering."

My palms get sweaty. My hands quiver slightly. I hide them under the table, tightening my grip on my thighs. I force them to stop their shaking.

Am I just terrified? I wonder. *Or ready to have this over with?*

The door opens slowly, creaking, then squealing loudly on its hinges. There stands Paydinn, entering first, cringing at the noisy door. He stops two steps in, and blocks the door from closing, most likely to keep it from smashing itself against our unwanted visitors.

Part of me wishes Paydinn would get out of the castle's way, and let it have its moment of victory. Smiling to myself, I find that the image wipes away my uneasiness.

Azabahk saunters in next. He waits for his king. But no King of Vitiosus is entering the room. Rather, it's Zymarc wearing Soren's face.

Talok sits up straighter. His nostrils flare. His face should be red, with how angry he looks. Instead, he's paler than even Quall. His paleness is akin to a Deathasyn's.

Casually entering the room, Zymarc initiates the talk, saying, "I hope you don't mind the change of face. I hadn't any idea that Soren's looks so disturbed more than merely myself. Had I been aware, I would've taken his face as my own decades ago. It would've been haunting. Indeed, disturbing, like a Nekrosyn spell bringing the recently deceased to life again."

No one voices a response.

Warren starts to lay his cards on the table.

But Zymarc makes a small gesture with his hand. "Don't end, on my account. It's considered bad luck to let the wolf go free. Even worse not to free the dyn. By all means, finish. Then we'll have this talk of releasing hostages."

Talok glowers at Zepharre, who's standing in the doorway, his hands still hidden. "Musgrae went to get Alpha Jasper. Go see what's taking them so long."

Without a word or nod, only fury in his eyes, Zepharre strides out of sight. Yet his footsteps are barely louder than a breath.

"One of you," says Azabahk, pointing to the two Vitiosyn men now waiting where Zepharre stood, "remain on the door's outside. The other, guard it from within."

One steps back out; the other moves farther into the room, to let Paydinn close the door.

Talok gets antsy. Obsessively, he smooths the fabric of his cloak, which conceals the Waking Dragon coat.

Zymarc strolls around the room, one hand stuffed in his pocket.

The three Paragonians continue playing their game.

His gaze observing the many things in the council room, Zymarc then stops at the sight of Siege's cards. He remarks, "You have the winning hand, Dragon's Voice. Can't you see the play?"

Siege shakes his head, wearily replying, "I've not played this all that much."

Zymarc brushes at some dust on the table, remarking, "That is painfully clear. Allow me to take your play, so that we may move on to other matters sooner?"

Siege hesitates and then lays his cards facedown. He moves, to let Zymarc take his seat.

Briefly making eye contact with Zymarc, Warren tightens his grip on the cards in his hand. "It's your move," he says.

Flicking and intermittently strumming the air with his fingers, Zymarc rearranges the faceup cards without ever touching them. He then plays two cards from his hand, outwardly intent on the game.

Voices come from somewhere beyond the door.

It's then that I have a nagging urge to ask Zymarc questions. His guard's down. And Jasper's already told of the desire Zymarc has to have me be his apprentice. That it's stronger than any of his other desires. I think to myself, *If there's anyone he'll answer, without concern, it will be me. Who knows? I could get some valuable facts out of him.*

I speak to Zymarc, "You mentioned Nekrosyn spells bringing the dead back to life?"

"Yes, what of it?" He doesn't look my way, instead readies to play his last two cards.

"What sorts of things are needed for those spells?" I ask. "Any objects the caster can't do without?"

Ryco sends me a glance of warning.

I Mensa-div, saying, *"Let me squeeze some info out of him. What harm can it really do now? Besides, don't you want to know if he actually knows about Awngeleik's dragon heart?"*

Looking away, Ryco cracks his knuckles. He says nothing.

"There are many things the caster must have," replies Zymarc, playing his third card.

Half of the strewn cards gather themselves up into a tidy pile. The dyn card then floats to rest atop that pile. Zymarc now eyes the other half of the deck, to the right of the wolf card.

Voices outside the room get closer.

The door opens.

Jasper strides in. Behind him is Mekka, entering too. But he's different, shorter, and proportionately smaller.

Zepharre enters last, softly shutting the door.

I speak more to Zymarc, "Would one of those things be a dragon heart, or is that used for some other spell?"

Zymarc's about to say something to Jasper, but his attention pivots to me. As if in a trance, he's saying, "No. Dragon hearts are not used for Nekrosyn spells. Dragon hearts do not hold life essence, once taken from the vessel. They are used for other spells." Coming out of his trance, Zymarc's eyes are unsettled. He looks over the game. Swallowing hard, he mutters, "I quite forgot what I was doing."

Alarmed, Azabahk says, "You were capturing the wolf."

Jasper sits at the other head of the table, opposite of Talok. Only a few seats away from where Zymarc is now. Intently, he watches the Vitiosyn Soren lookalike playing a game.

Zymarc quickly finishes his turn, laying down his last card. He rises out of his chair, even as the cards finish rearranging themselves. Twelve cards, each with a different symbol on them, surround the wolf card. Colorful fire flares from all the cards on the table. They then neatly draw themselves into one pile. Warren picks up the deck, and puts it away in his supply pouch.

Zymarc taps Azabahk's shoulder, as he's passing him.

The Prince-General startles, then stutters, "N-no. What's the matter, Zymarc? Why are you asking me that?"

"What about the other one?" queries Zymarc calmly, even while his eyes are riled up.

Azabahk replies, "We dissected . . . it, looking for how. You know. But, no, it didn't have it."

"Very good," says Zymarc quietly, taking a deep breath. He looks to my cousin. "Before we begin, allow me to release one-quarter of the hostages, as a sign of appreciation, for letting me and my men pass unthreatened through the city."

Talok, preoccupied with his thoughts, just motions behind to the bay window.

Zymarc stops, right as he's about to touch one of the windowpanes, asking, "Any, in particular, whom you want released first?"

"I value all my people equally," says Talok, sounding angry.

"Very well," replies Zymarc, touching the glass. "Caleiso, tell Belzara to release one-quarter. And be sure that more warriors and men are among them, than women and children."

A wave of white-wind bursts out from the castle, and heads in the direction of the city gate.

Gemma nervously twirls her strand of hair, before asking, "Why does that matter? Releasing more warriors? Is it that you want a fair fight?"

Zepharre precariously sets a small stack of papers in front of Talok, then sits at his right side, even while Zymarc confidently comes to settle down beside the nervous head adviser.

"A fair fight is a subjective viewpoint," replies Zymarc, to Gemma. "Rather, I like to take away things. Hope. Resources. Potential allies. These are the things that help to win wars. And I've obtained the greatest ally of all. The Onyx. For it is written in the races' accounts of history, any declared as Onyx Victors never lose. The Onyx never lose a war. Battles, yes. But they win, in the end. So, you see, I took away hope and a great ally from Paragon, in the same day. Years of planning. But it paid off."

I mutter, "Only because of Caleiso."

Elbows propped on the table, Zymarc massages his left wrist and hand. "It's true. She did help a great deal, in making everything line up nice and neat. Got me a snippet of Awngeleik's mane, and a feather or two. I took the evidence to King ReNovak, immediately. Almost got caught in the thick of a storm upon leaving."

Kent divs, saying, *"That must be why she opened the window, waking us all up. Could that have been Zymarc Talok mistook for ReNovak, leaving the castle?"*

"Probably," I div back, *"but don't say anything about it."*

Zymarc, pleased with himself, balls up his left hand and then grips it with his other. He addresses Talok. "In times of peace, you are right to view your people in light of equal worth. Wartime, however, is different. Warriors are valuable, yes. But in wars lasting years, decades, or centuries, it's those able to multiply your numbers that hold true worth. Your women. They have the dual value of bearing offspring, and fighting for their home country, no? Women who are not warriors, can be taught and, indeed, be trained to perfection. But, no matter how hard you try, a man cannot be trained to carry his unborn offspring for nine months, nor for the Sorsryns' time of eighteen." Pausing, Zymarc motions to Paydinn, saying, "Unless you're of the Metimoran physiology. Did you ever carry any of your children, Jokryn?"

"Uh, no," replies Paydinn, flinching. "I'm merely half Metimoran. Therefore, it would've been quite impossible. Fortunate for me; but perhaps a, um, little upsetting for my wives."

"Cousin Tyler," Talok says, abruptly looking to me. "If you would, please lay out the items for our visitors to look over."

I stand, and do as he says. Taking out the golden-bronze journal first, it grows to full-size.

At the same time, Mekka snaps his attention to Azabahk seated beside Zymarc. "Have you personal issue with me, Deathasyn?"

"Not a bit." Azabahk smiles. At least, I think it's meant to be a smile. It resembles more of a grimace.

Mekka's irate over the response, saying, "Then why has your gaze wandered to me, one too many times? It's against Greyvon etiquette, to look more than six times without permission."

"I wished to give an apology," says Azabahk, "for hitting your face with the dearest of hammers. It wasn't my choice. It solely, rather, happened in a flash of dyn flame."

I slide the journal over to Zymarc.

He grips the spine, but he's focused on the exchange between his man and Mekka.

"Apology?" queries Mekka. "Hadn't a clue Deathasyns were capable. I wonder, can you say it to my face?"

Azabahk stutters and stammers, and sweat glistens along his thin brow line.

Mekka strides forward. Upon reaching the Prince-General, he pulls out the chair.

Jasper has clasped his hands together. He then rests them on the table. No sooner have his hands met with the surface, than Paydinn takes a single, silver cup out and sets it in front of Jasper. The alpha scowls at nothing in particular, just empty space. He does not touch the cup.

Before Azabahk can stop the Von, Mekka straddles his lap, swiftly sitting down upon him.

Azabahk grunts and pants and frantically screeches his displeasure. "Zymarc! Is this allowed, at the Negotiating Table?"

Looking away from the two, Zymarc replies, "I will permit it. You *did* break their etiquette, after all. You're old enough to know better." With that, Zymarc opens the journal, feeling the black-edged pages.

"As well, did you," Azabahk argues, "bowing to their Arkivara. They didn't like that, you know. Nor did she."

"Withrasyn etiquette," states Zymarc, quickly flipping through the pages, "requires foreigners to pay homage to places of history. Especially to libraries. The Paragonian equivalent—as they keep no extensive libraries filled with books, scrolls, and papers—would be their Arkivaras, where living memories rest forever, never to be forgotten."

During Zymarc's clarification, Azabahk clenches his jaw. His face turns even paler than normal.

Mekka, as if hoping for a snack, subtly licks his lips. Intently, he eyes the Prince-General over.

"Yes, yes! I know," says Azabahk, squirming with Mekka still upon his lap. "I had forgotten that, though I was never invited to the Monel. Nor their capital city of Waykron."

Mekka laughs. "You couldn't have ever been invited, Deathasyn. Those cities were lifeless, long before you were born. You cannot be more than seven hundred, based on your stature and bone structure."

Azabahk stops his squirming and mutters, "Perhaps not, in this life. But, rather, in one of my past ones, for I've been through ReNovamen. Now, get off, Von. You're crushing me, and my bone structure you've taken liberties to comment on."

Warren chuckles.

Mekka joins in, glancing over his shoulder to Warren. Turning serious, Mekka focuses back on Azabahk. "That's what he said." Deepening his voice, Mekka adds, "Before I *ate* him. One of your Vitiosyns. He was quite tasty. Crunchy too. I see why my alpha didn't want to share. Only difference is that the one *I* ate was no traitor's flesh."

"King Zymarc," Azabahk says, "are you going to let him talk this way?"

"Yes, but now I've heard enough." Zymarc doesn't raise his focus. He just keeps leafing through the journal, calmly saying, "If you would be so kind as to remove yourself from my man, Von."

When Mekka remains where he is, Zymarc pivots his attention to him.

Mekka stares back, chewing on his lower lip, before he clamps his mouth shut. Slowly, he nods. He takes out a leather cord, with a single, metal pendant on it, and then drops it on the journal. Removing himself from Azabahk's lap, Mekka goes to sit beside Jasper.

The Prince-General is left to recuperate.

Zymarc takes hold of the cord, lifting to show the pendant to Azabahk.

Scoffing, Azabahk says, "I told you that one was doomed for death. Stupid, ambitious idiot. Fancied himself a spy."

Tucking the piece away in his inner coat pocket, Zymarc reads more of the journal, seeming disinterested. He gets about halfway, when Azabahk grips his arm to stop him from turning another page.

"Zymarc," he says, "that symbol there"—Azabahk points—"I've seen it before. Don't you recognize it?"

"Yes, Azabahk. It's the Dei-Athos-Kree symbol for Vardiyas." Pushing the journal over to Azabahk, Zymarc holds his hand out to me. "The next one, if you please."

I give him the blue one next, wondering what he may find in it.

Azabahk returns the bronze journal, then peeks at the one Zymarc is perusing. Gasping, he exclaims, "There it is again! But what languages are these? I know them not. Do you, Zymarc?"

"I'd rather not say, for certain," he replies.

After a while, Zymarc asks for the third journal, and I give it to him. The one written in English. Zymarc and Azabahk study the shield crest upon its cover.

"Is that . . . ?" Azabahk trails off.

"It's a chain of command," remarks Zymarc. "Either that, or it's a family tree. Regardless, it needs another piece, to decipher the member names." After he opens it, he pauses. He looks in my direction, stating, "This is a rather personal account of your father's life. You're sure you want me reading this?"

"If it means you'll release the hostages, then yes," I reply. "I'm sure."

Zymarc studies me, then closes the jade-colored journal. "You should know, then, that I've left the most valuable hostages back at my home, near the Pools of Vosh-Perida. One-quarter of them, to be precise. The blacksmiths. The architects. The mages. And the women, who are also warriors, tailors, and mothers for many. It's only fair, since you are likely withholding your most valuable piece. You're sure you still want to refuse letting me see that Rubidyn-Greyvon journal?"

"*Tell me* what you want with Awngeleik, and I might reconsider it."

Zymarc's expression darkens, as he's saying, "She is mine. I want her back."

"You gave her to my dad, as a peace offering," I state. "Then he died. And, now, you want her back? Why? What do you need her for? Can't you just get another one? Make another dragon-horse?"

"It's true," replies Zymarc. "I could breed another one into existence. But I've spent over seven hundred years bringing that one into existence. With

LanSoren gone, ownership reverted to me. I'm her rightful master. I was at her beginning. And I will be at her end. Or until I'm gone. Whichever transpires first."

"Then call for her," I state. "See if she comes."

Azabahk snorts and coughs, then sneers a bit.

Zymarc starts to talk, but I cut him off, saying, "Or, answer this. Why didn't you just take her last night, rather than collecting evidence to show ReNovak?"

"Forcefully taking her," he replies, "would've resulted in many Paragonians being slaughtered. By the Onyx Rules of Engagement, I could not do that. Nor could I sneak her out of the city unnoticed. Again, Paragonian blood would've been shed, during a time I was required to give my enemies two days to assess their positioning. With the evidence of her being in Paragon, however . . . that did allow me the legality to attack the city, without Onyx interference."

Zymarc goes back to the jade-journal.

I interrupt him again, to ask, "Are you bound not to tell us why you need Awngeleik, or something?"

With a murderous gaze rivaling Soren's, Zymarc stares me down. At last, he says, "Vitiosyns cannot be bound, in the usual ways."

I ask, "Then why not tell us your need for her? Regaining ownership of her is what you want. If there was any chance of that happening by you being honest with us, then why won't you do it?"

Slightly confused, Zymarc looks from me to Talok.

My cousin has recovered some color to his face. In fact, a little too much. He appears as if he's going to burst out in a raging fit at any second.

"Cousin Tyler," he starts, sounding quite tense, "we are negotiating for the return of our people held hostage."

"But don't you want more than that?" I ask. "Don't you want to stop a war from happening? What good is it getting them back, if they're just going to die tomorrow, or sometime soon after that?"

"There *will* be a war!" Talok shouts.

I start to argue, but Talok pounds his fist on the table, and shouts again,

"As I am King of Paragon, not you, you will hold your tongue, Tyler! Say no more of Awngeleik."

Inhaling sharply, Gemma grips my arm under the table, and digs her fingernails into my skin.

I take Gemma's hint and go silent.

Zymarc queries, "Would you like for us, Vitiosyns, to take a brief respite outside?"

"No," says Talok, calming down. "Sorry for my temper. Carry on with your reading."

Clicking his tongue, and then folding his hands on the table, Zymarc asks Talok, "Permission to be honest with you? Perhaps even a little *unconventional*, at the Negotiating Table?"

Talok huffs. "It can't be any worse than what's been said or done before."

"I don't want to go to war with you Dragon Tamers," Zymarc confesses. "But there are things I want more than my desire not to war with you. If you were in my position, you would've done the same."

Quall states, "Stealing dragons, and committing genocide, you mean? No, we would *not* do the same."

Zepharre adds, "We don't know the nature of your relations with LanSoren, but if he were here—"

Interrupting, Zymarc says, "He wouldn't have even let me pass through the gate, knowing what I've done. Let alone, enter the castle. Yet here I am, while he is not."

"Speak carefully, Vitiosyn," Jasper warns. "We are losing our patience."

Zymarc pushes the jade-journal back to me. "Out of respect for your father, I will not read more of this. Now, all that's left are—"

Interrupting, I state, "The daggers."

Slipping them off my belt, I carefully set them in front of Zymarc.

At the same time, Azabahk retrieves something from one of his pockets. Whatever it is grows to full-size in his grasp. He hands it to Zymarc. The marred metal mask. Marred by Soren, using one of the very daggers now in front of the Vitiosyn King.

He first takes hold of NeiSator, and slips it into the cut groove. Nothing happens. He trades it out with RotaSyn, repeating the motions. He tries a little harder to make it *do* something, even making a spark of magic flash from it.

"Well." He sighs. "It was worth a try."

"Guess it'll be back to using the old spindly, black mask?" queries Azabahk.

"So it would seem," replies Zymarc, reluctantly standing up. "As you have upheld your end of the bargain, LanSoren's Tyler, I will uphold mine. All hostages I've brought with will be released, as soon as I and my men have made it to the gate. The last quarter, however, will remain in my hospitality, back home. Unless . . . there is something you have of equal worth to one-quarter of those most valuable hostages?"

I ask, "There's nothing else you want, besides Awngeleik or a look at the fourth journal?"

"No," states Zymarc, as he heads for the door.

Desperate, I try to think of something valuable to give him, which won't cause too much harm. But nothing comes to mind. It's not as if I can give myself over to him. That's what he wants.

I muse, *Talok would never allow it, anyway.*

Zepharre bolts up, striding to take the lead. EmiKal's close behind.

Everyone exits the room, in single file. Gemma and Jasper, however, remain seated.

"Shouldn't we go with them?" I ask Jasper.

He shakes his head. "I'd rather not. Hostage exchanges, and whatnot, only feel like half-wins. I also don't want to lose my temper. And with Zymarc wearing Soren's face, well, that may not be too easy to control. Then there's the chance of Mekka doing something else, to bring out the worst in me. It would all be too much, at the moment, for me to handle."

"Did Rorka make it back?" queries Gemma.

Jasper replies, "She and Musgrae are down, tending the sleeping beauty."

"The Dark Prince, Tyler!" Gemma exclaims, suddenly grabbing my arm again. "You could've let him look over that children's book. No one knows what good it's for. Maybe there's something he could've given away about it, without even realizing it."

"Think it's worthwhile to offer it, before he goes?" I ask.

Jasper stares at his reflection in the silver teacup, then replies, "If it will give you some peace of mind, then yes."

I rush for the bay window, and undo one of its latches. Pushing the windowpane open, crisp air creeps in. Looking down, I spot Zymarc collecting Deezalo's Hammer from his fourth man waiting outside the castle.

I call down to him, "I forgot to mention this short children's book he left behind. Care to have a look, before you go?"

Zymarc cranes his neck, to look up at me. A crooked grin on his face, he divs, saying, *"Show it to me the next time we see each other. For we will see each other again, before that cousin of yours is dead. Until then, Ravier.* He gives one wave goodbye, then carries on down the path leading out of the city still in shambles.

12

Arguments in Eyo'el

Sometime later, outside the castle . . .

Gemma and I watch, as exhausted hostages settle in groups with their loved ones. Some cry in relief, hugging each other. Others chatter frantically, relaying the happenings the others missed. Especially the night of the festival. Though it warms my heart, it doesn't last. Many sit silent. A deep apprehension clouds their faces, making them appear as empty shells. Paragon isn't safe, anymore. And they know it. Jasper has already asked that I help persuade them to flee to Vondurheil. I convinced Talok, twice, that we should flee Paragon.

But can I convince a nation of people? I wonder.

Some distance away, I spot Zepharre and EmiKal talking amongst the Arkiveis and other advisers. I know it starts with persuading them. But I'm afraid of how it will end.

"Go on, Tyler," Gemma whispers. "They'll listen to you."

"You sound so sure," I reply, looking down at her face smudged with soot.

"Well, aren't you? You did put up a good fight against Soren."

"Only because I'm on borrowed time," I reply. "It's from a gift of power I'm not supposed to have yet. It'll be gone soon. I'm just not sure when."

"Then hurry. I'll stay near Talok. Tell him that you're keeping your end of the bargain." Gemma nudges me toward them, and I go.

Step by unsteady breath, I approach them with no idea of what to say. Inaudible, Nyrim voices something.

"Journey to the Silverians?" queries Grover, a bit open to Nyrim's idea.

"Absurd!" Eishal shouts, striking the bottom of his black staff down. "They'll not help us. Stingy, skinny, sticks of stature. I don't care if some seem as tall as first-year trees. Besides, I must be away to Trauvo soon. She'll be needing her dose of memories. Why not transition there? We will be protected, for Trauvo is strong."

"Perhaps a little too strong," says Lokasi quietly. "No, we must be away to Kirja or Veldar, for they are the farthest from threatening neighbors. And less demanding than Trauvo."

"They're also closed off," EmiKal argues. "Unless you want to take to the Sea of Gradoelin."

"No." Zepharre clenches his fists, before hiding them between the folds of his long coat. "Only those of Kirja are well versed in sailing. We well could all drown, trying to escape that way. And what for the matter of where would we *sail* to?"

Drauggen scratches the back of his neck, suggesting, "Down to the Amethysyns. To their homelands of the Zotek. It's quite easy to access, by way of water. Isn't that right, Arkivy Ragaz?"

Grover exclaims, "Why, that's an idea!" He smiles, then frowns as he focuses on the water spots upon his spectacles. Huffing, he begins his fervent cleaning of them.

Drauggen rolls his eyes. "Yes, Arkivy Grover. That's *why* I said it."

Grover continues, as if Drauggen hasn't spoken, rambling on, "For the Amethysts are quite safe. Vitiosyns would have to go through the Silverians' forces, to get to them. And, who knows? Perchance they've seen our Siveyra Avilon. Ragaz of Kirja, how quickly could we be there, from your home city?"

Starting to panic, I step forward. "Actually, I was hoping you'd be open to going to Vondurheil. The Greyvons are Paragon's ally. Are these Amethysts allies, as well?"

Hesitating, Zepharre flatly says, "No."

"Then why risk them turning us away?"

Impatient, Zepharre replies, "We wouldn't be sending a multitude. But the most vulnerable would certainly go. They wouldn't dare refuse our frail."

"Don't be too sure," says Jasper, approaching our circle.

"And why ever not?" queries Zepharre, scrunching some of his coat's fabric in his fist.

"Because," Jasper replies, "the Amethysts have a history of facing the named Onyx Victor. Twice, if my memory serves correct. Their losses, during both wars, were heavy. Though none among them has firsthand memories of those wars, their queens have kept it fresh in the records passed on down the generations. Zymarc will be spreading the word, and rather quickly, that Vitiosyns have been named the victor."

EmiKal mutters, "Most likely, he has already started."

Jasper states, "Their fear of the victor, alone, may make them refuse you."

"Even if, in fact, they want to help?" queries Nyrim.

"Yes," Jasper replies, forlorn.

"Well," says EmiKal, "I still say we send some scouts, to make inquiries of them. Do you agree, Zepharre?" EmiKal looks to him.

But Zepharre seems to have not heard him. He merely stares at a lonesome twig, a few feet in front of him, which rests on a patch of bare ground.

EmiKal's gaze darts about. Then he states, "At least with the Amethysyns we wouldn't have to worry over being eaten, should the food supply run short." Blushing some, he grins tensely at Jasper.

Jasper's lip twitches a bit, though he remains silent, clasping his hands behind his back.

Lokasi clears his throat. "Zepharre, what are your thoughts on the matter? To Vondurheil or The Zotek?"

Startling, Zepharre exclaims, "What? Food supply? Yes, a good idea, EmiKal. I will go start documenting our reserves. See how much we have, how long it can last for our current headcount." With that, he's rushing away, leaving us speechless.

As Zepharre races up the castle's thirteen steps, EmiKal proclaims, "That's never happened before."

"Perhaps," says Nyrim, "we should ensure that Zepharre is well. Have his head checked. Make sure he didn't take a severe blow to it."

EmiKal scratches at his forehead. "I shall go see what Ryco suggests we do." The small adviser starts turning around, but he nearly walks right into Ryco. Stopping short, he looks up into Ryco's bright-yellow eyes, and gulps.

Ryco steps away, to give EmiKal his space, asking, "Where does Zepharre think he's going in such a hurry? Have you made up your minds, on the beginnings of a plan?"

"Not quite," I reply.

EmiKal states, "Zepharre's acting a bit absentminded. It's unusual."

Grover blurts out, "Nyrim says we should take turns beating some sense into him, with our Arkivara staffs. But how ever will that work? Nothing will come of it, except to possibly make him *more* absent."

"That's not what I said," Nyrim says defensively. "At least, not aloud."

"Never mind that," says Eishal, flapping one of his hands impatiently. "He's gone off to document food reserves for the current headcount."

"If you can believe it," Nyrim adds, crossing his arms in skepticism.

Tapping two fingers to his mouth, Ryco says, "We've not gotten an official headcount. Quall has the scouts working on it now. EmiKal, go get him. Bring him back. It's imperative to settle on a plan of action. I'll not have him arguing later, about what's decided now."

EmiKal replies, "I think he's been getting an estimate of the headcount, for a while. As for going and getting him, uh, well, I don't think I can persuade him in his present state of mind."

Pursing his lips, Ryco then says, "What would you have me do? Zepharre has never faced a scenario like this."

Jasper states, "Indeed, none of you have. But there are a few old Von-dogs left who have. Survivors from the War of Ichors Von. I ask that you let us help you, through your ordeal of a home destroyed."

Arkivy Eishal scoffs. "We can't abandon everything. My Trauvo wouldn't have it. She needs a keeper for company. As does Eyo'el. Then there's Yharss and Dysarda. They're deep in their grief. Their keepers must go back to them. And what if something goes wrong? We may well need many Arkiveis-in-training to stay with each, in the Arkivaras."

"Then choose a group to stay in each city," is my suggestion. "The bare minimum, to tend every Arkivara."

"The people will not like it," says Ragaz of Kirja. "How to, for this? Drauggen and I take half of the three cities' survivors, and head for Kirja, by which we will sail for The Zotek. Then we will *implore* the Vardiyas that the Amethysts not turn us away."

"You still have to run it by Zepharre," says Ryco.

"Why not have us all go to him," Grover suggests, adjusting his clean spectacles. "Perhaps Zepharre needs a bit of encouragement. A show of concern for his person. He might very well be in shock."

Lokasi's eyebrows draw together. "I'm surprised you're not in shock, Grover. Look around you. At The Eye of Pawv'Ragaen. It's gone."

"Yes, yes!" Grover shouts, tossing up his hands. "I know! I'm not blind, Lokasi. I have two eyes set in my head. Two prisms in front of them, for further focusing. I *know* that it is gone. But I've promised Eyo'el that rebuilding of her city will be done. Some must stay and start on this task."

Clutching his staff with both hands, Eishal shouts, "You had no right, making that promise without us, Grover!"

"But I had to," Grover defends. "She would not let me leave her, without some sort of promise that all will eventually be well. I even had to give her some of my fondest memories, as a bribe to get out. I don't remember what they were. But they were memories most precious to me. And, now? They're gone!"

Drauggen rolls his eyes again, then starts striding purposefully for the castle.

Ragaz sucks in a breath, then follows Veldar's Arkivy.

Without prompting, Grover and Eishal fall in line behind them, arguing in hushed tones of their native language. Then they seemingly continue their argument in Mensa-div, as there are no more words said to each other. Rather, there are many scoffs, glares, and hand-gestures thrown between them.

We all make it inside the castle's entryway, still devoid of its red vines scared off from earlier, when Jasper says, to no one in particular, "I will be off, relieving Musgrae and Rorka. Come find me, when you've need of me."

"I'll make sure that it isn't long," states Ryco.

"Mind if I accompany you?" queries the calmest of the Arkiveis. Jutting his callused hand out, he introduces himself. "I'm Yevolta of Bethsaide. We've not been formally introduced, Alpha Jasper, as I was not Arkivy during the years you frequented my city. I've a mind to speak to Musgrae, regarding weapons and whatnot. I would, however, greatly appreciate hearing your knowledge of which weapons, enchantments, and such will be most valuable in our current predicament."

Rather than shaking his hand, Jasper takes a small, sheathed dagger from his belt and presses it to Yevolta's roughened palm, saying, "Enchantments such as this will do."

Yevolta studies the dagger a moment, then smiles in satisfaction.

Jasper continues their conversation, walking down toward the bunkers. Yevolta's not far behind him.

Meanwhile, the rest of us—eleven advisers, six Arkiveis, Ryco, and myself—make for another wing of the castle, one that's on the opposite side of it from the infirmary.

13

Aid the Alchemist

I t's awfully quiet, during our passing through of many corridors. Countless rooms line our path. But they're all empty. Barren of food, drink, cloth, and weapons.

A knot starts forming tight in my stomach. I'm really starting to worry, now understanding Zepharre's concern a little more. It's likely, however, that most of his concern is self-serving in nature.

When Ryco slows his pace ahead of us and stares into a room, we stop.

"Zepharre," Ryco begins. "Is everything all right? EmiKal said something to the effect of, you forgot to give your vote on a plan of action. Is that true? Are you feeling well enough to perform your duties?"

"My duties?" queries Zepharre, disheartened. "Duties. Abilities. Strategy. They're worthless to us now."

Ryco, EmiKal, Eishal, and Grover enter the small room. With the others behind me, I go to stand in the doorway. We take in the sight before us. All the smells, and underlying truth too.

Zepharre's the first to say it: "There's not food enough to feed us. Nor even enough for my abilities in alchemy, to assist in staving off the starvation."

Zepharre observes the dozens of barrels, barren. Then the smashed kegs and spice bottles, upon the stone tiles, their powdered or dried contents strewn about. A deep, frustrated sigh escapes him. He bends down to pick

177

up burnt flowers and herbs. In his grasp, he crushes them. He lets them fall like dust to the floor. His head sinks, in defeat.

"What of the other storerooms, farther down?" queries EmiKal, somewhat cheerful. "Certainly, there must be more, down farther."

Zepharre stands up straight. He looks hard at EmiKal then Ryco, before saying, "There is." But he hesitates, anxious to say more.

EmiKal proclaims, "There! We can all give you some of our magic, and find our other alchemists to assist you in multiplying the supply. All will be well, Zepharre. We should tell Talok the good news. We won't be starving unto our death."

During EmiKal's cheery rant, Zepharre's neck tenses, his breaths turn shallow, and his face goes red with rage. Without saying a word, the head adviser takes a crinkled note out from his pocket, and hands it to EmiKal.

Ryco queries, "Well, what's it say?"

Terror washes over EmiKal's face. The note falls from his wobbling grasp.

Zepharre's voice is deeper, and cold, as he states, "Caleiso gives her condolences, regarding our poisoned food stores. Warned us that we shouldn't eat any of it, except for what's in this very room, the infirmary, and the kitchenette, lest we die before our king is laid to rest with his father, King Sosha."

Eishal scoffs. "Fool of a girl! She must not know that the destroyed trunks of the trees outside can feed us for many days. It's not ideal, but they'll tide us over. We merely need pots and water, to boil the chunks in."

Abruptly, Lokasi steps forward. "What a fool I've been! She's been learning of our entire infrastructure, for three years. Particularly in regards to food. Many of her questions had to do with seasons, gardening, storing, and the like. I thought nothing of her questions, for she was a child."

Ryco states, "Then we must assume the usual food was tainted by her, or other Vitiosyns, during the attack."

Drauggen adds, "That surely explains why we had to wait so long for the ceasefire. It's a lengthy process, to taint that amount of food stores."

Frantic, EmiKal queries, "Is there food enough to make it to one of the other cities, Zepharre?"

"No," he replies. "Warren and Ben gave their assessment of the infirmary's supplies. Kent, as well, of the kitchenette's stores. A more serious matter, however, is this. The trees are no longer synthesizing magic, leaching it out into the air. I've taken a reading of it. Rather than what little magic is contained in the air replenishing our Mazhrein, it's in fact draining us. Whatever curse is upon our trees and air, or indeed us, is altering the normal order of things. Like any sickness related to Black or Death Magic, it will take days for it to leave our bodies, if even we left the vicinity of contamination. Which, by and large, we do not know what the contamination's radius is. But we need a source of magic, to restore what we're losing every minute."

"Why!" exclaims Grover, his eyes widening. "If what you're saying is so, Zepharre, we have one day before our frail start collapsing unto death. Two or three days, for the strong. That isn't much time at all."

"Truly, it's worse than that," Zepharre states. "Half a day is left for the weak. A day for the strong. Two, for the exceptionally strong. Only Tyler and Gemma will survive, due to their bodies not needing magic for survival. The rest of us will collapse from exhaustion, ending in death."

Ragaz starts sniffling. "Then it does not matter where we try to go?"

Zepharre scowls at the floor. He shakes his head, in answer.

Rendered speechless, the others attempt to keep calm. But, looking to each other, hope drains from their eyes.

Even Ryco's defeated, sinking to sit upon the floor, before resting his back and head against an upright barrel. Slowly, his eyes close. He tries to keep hold of his composure. But the quivering of his chin gives away how afraid he must be.

Zepharre joins Ryco's example, in sitting on the floor. Gripping his head, he hides his downcast face.

My throat burns. I want to scream. I want to tear Caleiso apart. *How could she do this?* I seethe, inside. *Doom innocent people, to die a miserable death?*

Suddenly, I get an idea. But I know time is running out for me to do it.

"Zepharre!" I exclaim.

He looks up, his eyes seeming like he's dead already.

I ask, "The food in here is usable, right?"

He nods weakly, and I continue, asking, "How much do you need, to counteract the effects of the sickness, so that we can make it to another city?"

Sulking, he stands up, then points to a half-filled barrel of grain. "I would need at least twenty barrels of that."

"What else?" I ask.

Frowning, Zepharre lifts an unbroken keg up off the floor. Setting it upon a nearby stone table, he pries its lid off. Inside is a glimmering, yellowish powder. "Ten kegs of this," he says, before picking up various flower, herb, and spice remnants off the floor. "Then I'd need two ounces of each of these." He motions to the dozen or so different remnants he's spread out on the table.

"Forget it, Tyler," says Ryco, propping his chin on his fist. "It's impossible. Not even your father could've done such a feat. Even a Siveyra possibly couldn't do it. It's a lot to ask, of just one or two, or even three, partnering together."

"What do you mean, partnering together?" I ask.

"When you partner together, for magic," he replies, "you can do more than when you're by yourself. But it takes years of practicing, as one unit. Learning each other's rhythm, and breath. Each other's aura. Your vibe."

"Our collective heartbeat?" I ask, with a grin. "Like what you and Rozeth have, being Dezarin's apprentices during the same time?"

"Yes," says Ryco, as a sad smile tugs at his lips. His eyes start to water. He looks down at the floor.

I muse, *Rorka and I have some sort of similar connection . . . I think. But are we enough, together, to do what Ryco says is impossible?*

I ask Zepharre, "If I can find a way to get you what you need, to feed Paragon, and outlast the sickness, will you convince them—all the people, dragons, and horses—that they need to leave? Whether it's to The Zotek by way of Kirja, or to Vondurheil?"

"Of course I would," says Zepharre, spinning around to face me. "But I don't see how you'll ever get it in time, Ravier."

"I have to at least try. I'll be back soon."

With that, I run out, and down the long passage. My footsteps strike the stone, echoing in the quiet corridors.

Before I know it, I'm bursting into the room with Awngeleik and her current caretakers.

Deep in conversation are the three Greyvons, Yevolta, and Musgrae, now stopping to look at me.

Awngeleik is curled up in a corner of the room, scowling at all the faces. When she sees mine, she looks away like a spoiled brat of a child.

Her grudge against me, for leaving her, is a little cute.

I hide a smile.

"Smooth things over with Zepharre?" queries Yevolta, folding his hands.

Catching my breath, I tell them, "The food stores have been tainted. And the trees poisoned. Possibly, Paragonians too. I don't have long to try to *do* something. But, Rorka, I think you can help."

Holding the door open for her, I eagerly wait.

"Of course!" She says, "I'll do what I can. Lead the way."

"Grae and I will stay behind, with the beast," says Mekka. "The rest of you go ahead."

Musgrae gives a reassuring grin. "You've got this, Ravier. But best of luck, just the same."

As soon as Rorka has stepped out, we rush back to the others waiting for impending doom. Jasper and Yevolta are close behind.

Along the way, I notice that Rorka's much taller than the last time I saw her, and I ask her about it. "What did you and Mekka do, besides eat Vitiosyns? First, he's shorter. Now, you're taller. What gives?"

"We came to a compromise. A sharing of our statures. I obtained some of his size and strength, and he got a taste of my magic."

I slow my pace, fighting the panic again. "What do you mean, he got a taste of your magic? Have you shared it with him?"

She dips her head down, in reply, and my heart drops to a loud, thundering beat.

I tread down the last passageway, leading to the storerooms, while thinking hard about whom else could help me in this moment. Mekka must have a deep connection with Rorka. But my misgivings over what his history may be, might stop me from joining my borrowed strength to his. With Awngeleik holding a grudge toward me, she's an unlikely choice too. Then there's Madeleine, who doesn't remember enough. And no one else is coming to mind.

"If that's the case," I reply, "I'm not sure how much you can help, Rorka."

Right then, someone's rushing up to my side, breathless, and grabbing my arm.

It's Khyra, saying, "Tyler? The castle said you need me. What is it?"

Shaking my head, I start to reply, "I didn't tell him that." But then I recall that Khyra was the one who passed through the magical barrier with ease. No one could explain it. Part of me wonders now, *Is she another one different from the others?*

"Actually," I correct myself, "I was about to go looking for you, but he saved me the trouble. This way."

I lead them into the storeroom, where the others are still in the same positions as when I left. It's as if they were afraid to move, perhaps even to breathe.

Looking to Khyra, I state, "We need to find a way to lift the poison from the food, and replenish the stores. Are you up for it?"

She nods, rolling up her snagged dress sleeves.

Before anyone can distract us further, I'm whipping up my right wrist, and speaking into the watch: "Illusion of death," as that was the other phrase I wrestled with using. It wasn't as fitting then; but, now, it most certainly is.

Impending death is only half a day away, unless I can stop it. Khyra and I *must* stop this. Or suffer a heartbreak I cannot bear. Not just the death of my cousin. But all inhabitants of the city.

The pressure to perform is immense.

Very quickly, the scene shifts to a place of in-between. Dim light. Muted colors. The others are also still like statues. Only Khyra and I are able to move about freely.

She looks around anxiously, but focuses on me for reassurance. "It seems you slowed time. But where do we even start?"

"Multiplying the food supply," I state. Offering her my right wrist, I cringe inside, only remaining calm for Khyra's sake.

She grips my wrist, and gasps in pain. "Oh! I don't like that at all. Do your work quickly. Faster! Hurry!"

With firm focus on the objects that we need to duplicate, I stretch out my free hand. It starts out slow. The grain replicates, making the barrel swell. When it spills over, I take a handful of it, and toss it into an empty barrel, repeating the process. Eventually, twenty barrels are filled to brimming. Then it's on to the kegs of yellow powder that Zepharre needs.

Khyra shakes my wrist, breathing out through clenched teeth, and in through her nose, sounding as if she's in hysteria.

It occurs to me then, that she could well be in hysterics, unable to speak.

"Almost done," I state, and she nods frantically, squeezing her eyes shut.

When I'm able to let go of her, I hunch over, and try catching my breath. My vision blurs a bit. But I shake my head, refusing to let this stop me from what must be done.

Khyra gasps then gags. Rushing to a vacant corner of the room, she starts vomiting.

Not fairing much better, I'm breathless, and fighting my own wave of nausea.

Staggering back, Khyra wipes at her mouth, grimacing when she swallows. "Was that all we needed to do?" she queries.

My head wobbles. I straighten to my full height. "We still need to multiply those." I point at all the herbs and spices on the table, saying, "But it shouldn't be too bad, since Zepharre only needs small portions of them."

She takes hold of my wrist again, and sighs dramatically. "Go on."

We start again. However, it takes just as long to increase the spices and such, as it did with the grain and kegs of powder. My casting-hand trembles. Khyra's arm shakes. We're both tired. But we're able to finish, quickly drinking in air, as we do.

Khyra starts for the doorway, her feet dragging the whole way. "Best we tell Talok the news of the food stores. Come, Tyler. Get us out of this dark, dreary place. It's making me feel even more miserable over everything."

I state, "Can't. We've still got the poisoned supply to try to mend."

"Right! I forgot. That dreadful pain rushing through me, struck away most of my thoughts."

We walk out together, unable to force ourselves to run.

Khyra reaches for the doorknob of the nearest poisoned storeroom.

But I stop her, saying, "I need a minute."

Her eyebrows lift, in humor. "A minute? I was thinking I need a whole year. Yet, you just need a minute. You are truly remarkable, Tyler Ravier."

"Not remarkable," I correct her, "just determined."

Shyly, Khyra looks away. "Ryco has asked me many times, when I'm frustrated with myself, and my slow learning, 'If the end result is exactly the same, was the path that led there really so different? So horrible?'"

Shaking my head, I reply, "I don't know."

"Ah, well," says Khyra, with wit, "neither do I. It just sounded good to say, here in this dim place."

I smile, telling Khyra, "You know, we just did something Ryco said was impossible. You and I."

In elation, her eyes widen. "Really? The impossible? I just stood there gritting my teeth, while trying not to faint, as you did the work."

"I think you're going to need to do more, with this next part." I ask, "You sure you're up for it? I might be able to get Rorka to help."

Khyra bites at her lip, then bobs her head up and down. "I'll be fine. I'm the City Architect of Paragon, after all. My parents may be gone. They weren't with the hostages, or among the fallen of Eyo'el. Neither Nyrim nor Lokasi witnessed them slain, either. But it's all right. I've still got Ryco and Talok. Now, you and Gigi and all the wonderful members of the Sovereignty. But enough of that. We should begin this last part."

Opening the door, she leads the way in. She freezes mid-step, gasping and gagging.

A bluish haze blankets the room filled with the stench of rotted wood and food decay.

The red vines of earlier lie writhing on the floor, in the barrels, or wrapped around the kegs of various sizes. Some seem to even be guarding the bottles of treasured ingredients. But it doesn't matter. It's all ruined. And the vines are now poisoned too. They turn sickly gray, then harden to stone.

I stride forward, fighting my fear. I'm about to rip a lid off a barrel.

"Tyler, stop!" Khyra shouts, rushing to grab my arm. "Don't touch the grain with your bare hands."

"Why not?" I ask.

"Unless you're a Diveyra," she says, "like Gyron, or someone equally as strong, it will kill you. My parents never allowed me to study Deathasyn Magic, not even to learn how to guard against it. But I still snuck in a reading of a book or two. You have to use an object to absorb the magic. Sometimes the caster even has to use a similar means, to cast poison into harvested or growing things."

"Would the daggers work?" I ask, unhooking them from my belt.

Hesitant, she nods. "I think so."

"You do this part," I suggest. "You know more about what you're doing, regarding poison; in fact, probably a lot more about many things than I do. I'll stand by, and let you take whatever magic reserves you need."

I offer her the choice of which dagger she wants, and she takes NeiSator without even thinking. Gripping it in her left hand, she says, "I have to cut one of your wrists a bit, to have better access to your magic."

I slit my left wrist a little and offer it to her.

"No," she says. "It must be deeper. See, you're only bleeding blood. Not magic."

"Do it," I state. "I want this over with, whether we succeed or not."

She jabs NeiSator's tip into the flesh of my wrist, and white-hot pain sears from the wound to permeate throughout my body. My legs want to give out. But I tighten my right hand's grip on RotaSyn, and watch, feeling like a ghost, as Khyra thrusts NeiSator into a barrel of poisoned grain.

My body shakes.

Khyra starts screaming.

I hear a clock ticking in the background. Faster and faster, it ticks out time.

When it stops, Khyra's skin rips open where Gemma and I sewed up her wounds of earlier, at the instructions of Quall and Ben.

Blood gushes from her. From her arms. From her nose. She coughs and gargles, then blood spews out from her mouth, covering the front of her dress, and the nearby poisoned grain.

Fear grips me tight in its impartial, unkind fist. Death does not care whom it takes, so it would seem. It only waits. For it must know that all living must one day die. And it's only a matter of time.

Khyra stops breathing. Her time seems over. And, drained of too much blood, she falls dead. Her head smacks the stone floor, and I nearly puke at the sound of her head cracking open.

I look away, to cry and scream and fall to my knees. Crawling over to be closer to her, perhaps even to try and comfort her, though she is dead, I pull her onto my lap and cradle her broken head.

Tears have seeped from the corners of her violet eyes. Now, blankly, she looks off into nothing.

Choking, and scared, I speak out, "Forgive me, Khyra. I shouldn't have asked."

Releasing the dagger, I feel my heart stop.

Ever so faint, the ticking starts again.

I look to the diver's watch of my dad's, and am reminded of him. Lovingly, I brush my fingertips across the watch face, before I'm drifting off to join my dad and Khyra in death.

The ticking stops.

Then there's a click.

All is grim.

All is night.

I sense a hot breeze. That breeze then turns to a fiery wind. Then a gale-storm likened to sheets of ice. A contradiction of sensation, even at the end.

But is it the end? I wonder, while longing for the in-between. *Or is it just another place to live?*

In this moment, I realize that if there were a devil to sell my soul to, I just might be bargaining with him. Begging for a different end. One where it's just me. Not anyone else. Not Khyra or Rorka. Awngeleik or Gemma.

Just me.

One life cut short.

That's when I think, *I could bear it. I really could.*

But you won't have to, says a dark voice, in my head.

It's not me. It's not Soren, nor Zymarc. Not like a Greyvon, or a dyn. But it is dark, and menacing. Masculine, and powerful. Consuming, decaying, and almost like the voice of death itself.

I go numb inside.

The watch's time begins ticking, but in the wrong direction.

It's reversing.

Actions rewind, reverting through all of it.

It stops, when Khyra is about to thrust the dagger into the grain again.

"Wait, wait!" I exclaim, like my heart's about to burst. "We did something wrong."

"How do you know?"

"Because I just watched both of us die. It seems we get another chance. We should hurry, but do something differently."

She grimaces, and takes shallow breaths. "Oh! I know! We need an outlet for the poison. If there's too much poison, even a powerfully enchanted weapon can't hold it all."

"How about drawing all the poison to one or two barrels," I suggest. "Better to sacrifice some of it than to fail completely."

"Good idea! Let's draw it into those two in the corner. Them being in the corner will make it easier for Warren to seal away the contamination."

This time, Khyra instructs me to place RotaSyn in a barrel of grain, before she thrusts NeiSator down into a different barrel of grain. We watch the bluish tinge in the grain fade, drawing up into NeiSator. It channels through my body like a ravaging beast clawing beneath my skin, seeking a way out, and it finds its way out through RotaSyn. The blue hue is deepened in my barrel of grain. But Khyra's appears as it should be: a soft wheat color, flecked with golden-yellow.

One by one, we transfer the poison from barrel to barrel, until it's only left in the two we want it in.

As we leave this storeroom, to head for the next, part of me wishes I knew what to do about the castle's vines. But there's no time for that.

The rest of the storerooms give us little trouble. Only, we're exhausted and sweaty by the end. We collapse to the floor, smiling, even laughing in relief.

"We've done it, Tyler," Khyra says, as she seals up my wrist wound. "We've cured it of the poison. Ryco will be so pleased. And Talok? Oh, if you were a girl cousin, I think he'd be so relieved he'd peck you on the cheek."

"Good thing I'm not a girl cousin, then," I state, wiping sweat off my neck.

Khyra laughs. "Yes, I don't think the Sovereignty would've put up with a girl talking to them as you do. It requires a bit more tact than how you go about it."

I'm about to ask her what she means, but then a wave of dizziness hits, even though I'm sitting down. The struggle of it all is getting to me.

"We should get back, Tyler." She stands, then helps me up. "You do know how to make time start back to normal again, right?"

"Hope so," I reply. "Otherwise, we're stuck here for a while."

"You'd better be joking." Khyra scowls at me.

When I shrug at her, she taps my chest with NeiSator's pommel. "As Gigi would say, 'Bad Tyler Malik Ravier.' Getting us into trouble, without knowing how to get out."

"Stop worrying, Khyra. I'll get us out . . . eventually. And alive too."

"Your relations with Gigi," Khyra says, "are starting to make more sense now."

"Relations with Gemma?" I look at her quizzically, as we head back to our starting point. "I'm not sure what you mean."

Khyra queries, "You have a complicated sort of friendship, no?"

"I suppose so." I shrug. "Hadn't really thought about it."

"Then perhaps you should."

We make it back to the first storeroom, where no one has moved, not even Jasper.

Hooking the daggers back on my belt, I slap my left hand over the watch, speaking words of, "Thirteen, Aysivak. We're done."

Khyra glances at me in confusion, her violet eyes luminescent in the dim light, akin to Ryco's citrine-yellow set of eyes glowing at night.

What signs of giftedness does violet stand for? I wonder. *Or was Caleiso making that up?*

Breaking my thoughts is Aysivak's voice, replying, "Very good, Ravier! And you didn't even have to use up all three attempts. But try for the first time, next time, if you would, please. You made me rightly nervous, for a moment."

"Who's that?" queries Khyra, quickly looking about.

"A Vardiya," I reply.

Colors start to brighten.

Khyra and I step back exactly to where we started.

Her eyes lose their luminosity, as she's asking, "You have a Vardiya? And it's been in your watch this whole time?"

"Sort of." I lift my shoulders. "It's a long story."

"Long story?" she asks. "Like Zymarc trying to kill us all, then helping to save us from Soren, long sort of story?"

"I don't know what his intentions were, Khyra. There are too many mysteries surrounding Zymarc. Even Jasper's baffled by him. But don't go telling anyone that."

The room finishes its transition, but no one's moving yet.

"You know what I think?" says Khyra. "I think that maniacal, red-eyed monster just couldn't bear the thought of Soren being the one to have the last spot on the stage of war and bloodshed."

"You could be right."

"Right of what?" queries EmiKal.

Zepharre glances up at me, asking, "Have you changed your mind, Ravier? Can you not go through with trying? We understand it, if you can't." He gets up, continuing, "At least allow us to give you and Gemma directions to the nearest functional portal, so that you may make it back to Earth."

Grinning at Zepharre, I point behind him. "Turn around, Zepharre of Paragon, and tell me what you see."

The head adviser, hopeful and anxious, does as I command. He leans forward, rushing to the first filled barrel. That hand of his, grabbing a fistful of grain, starts trembling. Zepharre fights back relieved laughter, slowly letting the grain fall from his grasp, and back into the barrel.

At the same time, Ryco bolts up off the floor, joining the Alchemist in examining the barrels of grain.

The Alchemist says, "The grain is as if it were harvested yesterday. With this, I will be able to multiply triple of my estimations. We'll have enough for the injured dyns, yet unable to hunt for themselves, as well. We most certainly will not starve."

Gripping an edge of an open barrel, Ryco leans forward, sounding so happy he can't decide whether to laugh, cry, or shout out our victory over starvation. Quieting down, he looks at Zepharre, who's still in shock, an arm's length away.

The room suddenly quakes. And a groaning, creaking of wood resounds within the storeroom.

"What was that?" queries EmiKal, fearfully watching the ceiling as if it's going to come crashing down on us all.

"Metsa," Ryco replies. "He's celebrating. It has been a long while since anything truly astonishing happened within his walls." Reaching out, Ryco squeezes Zepharre's shoulder. Turning around, he strides forward to me. He grips both of my shoulders with his strong hands. "Sleeping Dragon, indeed," he says. "We can never thank you enough, Tyler."

Jasper watches from the doorway, asking, "Shall we tell Talok the news?"

Hesitating, Ryco replies, "No. It was too close of a call."

Remembering Khyra dying, I think to myself, *Ryco doesn't even know how close it was, either.*

"Are you saying," Zepharre starts, "that we should tell him later, or not at all? I thought you didn't want to hide things from him? Even to protect him."

Sighing, Ryco's lost on what to say.

Khyra speaks up then, saying, "I've known Talok for a while. There are limits, on what he can take. He will start berating himself for not sending more warriors down here, to guard the food in the first place. Guaranteed, that's what he'll do."

"Yes, yes!" Grover pipes in. "That is a habit, most bad, of his. Self-doubt. Tell him later, Ryco, when his mind is less fragile."

"Now that the matter is cleared up," says Ryco. "Shall we go up? Or have you forgotten your end of the bargain, Zepharre?"

"Of course not!" Zepharre exclaims. "What of this? Giving them three choices of where to go? We, Paragonians, like choices."

"What have you in mind?" queries EmiKal.

Zepharre replies, "Vondurheil, The Zotek, or staying here in Eyo'el for rebuilding. As for us, advisers, we should make for Yharss-Rawshuen and Dysarda-Reine. See what can be salvaged or brought back here."

* * *

Before long, we're back outside.

Zepharre makes his way to a pile of rubble, to get a better position for garnering attention. "People of Pawv'Ragaen!" he calls out.

Paragonians gather round, to listen.

Zepharre begins, by saying, "I and your Sovereignty have come to a decision. And we're giving you three choices, as to where you will go."

Horses assemble, shoving their way forward, while looking to Zepharre.

"You may," he says, holding up his index finger, "of course, travel to Vondurheil with our allies: the Greyvons." Now holding up two fingers, Zepharre continues, "Second choice: you go with two of the Arkiveis—Drauggen and Ragaz—to Kirja. By then which you will carry on to Veldar, or take to the Sea of Gradoelin, porting on the shores of The Zotek, where we hope to gain an additional ally, in the Amethysts."

"And what of the third?" someone shouts, from the gathered crowd.

"Patience!" Zepharre shouts back, starting to toy with his coat's fabric. "I was getting there. The third option is this. To stay with The Eye's Arkivy Grover, and our young City Architect, Khyra, for the rebuilding of Paragon's center."

"But where are you going, Adviser Zepharre?" another in the crowd shouts.

"Look!" Zepharre holds his hands out, in a pleading manner. "You can't go where I and the other advisers are going. To Yharss-Rawshuen and Dysarda—"

Someone cuts him off, shouting, "Where you go, Zepharre, we shall follow."

Many shout or nod their agreements, starting to sound like a mob.

Glancing down at Ryco, Zepharre mutters, "I've no idea what I've done to gain this reaction. This . . . loyalty? Is that what it is? It feels weird." Finding his voice again, he shouts his last attempt to convince them. "You're not going to Yharss or Dysarda, and that's final!"

The mob isn't listening to him anymore, however. Rather, they are busily rushing away. Most likely to pack for the journey they think they're going on.

Standing beside the rubble pile, Ryco says, "Come down, Zepharre. I will handle this."

Striding forward, Ryco draws out his two blades, and clangs them together a few times, shouting, "Whomever can defeat me in a duel, may go to Yharss or Dysarda. Have I any takers?"

The mob returns, some stomping, others scowling, and a few even sniffling and crying.

"That's not fair!" shouts a woman, in blue. "No one can beat you, unless they're actually intending on killing you. Even then, it's doubtful."

Nodding, Ryco says, "That is true. Since none are brave enough here to duel with me, you will pick one of Zepharre's three choices that he was so kind as to announce to you. To Vondurheil, The Zotek, or, if you're one of the lucky ones we choose, you may stay in Eyo'el."

The mob starts to disperse, though they do so while grumbling.

Zepharre makes his way down, but then motions behind Ryco, whispering, "Ryco, I think you have a taker."

In quiet humility, a voice says, "I will duel, for a chance to see my city of Yharss-Rawshuen. Though I could never defeat you, Ryco'el de Pawv'Ragaen."

14

Gift of Gloves

Smiling, I watch as Ben shyly stands his ground. "What is the longest a person has lasted in a duel with you?" is his question for Ryco.

Ryco faces Ben. "Just over two minutes. It was Musgrae, in fact. Think you can beat his time?"

"I am unsure," says Ben, quietly confident. "But if I cannot resist you for more than three minutes, then I have not earned my way home."

"Then let it begin," says Talok, coming to stand by me. "Three minutes. Lokasi, keep track."

"Draw your weapons," says Ryco, readying his grip on his own.

Ben swiftly slides his blades out, and they grow to short spears with sharp, curved blades at the end of each one.

They start. Ben lets Ryco come at him, and he defends himself rather well. Fast too, he hits Ryco many times with the handle-end of his spears.

Ryco doesn't flinch. His focus is on the sharp ends. Relentlessly, he clangs his blades against them. Step by calculated attack, he pushes Ben back.

Musgrae watches from the sidelines. Intermittently, he whoops and hollers, encouraging Ben.

The crowd screams and cheers for Ben to beat the clock.

Musgrae shouts, "Two more minutes!"

Ben gets faster, dodging half of Ryco's swings altogether, then repositioning.

Ryco crouches down, altering his tactics. His movements are akin to Caleiso's, circling me like a crouching cat. Only, much quicker. This time, I get to watch someone else's reaction to the animalistic movement.

Ryco jabs and pokes and prods, then retreats as if to antagonize Ben in lashing out without thought.

Ben remains calm, until Ryco goes for his twelfth jab or so. Then Ben goes ballistic, rapidly clashing against Ryco's jabbing blade.

Lokasi whispers, "He's almost to three minutes."

Zepharre, watching the two dueling, gently grips Lokasi's arm. "Let it go on for a little longer."

"Why?" queries Musgrae.

Talok is also eyeing Zepharre oddly.

"Because," Zepharre replies, "I think Ben is going to bring out Ryco's other form. His Paraso—well, you know. His sort of . . . dragon form."

By now, Ryco looks more than frustrated. Smoke starts emitting from his nostrils.

"You mean that smoke?" queries Musgrae, pointing at Ryco. "He's done that loads of times. Especially with Eli around."

Zepharre states, "No. I don't mean that. I meant *that*." He motions to Ryco, who's beginning to grow in height.

Ryco's nearly the same as Mekka's stature on two legs. His showing skin is heating up, but not turning red. Instead, grayish-brown scales form, accentuating the contours of his face, especially around his eyes and cheekbones. Steam emits from his scales, and his breath deepens, sounding reptilian.

Alarmed, Ben hesitates in his movements. He's no match for Ryco's strength now. Yet, he still puts up a good defense, and gets one slice across the back of Ryco's hand, and Ryco goes into a rage, yelling one long, drawn-out cry directed at Ben. His teeth are sharp and menacing.

The scent of pinesap swirls all around, oddly making me feel calmer than before.

A wind starts from Ryco, during his slow approach toward Ben, who's cowering away. The Sylvadyn begins a chant, and the dyns around sound as dogs unsure of whether to whimper, bark, or growl.

Ben sinks to the ground, grimacing. He breathes hard, as if a heavy weight is pushing him down.

Ryco's chant ceases, as soon as Ben kneels, his palms pressed on the dirt. Quickly, Ryco shifts back to his usual self, and helps Ben stand.

Like a great cheer, Lokasi shouts, "Five minutes for Rueisvben'el Yharss-Rawshuen, against Ryco of Paragon!"

The crowd applauds. But none clap harder than Musgrae.

Ryco lifts a hand, to quiet them. "Whomever Ben of Yharss-Rawshuen wishes to take with him, to his home city, will be permitted to go."

"Yes," Talok agrees, "for he has earned that right."

Ben shyly looks up to Ryco. Then to the ground. Then around at the many faces directed at him.

"But," Ryco says, holding up his hand again, "if Ben wishes to go alone, or with a select few, you will *not* argue."

The crowd takes to kneeling, each upon one of their knees. The multitude shows respect for Ben. And he smiles, saying, "I will go with few, as it may not be safe for all of you."

They rise, and disperse. But there are no murmurs among them. Only pride in their eyes for their young Ben'el Yharss, now possibly more of a warrior than a rookie, if ever he truly was a rookie.

Approaching, I congratulate him. "Good fight. We'll miss you."

"Take care of Talok," he says, shaking my offered hand.

"It goes without saying," I reply, while trying to think of what parting words to voice. Or what I can give, for good luck. Thinking of nothing better, I just say, "I wish I had something to offer, to help protect you. If I didn't think I'd need them, I'd give you my dad's daggers."

Gemma, Talok, and the guards approach right then, and the conversation is quickly stolen away by chattering praise and goodbyes. Only Talok is less than enthusiastic, looking tired beyond words.

Ben's about to leave, to go select a horse for the journey.

But I stop him, saying, "Hey! What about the gloves? Do you want them?"

Digging them out, I freely offer them to him.

His eyes sadden, in that happy, overwhelmed sort of way. But he shakes his head. "No, I couldn't."

He heads for the horses grazing nearby.

I follow, insisting, "Yes, you can. It'd make me feel better, knowing you'd have them with you, no matter what may happen."

"I'd rather take Awngeleik to my home city," says Ben, glancing at the gloves I'm still holding out to him.

"Come on." I grin, shaking the gloves. "Try them on for size."

Ben grins back, looking charming and amused. "Does that mean you wouldn't let me take Awngeleik to Yharss?"

I cringe a bit, saying, "I think it would end up being a bad idea."

Ben takes the gloves reluctantly. "You are probably right. But it couldn't hurt to ask. She is rather fast. Yet, I will find one adequate among these, I'm sure." He starts petting a nearby nein of average height on the shoulder.

Unfolding his wings, that dark-gray nein dappled with colors of umber and white lifts his head high. When he sees me, he comes to nudge me on the chest. Proudly, he lifts both of his thick, feathered wings. Then it registers where I've seen this winged-horse. He's the one I healed of two broken wings, during the night.

Ben carefully slips the gloves on, as he assesses the other horses he could take on the journey.

"Take this one," I tell him, as I scratch the horse's forehead. "He's got a strong spirit."

Ben looks over his shoulder. "How would you know?"

"Well," I start, "I would tell you, but then it would lead to you asking questions. Then your journey would be delayed. And—"

"Yes, Ravier," he interrupts, before coming to reassess the dappled horse. "You have formed a special bond with this one, haven't you?"

I'm about to answer.

Ben continues, "As such, I will name him with a name that will remind me of you. Can you guess what it is?"

He beckons the chosen horse companion to follow him, then heads back in the direction we came from.

Walking alongside Ben, I reply, "I have no idea."

"Brash," is Ben's smart-alecky remark.

"How do the gloves fit?" I ask, ignoring his name for the proud horse I healed.

"They fit perfectly." He grins in his charming way. "Tell Nyrim, Lokasi, and Eishal I've already packed for five, and miniaturized it all to fit in my pockets, in case we should be allowed to go."

"All in the pockets?" I look him over, in surprise. Then I point at him, asking, "Did you use the weight reduction spell too?"

"You got it."

Gemma's the first one we approach, on the way back. Timidly, Ben glances at her. Pausing his stride, he holds one of his arms open, silently inviting Gemma in for a hug. She rushes to accept the invitation.

"Thanks for the walk last night," she says, squeezing tight round his waist. "I'll remember what you said, and the lessons on potions."

Ben suppresses a smile, telling Gemma, "You will mostly need them for Tyler, I think, as he is the one dashing into harm's way often." Taking out a clean cloth, which he always seems to have, Ben wipes the biggest soot-smudge off Gemma's face. Then he chuckles, when she blushes and takes the cloth from him. "Goodbye, Gemma Galloway," he says, letting go of her. "I hope to see you in eight days. For eight, to us, is fate. Most lucky."

And just like that, Ben's turning and leaving. Mounting the proud, healed horse, they ride off, and out of sight.

"He taught you potion-making?" I ask Gemma.

She sniffles, and wipes her face more, then nods.

"What else did the two of you do last night?" I ask. "And when? I don't remember seeing Ben around the fire pit."

"It was before that," she replies, "after you and Eli fell asleep. The others too. I couldn't sleep, and neither could Ben. So, he showed me around the castle and whatnot."

Gemma looks away, seeming guilty over something. But I don't really know what guilt looks like on her. Only her openly feeling bad over framing me for a prank, after my dad died. And that's not really the same as suppressed guilt.

Catching sight of Khyra chatting away with Rozeth, Ryco, and all twelve King's Advisers, I think it odd that Ben didn't even wave goodbye to her, since he practically wanted to be betrothed to her, before Gemma and I arrived.

I push the thought aside, focusing on more important things than whether Gemma has a crush on a foreigner or not. I scan the crowd for Paydinn.

He's headed straight for me.

"Ravier!" He beams. "How ya feelin'? Good, bad, faint?"

"Why would I feel faint?" I ask.

"Ah, well," he says, exaggerating the roll of his wide-open eyes. "That borrowed power's about to, erm, fade. But, no worries! I wrote to my mother, RayVora, as well as my wife and many children. They should be headed this way, in a few days' time. Could be a bit before they all make it here, though. Now, I must know, before you pass out for . . . indefinitely. Where do you wish to go?"

"Vondurheil, with Jasper," I reply. "Awngeleik too. I want her there, not here. And what do you mean about indefinitely?"

"Agreed, regarding Awngeleik!" says Paydinn, louder than is necessary. "That is best. I'll see to it. And, look, the Emeralds have arrived. They're in for a wind blast of a frightening surprise."

"Paydinn," I remark, "you didn't answer the other part."

"That's because I don't wish to." Paydinn holds up his hands, in surrender. "If you must know, though, this sort of affair hasn't happened previous to now. You could be out for hours. Days. Months . . . Years. Hard to tell." He lifts his shoulders.

My throat goes dry. I try to swallow, but cough instead.

Paydinn makes a chair appear out of nowhere, and motions for me to sit in it.

And I do, sweating profusely.

Licking his lips, Paydinn then speaks in a rhyme, "Sleep-slumbering-sleep! Here's to seeing you in Vondurheil, Ravier. I'll pass Ben's message along, on your behalf. Now, mighty-night, too bright for the Kyanite. Goodnight."

Paydinn's amused face is the last I see, before it all goes gray.

15

Equal to Vons

There's movement around me. I sense it. Yet I cannot move one bit. Shuffling footsteps traverse, scraping along dirt and rock and dried grass. Water sizzles, as if it's putting out a fire. Then words come.

Conversation.

"We can't wait any longer for him to wake up," says Jasper.

"No worries, Alpha," says Musgrae. "I'll hold on to him."

"You'd better," Gemma threatens, "or you're only eating off silver when we get there."

"That's cute!" Mekka snickers. "A little girl's bossing you around, Grae."

"Yeah?" Musgrae says. "Well, you haven't had to deal with that girl kicking you in the chest all unexpectedly."

"She's got a mean kick," Kent adds.

Eli says, "Can't see it coming, neither."

I fade out again. Mostly, anyway. I have the sense of being moved about, from one place to another. Then I limply have to endure a jostling ride, with presumably Musgrae holding on to me.

When I start to have a dream of falling, I black out completely.

In the distance, Awngeleik screeches.

A cold sweat claws at me.

I toss and turn against my will, wanting to wake up.

When a boom goes off, I jolt awake. Sitting upright in a small bed that's low to the ground, I look around.

I'm in a large, white tent. Its peak goes upward, to eighty feet or so. Wooden cots, covered in fur bedding, fill the tent. There's space enough, and beds aplenty, for a group of at least a hundred. Yet, no one's around except for a man, youthful in appearance, seated four feet from my bed. Flipping through a book, he's not noticed I'm awake. His sharp features remind me of Greyvons. And his eyes resemble the intensity of wolves, more than any other Von I've seen in human form. Jasper included.

Not looking up, he says, "I told them that you'd stir, once they left you unattended with a stranger. See, your subconscious is likelier to perceive me as a threat, and wake you up."

"Glad it worked," I remark, shifting on the bed. I suddenly realize only the blankets cover me. No clothes. Not even the diving armor.

Where are my clothes? I wonder, looking about. *My things? They're not here either.*

The man stands up, as he introduces himself. "I am called Droediin, eighth male heir of Merlynite. Jasper and my father instructed me to take you to the main lodge, if you should wake."

"That's fine. Except that I need clothes, first. And where have my things gone?"

"Clothes?" Droediin's amused. "Jasper said nothing of clothes. Although, Gemma *did* bring a pile of something in here earlier." Droediin tosses me a canvas sack.

Catching it, I rummage through its contents.

"Any luck?" he asks.

"Well, they're made of furs and leather," I reply. "Not my things, but they should do."

Droediin waits outside for me to change.

The soft warmth of the thick, Von clothes and boots is comforting, until I pull back the tent flap, and am assaulted by the freezing temperatures.

The day's blindingly bright. Snow's all around, glittering where it's undisturbed.

"This way," says Droediin, leading us onto the dark-turquoise stone path. Strangely enough, not a speck of snow or ice is on it. It's as if the stones themselves are heated, keeping the path dry.

Tents are scattered all over. Massive ones. Bigger than the one we've just left. The farther we go, log structures of brown and tan wood are set several feet back from the main path. Rather than doors, for the lodges' entrances and exits, both little and large round holes are cut into the structures.

In clearings filled with snow, Vons of all sizes romp and bark and yap. Some are likened to werewolves, chasing after young pups, and scaring them. They laugh out growling sounds, then back they shift to their catlike wolf forms. Proudly, they prance along, and herd the lively, yipping pups.

"Let me guess," I ask Droediin, "those are Vonsai?"

"What?" says Droediin, in sarcasm. "You mean the big black-and-brown ones, on two legs? Yes. That obvious, was it?"

I nod, still following a step or two behind Droediin. "How long was I out?"

Droediin replies, "Three days, I believe. Not too bad, considering all you've put your form through."

"What did they tell you?" I ask.

"All of it," he replies, with a straight face. "It was rather impressive. More impressive than that, is the fact that even my brute of an opponent is in awe of your abilities."

"Who's your opponent?"

"Mekka," he says, in a deeper voice.

"Rorka implied that there are numerous alpha candidates," I state. "Yet, you only see Mekka as your opponent?"

"Undoubtedly, he is my *only* opponent. The last of the dog fights are over. They transpired, while Jasper was in hibernation. Only Mekka and I remain, to be the next Alpha of the Greyvons. But our duel will have to wait for this war with Vitiosyns to conclude."

"What about Rorka?" I query.

"What of her?" Droediin queries back. He has his head held high, as his mysterious gaze sweeps over the expanse ahead.

"Does she not get to compete against either of you?"

"She could," he says. "But it's unnecessary. Whoever is left of the alpha candidates is expected to become her mate for life. She doesn't like it. Mekka *hates* it. And I am indifferent. To that aspect of the future throne, at any rate."

"What if one of you wanted to partner with outsiders? Non-Vons, I mean." Waiting for his answer, I cup my hands over my mouth and breathe hard, trying to warm them up again, as they've gone stiff from the cold air.

Droediin eyes me critically. "You're a bit young to be vying for Rorka, aren't you?"

Snickering, I cross my arms. "Not me, Droediin. Someone else. But you don't look much older than me. Maybe not even older than Talok."

"My nineteenth year is what I'm in," he says, with a half-grin.

"Then you're old enough to have met my dad?" I ask. "In fact, Jasper said he often took you with him to Earth, to *visit* my dad."

"Rorka warned me of your questioning nature," says Droediin, amused. "And how you seem able to make anyone reveal whatever you wish. But I am different, in the world of Vons. I'm not Rorka. Nor Mekka. Nor Jasper. Eighth generation, of my father's line. And eightieth, on my mother's side. Of my father's line, only sons of the eighth male pup are in my lineage, until you've traced all the way back to my grand sire."

"Then, you must be especially lucky."

"No luck," he says, slowing to match my stride. "Purely gifted. Such as you are. So, you can forget about Mensa-div, unless I wish to engage."

"At least I know where I stand with you," I remark, uncrossing my arms. I try to appear open. Underneath the appearance, however, is suspicion.

He's guarding something, I muse. *But what, exactly? Toying with Jack Wayeland? Why would that matter, when no one was actually hurt? Is it possible he was the one leaving me all those notes?*

After we take a turn in the path, and trudge uphill for a ways, the view breaks over the whole of Vondurheil, and I stop to take it in. It goes on, as far as my eyes can see. In the distance, white mountains tower high. Closer to us, there are rolling hills fully covered in snow. Trees, seemingly made of blue glass with quills reflecting like silver, clothe the landscape too. A colored wind wisps through the air, a soft trio of sky-blue, sea-green, and gray. Enlivening the scene, however, are hundreds, perhaps even thousands, of Greyvons. Paragonians have joined many of their clusters, engaging in varying games of fetch.

I then look to where more lodges lie. So many, I won't even bother counting.

Not too far from where Droediin and I are, is what must be the main lodge. Except that calling it a *lodge* seems tasteless, for it looks to be made of ice, crystal, and pale stone. It has not the humble look of home. But, rather, of grandeur. Its footprint must be of eight hundred feet or so, and its height at least six stories, if taking the centermost steeple into account. It's the one structure that matches the magnificence of Vons; of Jasper, when he's charging at his victims to tear them apart.

"Wait until you see the inside," says Droediin, now leading me down the slope to get there.

When I feel a creeping, clawing sensation across my forehead, I know Droediin's pressing into my mind, and I push back in anger. Yet I remain perfectly calm, outwardly. Not even do I let my breath change its rhythm.

Droediin falls out of sync with my step for two strides, then is back to matching my gait.

I smile inside.

When he remains silent, I let the smile show through ever so slightly. "Though I don't know what my lineage is, Droediin," I tell him, "I know that I'm no ordinary Paragonian. Unless I want you browsing through my thoughts, I'd appreciate it if you wouldn't try."

"Oh, but I won't be trying, Tyler. Eventually, you'll slip up around me. And it will be then that I will steal a thought away. It's what Vonsai practice on each other, to keep one another sharp. Greyvons continue the mental practice. Always, we do test our equals. You should be honored to be my equal. For you were not, till just now."

"I don't really know what it means to be equal to Greyvons, Droediin. I'm still very new to all this."

"To be our equal," replies Droediin proudly, "is to be free to roam, wherever you wish, in Vondurheil. To come and go, as you please. To be protected, even before any of our allies."

"Then Greyvons went to Earth, to protect my dad?" I ask. "How is it that they failed?"

"Who said LanSoren was our equal?" queries Droediin, sounding defensive.

"No one. I just assumed—"

Droediin cuts me off, saying, "He was far above us, in practice. Able to summon a dragon storm of Mystadyns; a flock of BlacKaidyns; an attacking forest of roots and vines; a crystal dome filled with webs of memories. He was such a soul, which didn't need protection. Or so many thought. Sadly, we were all wrong. Even the greatest can fall. And so mysteriously too."

"Well," I state, "that kind of explains why Zymarc wouldn't attack Paragon until he was gone."

Nodding his agreement, Droediin steps off the path. We take to the steps of shimmering, yet roughened crystal.

The main lodge's double doors crack and hiss, then fracture like cut gemstones. The triangle and diamond shapes slip back and out of the way, to allow us entrance.

Entering ahead of Droediin, I don't know what to expect. But what I find certainly wasn't anything I could've imagined. Familiarity. Like I'm at home, in my father's study. Instantly, I know from where his inspiration for its rich colors of brown, and shelves filled to overflowing, came. Yet, in here, the books won't be anything I can read.

Scents of leather and fur are overwhelming, even in this cavernous room. But then burning wood chases away other smells. Dispersed along one wall to my right, fires are lit in little trenches. Their flames rise to near six feet. Flaring, they light the next trench above. Then it's seven feet high, eight feet, and on like that, until it reaches the room's ceiling. The fires go out. It then starts all over.

Droediin passes me, without making a sound. He puts a silencing-finger to his lips. "Let's surprise them, shall we?" he suggests.

I nod, asking, "Where are they?"

"Eating, or just finishing up, downstairs." Silently, he traverses along the wide, gray furs laid out as a long, carpeted walkway.

Along the rear wall, which is blanketed by tapestries containing depictions of many creatures, are thirteen chairs glistening similar to ice. All are of equal size, except for the center one. The seventh one from either side—it's larger, sculpted with ornate, geometric designs.

Droediin leads us around the elevated space, where those empty chairs are. Opening a door behind the stage, we go down spiraling, wrought-iron stairs.

Boisterous noise becomes audible, the farther we go down. Music's playing; drums, wind instruments, and other sounds too. Laughter rings out, and rhythmic clapping.

Droediin slowly emerges into view of the room. Glancing at me, his mouth twitches upward, as he's saying, "That Gemma friend of yours certainly knows how to have a spot of fun. Come see."

Very nervous all of a sudden, I go stand beside Droediin. The pale room is warmly lit by torchlight. The snaking fire along the ceiling too, illuminates the space. Within the open floor, surrounded by an audience seated at many long tables, is Gemma dancing, as if she's back home in one of our school Broadway shows.

She's dressed in the diving armor, as well as dark-gray clothes, and a white top hat. Her steps and swaying hips are timed perfectly to the beat and clapping. Out there with her are Eli and Siege, weaving round each other, and stealing Gemma away for a partnered dance. When not dancing with one of them, she twirls a black-and-silver baton, sometimes striking it down on the ground. Fire sparks at the point of contact. Her free hand switches between resting on her hips, fiddling with the top hat, or toying with her hair. Then there's her big, brown eyes taunting Siege and Eli, as she's running away. She only stops the alluring game, when one of them catches her by the wrist.

Droediin thrusts his arm out. "Grab on. I'll make us invisible to them all.

Then you can *really* surprise them."

Absentmindedly, I grab hold of his forearm, and let him lead us out to the room's center, where Gemma and her partners are. My chest tightens at the sight of them holding her close, gripping round her small waist, and sometimes picking her up to pass her to each other. It doesn't matter that they're all laughing, having a good time. I'm jealous. And I hate it.

Why should I be jealous? I wonder. *It's not as if I want her as anything more than a friend. Do I?*

Still, the feeling persists. Fire ignites in my chest. Heat creeps up to my cheeks too.

Droediin interrupts my fixation, Mensa-divving, *"See? You should have listened, and let your friend stay home."*

I'm only six steps away from Gemma, when my heart drops to a loud, hammering beat. I glance at Droediin, eyeing me with those wolf-like eyes. He grabs my hand, which has a grip on his arm, and holds tight.

Smoke- and mist-like substances wisp off our skin, giving the two of us a spectral appearance. It's as if we're here, but not really, because no one notices us.

I try to pull away. Physically. Mentally. Either one. But it's too late. I had let the distraction of jealousy bring my guard down. It's pathetic, really, how little time Droediin had to wait for me to falter.

His divving continues, speaking the words, *"To spells, binding and whole, not to tell, nor to say, and* absolutely *not to think the name: The Phantom of Muraine. Am I he? What do you think?"*

I try replying, "Yes," but it's no use. He's bound me not to say. Instead, I div back, asking, *"It's that easy, then, to bind someone?"*

"Of equal strength, yes," he divs. *"But only if you know what you're doing. Apologies for the act. I had to, you see. Can't have you showing those notes to my Alpha Jasper. But I left that glass shard, with Rorka's blood on it, alone. There's no harm in letting you keep that."*

I div, asking, *"So you lied, when claiming to be at my service?"*

"No lies. I simply don't like to leave my fate, in someone else's grasp. I'm sure you can understand that."

"Fine," I div. *"But I'll find a way to break it, if your secret becomes too bothersome not to tell."*

"Yes, break it," Droediin divs, daring me. *"It'll be good practice. Breaking a friend's spell, in comparison to a true foe's. If the time comes, who knows? You just might be able to do it."*

I ask, *"Are you finished? Can we get on with this, now?"*

He steps forward, closer to Gemma, then motions for me to make the next move.

Instruments cease their song.

Applause begins.

Gemma smiles, then giggles somewhat, at Eli and Siege. She practically glows, looking quite proud of herself.

With my left hand, I reach up and pluck the top hat off Gemma's head. Slowly, I set it down atop my own.

Gemma's face goes blank, as she watches the hat move seemingly all by itself. She scowls back at Eli, and swats at his arm. "Cheater, Eli!" she exclaims. "I can't use levitation magic yet."

Eli holds his hands up. "No magic-use here, Gigi. It's not me."

Siege, still catching his breath, glances over at Talok sitting beside Jasper. The two monarchs shake their heads.

"It's not anyone over here," says Jasper, studying the space where Droediin and I are standing.

Gemma points at Eli, in accusation. She starts berating him once more.

I let go of Droediin's forearm, right then. The smoke and mist appearance fades.

Talok sits up straighter in his seat, looking to me and then to Gemma. He waits for her reaction.

Eli peeks past Gemma's head, and grins as a vampire would, though he's not a drinker of blood.

Gemma stops talking, and whirls around. When she sees me, she blushes, then shrieks out my name and throws her arms about my neck.

In her haste, she's knocked the top hat off my head. But I catch it, then set it down atop her tousled black locks. Briefly, I hug her back, using one hand.

Stepping away, she happily adjusts the hat.

"Finally," says Eli. "You're awake. Took you seemingly for-e-ver."

Gemma glares at Eli, but she beams at me. "You must be starving. Go sit down. I'll fix you a plate." She rushes away, toward a corner of the room.

Eli claps me on the back, as Siege says, "We had hoped you'd be up soon. Your timing could've been better. But we feared you'd be unconscious for weeks."

Ryco pulls a chair out that's across from Talok, then sits next to it. "Sit, Ravier," he commands, before gulping down the rest of his drink.

Taking the seat, I ask, "Ben make it home all right?"

"Don't know," Ryco replies. "I convinced Rozeth to go with him and the others. She should be sending word, soon. Want me to ask about Brash, in my next letter?"

I ignore his question, glancing around for the new person of interest. Not seeing Droediin nearby, I look over my shoulder, and spot him trailing back with Gemma, as he carries his own plate of food.

"I am glad you are all right, Cousin," Talok says. "We were very worried for you."

Looking forward, I survey my cousin's appearance. He's thinner. Paler. An unfamiliar wildness has settled into his eyes too. I can't help but feel that something very wrong is happening to him, the longer that Geldryn device is on his wrist.

I reply, "After three days of rest, I feel fine."

Gemma sets down a plate piled high with food in front of me, then takes to the adjacent seat.

Droediin sits by Ryco, and starts up his own conversation with others near him. He seems unconcerned with anything else, until Rorka, Mekka, and a few others approach from the base of the staircase.

"Eat, Ravier," Ryco commands, tearing into his dinner roll.

Sighing, I look down at the food. It seems fine: root vegetables; odd, glistening cubes that look like gelatin desserts; and, perhaps best of all . . . meat. Dark meat. Light meat. I dare not ask what creatures they were. I don't want to know. I hesitantly reach for a thin strip.

But Musgrae's clearing his throat, saying, "At least yours isn't served on silver."

I glance at him, two seats down from Talok.

In front of him is a moderate-sized silver platter, still half-filled, but with most of its contents picked over.

"I suppose that means you dropped me," I remark.

Cringing, Musgrae nods.

"Serves you right," says Gemma.

"Is that what led to me losing my clothes?" I ask, in good humor.

"Yes," Musgrae says, in resentment.

"He didn't just drop you, Tyler," Gemma explains. "He dropped you in a puddle of freezing water."

"In my defense," says Musgrae, "it was really hard holding on to Ravier, after he had started his squirming, the same time I was reining in a frightened horse stomping at the Vonsai greeting us at the gates. Is it any wonder that I didn't drop him sooner than I did?"

"That's no excuse," says Quall. Winking from several seats down the line, he raises his glass to me.

Eli says, "You were stiff as a frozen stick."

"Took Warren a while to thaw you out," Siege states.

"But, no worries, Ravier," Kent reassures, "when it came time to rip the wet clothes off you, Warren and I made sure you were covered."

"All nice, cozy, and content," Musgrae says. He then adds, with a sneer, "Unlike me, eating off silver."

Taking several bites of meat, I push the plate over to Musgrae.

His face brightening, Musgrae says, "Told you Tyler would be on my side. You're the best, Ravier."

"I try," I reply, before standing up, and resting my hand on Gemma's shoulder. "Care to take me to collect my things, or to visit Awngeleik?"

She pushes her chair out. "Your things are with Warren, who's also with Awngeleik. Your pouches may not be thawed yet, though. Warren's taking his time with them, since the journals probably got wet."

Resisting the urge to glance at Droediin, I state, "Knowing Warren, I bet he's finished. Come on." I walk away from the table, and head toward the stairs and approaching group.

Rorka, back to her usual stature, is passing by, but stops when she notices that it's me. "Tyler? Good! You've recovered. I want to introduce you to one of Paydinn's brothers. Siveyra Zeekryn. Their mother, RayVora, is soon to arrive here too. Were you going somewhere?"

I glance at this distinguished man, clothed in ample black, gray, and teal robes. He couldn't appear more different from his brother, Paydinn, even if he had planned it. And, perhaps, he did.

He presses his gloved hand to his opposite rib, and bows slightly in greeting.

My head dips down in respect, before I look up into his calm, burgundy-red eyes, and feel a sense of slight alarm. I ask him, "Are you a Borrower of Time, as well?"

"Certainly not," he replies, in a silky-smooth voice. "Only the firstborn of my father, GrawVadian, could ever hope to be a keeper to a book of time. Unless my brother had the misfortune of dying, us brothers-three will never possess our own book of time. Besides, being a borrower isn't all it's made out to be. Such a great responsibility. I'd rather not have it."

Interrupting, Rorka says, "That reminds me. Alpha Jasper said to tell you, Zeekryn, that he has your brother's results in, for that genetic test he's been asking about."

Zeekryn's calm eyes unsettle. "Genetic test? Now, I'm a bit intrigued. Don't go too far, Son of LanSoren. Warren informed me of many things. But I've questions for you. And my mother implied that you've questions for her that need answering." He saunters away, with a sort of serene air, as if he isn't in any hurry.

"Quite different from Paydinn, isn't he, Tyler?" queries Rorka, before following in his footsteps.

Mekka and another Von (a much older one) follow them, not sending me even one glance.

Someone grips my arm, and I flinch.

Now wearing a coat of fur and leather, it's Gemma, saying, "You really should rest, Tyler."

"A visit to Awngeleik, while collecting my things. Then I will rest. Deal?"

Huffing, she glances to Talok, then to me. "Talok says that's fine. But we're under orders not to wander. At all. Between visiting Awngeleik, and going to bed. Deal?"

Reluctantly, I reply, "Deal."

We take the way Droediin and I did, until we're back on the path outside. Gemma and I continue traversing farther into Vondurheil.

After a while of silence, I ask, "What'd I miss?"

"Lots of riding, on stubborn horses," she replies. "Or some of Jasper's new members of Thedaesiim. You should've seen his reaction to them. Four Vonsai. He was livid, until one showed a lot of promise. Taeso. Musgrae said he matches your daggers quite nicely. He's an unusual tortie-calico color: black, orange, and white, with eyes of blue and green. He was my ride, for most of the way. Talk about fast."

Smiling, I then brave the question, "How's Talok? And be honest."

She frowns. "Not too good. He can't keep much food down. Only drinks. Quall's been brewing concoctions that help a little. But today's been especially bad." Gemma fights back tears. "Talok's afraid. Worn out. Overwhelmed. We're glad you're up. Maybe it'll cheer him. We don't know, though."

I state, "Let's hope Jasper can figure out how to get the device off."

"Yes," she says. "He's going to his observatory with Talok, once finished with dinner."

"Can't we go there, after visiting Awngeleik?" I ask.

She shakes her head. "Talok doesn't trust you to keep your hands off things in there. He talked to Warren about making restraints for you, before you could wake up." She laughs. "He was mostly joking, though."

"They haven't told him what Khyra and I did, have they?"

"No. But Ryco told me." She takes hold of my hand, sending warmth up my arm. "In place of Talok: thank you, Tyler," she says. "You've saved Paragon. And, one day, they'll know just how much."

Gemma starts to loosen her grip on my hand, but I tighten my hold. She smiles, asking, "Cold?"

Although I'm really not, I lie to her with a single nod of my head.

She crowds closer. My heart beats faster. I like her close. *But don't friends enjoy each other's company? I muse. Each other's warmth, when things are just hard and bleak and uncertain?*

Before I know it, Gemma's opening a door to one of the few lodges with actual doors.

The inside is just like any other pine-built barn, except cleaner; newer-looking with its un-aged wooden structure, and lack of dirt and grime.

Warren pokes his head out of one of the stalls, smiling his wide grin. "Yo! Ravier! You's just in time for your stuff. All thawed, and like new again. Awngeleik's mighty happy too. Mind taking her out for a run?"

"No!" Gemma shrieks. "She'll be a little kamikaze, and take us right to all the naughty Vonsai."

Warren laughs. "What? You don't want to be the dragon's bait?"

Gemma glares. "Hmm? No."

Opening the stall gate, Warren lets us in. "Stuff's over there, in the corner." He points. "I've been training Awngeleik to resist the temptation to chew on any of it. And it has gone rather well. Now, I'm off to meet up with Zeekryn, talk more spells and stuff. Can the twos-you handle her, do you think?"

Swallowing hard, Gemma says, "We were supposed to go to bed, after visiting her."

"Then sleep in here," says Warren. "There's a bed in the loft. A cozy one, with loads of furs for warmth. Doubtful you'll need all of them."

Warren leaves us. Specifically Gemma, still stammering and explaining Talok's instructions.

"My word!" she shrieks, stamping her foot, when the door has closed. "No wonder Quall's driven to drink herbs every night. They don't listen! Stubborn men."

I hold back a laugh, envisioning what the three days I've missed must've been like.

Awngeleik comes over to Gemma, her long neck hanging in defeat.

Gemma pets her, combing fingers through Awngeleik's dirty, ratted mane.

When I brush my hand across Awngeleik's forehead, her spirit brightens. She jerks her head up, and looks me straight in the eye, unwavering. It's almost as if she's trying to Mensa-div.

Her sadden eyes look away.

"She's sad," Gemma whispers. "She overheard Jasper and Talok talking about how we have to leave her here. If Jasper can't find a way to remove the device, we're to head for the Laykonian city. It's quite a ways to get there. And it's too risky to take her with us."

"Definitely," I state. "You'll be safe here, Awngeleik. And we'll come back for you."

Awngeleik snorts, then struggles to release her wings from the harness. Her eyes beg me to remove it. And I start to.

But Gemma quickly stops me. "Under no circumstances are you to remove that harness, Tyler. She's gotten better at using magic. And her wings are what allow her to wreak havoc. Just before we left, she shocked Khyra. Then Rorka. She delayed our journey by five hours, because of it."

"She didn't shock anyone else?" I ask, a little confused.

"No, but it was serious."

"What were their symptoms?" I pry.

"Out cold for five hours," replies Gemma, giving me an odd look.

"Just curious," I reply. "Don't go getting defensive, Gem. I haven't even asked you more about Ben, and your nighttime tour with him." Grabbing my stuff from the corner, I head for the loft, leaving her squirming on her feet.

She follows me, but stops, to ask, "Are you going to rest, or just sleep for a bit?"

"Going to change back into my clothes, first. I'll tell you when it's safe to come up."

Blushing, she turns on her heel, and strides back to Awngeleik.

The loft isn't like home. No straw. No storage trunks. Or piles of worn blankets. Just one small bed, in the center of the room, overwhelmed with at least four furs, three quilts, and two pillows.

Quickly, I change. But I leave the Sleeping Dragon coat off. Feeling a new sense of comforting warmth, I call down to Gemma. While waiting for her, I peel the bedding off to make my place on the floor for a few hours. Perhaps, even for the night.

I hear her behind me, making her way up the ladder.

"You really want to know what happened?" she asks quietly.

"Only if you want to tell me," I state, when, really, I desperately want to know.

Smoothing out the furs, I'm about to lie down on the floor.

"You're not sleeping on the floor, are you?" she asks.

"Well," I hesitate, shrugging, "yeah. You can have the bed."

She sits on the floor-bed I've made rather than the actual bed. Then she draws her knees to her chest, and hugs them. Her eyes well up with fresh tears.

I sink down, to sit beside her, dreading what she's about to tell me. I can feel it. Some confession. Suddenly, I don't want to know. I want to be ignorant of what she may or may not have done with Ben. My stomach churns, during what seems like hours before Gemma's saying another word.

At last my fears are confirmed, when she says, "Ben and I kissed that night."

I clench one of my fists, the one out of Gemma's sight. Quietly, I ask, "Is . . . that all? That's not all that bad, Gem." I look over at her.

"It was a lot more than once. But, no, it's not that," she says, looking less tense. "It's wondering why I like him so much. I'm not Kaida, attracted to every boy who's even a little nice to me. But it's different with Ben. I can't stop thinking about him."

Licking my lips, I feel that jealousy reemerging. Except, this time, I know Gemma's feelings for another person outweigh her own for me. Ours is merely friendship. But Ben actually has a chance to win Gemma. *Yet, he's many miles away,* I muse. *And what if something happens to him? I couldn't stand losing him as a new friend. Then there's Gemma's heart, which would definitely be broken.*

"You're worried about him?" I ask.

She nods. "More than I think I should be."

"With Rozeth for company," I point out, "he should be safe."

"I've tried reasoning it all out," she says. "It doesn't help one bit. I still feel sick, in the end."

"Does anyone else know about you two?"

"Musgrae caught us, after the third round," says Gemma, blushing a deeper red this time.

"Round?" I laugh tensely. "Say no more. I don't want to know."

Gemma cringes. "I know! I know! We probably shouldn't have. But we didn't want to stop. So, we didn't."

Nudging her shoulder, I stand up. "Well, I'm taking the bed, after that confession. You can share it with me, or have the floor. Your choice."

I crawl under the two furs and single quilt left on the bed. Then I throw one of the pillows down to Gemma. It gently smacks her in the face.

She scoffs, jolting up to beat me a few times with the pillow.

Rolling off the bed, I tightly hold my pillow. I dash away, and titter the entire time.

She chases me down, beating me repeatedly. And I let her. It's not like I have much choice. I laugh so hard, all strength leaves me. At the end, I collapse on the bed in a fit of hard, silent laughter, still clutching my pillow.

Gemma leaps onto me. Straddling my waist, she tickles my sides.

I thrash, grabbing her hands to stop her.

But she wrenches free with ease, gripping my wrists and pinning them down to the bed.

In that instant, it turns serious.

My laughter fades.

Gemma's humor disappears too, before she's declaring, "I win, Ravier. But we can share the bed, I think. So long as there's no sneaking out like a Demon in the Night."

Releasing me, she gets off. Then she pinches my side. I flinch, smacking at her hand.

"Deal," I reply, before digging my way under the blankets again.

She takes off her boots, and clambers in, to face me.

My stomach flutters. I don't want it to. But it betrays the calm I'm desperately longing for. I'm thinking of asking her about her spell-book. But she playfully blows in my face, giggling when a hair strand of hers ends up partly in my mouth. I pry it away, glancing at her red lips. When Gemma just smiles at me, I roll over. I hate her looking at me that way, when I can't test how I really feel by kissing her. I want to. Yet I can't. It goes against the code. Ben got her first. And it's not fair to get in the way of that.

I sigh, hoping Gemma doesn't guess my thoughts.

"Sleep well, Tyler," she whispers in my ear, while wrapping her arm around my waist.

Now, I'm the one who feels sick.

I grip her small hand, and softly brush my thumb along the back of it.

After a while, her breathing evens. She's drifted off to sleep.

I gently lift her arm up by the wrist, and slip off the bed to freedom. Freedom from the feelings welling up, driving me mad. I tuck her in. Then I sit on the bed's edge, and watch her sleep.

Sighing in regret, I get up to fetch the rest of my things. I dig through all the contents, to ensure that Droediin didn't perhaps miss one of the notes. He didn't. Only left the glass shard.

I head for the ladder, thinking, *A lot of good that does me now.*

Someone opens the lodge door.

Awngeleik screeches, startling Gemma awake.

Talok calls out, "Tyler? Gemma? Jasper's finishing up going through his tomes on Geldryn history. He said it won't be much longer, before we know the next course of action to take."

Looking down at Talok, I ask, "If he doesn't find anything to work on the device, will we be leaving today?"

Talok nods. "I hope you got some more rest. If we must leave, it'll be a long journey to King Lemara's underwater city of Deivahl."

16

The Horse in Winter

Within the cavernous room of the main lodge, we're all seated at a table across from the trenches of fire. Awngeleik, insisting that she come with us, prances around the room, and chases after Droediin and Mekka, who are in Von form. They're kind enough to entertain her. Soon, however, I realize that it's more than entertainment for them. They're wearing her down. It's not working too well, yet. It's merely making her furious. She chases them harder, and kicks at them too.

"There's nothing," says Jasper, with some sadness. "No history of that particular device. I have histories describing newer makings. But not one as old as that. I've no idea of how to deactivate it, without it immediately killing you, Talok."

"We're deeply sorry," says another Von, in human form.

I do believe he's the one I saw earlier with Mekka and Rorka. Closer now, he appears to be older than Jasper. His hair's a wiry gray mixed with white. The lines on his face are deeper set than Jasper's too. But there's a genuine calm about him. Jasper always seems to have a storm, barely contained underneath it all. Yet this Von is relaxed, amidst our apprehension and Awngeleik's racket.

"It's not your fault, Merlynite," Talok says. "We knew it was a possibility that there wouldn't be anything here to help me. But it got me out of

Paragon. Indeed, many of my people are making their way to safer areas. And the ones here can be at rest from trouble."

"Undoubtedly," Merlynite replies, sitting up straighter. His chest lifts. His neck appears elongated. His posture is stately. His eyes never move. Merely, he moves his head to change where he is looking, except for when he side-glances at Jasper every so often. "What sort of supplies have you need of, for the journey to see that old king hiding in the depths?"

"Potions," Quall declares. "And ingredients for potions, especially ones to clear the water of contaminants."

"You then mean to make it to the eastern shoreline," queries Merlynite, "by way of the Metsundai?"

"He means the Forest Lake," Quall clarifies for Eli, poised to raise his hand. "And, yes, that is the way we wish to head."

"Then allow me to accompany you," says Zeekryn, sauntering toward our table.

Awngeleik doesn't notice him. Too intent is she on biting Mekka's front leg, and making him bleed.

Musgrae cups his face, slouching in his seat, until he spots the person beside Zeekryn. He straightens, grinning at the especially beautiful woman, whose skin is darker. Her hair reaches well past her waistline.

Like Paydinn's brother, her eyes are burgundy-red. She must be their mother, RayVora.

Intently, she looks to Talok. When he simply sits there, picking at his nails in that bored sort of way he's taken to, she says his name.

Startling, he pushes out of his chair. He rushes to her, then wraps his arms around her.

"I received Paydinn's letter," she says, embracing him as a mother would. "And here I am, to comfort you. Assist you, with whatever you need. Be it even knocking at Zymarc's door, myself."

Talok steps back. "I can't tell you how happy I am that you're here, Matron RayVora."

After smoothing her dark, floor-length coat, RayVora takes a seat, and slides her chair in. "I'm merely happy I made it here in one piece. Anyway,

I was saying . . . as I still have some friends in the Vosh-Perida, Zymarc may accept me as a temporary guest. But I will only get one request. Also, I must take something of value."

Zeekryn suggests, "What of that coveted book of the Dei-Athos-Kree King Vit'Dod gave you, when you were a young girl, Mother? Only, put a curse on it, for when it's opened."

"It's not the sort of thing you can put a curse on," says RayVora. "Besides, Zymarc will detect a cursed object, as soon as it's at his gates."

"True," Zeekryn replies. "You are likely right."

"Of course I am, darling," RayVora says. "Even that Azabahk would sense it. He's rather gifted, even if he doesn't seem overly intelligent at all times. No. That book is too essential to be giving it away."

I ask, "Would Azabahk be intelligent enough, to know Death spells that involve dragon hearts?"

Surprised, RayVora takes a moment to answer.

Even Zeekryn has lost his air of calm, suddenly fidgeting with his hands. "What sort of question is that?" he queries.

"Awngeleik has a dragon heart," replies Talok carefully, "in addition to an EquiNein heart."

RayVora and Zeekryn turn to look at Awngeleik, both seeming unaware of this news until now.

Merlynite side-glances at Awngeleik toward his left, then to Jasper on his right. He looks directly in front, to where I'm sitting. The two old Vons seem to have shared a thought. Unless it has to do with Awngeleik, I've no idea what it could be.

Talok starts sauntering around the table. He stops to take a sip of Ryco's unfinished drink contained in a glass mug.

"We had wondered," states Ryco, trying to ignore Talok, "what sort of spells involving dragon hearts could be performed, if the entity never dies from the loss of its heart. As far as I'm aware, it's never been a viable option for Dei-Athos-Kree spells. To have a host survive."

Talok stares down into the mug, moving his hand enough to make the liquid swirl.

"It's hardly been done," says RayVora, sounding quite serious. "But it *has* been done before. The one I'm aware of is the spell that bound the Warrior of the Nyxane, to his Onyx King and any of the monarch's heirs. Only a new house of rulers allows the warrior his freedom of choice again."

Talok takes a giant gulp of Ryco's drink, finishing the last of it. He gargles before swallowing.

"So, if Gyron," Gemma starts to say, "wanted to leave his position, ReNovak would—"

RayVora nods, even before Gemma has finished. "Yes, dear," she says. "He and his entire family would have to perish for Gyron to be free, and another warrior be given the opportunity at the title."

"Who was owner to the heart used in that spell?" queries Quall.

"No one knows for certain," replies Zeekryn, as he pours himself a glass of water.

Talok sets Ryco's empty mug down, then eyes the bread roll Kent is about to finish. Slumping, Kent tosses the remains to Talok.

RayVora says, "It's been suggested that Nyxane's mother was the one whose heart was used."

I ask, "How could she live without her heart, though?"

"She could've been given someone else's heart," replies Zeekryn, sliding his glass over to Quall. "It's a way around the Laws. Kill a poor soul. Transplant the heart. Continue on with spiteful spells or rituals."

Quall gulps down the water, then lets out a hushed sigh.

"Not all spells of that sort," says RayVora, flashing an angry look at her son, "or rituals are spiteful, Zeekryn. Some are deserved. You are well old enough to know that."

"I am advanced enough to know, too, Mother," Zeekryn states, "that lowering yourself to your enemy's tactics does not go without consequence. Shadows, fighting darkness? Single slayings, to avert massacres? Where does one draw the line?"

"All right, Zeekryn." RayVora sighs. "You've made your point."

Satisfied, he looks to Jasper, then Merlynite, asking, "Has my brother arrived yet?"

"Not yet," Jasper replies.

Zeekryn leans back in his seat. "Mother, you really must sort him out. He made it clear to you, and Giveidra, the importance for haste. Now, he is late. Again. YaeVorkk and I have decided—"

"Decided what?" RayVora snaps, then plasters a sweet smile upon her face. "Decided, perhaps, to have families of your own? Do you wish for Jasper to do genetic testing for you too? Find you a lovely Metimora, who complements—"

"I do not wish to have a Metimoran wife," Zeekryn replies, in his smooth way.

Talok finishes the roll, then goes to steal one of Eli's pieces of dessert set atop a plate.

RayVora asks, "Then why not a Sorsryn, of one of the nonviolent clans?"

Eli, even while chewing, cups his hands over his remaining dessert squares.

"I do not wish to have a wife at all," says Zeekryn impatiently.

Warren reaches over and flicks Eli on the back of the hand, making Eli shake that hand out. Talok takes the opportunity to snatch up a dessert square. He stuffs the whole thing in his mouth.

RayVora rests her clasped hands on the table. "Then I want silence, Zeekryn, in regards to what you and YaeVorkk have decided. And where *is* YaeVorkk? He was summoned by your brother too, I do believe."

Eli scowls darkly up at Talok, who then wipes off the bits of sugar stuck to his fingers in Eli's perfectly groomed, strawberry-champagne-colored hair.

"Asleep," Zeekryn replies.

"Asleep? Where, asleep?" RayVora fumes.

Eli stifles a scream, feeling his hair, before reaching to claw at Talok.

My cousin dashes away, to sit back in his seat.

Quall stares at the empty glass he's set down on the table. Part of me wonders if he's longing for a nice herbal drink about now.

Zeekryn glances around in guilt, saying, "In his chair. His favorite one. I cast a spell on it, over three years ago. As a joke. Then YaeVorkk didn't sit in it, until ten months ago. If you must know, Mother, he's been asleep for these past ten months."

RayVora's face goes rigid, her eyes seeming to turn demonic.

Zeekryn continues calmly, "I went to his little cottage to fetch him, when the Vitiosyns started expanding their territory. That was six months ago. Or was it eight? I don't remember. However, he was gone. It is *quite* possible he's in a Vitiosyn prison cell. Still asleep, though. I've not felt the spell break."

"Do you feel better, my dear," queries RayVora, "now that you've cleared your conscience?"

"That depends on whether you want me to go see about fetching my brother from a Vitiosyn prison or no."

"Are you making an offer?" queries RayVora, lifting an eyebrow.

"Not really," Zeekryn says. "My chances of escaping unscathed are nil. As for you, Mother, you are as tactful, as you are beautiful to behold. You can charm your way out of any unpleasantry."

"It *is* somewhat true, RayVora," Jasper agrees. "I will go through my stores. See what I have that he, or Azabahk, may value that isn't of terrible importance. That is, if you're daring enough to step foot on Vitiosyn territory."

"Guts has got nothing to do with it," says RayVora. "It's reputation. A call to honor from Zymarc. To appeal to that reasonable Onyx side of himself. Remind him that Talok is barely older than a boy. And that the premise of this war is ridiculous."

Zeekryn grimaces. "Best you leave the war-premise bit, out of the conversation. No need to get yourself killed, talking to him like that."

"Oh, so you do care whether I live or die?" queries RayVora. "Sometimes I wonder about the four of you boys. Now, back to Awngeleik's heart. Has Zymarc hinted that this is how he intends to use her? For one of her hearts?"

I reply, "We think he doesn't know that she has two hearts. And he said something about Nekrosyn spells not using dragon hearts."

"That is true," Zeekryn agrees, leaning forward. "But were some of you thinking he wants to bring a life back from the dead?”

Quall and Siege share a look of dread.

“We don’t know,” Ryco replies. “Zymarc is holding fast in refusing to tell us what he wants with her.”

“Therefore,” Zeekryn says, seeming thoughtful, “you are trying to ascertain his motives, for getting her back.”

“Zymarc is too methodical,” says Ryco, “to simply want her back, for the sake of *wanting* her back, don’t you think?”

“Absolutely!” RayVora exclaims. “He *is* still Onyx at heart. He’s shown it to be true, with wanting to win the title of Onyx Victor. After all these centuries, I had wondered if he still yearned to go back to his roots. His home. The Nyxane. Especially its capital city of Oniva.”

I state, “He’s already been back there, I think.”

RayVora looks at me, blinking rapidly.

Zeekryn touches his mother on the shoulder, saying to her, “Warren relayed that Zymarc’s taken a liking to wearing Soren’s face, as well as someone else’s, for going where he pleases.”

“My word,” says RayVora breathlessly. “He could be one of the Onyx Warriors.”

“If that’s the case,” Siege queries, “any ideas of which one?”

“I’ve not seen them recently enough,” replies RayVora, “to make my guess.” Perking up, she grins deviously. “But I think I’ll be paying ReNovak a visit. See if I can find a likely suspect among his ranks.”

Zeekryn points out, “Mother, they are at the start of a war. You can’t go to the Nyxane, as you have in the past, freely and without fear. He could imprison you. Hand you over to Zymarc, himself.”

“Well, then, I could be sure whether YaeVorkk is there or no. But he won’t be doing that,” RayVora reassures, before looking to Talok. “Tell Paydinn not to make any official agreement with Paragon. Perhaps I can tempt ReNovak with a false offer, as I am the Queen Mother of the Jokryn, and hold negotiating power on behalf of my head son and his wives.”

“Wife,” Zeekryn corrects. “He only has one, now, remember?”

“Yes, how thoughtless of me.” RayVora cringes. “Poor Illveidra, being forced to begin her transformation early. We won't likely be seeing her, for several decades more. And that's if she wants to be found, after her new form has taken on life."

Jasper asks, "You are talking of the Metimoran snakes?"

RayVora nods.

"Among the Metimorans," says Jasper, "is there any significance of two black snakes being latched on to a neck?"

RayVora happily shifts in her seat, replying, "Oh yes! Not two snakes. But one. They're companion snakes for Metimoran explorers when they go out from their homeland. The practice heightens senses, magic, strength. The immune system. Honestly, Jasper, I thought you knew near everything." RayVora gently laughs. "I rarely hear you ask this sort of question. Why did you wish to know?"

Talok leaves his seat again, walking too far away for me to still see him from where I sit.

Jasper swallows, as he tightly grips the edge of the table. When he flicks his intense gaze in my direction, I answer for him, "Zymarc is using two black snakes, as a means to communicate over distances, and control some of his warriors. Warriors like Belzara."

Akin to a slap on her face, all humor is struck from RayVora. "That is Metimoran Magic," she whispers, turning a few shades lighter. "How has he learned Metimoran Magic?" She abruptly stands up, practically running for the door of the main lodge. "Zeekryn!" she shouts over her shoulder. "Send word to Paydinn. I'm going to Oniva. Come what may, I will be getting answers out of ReNovak. Even if I have to resort to seduction."

Talok now stands near the table. He plants his fists on the surface and leans forward. Looking over his shoulder, he watches her go. "RayVora!" he calls, before she's gone. "Just, please . . ." He trails off.

She stops at the door, to look back. "Don't you be worrying, King Talok. I was raised by the most fearsome of Deathasyns. So formidable were they that near every Geldryn trembled at the sight of them. I *will* come back."

No sooner has RayVora left than Rorka approaches our crowded table, and bows her head.

Jasper says, "Rorka tells me that everything's packed, and near ready to go. I went ahead and let her know the bad news regarding the device. If you're not against it, a few of us will accompany you to the border of Metsundai. From there, you're on your own, to traverse your way to the Laykonian city."

"I, too," says Zeekryn, "will go that way with you. And, even better, I'll help guide you through the forest. It changes slightly, every year. I went through there not long ago, looking for YaeVorkk. Evidently, I had no luck finding him."

Gemma looks concerned. "Shouldn't we wait for Paydinn?"

"We could all well die, waiting for my brother to be on time," Zeekryn replies. "I'll write to him. Tell him to find us in the Metsundai."

"Then let us be off," says Quall. "It's half a day's journey to the forest."

Oddly enough, Awngeleik's racket has quieted down. In fact, she's no longer in the main lodge. It's not until we get outside that I spot her, on one of the snowy slopes, chasing after Mekka and Droediin.

I think to myself, *I hope she zaps the ego right out of Droediin. It'd be well-deserved, for everything he's done.*

Still, I can't really blame him for his actions.

I head in Awngeleik's direction. Her tantrum ceases when she sees me. Prancing over, she performs that head-waving of hers, screeching happily.

"See," I tell her, petting across her forehead, "you'll be happy here. Bet you won't have even missed us, before we're coming back to get you."

"I'll take good care of her," says Rorka, from behind me. She comes to pet Awngeleik on the neck.

"Gemma mentioned what happened to you and Khyra. Are you okay?" I ask, while still petting Awngeleik.

Rorka presses her lips together. She steals a glance at me, then whispers, "Something's changed about me." She licks her lips, before continuing, "I've started having visions, when I sleep. Since they don't play out fully, I don't know what they mean. They seem to be telling of a horrible end or beginning of something."

I pull my hand back, to readjust the watch on my right wrist. "Have you told anyone about them?" I ask.

"Just you," says Rorka, starting to stroke Awngeleik on the forehead. She traces the lines of the Equidyn's facial scales.

Awngeleik contentedly sighs, then lowers her head. I reach to pet her again. But I take that moment to bravely satisfy my curiosity, instead. My left fingers brush against Rorka's right hand. Where my fingertips touch her, her skin darkens, black like ink slowly seeping into her flesh.

She jerks her hand away and inhales sharply. When she grabs hold of her left bracer, the black stain fades. She swallows hard, not saying anything more.

Meanwhile, I smile to myself. There is another like me. And I find that comforting. She's in those beginning, frightening stages, afraid of change. Especially an unexplainable change.

I lean over to whisper to her, "Come with us. It'll be fun, making that stain grow."

She stares at me wide-eyed. "You know what this is?" She glances to her hand then to my face, as she calmly resumes petting Awngeleik.

"Not exactly," I reply, letting that grin creep into my features. "But I've got it too. Whatever it is, it stains half my arm, now."

"Half your what?" she whispers, in a rasping voice.

"It has its perks," I add. "An undetectable magic, it seems. Haven't you noticed the stain I sometimes get on my left hand?"

Rorka shakes her head. "I've not noticed it on you. And no one has mentioned seeing it, either."

"Well then," I reply, "it must only be visible to those with its gift. What do you say, Rorka? Will you come with us?"

She confesses, "I greatly desire to, Ravier. I'm certain that your father avoided meeting me on purpose. And that you and I share a bond for some reason. I cannot uncover the truth of it, though. You are not a Von. Nor was your father."

"But I'm your equal, aren't I?"

"That is Droediin's claim," she says. "And I want to believe it. But Vons do not ever fear their equals. Only compromises between our equals. Yet

. . . I fear you, Ravier. On the other side of the matter, I do not wish to let you leave. I do not wish to stay. However, I've been ordered to. It is my duty to help our allies settle in. Also, I must further train with my Von pack of Theocktras. Alpha Jasper wants us as ready as we're able to be, for the coming war. Many Vons have never faced a true battlefield. There's much to be done."

My sudden glee plummets. Still, I turn to Rorka and offer my left hand. "Then I wish you the best fortune, Rorka."

"Goodbye, Tyler," she says, shaking my offered hand. "Be safe."

Though I'm gripping her left hand, it's her right that's starting to stain with the Prismatic of Magic. Hers is colored differently, however. Equal parts of white and black paint along her hand and part of her arm. Her nails turn black, as if all her fingers got smashed. She lets go of me, when her right palm courses with color. Not as many colors as my hand does, but the primary colors of magic: brass-yellow, ruby-red, and cobalt-blue. She grips her left bracer again, and the stain is erased.

Somewhat chuckling, I ask, "Enchanted bracers?"

"Yes," she says, turning to stride back toward the group. "Magic Neutralization. I don't want anyone asking questions about this sudden change in me. Initially I thought it might have had to do with Gyron and I—" She stops short, blushing. "Well, with us dancing and such, at the festival. Then later getting to know each other better."

When Rorka looks over her shoulder, I tell her, "I bet that's why the visions won't finish. You're starving your body of the proper magic. Take the bracers off tonight. See what happens." Pausing, I add, "Or are you afraid?"

Rorka faces me fully, replying, "I'm afraid of many things, Ravier. Things Vons just aren't supposed to fear. I cover it up well enough. But it's there. Mekka and Droediin know it too. They hide it from Jasper. They want the Greyvons to get their Matriarch. I'm the only candidate for that. And that reality is alarming."

I nuzzle my face against Awngeleik's neck, hugging her, before innocently saying, "I don't think that's why you're scared."

"Then why?" Rorka crosses her arms over her chest.

After a quick pat on Awngeleik's shoulder, I reply, "Your lover's now on the enemy side, whether he wants to be or not."

Rorka hangs her head.

I ask, "Will you do us a favor, while I'm away?"

She meets my gaze. Tears have welled up in her beautiful, juniper-green eyes.

"Start reading through texts, searching for a way to free the warrior from the Onyx King."

Her eyes grow wide again at my request. "That is impossible, Tyler."

"For most, maybe." I grin. "But not for us. For we are different, are we not? How can I stand by and let Gyron be fought over by two kings? Neither of which he even wants to serve. Help me do this, Rorka. Find a way, even if your mind tells you it cannot be done. I'll do what I can, when I get back."

Tears spill down Rorka's cheeks, as she smiles. She throws herself against me, in a tight embrace.

Losing our footing, we slip. Then we fall into the snow, laughing.

Turning serious, she says, "You have my word. I will not rest, until I have found a way."

Rorka pushes herself up, to dash away with revived energy.

Regaining my footing, I jog in the snow, chasing after her. But Awngeleik gets in my way and pushes against me. She stamps her feet.

I'm stern, in saying, "Awngeleik, no! You're safe in Vondurheil. You *must* stay."

She furiously pounds her hooves on the ground, yet does not land on either of my feet.

Several Vonsai on two legs have gathered round to watch.

She spots them and charges, snapping and stamping and screeching. Most run away from her, in fright. Only one wrestles with her, until she bites him on the ear. That werewolf-looking Vonsai yelps and whines, then gives up and runs off too.

I glance to Droediin and Mekka, both in human form, while hollering across the distance, "Have fun with that."

Mekka hollers back, "You've no idea the torment we're going to let her inflict on weak-willed Vonsai. We're hoping to see that demon form Musgrae mentioned too."

Droediin calls out to me, "Best of luck to you, Tyler, if luck is *indeed* what you need."

Before I know it, we're all mounted on the horses from Paragon, saddled and ready; some sit astride Greyvons willing to make the half-day journey with us to the border of the Metsundai. I take one last look over my shoulder, at Awngeleik and Rorka, deeply hoping to see them once we've found a way to save Talok.

We trail on the stone path, able to have three mounted riders adjacent to each other. After a bit, we're out of the city, and going up, up, and higher on the seemingly endless slopes. Jasper, in Von form, takes the lead at the front. He breaks into a run. It's blindingly bright, ahead. I close my eyes, and the sound of swirling sand fills the air. The whole group of mounts bolts forward.

The light suddenly dims to bearable levels, and it's no longer frigid. Rather, it's hot and dry. I open my eyes, quickly wishing to close them again, and wake to a different sight than the one before me.

17

Creatures in Water

Endless, snaking sand dunes lie ahead and behind and to the sides. Sand everywhere. No sight of a forest edge is anywhere.

Our mounts slow to a steady trot.

To Gemma on her Vonsai mount, I glance. She gives me a knowing look.

"Be happy you missed the ride here, Tyler," she says.

Talok adds, "Now he has to suffer this sight and heat, like the rest of us."

Tugging the reins, I position my horse closer to Talok, on his own mount.

My cousin eyes me mischievously. A light I've not seen in him since the festival is suddenly there again.

I dig my heels into my horse's sides, and he bolts forward.

But Talok's anticipated my intent, and is already there alongside me, neck and neck.

Jasper, slowing down, presses his ears back. He listens to us approaching from behind. His pace quickens, once more. The other Greyvons follow Jasper's example. All of them are infinitely faster than the horses trying to keep up. Consequently, Gemma speeds by us, on her Vonsai. But her Von's unable to keep pace with the full-grown ones.

Fastest of all is Jasper. Only Zeekryn's young winged-mount can keep up with him. The two run side by side, going faster and faster. Zeekryn presses down, and his robes whip in the wind. He lets his horse take the forceful brunt of going forward at such velocity.

After a short while, Talok reins in his nein. They slow to a trot, before the rest of us do the same. Circling around, Jasper comes up to Talok's side.

Trotting beside Talok's mount, Jasper says, "A safe journey to you, my young ally. We shall look for your return. Guarding your people, all the while."

Gemma reluctantly transfers to a horse.

We then wave goodbye, watching the Vons follow Jasper back home to Vondurheil.

By the time we get to the forest edge, we're all hot and tired, drenched with sweat. Ryco's at the lead. Zeekryn's beside him. They dismount, to go study the forest. They seem suspicious of something.

"What's wrong?" queries Talok.

"Ryco feels uneasy," states Zeekryn, holding the reins of his horse as it's trying to pull away.

"It's not my imagination," Ryco defends. "Something's not right with the forest."

Sweeping a glance across it, I don't know what Ryco means. To me, it looks like any ordinary tropical forest. Perhaps the palm trees are taller. Colored differently too, with their gray trunks, and darker green leaves edged in black. But, then, what is ordinary on Muraine?

"Is there another way to the shore?" queries Kent.

"Only if you want to fly over the forest," Zeekryn replies. "Or take a detour, and add an additional five days to the journey."

"It'll take five days, as it is," states Quall.

"Then what choice have we got?" queries Talok, urging his mount forward. "Not all our horse companions have wings."

Ryco sighs, but turns to tug his non-feathered horse onward. They enter the Forest Lake: The Metsundai.

Talok's next to enter. Then Zeekryn, sauntering in much like Ryco. Downward, we wander into the forest, steadily stepping and sliding our way down a steep slope. Partway in, it becomes obvious why it's called the Forest Lake. Water, at least four feet deep, covers much of the forest floor.

Taking in the sight ahead, I know the journey will be a steady one. No boats have we, to traverse this winding habitat. Only us and our horses.

Ryco and Zeekryn are chest-deep in water, before they mount their neins again. The group relaxes some, especially when birds chirp cheerfully overhead. They're undisturbed by us. More importantly, they don't seem to sense what worried Ryco. Surely, the creatures of the forest would know if something were amiss.

Below us, beaver- and otter-like creatures swim about in the water. Fish too. Fish of many shapes and patterns. Unconcerned with blending in, they brag of their flamboyant colors. Our horses startle, at the slippery creatures brushing up against their legs, and trot forward.

From above, light rays catch on water as it sprays down on us, glimmering in the way a refreshing mist would. After being out in the scorching sun of the desert, nothing could feel better. Instead of the mist dissipating, it collects on a majority of the palm trees' trunks of gray. I brush my hand along some. Most are akin to rubber, slick and resistant to water. Others are spongy, and retain impressions of my nails when I dig them in. Glancing again to the water below, I expect it to be murky from disturbance. Yet, it isn't. It's clear, flaunting long, bright plants and grass that have made their home on the forest floor.

A creature swims among the long grass underwater, nibbling at the flowers and such. Its stiff ears remind me of rabbits. But its longish body is likened to an otter. Yet, it's the color of sand, with green stripes running down the length of its body. I almost didn't spot it amid the grass, so well does it blend in. When we get too close, it uses its long back feet to push off from the forest floor. It propels away, paddling its four webbed feet wildly.

The water level deepens. Our mounts grimly begin the swim. It's slow going. But peaceful. The scents around us are as fresh as flowers and sweet as fruit.

Zeekryn slips his legs up out of the water, then turns around on his horse to lounge back. He wrings water from his robes, while asking, "What is it you hope to get from King Lemara of the Laykons, Talok, if you don't my asking?"

Talok replies, "Jasper said he's the oldest mortal on Muraine. Older than even the former Matriarch, Shena, would be now. He's hoping Lemara will have useful information on removing this Geldryn device."

"I don't see why he would," Zeekryn states. "Lemara has kept to himself, in the depths of the sea, for much of his life."

"That's not Jasper's claim," states Quall. "He took in a Sorsryn woman for his wife, centuries ago. Lemawr's mother, so Jasper said."

"Gyron's nephew, Lemawr?" Zeekryn asks, in surprise. "Is that how Lemawr has ties with the Laykons?"

"That appears to be the case," replies Warren.

"I hadn't any idea," says Zeekryn. "Well, you should know, then, that Lemawr's mother was surmised to be part Kyanite. My mother often talked of the Kyanite King, Guyheiz, and his numerous adopted children. Many Sorsryns, over the centuries, have thought Vayohl was one of his daughters, and that's why Lemawr was always so respected among the Onyx. He's a prince. Twice over. Thrice, if you account for when he was named the Onyx Prince. I'm unsure of whether that naming was before ReNovak's son, or after."

Gemma states, "Gyronawv talked about Setharyn dying by Vitiosus. Was it Zymarc who killed him?"

Zeekryn stops wringing out his robes. He looks to Gemma. "We don't think Zymarc had been born yet. No one's too sure how old Zymarc is. Many interested parties think he's not yet the age of Siveyra."

Warren's face takes on a serious expression. "Petition the Vardiyas he never reaches that age."

Zeekryn agrees, "It would be devastating for his enemies, wouldn't it, Warren?"

The forest quakes, then. Ripples spread out across the water's surface. It goes quiet again.

Hesitant, Eli asks, "Is that normal, Siveyra Zeekryn?"

Zeekryn glances about. He repositions himself, to be ready for his mount to run. "I'll take south," he says. "Ryco? Go north."

"I'll stay here at the front," states Quall.

The two head off, in opposite directions. Slowly, the sound of their neins wading in the water fades.

Something heavy, much heavier than a bird of prey, flutters overhead. It's a large blur of black, making its way over us.

Eli forms an ice spike, within his dominant grasp. Closer, he crowds to Gemma. Talok, as well, is protective of her, taking position at her other side.

There's a commotion farther ahead, in the direction Zeekryn took.

White flashes, and water splashes.

Thunder booms out, then red-fire hurls across our path.

Our horses screech and scatter. There's lots of shouting, and Quall is giving commands. But, in a panic, I don't catch any of it. As soon as my mount has found shallow waters, he bolts. It's all I can do to stay on, during the tumult of him galloping across soggy mounds, and slushy dips.

Howling echoes out, low and hoarse.

The black creature growls from somewhere above me, scaring my horse into rearing up. I'm tossed into the water. When I surface, spitting and sputtering, my ride is gone. Swallowing hard, I look to where the black creature is crouched down, watching me from his place in the tree canopy.

It has the body of a horse, and wings of a bat. It yawns, showing all its wolfish teeth. Its snout, too, is likened to a wolf. Then there's its catlike front paws gripping thick tree branches.

Still treading water, I start a dialogue with it. "I suppose you're going to eat me, now?"

It laughs, sounding metallic and hollow. "No, no," he says, in a deep voice. "But there *are* creatures in the water that might want a sample of you."

Easing up, he glides down to a little mound of soggy ground that's protruding out from the water. Like a proud dog, he sits upon that mound. Then he wraps his bushy tail round his back legs. "You had better swim out of the water," he says.

"So you can eat me?" I ask again.

"Boy!" He snorts. "If I wished to eat you, you'd be half gone already. Your friends too."

"What?" I tease, joining him on the mound. "You only like half? Which half? Upper or lower?"

The black creature eyes me curiously. "You know, I've never had a soul ask me that. But since you asked, I'd say the lower half. Then the upper half would still have a voice. Therefore, the ability to engage in interrogation. Or beg. Yes, they would likely beg for their legs back. Unless they are gifted like Greyvons. Then they could grow their own legs back . . . I think. Never ate Greyvon legs before." He tilts his head, seeming to envision it.

Suddenly, I have an idea of who he might be. Mekka's cousin. Part Von. Part EquiNein.

"Gifted Vons, like Mekka?" I ask.

He laughs his empty sound again, saying, "That cousin of mine? You've met him? Small world, eh? But who be you, boy? I know not your voice, nor face."

"Nebukahn?" I reply, in question.

"That'd be *my* name, boy." He snorts again. "I was asking you, for yours."

Toying with him, I state, "I'm bound not to say."

He squeals and stands, then stomps his front paws, as his bushy tail whips me in the face. "Not to say your name? No!" he shouts. "Of course you can say your name. You're just stingy, refusing to tell. Have you a bet with my cousin?"

"I've a bet with a Vitiosyn."

Nebukahn's beside himself, rushing off the mound and flying back to his spot up in the tree canopy. "You devil tyke! Made a deal with a Vitiosyn? And here I was, thinking to save a poor boy from the guiles of water creatures. And, listen, here be one come looking as a ghastly girl, to see the end of your Vitiosyn bet!"

Someone comes splashing and swimming toward me. It's Gemma, calling out, "Tyler! There you are. What are you doing?"

"Bets!" I proclaim, smiling up at Nebukahn.

He scowls down at Gemma.

She joins me on the mound, confused. "Bets with whom?"

I point up at Nebukahn.

His scowl deepens. "Selling me out to a Siren, are you?" he spews.

Gemma tears her wide-eyed gaze from Nebukahn, fixing her eyes on me. "What is that?" she whispers.

"He's Nebukahn," I whisper back. "Mekka's cousin."

Looking to Nebukahn again, I watch him as he starts to leave. "Where are you going, Nebukahn? Don't you want to meet one of my friends?" I ask, in good humor.

"Oh, you know that one, do you?" he queries.

I nod.

"So . . . she's not a ghastly water creature in disguise, then?" He's skeptical.

And I'm skeptical of him. At least, in how he appears. *He can't really look as odd as that, can he?* I wonder.

Gemma looks herself over. Her eyebrows draw together. "I don't look *that* bad, do I?"

She's soaked head to toe. Her black hair's stringy, sand clinging to the strands. Grass and flower petals dot the fabric of her coat. And she's a bit flushed from getting too much sunlight.

Shrugging, I reply, "Never looked better."

"Nebukahn, come down from that tree," demands Zeekryn, wading into view.

"I'm not listening to you, nasty master Zeekryn," says Nebukahn, huffing.

"That's hurtful, Neb." Zeekryn tears up a bit. "Nasty *and* master, said with the same breath."

"Are you crying?" queries Neb, his expression contorting. "You never cry. What has happened? Has someone died?"

Zeekryn's face goes blank, then he's saying, "No, Neb. No one's died. Just switched places, is all. It's me, you idiot. Zeekryn's back there, somewhere, in my body. Anyway, the twos-you must be from Paragon," says the Zeekryn-impersonator, approaching us.

Gemma's utterly confused, stammering, while no actual words issue forth.

I just shrug and stand up, then wade out into the water. I make for a large clearing, in the distance. Now wordless, Gemma follows.

"Say!" the impersonator shouts, tripping over his feet. "Where are you going? Aren't you going to introduce yourselves?"

"No," I reply. "I think I'm hallucinating. I think *you* are a hallucination. That thing back there too. It's probably the freakiest thing I've ever seen. I can't imagine that's how he really looks. Possibly, he's not even there."

"Hear that, Neb?" queries Zeekryn's impersonator, trying not to laugh. "He thinks we're hallucinations. Never been accused of that."

Gemma and I get to the large clearing of dry grass. A small, nearby waterfall fills a pond in the middle of it. I lean at the edge, and cup my hands to get a drink, utterly parched am I from Pariah's hot sun and the Metsundai's muggy air.

Nebukahn and the pretender cautiously follow, more curious than anything. When someone snaps their fingers, Zeekryn's impersonator collapses to the ground, unconscious. Nebukahn spooks, before coming back to sniff Zeekryn's hand.

Gemma fills her canteen. While capping it, she looks up in alarm. "Talok? Are you all right?"

I turn, to see Talok looking over his shoulder. Hearing Gemma, he startles.

"Do you know where the others are?" I ask him.

"No," he says, sauntering over to us. He flops down in a lazy sort of way, before inspecting his fingernails. "I have no idea where *they* could be."

Gemma suggests, "Should we go look for them, now that you're with us?"

"Why?" queries Talok, smiling wildly at Gemma. He fastens his hands together, behind his head.

"Because," she says, "Tyler thinks the forest is causing hallucinations. And I'd feel better having Warren with us, to ward off that sort of thing."

Talok bolts upright, first eyeing Nebukahn, then us. "My word! You mean that? Yes, a hideous hallucination, most definitely. It should go away in a bit."

Nebukahn rolls his eyes, then walks out of sight. But he's quickly rushing back, with someone chasing after him. Someone quite angry. Some blond-haired man, clad as a warrior in a white-and-black coat, screaming, "Brother! What is the matter with you?"

"I don't know, Zeekryn," Talok replies. "You tell me. You're so good at Mensa-div."

The man's arms cross. He demands to know, "Where's Talok? What have you done with him?"

The one looking like Talok points at Zeekryn lying in a heap, surrounded by the fullness of his robes.

"You put him in *my* body, Craesha?" the man fumes. "Well, trade places. And now!"

Talok snaps his fingers, then falls to his hands and knees, gasping.

Craesha, now in Zeekryn's body, slowly gets up, rubbing at his forehead. "Wow," he says, "how do you stand the weight of all these robes? No wonder you're so hot-tempered, big brother. I think I'll lighten your load for you." Craesha starts whipping off the robe layers.

Zeekryn, stuck in his younger brother's body, tries to stop him. The two end up wrestling each other to the ground.

Nebukahn lies down, and sighs heavily. "Jokryns! Can't ever have a pleasant brother reunion."

"What should we do?" queries Gemma.

"Help me up," says Talok, still on the ground.

I grab one of his arms; Gemma, the other. We help my cousin regain his feet.

"You all right?" I ask him.

"No!" He shakes his head, and rather violently. "I'm starving. Thirstier than I've ever been too."

Gemma hands him her canteen, which he empties. When finished, he seems sick. Trembling, he starts to hyperventilate.

The others emerge into the clearing—tired, dripping-wet, but relieved—as the two brothers are finishing up their wrestling reunion.

Ryco looks to Zeekryn, stating, "Told you something was wrong with the forest."

Zeekryn starts slipping his many robes back on his now-reclaimed body. "You might have said, Sylvadyn, that you suspected it was my kid brother and his pet horse."

"I am no one's pet, Zeekryn," says Nebukahn. "Once EquiNeins find their voice, they belong to no one."

"Shall we carry on?" queries Kent, interrupting. "We've still got a lot of daylight left."

Talok's eyes suddenly fill with hunger. "No. I can't. Not until I eat something I can keep down."

Siege suggests, "Let's set up a day camp, here. Cook a bit of food."

The rest of us agree, and start unpacking.

Musgrae and Eli are in charge of the food packs. Near to them, Talok lingers, fidgeting with the cloth that still conceals my father's coat beneath.

Musgrae hands Talok some bread, then continues his task of selecting food for dinner.

Talok scarfs it down, and then his complexion grows deathly pale.

The warrior-clad Craesha approaches, in concern. "Talok, whatever is wrong?"

"He can't keep food down," Gemma states.

Craesha queries, "Has that device got anything to do with it?"

She nods, before helping Kent unpack pans.

I add, "King Zymarc's apprentice put it on him."

"Was that the bet you were referring to?" queries Craesha. "Getting it off Talok."

"No," I reply. "It was a bet that I wouldn't become the next apprentice."

"My word!" Craesha grins at once. "You must be the cousin. Tyler Ravier. Now, what's this? He wants you as his apprentice?"

Nebukahn hisses, making his snout contort. "Greedy silt, that Zymarc."

Before I can add anything else, Eli lets out a scream from somewhere nearby.

My cousin has latched his teeth into Eli's neck. He pushes Eli up against a tree trunk, then restrains that Kirjan's flailing hands.

Musgrae clutches a bundle of food. He stands by unmoving, mouth agape in shock.

Ryco and Quall are there in an instant, prying Talok away from Eli. When Talok's teeth rip out a chunk of Eli's skin, blood goes everywhere. Kent tries to stop the bleeding. Gemma helps Kent however she can.

It takes several minutes to calm Talok down. His color starts to look better. But then he's coughing up the blood he just drank, and looking all the worse for it. He shivers and shakes and coughs some more. I help Siege prepare a bed of blankets, then watch my cousin drift off into a fitful sleep.

"Does anyone know what's happening to him?" I ask.

Craesha taps the device. "It's this. It's changing his physiology. If he's craving fresh blood, well, it's not something you're going to like."

"Deathasyn," says Zeekryn, under his breath. "He's turning into a Deathasyn. This blood-craving confirms it. Mother didn't want to say it, in case she was wrong."

Ryco states, "Consuming blood will kill him. He's of Vaegon descent."

"Yes, Ryco," Zeekryn agrees, "we know."

"No," Kent replies, "you don't understand. Vaegons cannot consume fresh blood, as Sorsryns can. It's like poison to us."

"Well, how do we stop him from biting one of us?" I ask.

"Find something to stave off his hunger," says Nebukahn.

"Easier said than done." Craesha paces back and forth, seeming lost in thought.

"What about meat that's not cooked all the way?" Gemma suggests.

"That possibly could work," Ryco replies.

Musgrae raises his hand, while voicing, "We didn't bring any meat."

Nebukahn groans. "Guess that means we're going hunting."

He and Craesha head off.

Zeekryn and Eli, meanwhile, work on catching fish near our little clearing.

After Craesha and Neb get back with several meat options, the rest of us help in preparing the food. We cut strips of animal flesh. Also do we light the fires, heat the pans, and tend to other such tasks. They vote on me, however, to be the one to wake him.

"If he jolts up, looking all crazy," Eli mutters, pressing on his bandaged neck, "run for it."

Gently, I shake Talok's shoulder.

Gemma stands by, holding a plate of the first pick. Fish. Three pieces. One raw, one somewhat, and the other one grilled.

Talok slowly sits up, groggy.

"Try this," I state.

Gemma offers him the plate with fish.

After a quick grimace, he takes a bite of each one and then knocks the plate away. "I'm going to be sick," he says, rushing off to spit it all up.

We make him try the rest. In the end, he vomits up every last bit, if he's even able to swallow it down, in the first place.

Nighttime now, it's getting cold.

"I don't know what to do," Quall whispers, taking a seat by the campfire.

Joining him, Ryco says, "He'll starve, if we can't figure out what will satisfy him even a little."

Zeekryn questions his brother, "Craesha, have you expelled your venom recently?"

"My venom?" queries Craesha. "What good will Metimoran venom do? It'll kill him faster than anything."

Zeekryn clarifies, "I don't mean to use your venom directly. Only, to make an antivenom. See if it can stave off his appetite." Zeekryn offers his brother a spherical glass, which has two holes at its top.

Craesha scowls. "Why, might I ask, do you carry one of these collectors around with you?"

"That's not important," says Zeekryn. "Just be quick in milking out every venom-drop of yours, you've got."

Snatching the glass from Zeekryn's grasp, Craesha leaves the group.

We're all silent and hopeful, waiting for him.

He ambles back, after a bit, now as pale as Talok. He hands his brother the glass containing a yellowish liquid.

Zeekryn sets up a small lap-table crammed with lots of little bottles. He begins the process for making antivenom.

To Talok, I glance, and spot Gemma sitting beside him. Gently, she rubs salve on his face, while he sleeps. I go join her.

"Want help?" I ask.

"Just sit with me," she replies.

When I do, she sets the salve jar down, and turns to me. She doesn't say anything, but I know she's scared. So am I.

What if it doesn't work? I wonder. *What then? He dies, or turns into a Deathasyn? Which fate is worse?*

Before anyone's ready, Zeekryn has finished the antivenom.

We wake Talok again.

Quall, not even telling him what it is, offers it to him. "Drink, Talok. And try not to worry. You'll be all right. We're here for you. Always, right here."

Talok forces a grin, weakly replying, "I know."

He drinks the antivenom. Slowly, at first. Then he gulps it down. Sighing contentedly, he lies back down, and drifts off to sleep.

"We'll know in a few hours," says Zeekryn.

We pass the time, listening to Craesha and Nebukahn tell of their adventures. Then Craesha begins playing a wood instrument softly. Colors emanate from the nearby plant life. Gemma curls up against me, hugging my arm, while watching the fire flare to the rhythm of Craesha's playing.

Three hours pass.

Still, my cousin sleeps.

18

A Summons

It's morning of the next day. We're packing everything up. Warren and Eli use spells to shrink things to smaller sizes; some things even small enough to fit in pouches and saddlebags.

Kent approaches where Gemma and I are re-saddling the horses. "Ryco wants you to wake him, Tyler. See if you can get him to eat more, before we head out."

"I don't mind, but why me?" I ask.

"Talok's more compliant with you," replies Kent. "If his temperament is changing, he's more likely to get upset over his guards telling him what to do than you. It can be against protocol for us, you understand?"

I give Kent's arm a squeeze. Then I fill a plate with remnants of this morning's breakfast, and amble toward Talok. Setting the plate down close to him, I gently shake him awake.

His eyes pop open. He fixates on the food. A piece of meat is snatched up by him, and devoured. Then another. All, until it's gone. Gradually, his color comes back. Kindness returns to his eyes.

"Better?" Gemma asks, sounding hopeful.

Talok grins. "I don't know what the lot of you did, but I feel like myself again. At least, for a little bit. Shall we be off?"

In a short time, we're urging our horses to brave wading through Metsundai's waters once again. They don't like it. But they go.

After the recent strain of everything, I'm not feeling much for talking. So, I take out one of my dad's journals—the jade-colored one, written in English. I've put it off long enough. Now that it's quiet, with plenty of time ahead, I might as well read it.

Hours pass. I'm only a sixth of the way through.

One day blends into the next.

A third of the way now . . .

The Metsundai is a chattering noise of birds and other creatures, during the day. At night, froglike sounds and low warbling echo around us.

We take turns finding where to stop for rest, and prepare dinner. Only one large meal do we eat, every day. After the meal's over—but before we sleep near the warmth of flames—we draw lots for who's to stoke the fire each evening, and all through the hours of darkness, into the next day, when we begin another very similar to what was before.

One night, Craesha's curled up on a blanket near me. He whispers, "Nebukahn thinks the singing is of Sirens. But I told him it couldn't be. They, with their guiles, are still asleep."

"They have a master, you know," Zeekryn adds, stoking the fire with a metal rod. "When that master enters the Metsundai, they will awaken, to bring forth chaos. So go the myths. Even being older than a new Siveyra, I've never had a Siren Sighting."

"Nor I," says Craesha. "And I don't wish to."

Zeekryn offers the venom glass to his brother.

In the dim firelight, I still manage to spot Craesha's glower.

"I don't wish for that, either," he says. "But if I must."

"Yes, Brother, you must." Zeekryn grins wryly. "Talok cannot keep food down, otherwise."

And so it goes. Each night, Craesha empties out his venom for Zeekryn to synthesize for Talok's consumption. Talok devours enough meat for two people. Gemma jokes that, even on her best day, she can't down that much food.

We're now on the fourth day. I'm two-thirds through the journal. Yet, I'm still no closer to knowing why he even left it for me. *It's nothing more, I* muse, *than an account of his life, during college. The years spent with my mom. Then life after me. How is any of it supposed to help me now?*

That's when I get to it, a section only a paragraph long.

It reads, *Entry: 233*

I went to have my watch repaired, today. Get it ready for Tyler, and everything. Saw my sister, on the way there. Bruce too. And . . . her. She's grown so much. Looks just like her mother. Oh, but the eyes. They caught me off guard. They're exactly like his. I wish, sometimes, that it could be different. That I didn't have to choose which one, well, you know. Which one must go, in the end: me or him? If I've a choice, it will be me. I do hope that Vak makes good on his promise. Then, at least Tyler will have someone to guide him. Still, I'm trying to outsmart fate. But will I succeed? Only time will tell. Or, rather, the phantom will. I still cannot find the truth of who, or what he is. Certainly, I know I must try. Try, or die.

The entry leaves me with so many questions. Who is this 'he' he writes of? And her? The possibilities are obscure. I decide that, the next time I see Aysivak, I'll ask him about it. He's mentioned in the entry, after all.

The fifth day's a blur. All the rest is ordinary in the journal's recounting of his daily life. I do love reading his voice. It's almost as good as listening to him. But not quite.

I finish the jade-journal on the sixth day, then put it away.

Talok asks, "Anything good?"

"All of it." I smile. "But nothing to help us now."

"Perhaps he was bound, in what he could write," Siege suggests.

"That's probably it," I agree.

"All hail everything right with the world," exclaims Eli, suddenly sounding set free. "We've made it to the end of this soggy water pit of trees."

Gemma taps her heels into her horse's sides. Her mount hastens forward. Eli starts a chase. Then Talok joins in, seeming more like himself each day.

Water splashes everywhere. We trot out of the Metsundai, and all its shade. The sunlight of Rentwaramein brightly shines down on us, and on the black sand speckled with golden flecks. The entire beach is like that, in appearance. And hot too. The horses quickly rush to the lapping shore waters, refusing to leave the coolness of it. We clamber off, and land in ankle-deep water.

"Quall," Eli says, scratching at his neck bandage. "There's no dock. Where's the dock? Why is there no dock?"

"Calm down, Skinny!" Warren booms. "I'm sure they've got something similar to a doorbell. Haven't they, Ryke?"

"They do." He says, taking off his coat. "It's called The Black Flame."

Zeekryn hisses out a breath. "The Black Flame? How's a Paragonian know that spell? Rather dark, even for you, isn't it?"

Craesha declares, "Brother, he's been apprenticed to Dezarin. Remember?"

"But Dezarin is an Emerald, not a Deathasyn," Zeekryn argues. "Why would he teach that dark magic to anyone?"

"You're jealous." Craesha snickers. "Someone actually knows a spell you know little of."

Interrupting, Ryco says, "I *was* hoping they would have something to call down to them. Perhaps all of you should go back to the forest edge. The Dragon Spirit can be rather threatening."

"Why not use a variation of Dragon Summon rather than The Flame?" queries Siege.

Kent replies, "Dragon Summon doesn't permeate water. Only carries it through the air."

All, except Ryco and Warren, head back to the forest edge. It takes some convincing of the horses to follow us. When Ryco speaks but three words in a deep, rumbling language, the stubborn beasts trot back to the trees. He then lets his coat fall to the ground behind him. Hands positioned at his sides, palms facing down, he does something, and the ground starts shuddering. Much sand bursts up a few feet, then drops down.

Sounds akin to drumming, beat from beneath.

Ryco speaks the word, "Invitas."

At its utterance, the sand stays hovering. It waits.

Performing various, artful hand-gestures, Ryco continues, speaking,

"Sasak-Concalos-Sadyn-el."

The hovering sand draws together. Like a storm, it races out over the dark ocean. It still has no form. Rather, it swirls round a black nucleus.

Ryco speaks the last word, slower, deeper, even demonically: "Sivondel." His hands go still.

The nucleus turns citrine-yellow.

The black sand separates from the flecks of gold.

Quickly, it forms a vast, astonishing dragon. His eyes are like gold, and his breath is akin to a consuming black-fire. If I thought Reign and his brother, Scepter, were large dragons, they are nothing to this one. They are as birds to dragons. Mere specks, in his shadow. And he is as a shadow of nightfall: distressing and dark.

Zeekryn whispers to his brother, "His name is—"

But Craesha cuts him off, with a mutter of, "Don't speak his name. He's about to get his voice and awareness. Trust me, Brother. You don't want him noticing us. Let Ryke and War keep his attention."

"Why *is* Warren out there?" I ask.

"In case things get out of hand," replies Quall, hunkering down. "Spirits don't know how to outsmart Blue Magic. But, from what I've heard of The Black Flame, he's quite resourceful."

"And cunning," Siege adds, while peering out from behind a tree to watch what unfolds.

"Ryco'el Dyn Pawv'Ragaen," growls the dragon, his mouth curving upward. He looks pleased, eyeing Ryco on his knees, with his head bowed. "I have missed you, Sylvadyn brood." He flaps his wings, and we can feel their wind all the way at the forest edge.

Rather than fighting its push and pull, Ryco sways with it.

Warren lies flattened, next to the discarded coat behind Ryco. The dragon has not noticed him.

"Why have you summoned me?" Sivondel growls as these words are said.

Ryco replies, "For a favor. A request. It isn't much. Merely to carry a message down to the Ruler of the Deep."

Sivondel flaps his wings slower, harder, then a crack of thunder booms out from them. "King Lemara of the Laykonians?" Sivondel's voice matches that thundering sound of his wings. "Why have you a wish for his presence, when you have mine this very moment? What can he give you that I cannot?"

"Answers," replies Ryco. "I know how you hate telling the truth."

"Did you discover that power?" growls Sivondel. "That power I told you would be yours?"

Hunching lower, Ryco deepens his bow to Sivondel. "Yes," he says.

Softly, Sivondel rumbles, "And was it all I said it would be? Vitiosyn Slayer. Summoner of The Black Flame. Parasogyn, born of a dragon's mistress."

Standing up, Ryco shouts, "It was more! Now, will you give me my request? Or must I swim down to the depths, and deliver it myself?"

Sivondel laughs, and it shakes the waters; the ground and trees tremble too.

"I hold the keys to death," rumbles Sivondel. "Yet you merely wish for me to be a messenger?"

"What do you mean, you carry the keys?" queries Ryco.

"Oh? Don't you know?" Sivondel asks, in return. "No matter! I thought you might have come to ask that I bring LanSoren back to life. But if a message is all you ask of me, consider it done. What do you wish for me to say?"

Ryco starts walking away from the shoreline, but turns back suddenly. "How could you bring him back? That breaks too many Laws of Magic, Sivondel. Surely, not even you are that powerful."

"But I am, Parasogyn." Sivondel's voice hums. "One life, every thousand years, is mine to return to the land of the living. And the laws you speak of? Why . . . haven't you guessed it yet? I *am* one of those laws. Death. How else could I hold its keys? She gives. And I take away. But, sometimes, *I* can give back."

Ryco challenges him, asking, "Are you offering to bring him back?"

I pick that moment to Mensa-div to Ryco, *"Ask how he died, Ryco. Please!*

I need to know."

Ryco flinches, then he asks, "Or tell me this, Sivondel. *How* did he die?"

"I know not," replies Sivondel, glancing to the forest.

I swallow hard, and hope with everything that he didn't hear me. That he doesn't see me. Terror crawls over me, like cobwebs touching my skin in the dark. For but a moment, my vision darkens. I see nothing. When it returns, I almost collapse on the ground.

"But you said you hold the keys of death," Ryco states. "Yet you do not know how that death is brought about, in the very land you tend?"

"Undoubtedly, I do," replies Sivondel, "when *that* mortal blow is dealt on Muraine. *His* mortal blow, however, was not given on this world. He merely died here. Then there's the matter of his bones. They were not buried here either. I have searched. But nowhere did I find."

Ryco questions, "Then how could you hope to bring him back?"

"That is my dilemma," Sivondel says. "I hope. And I can try. Yet, there is no guarantee that I am able to summon him to life, once more. To forget death, brought about on another world. And walk from my shadows into the light. Her light. It seems impossible. Yet for you, Ryco of Paragon, I would but try."

"Who is this 'her' you talk of?" Ryco asks.

"Stag of the Forest. Tree Stag," rumbles Sivondel. "You know her *quite* well. All tamers do. Eight hearts. Six beating. One sleeping. One wallowing in death."

"My word," Kent says, under his breath. "He means the Arkivaras."

Sivondel continues, explaining, "She is life. I am death. Yet we are both tied to the forest. Aeowneis-teras-metsas-sadora-vyn-kryn-dei-Sivondel. Forever, we are having to share. She gets memories of lives lived. I get their flesh and bones. Their life essence. I am free to roam. But she is tied to the land. Chained to her children. Their dyns, neins, and other creatures, also."

Ryco asks, "Why are telling me this, Sivondel?"

"Because you said I hate telling the truth," he grumbles. "But there is a matter of which I must tell you. You were not likely to believe me, if

I hadn't confirmed something you've long suspected in your heart to be true."

"Then tell me," says Ryco. "The sooner you do, the sooner you can send down the message."

Sivondel lowers himself into the ocean waters, letting his great big wings rest upon the surface. He bends his enormously long neck down, bringing his head nearer to Ryco. Appearing almost saddened, he growls out, "Zymarc of Vosh-Perida summoned me late last year. He hurt me. Tried to bend me to his will. It should not be done, to a spirit. To hurt it. *I* should be incapable of being harmed. But his power grows. And it hurts even us. The Laws of Magic. He means to wield them. To wield me. Aeowneis. The other elements. All of it. To destroy the order of things."

"What did he want from you?" queries Ryco.

"I cannot say. But you must know. He is smarter than Deezalo ever was. You should be afraid."

"I am a Sylvadyn," Ryco states. "It's not in my nature to be afraid."

"For imperials, no. But you're only one-quarter." Sivondel's mouth curves upward again. "One-quarter fearless. One-quarter arrogance. The other half afraid."

"Sounds balanced to me," Ryco says. "Now, tell that King Lemara, he has an important visitor. King Talok of Paragon. We would be *very* disappointed, if he refuses to see us. A party of thirteen. And, no, you may *not* know their names."

Sivondel thunders out a raging fit, as he rises up out of the water, angrily flapping his wings. The beach is pelted with water droplets. Ryco then Warren, still on the ground, get drenched from it.

With a nod of satisfaction, Sivondel quickly dives down below.

Waves start to crash toward the shore. Ryco snatches up his coat, as he and Warren rush for the forest, barely getting there before the water gets a chance to sweep them away.

Gradually, the waters recede.

"What now?" Eli asks, when the ocean settles.

"We wait," Warren replies.

Zeekryn steps toward the two, asking, "I am curious, Ryco, did Dezarin tell you The Black Flame's name?"

Still catching his breath, Ryco shakes his head.

"Then how did you come to learn it?" queries Zeekryn.

"I'll keep my secrets, Zeekryn, if you don't mind," replies Ryco. "Just as I know you'll keep most of yours."

Zeekryn turns to his brother. "How did you come to learn the name, Craesha?"

"By watching Ryco, the last time he summoned The Flame."

Talok's suddenly asking, "What reason, Ryco, did you have to summon him the last time?"

By the wild look in Ryco's eyes, I know he doesn't want to answer. But, for Talok, he does anyway. "It had to do with my mother, when she was dying. I didn't want her going to the usual place of death: The Kievas. The Flame told me of another place, and how to ensure she got there."

"Did it work?" queries Siege quietly. "Was she able to go to the other place?"

"I don't know for certain," says Ryco. "But I suspect that she did, since Grover couldn't collect a single memory of hers, in the days after her passing."

When the beach begins to quake, we look to the ocean.

Sivondel bursts out of the water, rumbling, "Your message has been delivered, Ryco of Paragon. Be cautious now, in how much you summon death. Three times in the span of one year, and your life is forfeit. You'd do well to remember that."

"All this truth," Ryco shouts, stepping out of the forest's shade, "in a single day? You must really be scared of that Zymarc."

Sivondel hisses, then roars, flying up, before throwing himself down on the beach. He returns to black sand. His face and golden eyes are the last to shift back to swirling grains of sand. He is gone.

Pressing on his neck's bandage, Eli winces. "Quall? I think my wound reopened."

Musgrae elbows Eli in the side. "You mean Talok's hickey?"

Eli scowls at Musgrae. He's about to give his retort.

But someone is running along the beach, headed toward us. A four-legged something.

Seeing it too, Eli shrieks. "Who's that? Can't they just go away?"

"It's Jasper," says Musgrae. "I can smell him from here. Something's wrong."

Talok rushes out to meet him. "Alpha Jasper, is everything all right?"

Jasper hacks and pants, finally managing to get out, "Something's been following us, all the way from Paragon. Droediin told me of its odd trail, spotted along the outskirts of Pariah and even farther away. I convinced him and Mekka to accompany me, to the northern section of the Metsundai. See if it followed you in, at a distance. Whatever it is, we caught its trail. Lost it last night, though. Droediin and Mekka are still in there, searching for it. But I had to find you. Make sure it didn't . . . well. Here you are, unharmed."

"Mostly," mutters Eli, even as blood soaks through his bandage.

Quall sighs. "Come here, Eli."

While he works on healing the Kirjan, we fill Jasper in on what's happened. Or, rather, Gemma and Musgrae do.

At the end, Jasper transitions into his human form. He scratches at his brow. "The Flame must've been coerced by Zymarc, to do something."

"My thoughts, exactly," Ryco agrees.

"But what?" Zeekryn asks. "What could he hope to gain, by betraying one of The Laws of Magic?"

A grin starts to form on Jasper's face. But then he scoffs, covering it up. "To learn a magical class, previously a mystery to him."

"Metimoran Magic?" I ask, actually impressed at Zymarc's resourcefulness.

Zeekryn takes in a giant breath. "Ah, that makes sense. Smart, on his part."

"But bad for us," Nebukahn says. "Nice to be seeing you, Alpha Jasper. It's been a long while. Wish to take my place, with the group hoping to go below? I don't much want to be taken down there. Afraid of depths and drowning, you understand?"

"And what will you be doing?" queries Jasper.

Neb declares, "Seeking my cousin in the forest, of course! Possibly scaring him out of his wits; his howl too."

"Just don't go killing each other," says Jasper. "Nor maim one another. Promise?"

"Hoof silt!" Neb exclaims, stomping his front paw. "I was hoping to eat his legs. See if he could, indeed, grow them back using Crae-Shand Magic. You take the fun out of it all, Alpha Jasper."

Amused, Jasper replies, "I'd have a lower Von population if I didn't, at times, draw the line. If you must know, Nebukahn, Vons *can* regrow limbs severed, so long as they're in two-legged form when it happens. If they are completely as themselves, once something's severed it's gone indefinitely. Will that satisfy your curiosity?"

"Hardly," says Neb, getting excited on his feet. "The ideas are just starting. But don't you worry a gray hair off your head, Alpha. I'll draw out whatever madness may be in there, before testing my ideas on Mek."

Jasper's amusement ceases. He's about to reprimand Neb. But Neb is already running off into the forest.

Jasper rubs his forehead, and his mouth draws into a tight line. "I had forgotten why I never miss Neb's visits to Vondurheil," he says. "But I remember now. Chaos, and the bloody hunts."

Zeekryn turns to his brother. "Well, aren't you going to go restrain your pet, Brother?"

"He's not my pet," Craesha spews. Then his eyes soften to thoughtfulness. "But, perhaps, we should assist in the hunt."

"That is your sort of thing," replies Zeekryn. "I've put in my time, as an adventurer and warrior. I'd prefer to get back to my scholar duties."

"It would please Mother," Craesha says. "And I *won't* tell her about some of the indiscretions which you engage in, with those Metimoran twins, whenever we go to honor Father's former status as King of the Metimoras."

"What do you mean *those* twins?" queries Zeekryn. "All pure Metimorans have twins."

"I'm aware," says Craesha. "But I meant those twins Queen Iissa, by proxy of Paydinn, forbade you to trifle with. You remember—"

"Yes, I remember!" Zeekryn shouts, tensing his hands briefly. "We're going." Addressing Jasper, Zeekryn says, "If we do find the emissary, we'll detain whomever it is. Be back on this beach, waiting for all of you, if you should be allowed to go down. We'll tend the horses too."

The two brothers mount the biggest neins. Herding the other horses, they depart while the rest of us approach the ocean shores again. We've almost made it there, when something moans from deep within the waters. It's metallic in sound. Not like a machine, but not quite like a whale's song either.

A wave rises just off the shore, and slams onto the beach.

We all get drenched.

Gemma smirks at Eli as he scowls out at the ocean, then to his coat that's soaked all the way through. "Look," she says, "no Ben to dry, or clean your stuff."

Eli complains, "I've had enough swimming, to last a whole year in Kirja. Quall, can't I stay on the beach?"

"Absolutely not!" Quall exclaims. "You'd be a target for whatever evil may be lurking in Metsundai."

A ways off, something breaks the ocean surface. It swims toward us. The closer it gets, the more nervous I am. For a fleeting moment, I feel those cobwebs brushing at my skin. I dread what is coming.

19

Ruler of the Deep

The moving object's nearer to us now. Clearly, it's a dragon of sorts. Nowhere near as spiked and jagged is it, compared to a BlacKaidyn. Nor as filled-out as one. Long and slender, it weaves like a snake in uncut grass. But rather than grass for its ground, it rides atop the water. Instead of wings that fan out far, they're shorter and fin-like, similar in appearance to black sails on a junk ship all folded up. Its dark scales are blue and teal, until catching sunlight of Rentwaramein. That's when it glistens like golden water. While still quite a ways away, it screeches an ear-splitting cry.

Siege drops to his knees on the beach, telling us, "He demands submission."

We follow Siege's lead and sink to our knees.

Siege further instructs, "Don't look at him, until he addresses one of us."

"You hath summoned," says the dragon gently. "And he hath answered, sending me. Dae'loog Dauger. Swim out, and climb onto my back. I will take the thirteen down to the docking station. From there, you'll be taken farther. To be sure, shown the city of Deivahl; home of Laepurians' Three."

"Are both of you good swimmers?" queries Ryco, glancing at Gemma, then me.

We nod, but Gemma says, "Tyler was on the school swim team, one year. Times weren't terrible either."

I add, "Jed practically made me join, since Jaxson wanted no part of it. Shouldn't have a problem swimming out there. It's not that far."

Quall and Ryco take the lead in swimming out. Their style is much different from what I'm used to seeing. Less strokes, but powerful enough that each propels them farther forward than I expect.

Gemma and I are about to go.

But Kent steps in front of us. "Hold a moment. They need to be sure it's not any sort of trap. We don't know these Laykonians well enough to trust them wholeheartedly."

Once Quall and Ryco reach the dragon's back, they signal for the rest of us to come.

Eli, even with his neck injury, is the first there, helping me out of the water.

Once we're atop the dragon's back, we rise and fall with each breath of his.

Then he takes in a giant breath, warning us, "Hold tight to any of my fins. We're going down a ways. Take a breath to last two hundred ticks."

"That's a tad over three minutes," says Siege.

"Can you hold your breath that long?" queries Kent, while securing any loosened straps or cords holding his gear on.

"Don't be concerned of that," states Warren, coming over to us. "I'll give them a jolt of air, if they need it."

"You can practice magic, while submerged in water?" queries Eli suspiciously. "Since when?"

"Since we were stuck in Metsundai for days," Warren defends. "That was plenty of time for practicing. Now, let's not keep a king waiting any longer."

Dae'loog Dauger perks his fin-like ears up, and looks to the forest. All of a sudden, he dives down. We scramble to find handholds. I get hold of a long, thin fin. The others manage to find their own, as well. But Gemma has the worst time of it, tugged back by the force. Her hands lash out, trying to grab hold of anything. I reach for her, grasping a fistful of her coat. But she slips away. The others miss her entirely. Then Jasper lets go, to fetch Gemma.

I'm a confident swimmer, under normal circumstances. But I panic at the thought of losing my grip. I can barely keep hold of the fin. And the water is getting colder the deeper Dae'loog Dauger takes us.

I look back, and hope Jasper has a hold of Gemma. He does. But she's gone limp. Warren's able to pull Jasper back, with some magic shot from his hand.

Seemingly an eternity later, we're spilling through a barrier. We land on a grassy platform.

Bent down on his knees, Jasper lets go of Gemma. Quall rushes to them. Right as I get to Gemma's side, she's sitting up on her own, and coughing. She spews up water.

"What has happened?" queries a girl, standing to the side of the platform, and looking up at us. "Dae'loog," she continues, "have you frightened them? That was not my father's intention."

"Ever so sorry, Princess Krina," says Dauger. "Something was rustling in the forest. I thought it best, to be out of sight. And fast."

The young girl turns her disapproving gaze, from Dauger to me. Though she has two eyes, two arms, two legs, one head, that's where all resemblance to the Paragonians ends.

I hold my hand out for an introduction. "I'm Tyler Ravier. Dauger said you're Krina?"

She accepts my handshake. Then, rather than gently shaking my hand, she smiles, and yanks me off the platform. I'm still sopping wet; as such, I practically splat on the stone floor. I look up at her, as she's cutely clasping her six-fingered hands in front of herself: each hand having four fingers, two thumbs, and webbing between them all.

"It's Princess Krina, to you, outsider," she says, tilting her head. Her hair colored of brown, turquoise, and navy falls across part of her pale face. Secretly, I wish it would cover the entirety of her face, as she's saying, "At least until you are no longer considered a guest. I'll expect your respect. Understood?"

I stand up, resisting the urge to smother Gemma if she doesn't quit her quiet sniggering. "Yes, Princess Krina," I reply, only too kindly. "I'm pretty sure we all understood that."

Her dark-blue eyes brighten. "Wonderful! Now, which of you is King Talok? I am most anxious to meet him."

Talok steps down first, bowing at the waist. "That would be me."

Krina states, "You, and only you, may call me Krina. Forgive my utterance, but you appear to be very young."

"As do you," states Talok, pulling his cloak tighter round himself.

"Thirteen, if it matters," she says, while turning on her heel and gracefully approaching what appears to be a domed, glass wall holding back the weight of water.

"Sixteen, if that matters." Talok follows her.

Smiling inside, I wonder, *We don't talk much about age? What is this, then?*

It takes great effort to resist Mensa-divving with Talok, telling him that he's not to give this girl any ideas. I don't wish for her to come to Paragon, in the coming years.

Then I think, *Why am I so offended? Maybe it has to do with Caleiso. Who knows?*

I push the feelings of ill-will away, as Krina places her hands upon the wall, and something launches down deeper into the ocean.

She asks Talok, "Your kingship isn't in full authority, then?"

"Not quite," he replies. "Two more years. If I survive that long."

"Who is your authority, until then?" she asks, walking back toward the platform.

"They are." Talok points to his guards. "Alpha Jasper, my ally, is a fearsome authority all on his own, though."

Jasper stands to his full height, acknowledging the princess with a single glance.

Krina's mouth parts, as soon as she's made eye contact with him. She bows her head respectfully. "The Flame did not say such a one was waiting. We must be on our way. My father will be quite pleased to see you."

To our left is a black marble trench, beginning to fill with water. A small ship is drawn out from underneath the platform, which we landed on. It's like a little hill, hiding many little ships. We manage to fit on one, yet with little room to spare.

Dauger passes through the glass-like barrier of the docking station. And, as would a guardian, swims out near the tunnel of space Krina created. The ship lurches forward into that tunnel, and we're off.

Talok cringes with every bump and shift, during our forward trajectory. Meanwhile, I enjoy the damp coolness of air within the tunnel. Krina stands at the ship's bow, leaning her arms atop the edge. Her focus is aimed frontward.

Where we're at now, no daylight from above can be seen. It's the blue and yellow lights, scattered about, which illuminate our surroundings beyond the tunnel. Tall, rounded structures of metal—fashioned of navy, teal, and white—come into view. Massive bay windows let us see in, and observe the Laykonians traveling within their city of Deivahl. Their skins have fish scales dotting some areas of their bodies; mostly their foreheads, forearms, hands, and feet. Many wear wispy clothing tinted of blues and teals and whites. And, though some splash about in fountains, their clothes never appear to be wet. Their skin scales, of shades unique to them, shimmer like glitter reflecting in daylight.

Connecting the structures together are many tunnels similar to the one we're presently in. The city exudes such peacefulness. Part of me hates the possibility that we're about to ruin it, by coming here to search for Lemawr, or some other journal translator, while also asking them to help us remove a device they may know nothing about.

What could go wrong? I wonder. *Everything? Nothing? Am I overreacting?*

My uneasiness tells me I'm not. I blame it on being far from home, on two accounts: Earth, literally worlds away, and no nearby Paragon, for a familiar retreat.

Dauger and other Water Dragons swim effortlessly around the tops of the buildings, as we approach an especially large, black platform. An eight-point star, outlined in white, is patterned in the way of a compass rose. At its center, it's painted with swirling blues and teals.

The ship slows, after passing through the filmy barrier ahead. It halts at a dock much larger than the one we left. It's as open as a cathedral made of domed glass walls and curved brass beams. Other ships about, separate in their own marble trenches, are being unloaded of plants, tree saplings, crates of fish, and such.

"It's the time of harvest," says Krina, to Talok, as she steps down onto a colored-glass walkway.

"Apologies for the interruption," says Quall. "If we weren't trying to avert a crisis, we wouldn't have called."

Krina's face goes blank. "The Flame delivering a message is a bit more than an interruption," she states. "But since you are in crisis, it's forgivable. However, Dae'loog Dauger was, well . . . perhaps I shouldn't say."

A Laykonian woman approaches, laden with weapons, and dressed in armor pieces, a deep teal tunic beneath for modesty. Nothing else. "So this is why you're skipping your daily lessons, Princess Krina? To be our new greeter to foreigners?"

Krina goes up on her toes, the four toes of each foot, then lowers herself to her normal height. "I got permission, Broena, from my father," she defends.

"I'll expect double lessons tomorrow, nonetheless." Broena's expression makes one thing clear: protesting won't be tolerated.

"Why not triple lessons?" Krina spews. "Then I could do fun things, the following day."

Broena's posture stiffens. "That'd be fine by me, Princess. Now, aren't you going to take our lovely, but worn-out guests to the allotted place?"

Krina looks about the room, in a panicked sort of way. "Allotted place? Um, I thought Father was supposed to meet guests at the docks?"

"Typically." Broena nods, struggling not to smile. "But he's helping to unload the wares. He'll be along, soon. Go on, now. Our guests must be thirsty, with all this inaccessible water floating about, tempting them to burst through the barrier to get in a gulp or two."

Krina mumbles, "I don't know where it is."

"Oh, don't you?" queries Broena sardonically. "Well, you might've, if you'd been paying mind to your lessons each and every time. That lesson was given, at the beginning of this year."

Krina glares. "You expect me to remember something I heard once, months ago?"

Broena scoffs. "If you had indeed heard it, yes, I would. But you didn't hear it, because you gave *distractions* an audience."

Eli mutters to Gemma, standing beside him, "That's something Zepharre would say."

Gemma coughs, barely stifling her laugh in time.

Krina and Broena continue their dialogue, right as I catch sight of a tall, male Laykonian standing about fifteen feet away. He has hold of a limp fish that's near three feet long. He wears a sleeveless, floor-length tunic made seemingly of Dauger's dragon skin. His tunic, which is slit on both sides up to the hip, reveals his long legs concealed by pants resembling my own diving armor. Worn by him, however, the pants look to be a part of his skin, as they do blend with the dark-turquoise scales upon his bare neck, face, arms, and feet.

He catches sight of me observing him, and I look down, not knowing how to show respect to this one, who must be the Ruler of the Deep. After the blunder with Krina, I don't want to give further offense.

Silently, he approaches. Only I've seen him, until he's at Broena's side, softly asking, "What is the matter?"

She startles, trying to gather words for a reply.

Krina's face goes colorless. She refuses to answer, as well.

He continues, saying, "I've been unloading wares, and have watched you waiting at the docks for several minutes. Why haven't you taken our guests to the banquet room, for rest and refreshments, Krina? They must be tired. And there were supposed to be thirteen. Why are there only eleven?"

"They had somewhere else to be," replies Talok. "As for waiting, it's our doing. We refused to leave the docks, until greeted by King Lemara, himself. Would that be you, keen Laykonian?"

The Laykonian's mouth parts. He's about to reply.

Interrupting is Krina, saying, "Yes, your kingship, Talok. This is my father: King Lemara."

"An honor," says Lemara, tilting his head down, then slowly closing his mouth. His breathing is slower than most, as if he's meditating. His aqua-colored eyes change focus from the different faces calmly. Even his blinking appears deliberate. Everything he does is measured and calm. But then he sees Jasper, and his breathing stops altogether. "Is this a formal meeting, Greyvon Alpha," he asks, "or an informal reunion of old friends?"

Talok turns around. "Jasper! You are friends with King Lemara? Why ever didn't you say?"

"Because, as you will recall," Jasper defends, "I hadn't planned on coming with you. But, to answer your question, Lemara, I would prefer informality."

"As would the rest of us," states Quall. "We're quite drained."

Talok clarifies, "Meaning: we'd rather not have to worry over saying the wrong thing and offending you."

"Very good," says Lemara. "Informality it is."

A much smaller Laykonian male comes by, carrying a crate half-filled with fish. He offers it to Lemara, saying, "I found a crate with some room for that one, Highness." He grins at his leader.

But Lemara doesn't grin back. Instead, he lifts his head high. With his longish neck stiffened, he appears stoic and stubborn. He tightens his grip on the fish's tail.

The younger Laykonian frowns, squirming on his feet and looking sheepish. "Actually, um, perhaps that one *is* too big for this crate. Shall I find Brinkorr, and have 'im prepare dinner for the guests?"

"Unnecessary," says Lemara, "as he's right over yonder." He points to someone standing at the start of a connecting tunnel.

He's garbed much like Broena, but with more weapons on, and less clothing.

Turning pale in the face, the younger Laykonian simply nods at Krina, then practically runs away, joining up with several others carrying crates off to various parts of the city.

Broena mutters, "Stop scaring the lads away from Krina, Highness. She may well end up alone forever, otherwise."

Brinkorr starts tapping his foot impatiently. Even from the distance of thirty feet or so, I'm able to see him sighing every couple of minutes.

"Unlikely," says Lemara. "Besides, they can wait two years, while she finishes her necessary training."

Several in the group glance at Musgrae, but it's Warren, who whispers, "Too bad you couldn't have waited, ay, Grae?"

Musgrae just lifts his shoulders, looking unashamed.

When Brinkorr meets my gaze, he stands up straighter, and Mensa-divs, *"Is he ever coming to introduce those The Flame demanded that we welcome, or what?"*

I div back, *"He and Broena are discussing Krina's future partner possibilities, and the training she still needs. There was something about skipped lessons too."*

"For fate's sake!" Brinkorr scoffs loudly, rattling my head a bit. *"They'll be going on forever about that. No worries! I'll break 'em up."*

Brinkorr snaps his fingers, and the limp fish in Lemara's grasp comes to life while he's mid-conversation with Broena.

It flails, smacking against Lemara's legs several times.

Lemara freaks out. He lets go of the fish, watching it flop and flail to being several feet away. He then scowls at Brinkorr. "You could've asked me to share it with you, Brink, rather than being dramatic, demanding attention."

"It's more fun this way!" Brinkorr shouts, across the distance.

Lemara strides over to the fish, picking it up by the tail again. He lifts it up, saying to Brink, "How shall we fix this, for our dinner?"

Before Lemara has finished his question, Dauger swims up close to the wall, and eyeballs the fish. He thrusts his head through the barrier. Water's flung all over, as Dauger snaps hold of the fish, with his front teeth. He pulls hard.

Lemara yells out, "Dauger! What are you doing? This is my dinner."

Dauger yanks harder, retreating back into the water. Lemara is dragged along, clutching the fish by the tail, before he slams against the barrier wall. The fish is dislodged of its spine and tail. And the flesh of it finds its home in Dauger's snapping jaws.

Lemara rubs where his forehead got smacked, while his other hand holds that dislodged fish tail, spine still attached. Blood has splattered on the wall, on the floor, and all over Lemara.

Pointing cautiously, Broena says to him, "The younger dyns love that part."

"Which part?" queries Lemara, back to being his calculated self. "Dauger eating my prized fish? Or me, hitting the wall, whilst losing that fish?"

"The spine and tail," says Broena. "You should, you know . . . throw it to them."

Lemara glances to the wall. Just beyond it, several smaller Water Dragons are gathered, swimming in place. Their eyes are wide, and their long tails sway. They look ready.

Lemara flings the fish remains out, and the young dyns go wild, making the nearby water turn frothy.

He strides back calmly.

Broena asks, "Would you like for me to catch you another one of that size, Highness?"

"That would be impossible," Lemara states. "There's only one of those, every harvest time. Therefore, merely two opportunities each year, to catch one. Then, even if that occurs, there's an unlikely chance whoever finds that fish will be sharing it with me."

"I would share it with you, Father," says Krina, cheerfully rocking up and down on her toes again.

"Yes, I believe you would, Daughter Krina, so you could get out of your daily lessons for an entire week."

Frowning, Krina ceases her rocking up and down.

"Come," says Lemara, sounding resigned. "The banquet room is this way." He starts heading for the tunnel where Brink was standing, but is now absent from.

Warren follows first, declaring, "I can get that fish back for ya, King Lemara. May take me a minute, but I can do it."

Lemara snaps his attention on Warren. "Oh?" he asks, skeptical. "And how? Never mind the words. If you are able, then by all means, do. The gesture won't go unrewarded."

Warren strides to where the fish blood still stains the floor.

Lemara asks Talok, "How can he know Time Magic, when he is not a speck of Metimoran? Who is he? Rather, *what* is he?"

"Warren of Veldar. Part Kyanite," says Ryco. "And it's Blue Magic he intends to use, for bringing your fish back."

"Blue Magic?" queries Lemara, drenching himself with water seeping from his hands. He clears away the fish guts that have splattered on him. "Haven't ever seen that practiced. My late wife, Vayohl, never used it here; rarely discussed it, either. This should be most interesting to bear witness to."

Quickly, Warren creates a crackling distortion that blurs his nearby surroundings together. After drawing two circular symbols, he moves his right hand counter-clockwise. Time reverts within the distortion. It's hard to tell exactly what happens. But, at the end, Warren is holding the flailing fish. By the time he makes the distortion dissipate, and comes back to stand in front of Lemara, the fish is still.

"Here ya go," says Warren, handing Lemara the fish. "No promises it'll taste the same, since it's essentially a clone of the one your dragon ate. But it should still make a fine entrée."

"I don't know how you'd be in other foreigners' cities," says Lemara, "but you seem rather cultured to me, Warren of Veldar. You may come and go from Deivahl, as you please. And, yet, that reward seems inadequate, given the current circumstances between Paragon and the Vitiosyns. How does a trinket taken from my armory sound, as payment for your efforts?"

"Excessive," replies Warren. "But I'll accept, so long as you take a look at that Geldryn *trinket*." He motions to the Geldryn bangle clamped on Talok's wrist.

I state, "It's one reason we're here."

"And the other reason?" queries Lemara, glancing at the bangle.

Gemma replies, "To translate his dad's journals, or hoping that you'll tell us whatever you can about them."

Lemara nods, in understanding. "Then come this way. These sorts of matters are best discussed elsewhere, in quarters more private."

"Aren't you going to ask who his dad is?" queries Gemma, as all of us follow Lemara into the long, glass tunnel.

"There's no need," he replies. "He is the Son of LanSoren. Fourteen years old. Not from the world of Muraine, even though he is cousin to the current Paragonian King. Did I miss anything, Miss Galloway?"

In shock, Eli asks, "How'd you know all that?"

"One word," says Kent, excitement in his voice. "Vardiyas. They are from this part of the world, no? Some later taken to the Pools of Vosh-Perida?"

Lemara starts to answer, then slowly closes his mouth. "Possibly, I shouldn't say," he replies, after we're partway down the tunnel. He commands, "Broena, take Warren to my armory. Answer any questions he has, on the use for each object."

Warren tags Musgrae on the arm, who then starts to follow. But Quall says, "Hold up, you two. Siege, go with them, report any inappropriate happenings or misconduct."

"What am I?" Siege complains. "A child watcher? Make Ryco go, if you're so worried over it."

"Or have them take Gemma," Ryco says. "I know for a fact that both of you will behave well enough—"

Interrupting, Gemma states, "No way am I missing journal translating. Or possibly seeing that wretched thing taken off Talok. Go on, Mooz. Don't have too much fun with Warren and Siege."

Musgrae silently chuckles, then follows the other three down a narrower tunnel.

"Father," says Krina, "may I—"

"No," replies Lemara, before she's finished. "And don't argue with me."

I take the lull in conversation as my chance to hurry things along. "King Lemara?" I ask. "Siveyra Gyronawv told us about his nephew, Lemawr, and that he'd be a good candidate for translating ancient Sorsrynian. With him being a sort of adopted son to you, would he happen to be here in Deivahl? We might need him, if you're unable to translate the journals. One, in particular."

Lemara shortens his long stride, replying, "I've no idea where Krina's half-brother may be. Nor have I a clue as to what happened to his mother, Vayohl. Ten years, she's been missing without a trace. I sent off correspondence to Lemawr, telling him of it. Never did get a response."

Up ahead is Brinkorr, talking with a group of young Laykonians. Most of them are males. When they see Lemara and us, they scatter. Only Brink remains.

"Stop scaring off all my new students, Highness," says Brink.

"Then teach them to be fearless," states Lemara.

Brink scoffs, then he sees the fish Lemara's holding. "How'd you get that back from Dauger? And in perfect condition too?"

"Not telling," says Lemara. "But take it. Cook it to perfection. Eat one-quarter of it. Let me know how it is. We'll be in the Driv-vell Den, where you shall deliver my dinner, and whatever our guests would like to have."

Brink takes the fish. "Yes, Highness. Whatever pleases you, it shall be done."

"Before you go," says Lemara, stopping him, "would you have ideas on where my 'sort of' adopted son might be?"

"Prince, twice over, Lemawr?" queries Brink, as his face briefly scrunches up. "He completed his Siveyra Journey, some decades ago. 'Twas magnificent too. He parted a portion of the ocean, so that he could draw out an Elemental Circle on the ocean floor. Said it would create the perfect conditions for an unbreakable weapon enchantment, or some such thing."

Lemara continues up the tunnel. "Where was I, for that?"

Brink's expression saddens. "You and Lady Vayohl were mourning over a miscarriage. Lemawr didn't want to get in the way of your grief."

Lemara stops breathing again, but then says, "It is in the past."

"Of course, Highness," replies Brink respectfully. "As for his current whereabouts, well, he could be anywhere. But he did rather love exploring the caves and night of north. He was always hunting those mythical Darklyre creatures. Never did tell me if he found any. He also loved spending leisurely time in the Metsundai. Does that help?" Brink glances to me.

I nod, stating, "It does. But what are Darklyre creatures?"

Crossing her arms, Krina proclaims, "It's a good thing you have the excuse of not being from Muraine. Darklyres resemble Sorsryns, except in that they are winged-creatures. It's said in the myths of them that they are descendants of eight offspring, born of Dragon's Mistress."

"Does the mistress have a name?" I ask coldly.

"She was a Withrasyn," says Krina. "Since she's most likely long dead, I had no need to commit her name to memory."

"Withrasyn, you say?" I ask.

Looking annoyed, she nods.

I state, "Well, there's a good chance she's not dead, if she was a Withrasyn, and somehow tied to Soren."

"What would you know?" queries Krina. "Did you grow up learning the various histories? The Legends of Soren?"

"No," I reply. "But I've learned enough to know that things on this world aren't as they seem."

"My word, Krina"—Lemara grips her shoulder—"someone is in need of expelling excessive combativeness. Your thoughts are everywhere. Most definitely *not* calm. Shall you smite the Son of LanSoren, in a game of thought and reason, while in the Driv-vell Den?"

"Most definitely," she says. "So long as that son is no coward, or fearful of losing, for he *will* be losing."

I shrug, replying, "So long as Gemma sits next to me for good luck, it won't be me who's conceding the win."

"We will see of that," says Krina, smug.

I hate to admit it to myself, but Caleiso's company is preferable to this Princess Krina's. Already, I can't wait for her to go away, or for us to be leaving Deivahl.

Gemma's face is tinged light-pink. "I don't know if my good luck transfers, Ty. But we can try."

"We're near to the den," says Lemara. "Are those journals easily accessible to you?"

Grateful for the diversion, I dig out the dragon-wolf journal first, and give it to Lemara. He flips through it, while he slows his stride.

Talok comes up beside him, showing him the ancient Sorsrynian sections we need translated.

Lemara states, "My apologies, but I encountered this language so long ago, I seem to have forgotten it. But Gyron is right. Lemawr may, indeed, be able to assist you. Give me another. Maybe we'll have better luck."

"Give him the blue one, Tyler," Gemma suggests, coming to hook arms with me. "The colors match Deivahl."

One-handed, I dig out the navy one, and see Gemma's point. Especially when considering the stoic figure on the cover that's colored of multi-shaded turquoise.

Glancing at Lemara, I think, *The figure actually looks like him.*

I ask, "Is this you, next to someone cloaked in white, on the cover?"

Lemara stops, to take the journal from me. "What's this? I was important enough to make it on one of the covers? Don't I feel special," he says, in sarcasm.

Lemara tilts the journal, and the faint gray outline of a beast's mouth fades in and out. While Lemara studies it, his facial scales turn a yellowish hue. He looks happy, yet sad. "This wouldn't be me, Tyler."

Jasper goes to stand beside Lemara, asking, "Whom would it be, then, if not you?"

Lemara replies, "My father, Liffa-Aroh. Not sure of the cloaked figure's identity. There's no fitting myth, to clue me in on whom he, or she, may be." He opens the journal, and stops breathing for the third time. "It's written in one of the Jextoran languages," he says.

"Jextoran?" queries Eli, lightly pressing on his neck bandage. "What's that?"

"Another world," states Brink, in place of Lemara, who's still speechless. "It's where Laykonians are originally from. Vardiyas too. Neither were meant to be on this world, near the start of Muraine's history. Yet, here we are, trying to remain unobtrusive to its dealings. Though we've mostly been successful, the Vardiyas have not."

Finding his voice, Lemara says, "Yet that unobtrusiveness seems harder and harder to sustain. Would you mind if I kept this for a bit, Tyler? It will take me quite a while, to go through all of it."

I nod, not sure what to say.

Another world? I wonder. *Does it still exist? And am I meant to go there, one day?*

Talok asks, "How long do you think it will take you, Lemara?"

Lost in thought, Lemara sways side to side a few times.

Quall nudges Ryco on the shoulder, who then slips a piece of paper out from one of his coat pockets.

He writes something on it, then hands it to Lemara. "When you've finished, send word to one of these locations. It'll reach us, within the span of a week."

Lemara takes it, tucking it away. "Thank you. I'll send word, the minute I've finished."

"Can we go to the Driv-vell Den, now?" queries Krina, glancing at Talok. "I'm most anxious to smite your cousin in a game."

"And I am most anxious to watch you," says Talok, smirking at me.

Lemara gives the journal to Brink. "Take this to my abode-room, where it will be safe."

As Brink passes me by, he divs, saying, *"The younger Vak says hello, and to remind you not to forget what's important. The one residing deeper within our city hasn't met you. But he feels that one day, he will. Vardiyas, I tell you, they're hard to get ahead of, with all that raw power at their disposal."*

I reply, *"I know what you mean."*

Brink's gone, out of earshot, by the time we arrive at a black door with white scrollwork winding upon it in a snake-like fashion. It's similar to the door I opened, which led into the Arkivara, Trauvo; the very place where I saw my dad.

So many things are familiar, I muse. *So why do I feel sick? Is it that I dread the opening of that door? Or is it being irritated with the fact that I have to best Krina in a game I've never played?*

Gemma tightens her hold on my arm, surprising me with a Mensa-div, saying, *"I'm right here with you, Ty. There's no need to feel the way you do.*

We're deep in the water. What could get us, down here?"

"Don't know," I div back, even as Lemara is searching for the right key, amongst many on the big key ring he's pulled out.

I div more, saying, *"Something doesn't feel right."*

"Like at the lake," Gemma divs, *"with the beast hurting Awngeleik?"*

I'm unsure. I've no response for Gemma.

Lemara's about to test a key in the lock, but Krina steps forward, and pushes the door partly open. "Father, it isn't locked."

Lemara takes in shallow breaths. "That's odd. This door is always to remain locked, after the daily time of Driv-vell Den is over." Pushing the door open the rest of the way, Lemara strides in confidently.

The rest of us enter the large, empty room a little more tentatively.

"This is the foyer," says Krina, "where we are to disarm ourselves. Weapons aren't allowed in the Driv-vell Den, for safety reasons. Some of the LeiHymurs hate losing, and they can get violent, when caught up in the moment."

Gemma points at a brass rack on one of the walls, meant to hold long-blades, daggers, and such. It should be empty. But there are two blades upon it. Onyx blades, crossed in an *X*.

"I think someone's already here," says Gemma.

Lemara approaches them, commenting, "The Onyx Sign of Neutrality. How very odd to see that here. Krina? There weren't others at the docks, who came down on a different ship, were there?"

"No, Mawfay'iiha," says Krina. "If I missed notice, Dae'loog would not have."

Lemara starts reaching for one of the Onyx blades.

It's then that I hear a voice in my head, loudly saying, *"To the count of: three, two, one."*

It's familiar, I muse. *Not Soren. Nor Gyron. Or Vak. But whom?*

I place the voice, right as Lemara grips one blade hilt. *It's when his voice was different without the mask,* I muse, then I shout, "Stop Lemara! It's Zymarc. He's in there."

But it's too late . . .

20

Thief Down Below

Lemara has removed one blade from the weapon's rack of the foyer. Someone in the Driv-vell Den immediately speaks a word. I look to the brass-pillar archway, which separates the two rooms.

"Done!" he proclaims. Hands stuffed in his coat pockets, he strolls into view. Under the archway, he stands. Again, he's taken Soren's face. Yet he wears the coat of Onyx. Surprisingly, he has not a single weapon with him, unless his hands count as two.

"You shouldn't have done that," says Zymarc. "Broken the sign of neutrality, I mean. I'm now permitted to attack, as are you."

Lemara unsheathes the blade. But Zymarc yanks his hands from his pockets, and uses magic to pull Lemara into the Driv-vell Den.

The group fires magic of their own. Once hitting the iridescent barrier, which Zymarc has set up in the archway, all of it fizzles out.

Krina rushes, attempting to grab her father. She slams into the barrier, screaming as if it burns her. She steps away, shaking.

Talok puts himself between her and the barrier.

Zymarc summons the other blade to his grasp. It slips through the barrier. Quickly, he slices at Lemara's hands.

Lemara, partially on his back, gets in a few good swings. He cuts into Zymarc's legs.

Talok bends down, and whispers to Krina, "Do Laykonians have an alarm? A call system, in case of an attack?"

She nods.

"Activate it," Jasper commands, as he watches the two kings fight each other.

Colored-glass table sets of teal and blue are hit, shoved, or overturned in Zymarc's enthusiasm to subdue Lemara. Lemara's desperate, using his magic, as well as setting, to his advantage. He does something, and the Driv-vell Den begins rocking like a ship. Within the den, the furniture slides all over the place.

Even amidst crying, Krina goes to the exterior wall that closes the foyer off from the hallway. She brushes her hand along that wall and then comes back to stand near Talok. Both intently watch her father.

Zymarc, when he loses his footing and slips a bit, laughs. Even after getting hit by a sliding table, he remarks, "It's like fighting on the back of a dyn, during a debris storm." The Vitiosyn King eases up, then toys with his blade. "I came here for a talk, is all, King Lemara. Cease this violence. I don't wish to kill you in front of your young daughter."

The room settles to stillness.

Irate, Lemara spits out the question, "A talk? You are here for more than a mere *talk*."

"It's true," remarks Zymarc. "This is my reply to RayVora's meddling. Her probing of King ReNovak, for information he simply doesn't know because I've not told him. Not told anyone. Still living, that is. Being Queen Mother to the Jokryn, she tempted him with a Jokryn alliance. When he refused, then told me all of it, what did the wench do the next day? Came knocking, literally, on my bedroom door. Threatened me with her reeking boot knife, demanding that I free King Talok of the device. Said I was a coward, for targeting someone so young."

"Well, aren't you a coward for it?" queries Jasper, in that overly restrained way of his.

Quickly, Zymarc corners Lemara, until the Ruler of the Deep has his back pressed against a wall. He's tired, bleeding bluish-blood rather badly.

Zymarc grabs Lemara by the throat, and pulls him up, stating, "Here I am"—he turns to face us—"fighting one-on-one, fairly matched, with the same weapon type. Yet, still, I've subdued a great king. Does anyone here have a good reason for me to stop? To choose not to kill him?"

I can't stand the sight a second longer. I know Jasper warned me. But I can't stop myself from a Mensa-div with Zymarc, saying, *"Kill him, and you can forget about ever having me for an apprentice. I know it's something you want. Me."*

"You misunderstand my restraint," says Lemara, coughing up some blood. "You cannot beat the stamina of a Laepurian. I could've deeply wounded you, four times over, already. But what good would it do me, or my people, to risk letting you bleed out, here? You are wise enough, Zymarc, to have forces nearby for saving you, should things not go your way. Am I wrong?"

"You are not," says Zymarc, wryly grinning at me. "Caleiso waits with the Prince-Generals and her warriors, on the surface. Many Vitasadyns, at Scepter's command, have Deivahl surrounded. And Azabahk? Well, he's my sniper. You won't see where he is, until it's too late."

"Seems you've thought of everything," I comment, coming up close to the barrier wall.

"Not everything," Zymarc corrects. "I hadn't any idea I would find Paragonians here. Certainly not any from Eyo'el. I thought you'd still be stuck there, watching them die. I'd be very interested in knowing how it is all of you escaped *that* death. The poisoned storerooms. Caleiso was quite proud of that deed. It was her idea. I raised her well."

"What is he talking of?" queries Talok, sounding angry.

Shoving Lemara away, Zymarc approaches the barrier. His face is inches from Talok's. "You are the King of Paragon, yet you were unaware of the castle's poisoned storerooms? Interesting, don't you think, that no one told you? Oh! It must've been your cousin who cleared it of poison. Look at his darker dagger." Zymarc points at it. "It glows green, in this lower light. The color is faint. But it is there."

I look, and see that Zymarc is right.

Talok's face turns stormy. Murderous, even.

Eli pulls me away as Talok lunges, clawing for me. He shouts.

Kent rushes to stand near us.

Ryco and Quall restrain their young, hungry king. His eyes flash burgundy-red, briefly matching RayVora and Zeekryn's eyes. Then his hands change. Claws start forming. Claws like what Soren had, when he killed one of Zymarc's Vitiosyn women.

Gemma, instead of being afraid in this situation, grabs hold of NeiSator. She places the dagger in my hand, and forcefully assists in thrusting it into the barrier wall.

With that first strike, Zymarc falls to his knees, gasping in pain. I assume the poison in the dagger has an added effect on him. He's quickly standing up, however, before Lemara can best him with a blade.

Two more times, I stab the wall, and it cracks like glass in all three places.

"*Enough!*" Zymarc shouts, in Mensa-div. "*I will take my leave, Son of LanSoren. Now, let me talk.*"

"*Then make it quick,*" I div back, stilling my hand.

Talok returns to being himself. But he's sweaty and pale again.

His chest heaving, Zymarc states, "I will tell you what I told RayVora. So long as you are the King of Paragon, refusing to give me back Awngeleik, I will not be removing that device. Name someone else as King of Paragon, in your place, young Talok, and I will happily transfer it from you to him. Or her. The gender matters not. Merely the title. What is your reply?"

"So long as I live," says Talok, "no one will bear this burden of mine. It is mine to carry, even if unto death."

"See, you are not a boy, like everyone thinks," says Zymarc. "You are a king. You speak like one, giving commands to get to safety. You lead like one, on the battlefield, calling for ceasefire. You bear burdens akin to a king, as well. And, underneath that ridiculous façade of a cloak, you're dressed as one too."

Talok rips the cloak off and then pounds his fist on the barrier wall. He punches right through one of the holes I've made, and yells.

Zymarc grins, looking Talok over, as my cousin pulls his hand out.

The two stare each other down.

The coat is more magnificent than words can properly convey. It's mainly of white dragon scales. But it appears as if ash and fire are in between those tightly knit scales. With each of Talok's breaths, the scales move with him. I liken it to being a part of him. An extension, the way the daggers are for me. Attached to the coat's back are five strips of fabric, partially overlaid on top of each other. The triangular, black ends of them stop at the back of his knees. Black dragon-eyes, with white pupils, are positioned, one on each shoulder. Then there are two, reverse in color and slightly bigger, at the bottom corners of the coat's backside. Black cording seals up the coat's sides, and the back of each sleeve. Small, various symbols dot inconspicuous places on the fabric. But a symbol, just below the high neckline, is unmistakably one for a Vardiya: an eight-point star.

"There," Zymarc says, proudly to Talok, "now you are the King of Paragon. A worthy adversary, as was King Sosha. Always hold your head high like that. You were right to cover up the Waking Dragon, for you were wholly unworthy of wearing it. Now that you've cleared up any question or doubt of who Paragon's king is, you may begin to make a name for yourself. Though it's likely you will die young, you will be great in my eyes. Greater than your uncle. For you have had to overcome more, during such a short life. An orphan. A pawn. A child-king. Horrible advice, from bad advisers. Pity those advisers resisted Alpha Jasper, as they did. You might have stopped me, otherwise."

"Enough!" Talok shouts. "We will leave Deivahl, if you will. Deal? Let us settle things on the surface. Leave the Laykonians out of it."

After a moment of silence, Zymarc is asking, "Do you give your word that I won't be attacked, if I bring down this barrier?"

"Whomever *dares* to," says Talok, glancing at me, "I will drain of blood, for I am very hungry."

Zymarc wryly grins again. "Spoken like a Deathasyn. It's a shame you can never complete the transition of becoming one."

Gemma comes to stand by Eli and me. Tightly, she grips my arm, and divs, *"Don't provoke Zymarc more, Tyler. I don't think Talok can control himself too well."*

Zymarc breaks the barrier, and steps out. He strolls for the exit.

Lemara saunters forward. "Wait," he says, "my warriors are standing by, outside. Let me exit first. They've started to flood the city. Unless you are well acquainted with Deivahl's waters, they're not likely to obey you."

Zymarc lets him pass.

I hate that we're just standing here, an arm's length from Zymarc, and not attacking him.

When Lemara opens the door, water gradually floods both rooms up to being knee-deep with the cold liquid.

Brinkorr waits there, outside, holding a platter of grilled fish, while standing in front of a multitude of warriors occupying the tunnel in both directions.

"Krina sounded the alarm," says Brink. "I thought you must greatly be in need of food and some able, witty minds for outsmarting our guests in the Driv-vell Den. Or did she simply want to give a demonstration of our defense system? Which is it?" queries Brink, offering the fish platter.

Talok rushes for it, tearing off a piece, and picking its bones away. He devours it.

Zymarc eyes the fish, then approaches.

"Who are you?" queries Brink, blinking in confusion.

"Just an Onyx," replies Zymarc. "Came here to present a deal. But the little Paragonians beat me here. Go figure. I was just on my way out." He reaches, to snatch a piece of the fish.

Lemara's livid. "You touch my dinner, and I'll remove that head from your shoulders, Onyx scum."

Brink's eyes widen. "What's happening? Krina, did you let someone in that you weren't supposed to?"

"Shut it, Brink," she seethes. "You don't know what we've all been forced to witness."

Zymarc steps away from Brink, to eye Lemara. He hands him his Onyx blade, saying, "I'll give you a free shot, at removing my head, King Lemara. I've told Azabahk, in div, not to retaliate. Get on with it." Zymarc clasps his hands behind his back, and waits for the strike.

Lemara unsheathes both blades, then traps Zymarc's neck between them, crossing them in an *X*. He takes a deep breath, then starts slicing them in opposite directions.

Zymarc's eyes go blank. They flash red. He stops blinking. The blades have actually cut into his neck a bit, spilling his blood. But then the blades melt at the point of contact upon Zymarc's neck.

He shudders, then starts blinking again, saying, "Now that we've cleared up whether or not I can be killed by beheading, I shall take my leave. A good day to you, King Lemara. You as well, Princess Krina." He lingers his gaze on Krina, then begins healing his neck of the cuts and burns.

Lemara motions to his warriors within the tunnel on the left, and they move to let Zymarc pass. In single file, we follow. We eventually enter another room, larger than where the docks are at.

Laykonian warriors start spilling into the room with us.

Jasper quickens his stride, cutting in front of Zymarc. "You're sure you did not expect us to be here?"

Gazing up at Jasper, Zymarc then lowers his head. "For what reason would I lie to you, Alpha Jasper?"

"To hide that you followed us to Vondurheil and then here," says Jasper.

Hesitating, Zymarc replies, "I don't understand why I'd be doing that."

"You like to stalk your prey." Jasper breathes faster. "Do you deny it?"

"I don't stalk my prey, Alpha." Zymarc takes a step toward Jasper, then shouts, "I turn it!"

Many rush forward in alarm. Ryco's the only one to make it in time, before Zymarc has put up a larger barrier. The Vitiosyn tears his coat away. It shifts into a lifeless figure. Then Azabahk is being summoned to that figure, to struggle against Ryco.

"Highness," says Brink, "do you wish for us to finish flooding the city? It'll tear right through that hindrance."

Lemara replies, "Not until the Paragonians have been taken to a safe room. Take them there, now. And get the ones still in my armory. The alarm doesn't sound, in there."

"No!" I shout. "Let us stay. Let *me* stay. Take the others there, if it'll make you feel better. Forcefully, if you have to."

Talok opens his mouth, about to defy my request, but I will his voice to give out, focusing on his throat. He starts coughing.

Brink hurries them away, getting several others to help him.

Gemma screams, "Tyler! You're not safe! Please, come with us. Jasper can defend himself."

I Mensa-div, *"I don't think so, Gem. Even if he can, I'm not letting Zymarc get away with this."*

Zymarc corners Jasper, near an enormous statue in the room's center.

"You can't shift into the Greyvon beast down here, well below the surface, Jasper," Zymarc says. "You've already expelled magic, at some point on the way here. And, now, the water will not let you access that magic. But go ahead. Try."

Jasper starts sweating. His breaths get even faster. His hands tremble. Yet, he remains in his two-legged form.

Many Laykonians watch in resentment, waiting to flood their city.

"I hope your friends are fast," says Krina, beside me. "Once we see Brink rushing back, those two won't stand a chance. My father assures he'll retrieve Alpha Jasper, if he's able to."

"What about me?" I ask. "I'm sure the rushing water will carry me off."

Krina glances at me. "That's why I'm next to you. To save you from drowning."

Great! Saved by a snobby princess, who, minutes ago, only cared about besting me in a game. I think I'd rather duel Caleiso all over again.

Ryco has about struck Azabahk down. I wish he'd be quicker about it, though.

Zymarc speaks to Jasper, "Down on your knees, dog, and I might consider not turning you into a rabid beast to do my bidding. Azabahk asked that I not kill you. This is our compromise. A Greyvon turned into a Vitiosyn. You've spent thousands of years, only concerned over exploring genetic testing. Didn't you once think it might be a good idea to reconcile with the Rubidyns? Now, it's too late. They cannot save you from this fate."

Jasper sinks to his knees. His eyes are sad, yet wild and hateful. He glances at me, as I pace by the barrier. His expression turns fearful.

Zymarc grips Jasper's face, with one hand. His other strokes the alpha's neck. "The bite won't hurt much," says Zymarc. "The turning will, in the days ahead, though. But Azabahk, even Belzara, have promised to look after you, during that time. Don't you worry, Alpha Jasper. You will become one of the greatest among us. Even my Vitasadyns will tremble, in your very presence."

To me, Jasper divs, saying, *"If I'm bitten, Tyler, you must stop at nothing to kill me, before I'm taken this day. Do you promise?"*

My face burns. The tears sting so badly.

Zymarc leans down. He's inches from biting Jasper's neck. The alpha's compliant. I don't know why. *Why isn't he fighting? Is he protecting me?* I wonder.

I press my hands on the barrier. Suddenly, I wish that I had my borrowed power again. Torturous is it, watching this happen, while there's nothing I can do to stop it. I glance at the diver's watch on my wrist. Desperate, I try to reason out what phrase will activate it. I mull over the word despairion. The different stories Gemma has conveyed. What Paydinn said, about how the diving armor protects me in more ways than I know. I think, *Surely, there must be something.*

I remember the reflective, metal disk Jasper put in one of my coat pockets. I feel for it. It's not there. My heart sinks as I assume it's one of the things Droediin stole from me.

Zymarc straightens his stature. He looks at me, then steps away from Jasper. "There is a way for me to spare him."

Jasper sinks farther to the ground, rasping. He's trying to speak. To Mensa-div. I can feel it. But Zymarc isn't letting him. Blood starts to drip from Jasper's nose. Then his hands rip open, at the knuckles. He's straining. He's fighting Zymarc's magic.

"Come now, with me," says Zymarc. "Come learn of the magic you crave, Ravier. I'll forever leave the Laykonians at peace. I'll never turn Alpha Jasper into a Vitiosyn. I'll even end the whole war with Paragon, and your young cousin will be saved. Best of all, I'll tell you everything I know about LanSoren. Together, we can find his killer."

Aysivak's words come to me; my own words, too, that finding my father's killer may have to wait. *But what if I don't have to? I wonder. Zymarc's deal is everything I want, in this moment. Everything, and more.*

Zymarc Mensa-divs, but it's different. He's projecting a conversation my father had, saying, *"When the time is right, tell him everything."*

"I won't have to, Lance," says Zymarc, in the conversation. *"Because you'll be here, to tell him yourself. He should hear it from you. Now, no misusing this Vardiya. Took me quite a long time to find one, who could serve your key intentions."*

My father asks, *"This is the one Soren used to talk with, centuries ago?"*

"The very one," replies Zymarc. *"Aysivak of the Pools of Vosh-Perida. He's been back and forth many times, from there to Deivahl. This particular one is from the future, in case you wanted to know."*

I whisper, "You're lying, Vitiosyn."

"What?" Krina asks, confused.

"He's lying," I state, my gaze fixed on Zymarc.

"Lying of what?" Zymarc smirks.

"That whole conversation is a lie," I seethe. "I bet you've just pieced together words you've heard, making it sound convincing. I won't believe it. My dad never would've trusted you, or your murderous heart."

"You don't have to believe it," says Zymarc. "All you have to do, to prevent future bloodshed, is to come with me this moment. Let me teach you magic, for four years. At the end of it, you're free to go where and do as you please. If you so desire, I'll even instruct you in the ways of Vitiosus. Teach you how to kill me. But that will not be forced on you. Do you accept an apprenticeship with me?"

I'm torn, now wishing I had Gemma here, to help me know what to do. It was stupid, sending them all away. *Why did I do it? I wonder.*

Ryco catches my gaze, as a shadow forms on the floor in front of Zymarc.

Zymarc and I both look up to see some smallish, winged-creature bursting through Deivahl's walls, without breaking the glass. It slips right on through Zymarc's barrier wall, as well. The black creature doesn't land directly on Zymarc. But its momentum carries it crashing into him. The two stop, after Zymarc's back has hit up against an exterior wall that keeps the ocean water out.

Jasper chokes and wheezes in deep breaths. "Neb," he says weakly.

Standing over Zymarc is Nebukahn, wide-eyed. "Onyx?" he jeers, narrowing his focus. "What's an Onyx doing here?"

Zymarc replies, "Came to make a deal. I was about to leave, Mister . . . ?"

"Mister Nothing, to you, Onyx," Neb spews. "For Onyx do nothing. Believe nothing. Are nothing."

Another creature, much larger, approaches from outside Deivahl's walls, casting a shadow over the entire room.

"Vardiya speech!" Krina cries. "What is that?"

A red dragon lands on top of the room. Quite quickly, it forms into a person, who then falls through, and lands near Jasper.

Nebukahn goes ballistic, running after the red-cloaked figure. There's no mistaking that the figure is in fact a woman, with her graceful silhouette and movements, as she dashes about the room to avoid Nebukahn's snarling and snapping at her.

Zymarc sees Ryco defeat Azabahk's decoy. Instantaneously, he rushes for Jasper.

"Nebukahn!" I shout, pounding on the barrier. "Protect Jasper!"

Neb startles at my pounding, and slips. He falls into the knee-deep water. But he can't recover his footing, not in time to help Jasper.

The woman gets a good running start, watching Zymarc. She slides down on one knee, splashing in the water. She positions herself in front of Jasper before Zymarc can make it there.

Ryco's beside her, in seconds. The both of them shield Jasper.

The woman removes her hood. Her bright-red hair resembles flickering fire. "You are to leave, Zymarc of Vitiosus," she says, pointing her long-blade colored of black and blood-red at him.

"You hold no authority here, Rubidyn," Zymarc says smoothly. "I know for a fact, Rubidyns haven't an alliance with anyone. You are merely permitted to protect your own. Jasper is not one of you. Step aside."

"I will not," says the woman. "I've been given the task of finding him. I have dealings with the alpha I've not yet completed. You will not get in the way of my King Rentwar's command, to find Jasper, which then leads to other tasks I have no obligation to tell you of."

"What's to stop me from killing *you*, Rubidyn?" Zymarc asks. "You are following a command that isn't bound in magic. I don't have to listen to you."

"That is true," the woman agrees. "But Rentwar knows my last whereabouts, as of this morning. The Metsundai. I told him of your infiltration of the ocean waters near Deivahl, last night. He'll be knowing what killed me, if I die this day. Even now, he has your main cities surrounded. The cities where you've few warriors, because most of them are here or elsewhere. King Rentwar is waiting for me to take my last breath, stolen away by Vitiosyns or their followers, so that he may utterly destroy you."

Zymarc tenses his neck. His mouth twitches with held-back hatred.

The woman stands. "Leave now, and your cities will be spared."

Zymarc looks around, assessing his options.

Outside, in the waters, a Vitasadyn approaches. It's Scepter, with the real Azabahk upon his back.

Zymarc sighs deeply. "A well-planned counterattack, Rubidyn." He nods. "I commend you." Then he strolls toward the wall, where Scepter and Azabahk wait beyond.

The Prince-General eyes Ryco. When they make eye contact, Azabahk issues his Deathasyn grin.

Ryco holds his head high. Smoke starts emitting from his nostrils. Menacing doesn't even begin to describe his stance. For a second, I think that he's going shift into his *Parasogyn* form, as Zepharre started to call it.

It's then that Jasper finds his voice, and shouts, "Neb! Stop him! He's taken Winter's Vondaen."

Nebukahn, scowling at the woman, startles and then starts running for Zymarc. But Zymarc bolts forward. The hilt of Jasper's blade barely pokes up above the collar of the Vitiosyn's coat. Nebukahn misses catching him by two steps, instead face-planting into a newly erected barrier laid in place by Zymarc.

The Vitiosyn escapes.

Scepter's quick in the water, pushing off from the main room, and swimming away.

The room shudders.

Krina steadies me, keeping me upright. Barely. Her hands are like ice. And I must feel like fire, because she's grimacing, pulling away immediately.

"Kaesh!" she curses. "You surface people are hot-blooded. How do you stand it? Don't you feel as if you're being cooked alive?"

"Only when walking on fire," I state, in sarcasm.

Her eyes get bigger. "You can do that? Walk on fire?"

Smiling, I shrug. "Sure. And on water. Air too. The possibilities are near endless up there."

"Surface magic must be vastly stronger than ours, then," says Krina, sounding less smug. "You must show me, if you are to stay."

"So now you want us to stay?" I ask.

"Well, no," she says shyly, turning especially pale. "You must retrieve that Alpha Jasper's possession, mustn't you?"

"Yes. But I'm not sure how we're going to get it back."

"Wherever is Brinkorr?" Lemara is irate. "He should've been back by now."

Since the barrier has come down, Lemara calls off the flooding of the city. "The immediate threat is gone," he calls out. "Disperse! Go find Brink, Broena, and the Paragonians. Bring them back here."

But they're already being brought back.

Brink's disheveled and bruised. The others are soaked through.

"We got trapped in the safe room," says Brink. "I think the system was tampered with. As soon as I did an area lock-down, it flooded in there immediately. I do believe that Onyx, Highness, has been in our city for a while."

"Are you suggesting something, Brink?" queries Lemara.

Brink replies, "It'd be best to retreat deeper within the ocean. Go to where our LeiHymids live. I scoped out the dyns that Onyx brought along. They can hardly move, or breathe at the deeper depths. Dae'loog Dauger and some others lured them there, testing my theory. Come, we must leave soon. There's no telling when he'll be back."

With the barrier gone, Ryco and the woman help Jasper to us.

"You must go, Lemara," Jasper says weakly. "As soon as the Rubidyn leaves, he'll be back. He's patient. He'll wait as long as it takes."

"What of you all?" queries Lemara, gently touching Jasper on the arm. "You are my friend, old dog, and I watched you nearly taken from the land of sanity. Watched him run off with your prized blade too. What's he want it for?"

Jasper replies, "It must have to do with wielding the elements. He's trying to become the master of famous weapons. Deezalo's Hammer. Winter's Vondaen. He can summon, and hurt, The Black Flame too."

"To what end would he need all that?" queries Quall.

"It doesn't make any sense." Kent is baffled.

Siege asks, "How are we supposed to prevent what's still a mystery to us?"

"I think that's the point," says Ryco, adjusting his weapons and clothes. "He has so many facets of war he's been planning. We have to pick the most important aspect, and not get distracted."

The woman steps forward that instant, to say, "I do so hate to add to your complications. It sounds as though you're caught in a maze of decisions."

Eli agrees, saying, "Truest statement I've heard all week."

"Which wasn't much," Musgrae adds, "since your head was in the fog of Metsundai."

"Why have you come, Rubidyn?" queries Jasper, whilst Quall heals his wounds.

"I was sent out, many months ago," she says, "to deliver a most important item to you. Rentwar was fearful of giving me a message to deliver, directly, in case I should be captured, and tortured into telling the truth." She pulls a small pouch out from a hidden pocket of her cloak, and gives it to Jasper. "Former master of me, now my King Rentwar, said you would know what is meant by the gifting of this item."

Jasper peeks inside the black velvet pouch, asking, "Then you'd be considered Rentwar's Recruit, if you are no longer under his pupilage?"

"Yes, my liege," she says. "May I know what the item is, which he hath tasked me in delivering to you?"

Jasper slips it out of the pouch, and onto his palm. Pinching the braided silver chain between his fingers, he lifts it up to view: a turquoise-stone pendant, encased in a wavy, eight-point star.

Neb comes to sniff it. "Alpha, is that . . . ?" Neb gets excited, and his wings flutter unexpectedly.

"Yes, Neb," Jasper quietly replies. "It's Matriarch Shena's star. The Star of Crae-Shand."

"What's that mean?" queries Gemma. "King Rentwar giving it to you now?"

Rentwar's Recruit seems to anticipate Jasper's reply, as do many of us.

Jasper stands, staring at it.

We wait for him to say something. To tell us what to do next. But all he says is, "Tell Rentwar it's too late. It is for another's time, not mine. Not ours, Recruit. Tell him she's been born. A Matriarch Candidate. Born in Shena's image too. It's for her that he waits. We wait. And you, it would seem. Two matriarchs, in the same generation."

"How old, my liege?" queries The Recruit. "Surely, you wouldn't have us wait for her to grow into adulthood."

"Twenty-three," says Jasper. "She'll be ready, soon. But what of you?" Jasper puts the pendant back in the pouch.

"I do not know." The Recruit bows her head, in respect. "I do not even have my own name yet, my liege, as I've never seen my first battle."

Jasper hands the pouch back to The Recruit. "Tell him to hold it, for safe-keeping. As I am an old Von-dog, I don't think I'll last through this war. His wait won't be long. Now, leave, Rentwar's Recruit. Go tell him what I've said."

"I cannot leave you, in good conscience," The Recruit says. "Vitiosyns will still be near the Metsundai. I'm obligated to protect you, for the entirety of this day."

"Can you look after them? Take them to the surface?" queries Lemara.

"I and my people must evacuate, to the safety of the depths. I will take that journal with. Have a look at it. Let you know what I discover. But we must go. Before those dyns come back."

The Recruit nods. "I am able to assist them to the surface."

Talok says, "Go, King Lemara. We will look to hear from you, in the coming weeks. Even months. If that's what it takes."

Brink states, "Head north, to get to those caves I mentioned. And best of luck to you, in finding that rascal Lemawr."

"Yes," says Krina, "tell that half-brother of mine, when you find him, that I would very much like to meet him."

We flee the city of Deivahl, after giving our goodbyes, to make for the surface, all while the Laykonians begin their descent deeper into the ocean. I know not when, or even if, I should ever see them again. I can only hope to meet with Lemara, in the future, and learn what is held within that navy-blue journal. The Jextoran Journal. Hardly can I believe there is yet another world I never knew about, till now.

21

North to Night

"**I**'m sick of this night," says Siege, holding a lantern tightly by the handle.

Paired together on the same saddled nein with Siege, Gemma has her grip on the reins. "It is dreary, isn't it?" she agrees. "I've kept track, and figured that we only have dusk for two and half hours, before it's dark again."

"Does real daylight ever shine here?" I ask Jasper.

"For five months, it does," he replies, while repositioning atop Mekka's broad, Von back. "But the other nine months are much like this."

"Nine and five months?" I ask. "Those don't add up to twelve."

Ryco responds with, "Muraine has fourteen-month years. Eight-day weeks. Twenty-two hour days. But our hours in a single year only differ by four hours, compared to Earth's. In case you wished to know." He flashes that sadistic look at me. But I realize now, it's his know-it-all smirk. It's the kind of look you just come to expect from Ryco. And if it were gone, you'd kind of miss it. At least, I would now.

Eli, positioned behind me, says, "I prefer this, to the Metsundai. If we need to make a quick escape, we can. Only need nuff light, to keep from running into these here gnarly, near-death trees."

"You're just sore about being bitten while in there," says Musgrae.

Warren adds, "So don't you go complaining 'bout nothing. At least

290

you'll not suffer the fate of those four neins we had to leave behind in the Metsundai."

Riding double with Ryco, Kent says, "I trust that Droediin will do his best to find them. But I doubt he'll find them alive and well."

I ask, "Why do you think Zymarc fled, before we could make it to the surface?"

"His home cities were at risk," replies Quall. "While he can be cruel to his own, he still needs an army of followers. He doesn't want to see them annihilated."

Ryco adds, "Especially not by Rubidyns."

"Do you think," I ask Jasper, "that you should've gone with The Recruit to meet with King Rentwar?"

He replies, "It would've been too dangerous, given the circumstances we were in. As soon as I've led you into daylight or, by chance, into the Darklyre's land, I'll reassess the best plan of action."

Talok, partnered with Zeekryn on one of the winged-horses, says, "Hopefully, one of those plans includes getting Winter's Vondaen back."

Jasper sighs. "It does. Though, nothing has a high chance of success."

Mekka, trotting along, grumbles, "Why didn't you send Droediin and me after it, Alpha? We're kilos faster than Neb and Craesha."

"Nebukahn's weighed down with guilt," replies Jasper. "He feels he was at fault, for it getting stolen in the first place. The distraction of him and The Recruit was all Zymarc needed, to slip it off me unnoticed. And I couldn't speak. Couldn't even Mensa-div. No one's prevented me from that for a few millenniums."

"I still think he was a bad choice," states Mekka, in a growly tone. "But you are Alpha. What you command, we do."

"Neb *isn't* under my command," says Jasper, "nor Craesha. Of these past days, only you and Droediin have been under my command."

Gemma asks, "Where's Droediin supposed to rendezvous with us, if he's able to find the horses quickly?"

"He's to take them to Vondurheil," replies Jasper, "where they'll be safe. You'll be able to make do with these seven, won't you?"

Talok nods. "I *do* think we should stop for a rest, though," he says. "We've been going for two days straight, since The Recruit left us. And the path ahead hasn't been cleared by her. The farther we travel in this darkness, the more I dread continuing. I hate to ask it, but would you and Mekka be willing to scout out the area? Make sure nothing too terrible is lingering near where we'll be passing through."

Jasper dips his head down, in answer. He clambers off Mekka, and makes the transformation into his Von form. The two trot off into darkness. As sounds of them are swallowed up by the eerie forest, my heart thumps harder in my chest. Our two greatest sources of strength have left us, not even audible now.

After we set up camp, I watch Zeekryn make more antivenom for Talok to drink.

"Will you teach me?" I ask.

He looks up. "I'm not sure that's a good idea."

"Why not?" queries Gemma, who sits on the ground, beside me.

Zeekryn rolls up the sleeves of his outer robe, then looks down into the bowl he's about to fill with his brother's bottled venom. "If you have any cuts or open sores," he says, "coming into contact with the venom could kill you. Since I'm immune to the venom, it's safe for me to handle."

Talok strides over abruptly. "Under no circumstances, Zeekryn, will you show my cousin how to make the antivenom."

I quietly say, "I just want to help you, Talok."

"I don't want your help, Tyler!" he shouts. "I want you safe. I want you back home on Earth. Somehow, I think *you're* the very reason you and Gemma couldn't go through the portal that day."

I ease up, and face my cousin. "You're right. I broke the portal. Not the first time. But the second. The creature that hunted Awngeleik on Earth, it was there that day. It was waiting for us to leave you. For me to leave. Possibly, it planned on going through with us. Gemma and I might already be dead. The way it is now, time's still suspended over there; and we're here with you, whether you like it or not."

Talok grits his teeth. His gaze turns lethal. "Get my cousin out of here. I want you out of my sight. The longer I look at you, the more I want to rip into your throat."

My breath catches, making my chest sting. "That's the device talking, Talok. You don't mean that."

"But I do, Cousin Tyler," he says, as he licks his lips. "I very much wish to know what your blood tastes like. Not that I would know how the other species taste, but *your* blood must be better than all the rest, given what you can do with such magical ease."

Ryco seizes hold of Talok's arm, and tugs at him. "Take a walk with me."

"I don't want to take a walk." Talok yanks his arm out of Ryco's grasp. "I want to sit and stare into this fire, until food is ready. I'll even help prepare it. That is, if all of you trust me to help make a bit of food." Talok's eyes glimmer with a few unshed tears, before they go dull.

Gemma's lower lip quivers. She looks from Talok to me. *"Why didn't you say anything about sensing the beast, Tyler?"* she divs. *"Someone should've known about it, before now."*

I shrug, saying nothing.

She jolts up, to stride forward. "I'd love it, if you made dinner, Talok," she says. "I'll go pick herbs and flowers, for you to use. Quall's been showing me how to pick the best ones in this area, for medicinal use. And Ben, before he left us, showed me which traits are shared among the ones used in cooking."

"That's fine, Gemma." Talok takes in a giant breath. "Don't wander farther than the camp light can reach."

"Want me to go with you?" I ask, desperate to get away from Talok for a little while.

"No," Gemma says sternly, as she picks up a canvas satchel.

"Someone should go with you," Kent states.

Beckoning one of the horses to follow, I approach Gemma slowly. Almost in the way a scolded dog would. Each passing day is harder and harder to find comfort. Some kind of solace in friendship. Gemma's drifting from me, and I hate it. I don't know what to do. Every turn. Every decision may be right for some, while hurting others. Each hidden truth seems bound to cut at least one deeply.

The nein nuzzles Gemma's cheek, and she caves. "Fine! You can come."

Quall commands, "Musgrae. Siege. Collect kindling. Our stores are running low. But stay within hearing distance of Tyler and Gemma."

Gemma and I leave the lighted camp. She thrusts a lantern at me. "Make yourself useful," she says. "And make sure our nein friend doesn't eat anything besides grass."

The lantern illumines a small radius. Otherwise, blackness surrounds us like a cloudy new-moon night. Gemma furiously picks little flowers and greenery, from the ground and around the bases of various tree trunks.

A short ways away, Musgrae and Siege break off dried branches from dead trees. Their lantern is a little brighter than ours, but not by much.

Gemma's on her knees now, still picking flowers. Though she's careful not to crush them, her quick movements and stiffened neck signal how mad she is.

"Come on, Gemma. You can't stay mad at me."

"Want to bet?" She springs up, to face me. "I thought we were past this. You lying to me. Hiding things from me. I get that you may not feel at home, here. But we've known each other for longer than we haven't. Thought I proved to you before we came, that I can be trusted too."

"I can't help it," I reply. "I don't want to see you get hurt, or more scared than you probably are."

She scoffs. "Too late for that."

"No. I mean *really* hurt, Gem," I explain.

"You're afraid I'm going to die?" she asks, sounding matter-of-fact.

I go sit upon a fallen tree, and set the lantern beside me. I cup my face, sickened by how this is all turning out. Completely opposite of how I wanted it to go. It seems so long ago that Talok was parading me around Paragon. Showing me off. Sharing a world and culture with me, which I never knew existed.

Gemma pets the horse, as he nibbles at buds on some tree branches. Finally relaxing, her shoulders slump; she comes to join me. Flowers in one hand, Gemma grips my left arm with her other. She dumps the flowers in my lap, before handing me some cotton twine.

I start bundling the flowers for her.

Sounding kinder, Gemma asks, "Why are you afraid of me dying, to the point that you won't include me in what you know?"

"Because I want to protect you. Knowing more of the truth may put you at risk. And I don't want you to be gone forever." I manage a pathetic smile. "Who would be there, to make me feel guilty for all my lies?"

Gemma pinches my arm. "Be serious, Tyler. Tell me your real reason."

I weigh the decision. Half truth? Or complete honesty? I shake my head. Losing my nerve, I just say, "You're my friend. And I care what happens to you. Isn't that reason enough?"

"I suppose," she says, starting to twirl her hair.

I finish tying the bundle, and hand Gemma the flowers.

Distracted, she doesn't take it.

A little annoyed at her reappearing habit, I drop the flowers in her lap, then ask, "Do you *have* to do that, with your hair?"

Her hand stops the twirling. Then she says, "For as long as I'm stuck with this hair I hate, yep! Not stopping anytime soon."

"You hate your hair?" I ask.

"I thought it was obvious? I want it short. But my mother threatened to take away my extracurriculars. Sports. Photography. Judo class. All of it. So, I put up with it. Style it the way she likes and whatnot."

I look away to scoff, thinking, *For years, I thought she had it all. I couldn't have been more wrong.*

Gemma awkwardly fiddles with the flower bundle in her lap, saying, "I didn't realize it bothered you so much. I'll try to stop."

"Does Ben like it?" I ask.

She grins, nodding shyly. "It's what I was doing, when he kissed me the first time." She cringes, closing her eyes briefly. "Sorry! Maybe you didn't want to know that."

"Well, if he likes it," I reply, "I can put up with it. In fact." I pause, to reach up and gently take hold of the strand. "I rather like your hair. It suits you. But it might look good short."

Gemma blushes, glancing away. But she doesn't shift away, as if she's uncomfortable. Her breaths get faster. Yet, she seems unafraid.

Still, I let go of the strand. Unable to stop myself, I sweep my fingers down her soft cheek that's facing me. I then brush along her angular jawline. In the lantern light, she looks worried, yet so beautiful. Slowly, I move my fingertips across her small, bony chin, before I tenderly graze my thumb over it. More quickly, I splay my fingers out to rest them on the side of her neck. My hand's positioned perfectly for the next move. But I can't take it yet.

Gemma inhales an unsteady breath, gradually closing her eyes.

Bravely, I take that next move, and cup one side of her face. I press my thumb to her lips.

She turns, to face me fully.

I look into her startled brown eyes, then glance to her full, red lips. Desperately, I want to taste them, to explore the feelings rising up in my heart for Gemma Galloway. All I have to do is draw her closer, for a quick kiss.

Is it all curiosity? I wonder. *Or more?*

When I soften my gaze on her, the fear vanishes from her face.

She touches her hand to my thigh, just above the knee.

A pleasant jolt pulsates through me. But then the sickness settles in my stomach. That's when I know I've fallen for Gemma.

How could I not? I ask myself. *She's strong and kind. Loyal, even when no one deserves her loyalty. She's smart too. Sees right through me, I swear.*

Suddenly nervous, I wonder if my thoughts are open to her in this moment.

She leans closer.

I hold my breath.

She cranes her neck, then kisses my cheek.

I lick my lips, taking in a quiet gasp.

"Thank you for bringing me with you," she whispers.

I turn my head just enough that my lips nearly brush across hers.

She moves away a mere fraction, and looks me in the eye.

"It's not like I had much choice," I whisper back. My hand pulls away. I rest both in my lap. "My dad said not to leave you. But I'm glad you came."

When her unsteady breaths tickle at my lips, I hold still. I don't even want to breathe. I want her to kiss me so badly. I want that choice to be hers. Not mine. Yet it drives me mad, waiting for her. I clasp my hands tight. I start getting lightheaded.

"Tyler," she asks, "what are we going to do?"

Make out, is the instinctual response in my head. Instead, I reply, "Do about what?"

"Talok," she says. "He's so different than when we first got here."

The dizziness subsides, and I take in a full breath. "Look for Lemawr," I reply. "Hope that the answer is in the ancient Sorsrynian parts of the journal. Aside from that, I don't know."

Suddenly, Gemma jolts up. She looks around frantically, whispering, "Do you hear that?"

My heartbeat plummets. The moment to kiss her is over. Now, she's concerned with every sound of the forest.

"I didn't hear anything," I state, easing to my feet. I retrieve the fallen flower bundle, and give it back to Gemma.

Now in distress, she takes it, but still listens for the sound. "It's coming from this way," she says. Seizing the lantern, she runs away.

"Wait, Gem!" I shout. "We're supposed to stay near camp."

I glance around, and notice the nein has left us. Musgrae and Siege's lantern light can't be seen nearby, either. No other sounds, besides the soft forest wind, can be heard. Then, even that sound ceases.

Given no other choice, I chase after Gemma. I get the nagging feeling that this won't end well. It's like the lake chase all over again. Except for, this time, it's unfamiliar ground.

How in the world is Gemma finding her way through here so quickly? I wonder. *She's never been here, same as me.*

When I finally catch up to her, the trees are creaking loudly around us. Then they go quiet, as Gemma peers through a thick infestation of them. It's a webbing made of branches. Beyond it, there's Jasper and Mekka in human form standing at an edge of water. More like a still pond than a rippling lake, it's eerie in the dim moonlight.

"Alpha, what are you doing?" queries Mekka. "We need to find the Paragonians. Let them know this forest is possessed, moving all on its own."

"It's not possessed," Jasper proclaims. "It merely wishes to keep us from getting to a certain location beyond the forest. East, if my perceptions are correct. Someone has something to hide. But it won't remain hidden for long. I think Nebukahn or another Von has hold of Winter's Vondaen. They're trying to make contact with me."

Jasper aims his hand at the water. The water bursts up. When it falls, figures are left seemingly standing or walking upon the liquid surface. There's one at first, facing Jasper. He turns, and strides to the far edge of the small pond. Jasper goes rigid, looking ready for a blow.

"Nice of you to join us, Alpha Jasper," says Zymarc, his voice muffled by a mask. Though the water figure of Zymarc is hazy as if he's surrounded in a fog, there's no mistaking Winter's Vondaen held in his grasp.

"Us?" queries Mekka. "Who is 'us,' you depraved soul?"

Other figures form up from the water; a near dozen, who then sit down at a table.

Only Zymarc and one cloaked figure remain standing. They're alongside each other.

"Any last words," says Zymarc, to the cloaked figure, "that you wish to tell your alpha, before I turn you by way of Vitiosus?"

The figure removes his cloak. It falls to the ground. Calmly, he looks at Jasper, then Mekka.

Gemma covers her mouth, whispering, "It's Droediin. He has Droediin." Tears brim in her eyes.

I just feel raging sickness in my gut, while thinking, *Droediin's either a victim or traitor. We have to get Jasper and Mekka away from there.*

I call out to them.

They don't hear me.

"Gemma, we need to cut through this tangled mess." I hand her the waking-dagger, RotaSyn. "And have you learned any spells that could help us now?"

"You're asking me?" She gawks. "I've barely finished reading my spell-book. Haven't even started on anything, besides potion-making."

"It was worth asking." With that, I start hacking into the web of branches.

She begins too, and quite violently. It's like watching Tadashi slaying the heads off ballistic dummies.

"Like father like daughter," I mutter.

"Shut up! I'm focusing."

Now through the first web layer, I tease her by saying, "No distractions?"

She gripes, "You're the biggest distraction on this planet, I swear. You arrive, and hell breaks loose. No offense."

"None taken," I reply.

"Forgive me, Alpha," Droediin says. "I let myself be captured, to ensure your safety. Nebukahn's as well. And my father, Merlynite. Will you give him my regrets? I know he had wished for me to beat out Mekka for the title. Consider this my surrender, Mek. You'll be a great alpha. Take care of Tyler. You and Rorka. And he'll take care of you."

At hearing my name, I stop slashing the branches, and dare a glance up at the unfolding scene.

"He is our equal," Droediin states proudly. "Do not ever doubt him. He's got good instincts. Von instincts, I dare say. Built to survive."

Gemma shakes my arm. "Tyler, crawl through. I've made a big enough gap."

Hooking both daggers on my belt, I bend down to claw my way through. The hacked branches snag on my clothes. I'm prevented from going any quicker. Gemma decides, then, to assist me. She plants her boot on my rear end, and drives me forward, hard. Splinters stick in the skin of my palms. Scratches get me on the face too. I scramble out, and stand up.

Rushing onward, I shout, "Jasper, you need to leave! Get away from the water!"

Jasper has sunk to his knees, looking heartbroken and old.

Gemma isn't far behind me, ordering, "Mekka, help him up!"

Mekka starts pulling Jasper up.

"Leave me here," Jasper whispers, collapsing to the ground. "I can't bear losing a Von like this. Please, Mekka, take Tyler and Gemma to safety. Leave me here to grieve."

I grip both daggers, ready to fight Mekka if he dares to even try to take me away. "You're coming, Jasper, or we're all staying."

"Tyler?" Droediin says, in disbelief, now standing nearer upon the water. "I am glad to see you again." He smiles.

Zymarc peers over Droediin's shoulder. Those red, piercing eyes of his look at me. Then at Jasper. It seems as if he can only see the two of us, beyond the water's edge.

Chills prick at my fingertips. Yet warmth heats up my arms. I feel the steps of the beast. It's almost here.

Before I can say anything. Do anything. Merlynite's running out from the forest, to growl and snarl and bark at the water scene ahead. He's loud and menacing. His coat is of metal fur, and his eyes are akin to hot coals. He's bigger than even Mekka was, that first day I saw him too.

Zymarc and Droediin can't hear Merlynite. He crumples beside Jasper, then curls his massive Von form round his alpha. Jasper buries his fingers into Merlynite's now-dense, furry scruff.

"I couldn't stop him, Jasper," Merlynite says. "Droediin knew I was going to offer up myself to Zymarc, and let him turn me with Vitiosus. He wasn't going to stop. He killed dozens of Vons, while you were hibernating, trying to turn them. But those were weaker. I knew it was only a matter of time, before Zymarc tried his magic on stronger Vons."

Zymarc keeps his focus on me, saying, "Tyler Ravier, do you wish to agree to my earlier offer? I will let Droediin go. All you have to do is agree to an apprenticeship with me. Four years is all. Magically bound to learn from me."

Ignoring Zymarc, I state, "Your father is here with me, Droediin."

Droediin's calm demeanor shifts to dread. "Turn me now, Vitiosyn, or I'll fight you. And we both know unwilling victims are harder for you to turn, aren't they?"

"Is there something, Droediin," I ask, trying to buy time, "that you want to tell me, first?"

Droediin flashes that mysterious grin of his, and those wolf-eyes dare me to guess what he's thinking. "Tell my alpha, it was me, who wrote those letters. The Phantom of Muraine. I spied on you and that girl, while on Earth. I went against direct orders. Strayed to the portal, after resupplying Mekka with food while he guarded the Cave of Ichors Von, and waited for our alpha to awaken, renewed. It was perfect. Until I got stuck there, for a few days; during which, six months passed on Muraine. Inconvenient. I know. But I was there to rescue you from that creature. Wasn't I?"

Merlynite watches his son in speechless disbelief.

"It doesn't matter now," says Droediin. "Once I've been turned, my memories of these past three years will be gone. Rorka helped me see to that, in case this very sort of thing should transpire. There's nothing this Vitiosyn can do, to make me remember. Awngeleik's whereabouts are safe. I've done my part, to protect her. Now, Ravier, what will *you* do?"

Zymarc shifts to looking like Soren, and takes off the mask. He's smiling. "Be my next apprentice, Tyler, and this all ends."

I'm at war with myself, not knowing what to do.

Droediin swiftly grips his own throat, and tears into it. Blood runs down.

Merlynite shouts, "Droediin, what are you doing? You're signing your own death warrant. We'll have to kill you, next we see you. Fight him. Try to stop Zymarc from turning you. It's against our laws, to surrender in this way. I'm old. I've lived long enough. I wanted it to be me. Not you. Never you!"

I speak to Droediin, trying to convince him. "Your father wishes for you to stop this, and fight."

"You'd best be turning me now, Vitiosyn," Droediin says, too calmly. "Turn me, before I change my mind, or Tyler changes it for me." Droediin removes his bloodied hand from his neck, and waits for the bite of Zymarc.

Gemma tugs on my arm. "Tyler, say something to make Droediin fight. Don't let this happen!"

Zymarc moves, to face Droediin. Tenderly, he grips one side of the Von's neck.

"This is my decision," Droediin says. "Please respect that."

Jasper stands up, heartbreak etched into his face. He turns away.

"Stay, Alpha," Droediin cries out, suddenly sounding frightened. "Don't leave me now."

In torment, Jasper looks back.

Zymarc glances toward the alpha too. "You see, in the end, I always get *something* I want."

Droediin closes his eyes.

Gemma screams, and digs her nails into my wrist. Horrified, she shouts, "Do something!"

Zymarc lunges for Droediin's throat, sinking his teeth in.

Droediin yells out in pain. But he doesn't try to stop Zymarc.

After a few minutes, Zymarc lets Droediin fall to the floor.

Transforming into his Von form, Droediin yelps and whines, before his eyes turn crimson-red. His fur changes to a metal coat. Instead of blackish-gray, the color resembles a blazing fire sweeping over him. He grows in size too.

"Tell me, Eighth Son of an Eighth Son," says Zymarc, staring at Jasper, "what do you think of your Alpha Jasper now?"

Droediin growls out, "Death be to them, whom stand in the way of Vitiosus. Whom stand in your way, my Alpha Zee."

I seethe at Zymarc, "I will never forgive this."

"You don't have to forgive," replies Zymarc. "Just agree. Those you travel with, know how to reach me. Send a letter. Name a place. Then we'll talk deals. You and I. Until then, goodbye." Zymarc sheathes Winter's Vondaen, and the scene on the water disappears.

It's an unmoving pond again.

Gemma bolts from my side, holding back sobs. She clambers back through the gap.

"Gemma!" I shout. "You're going to get lost."

"I don't care!" she screams, already sounding far away.

"You'd best go after her," says Mekka. "I'll catch up, after widening that break in the trees."

Jasper orders me, "Go, Tyler! We won't be long. Just have to catch my breath."

Still torn, I exit through the gap with haste, sprinting back along the way Gemma and I came. I hear her gasping for breath, and running. Even faster, she runs. I'm barely able to catch up, while stumbling around in the dark forest.

"Gemma, slow down," I plead.

"Just let me be, Tyler!" she yells, enraged.

I shout out, "I think Merlynite is the beast that hunted us. And I just left Jasper and Mekka back there with him."

Stopping, she breathes heavily. Once bent over, she places her palms on her knees. "What?" she asks, in disbelief.

I state, "Just before Merlynite showed up, I got the same feelings as I did near the lake back home. What if it's him? What if he's already joined Zymarc, and this was all a ploy? But he stopped, because he didn't plan on you and me being there?"

"That's not possible." Gemma straightens to her full height. "Merlynite was in Vondurheil, for those six months. While waiting for you to wake up, several of us talked about what went on during Jasper's hibernation."

"Vitiosus strives to break magical laws," I point out. "If he was already possessed by Vitiosus, couldn't he have found a way to project himself in Vondurheil, while actually being somewhere else?"

Gemma crosses her arms, lost in thought. "If that's a possibility, we shouldn't go back to Jasper and Mekka. We should focus on finding the others."

"How are we going to do that? Mekka said the forest moves on its own."

"Again, you're asking me?" she queries.

"First, you want me to include you," I complain, "then you resent me, for insisting on that inclusion? Make up your mind."

"I'm a girl, on a foreign planet, Tyler. Get used to it."

When dusk starts lighting the forest, Gemma and I sigh in relief.

I comment, "At least we'll have a sense of direction, now."

"Jasper mentioned that the east is hiding something," says Gemma. "Want to head that way?"

"Why not? The others are probably long gone from where they set up camp anyway."

For over an hour, Gemma and I amble toward the east. At least, what we figure is east.

The whole time spent in silence, I pick at the splinters in my hands.

"You wouldn't actually do it, would you?" queries Gemma, ending the silence.

I rub at my tired eyes. "I'm not sure what you mean, Gem."

"Agree to become Zymarc's next apprentice," she states.

I cross my arms. "I don't know. I want to say, 'No, I never would.' But that's a lie. I don't know what I would do, if Zymarc had everyone I care about at knifepoint."

"Then I guess we'll have to protect ourselves from that, won't we?"

"Guess so," I agree, starting to pick out the last of my splinters.

"I have a potion, to help with that," says Gemma. "Want some?"

I scowl at her. "You couldn't have shared that an hour ago?"

"I rather enjoyed watching you in slight pain," she remarks. "Now I'm just annoyed at your skin picking, much like how you hate my hair-twirling."

I scoff. "I don't hate it, Gem."

"But you don't like it," she says, handing me a small bottle.

As soon as I rub some of the liquid gel onto my hands, the remaining splinters slip right out, and the skin heals itself.

Gemma takes the potion back, and slips it into her satchel. "Now, not to give you a sense of déjà vu," she says, "but I'm hearing something again."

"What is it, now?" I ask. "Let me guess. Scepter's come to eat one Ravier and one Galloway?"

"No," replies Gemma, stopping in her tracks. "It sounds like a song."

I lean up against a tree, and stretch out my sore back. "I don't hear anything."

As soon as the words have left my mouth, that's when I hear it. A feminine voice. High and clear, but far away. The words aren't a language I've ever heard.

"Think we've gone far enough eastward?" I ask.

Gemma looks past me. She goes pale. Pointing behind me, she says, "Tyler, look. It's dawn, a real dawn, with daylight and everything." She laughs.

I turn to look. It's true. Full daylight. "Let's hope the others are near," I reply. "I'll race you."

We tear off toward the daylight breaking through the dead trees. The farther we go, everything comes back to life. The tree trunks appear as gold and silver, streaked with black veins. Their leaves are a fuzzy white, akin to freshly fallen snow. The grass is lush and green, its appearance like untrimmed hair flattened by a gale-storm.

Birds of many types and sizes flutter about, in the trees. One, in particular, stands out. Bigger than an eagle's, is its red face with a black stripe that runs down. A slight crook is in its beak, and on the bottom of that beak is a tuft of feathers that resembles a goatee. From head to tail, it's four feet in length. Feathers of black and gray are upon its wings. Reddish-orange tints its underbelly. And red feathers encase the legs. As we pass under it, only its pale-yellow eyes stir, following our every movement. It then flies off.

While that creepy bird flies away, a vastly different, smaller bird lands atop Gemma's shoulder, and startles her. She swats at it. But it turns into a letter, when she touches it. She just stands, staring at the envelope now perched upon her shoulder.

"Well, open it," I mutter.

She does, quickly reading the note.

"What's it say?"

"It's from Ryco," she replies. "He says Jasper and Merlynite found them before dawn, but Mekka's missing now. He hopes that the three of us are together, so Mekka can call out our location to Jasper."

"No such luck." I sigh.

"There's more," she says. "If it's just me, or me with you, Ryco says to stay put. That is, so long as we're not in immediate danger. Us moving about makes it harder for them to track us. Eli's picked up our trail, and lost it, half a dozen times." Gemma chuckles.

"How's that funny?" I ask.

She waves her hand. "No, it's not that. Ryco said Eli's getting bossy like Khyra, when she's planning parties. They all want to wring his neck. He's complaining so much. Musgrae hopes Talok bites him again. Even Kent and Siege are ready to knock him out. They miss Ben."

Slowly, her smile fades.

"One thing at a time, Gem. Worry about Ben later."

She tucks the letter away, then indicates that we should sit.

But the song restarts. Nearer now.

Gemma and I slowly make our way toward it.

We stop right before a clearing.

A girl, not quite five feet tall, occupies the edge of a small, gray-stone fountain. Softly, she sings. Her back to us, her musical voice fills the clearing, and she sways with the slight breeze. Her bright, iridescent, feathered wings drape gracefully behind her. So does her long, blonde hair. Except for the wings, she resembles Caleiso.

My pulse quickens.

Has she followed us? I wonder. *Waiting to tempt me, force me to make a choice?*

The girl sweeps her hand across the liquid surface. To the rhythm of her voice, she swirls her hand around. Continuing her song, she gradually lifts that hand in motion up out of the water. The fountain's water creates a small water funnel. She stops singing, and stands up, but keeps her hand moving.

Gemma whispers, "I think I hear Eli and Siege, in Mensa-div. Will you be fine, while I go to them?"

I nod, and she quietly leaves.

As soon as Gemma's out of earshot, the girl whirls around.

Her glowing, white eyes sear into my soul, and it burns.

Panic fills my heart.

The waterspout in the fountain grows to well over ten feet tall, as the girl sways her hand and body faster to its rhythm. Her light-blue dress is tossed about by the wind created from the swirling waterspout.

I take hold of NeiSator, ready to fight this girl who could very well be Caleiso, shifted into a new form.

I think, *Who knows what abilities she's gained, since I last saw her.*

The girl shouts, "Oonda-cantawr!" Black-and-blue fire shoots from her moving hand to hit the waterspout. While the flames still connect her to the water, she pulls her hand back, then looks to me again with those white eyes.

I try to scramble away, but I can't move. I can only watch as the waterspout rushes forward, and shifts into a giant wall of water. Still focused on me, the girl takes out a knife. The water hits her, and continues onward, carrying her, with the knife in her grip, closer to me.

So much for being fine . . .

22

Friend or Foe?

The waterspout hits, and the force slams me back against a tree. I drop NeiSator.

The girl lifts her knife and points it at me. "Intruders aren't allowed!" she yells.

I scuttle through the soaked grass. Icy water seeps through all layers of my clothes. It stings.

She lunges, and I kick one of her legs. She's thrown off balance, but flutters her wings to remain upright.

Scrambling to my feet, I shout, "I'm not here for a fight! Just looking for someone. That's all." I hold up my empty hands.

She studies NeiSator, then me. "Why draw a weapon, while watching me, then? Did you intend to kill me, before I could sense you?"

Hesitating, I wonder, *Is she Caleiso? Hard to tell, with her features partially shaded.*

Sounding as calculated as King Lemara, I state, "No, Caleiso. I would let you explain yourself, before putting up a real fight against you."

The girl's face contorts. "Who's Caleiso? Some long-lost Geldryn, come back to life? Or did someone name their daughter after one? Poor thing, being named after a revolting Geldryn." The girl lowers her knife. "They were horrid, you know? Painted Deathasyns, Withrasyns even, to be savage, when, in reality, it was they who were."

"I wouldn't know." I shrug, wishing to have NeiSator back in my grasp. "I've never read the history books."

"What?" the girl exclaims, as her wings quaver. "How did you manage that? My father never let me skip a day of reading of the past. 'History is where you learn the most,' he often says. Other times, he claims that it's *experience*." The girl shifts her weight. She then sticks her hip out to the side, resting one of her hands on it. "I've surmised that 'history' and 'experience' have equal importance, in my father's mind."

"Mine never shared the histories with me," I state, wondering what's taking Gemma so long.

The girl bends down, to pick up NeiSator.

I can't stop her.

As soon as it's in her grasp, I feel nauseated.

Hurry up, Gem, I think to myself. *Before this girl decides I'm a real threat, and things get ugly.*

The girl's eyebrows draw together. "How sad that he never did. I can tell you a lot of it, if you like. I love talking. A little too much, according to my father and fellow Lyres. The name's Skylin of the Jhire Clan." Suddenly happier, she holds out her left hand in greeting. In her right, she grips NeiSator.

I start to tell her my name, but hesitate. I then shake her hand, ready to pull away at any sudden movements. My chest becomes unexpectedly heavy. I feel pushed down. I'm overwhelmed. I can't help but think that this Skylin is doing something to me. When her blue eyes fill with tears, then those tears roll down her freckled cheeks, I know she's not doing anything intentionally.

She drops NeiSator, and begins weeping. She covers her face with both hands, and cries some more.

I pick up my fallen dagger, content to have both back on my belt. But I don't know what to do about Skylin. *Why is she crying?* I wonder.

She starts to quiet down.

"What's wrong?" I ask. "Did I hurt you?" I cross my arms, braving a glance around for Gemma and the others.

Skylin wipes away her tears. "Hurt me? No. I've just never seen her face. My mother, she died when I was too young to remember her." Her voice trembles, asking, "Who are you?"

I keep my arms crossed, and reply, "Tyler of Ravier," since I don't feel it's safe to mention Paragon, at the moment, if ever, to this girl.

"Ravier?" she queries. "That sounds familiar. Where have I heard it, before?" Skylin huffs. "Bet it'll come to me, in the middle of a fight. But I wanted to ask you, who's Gem? A friend of yours?"

"You read my thoughts?" I ask. "Is that appropriate to be doing, to someone you just met?"

"Well, no," Skylin defends. "But you're not a Darklyre, so the rules don't really apply with you."

"Does that mean you could kill me without consequence?"

Skylin puts a finger to her lips. "Yes, I guess it does." She tilts her head. "What an odd thing to say."

I shrug. "I have trust issues."

"Oh, but you can trust me." She nods.

"Where's the proof of that?"

She replies, "We're right outside of RawZend's Clan Territory. And they execute intruders. They don't want Sorsryns knowing where to find them, see? If I wasn't trustworthy, I would've already Mensa-divved to one of King Aygorinaith's Crown Sentinels to come get you. Take you away, for execution. Doesn't matter that you're young. Those old laws were written to protect Darklyres, after the firstborn of the dragon and his mistress had an attempt made on his life: Jhire, the Darklyre absent of a wing."

A woman's voice adds, "He was known for a lot more than the loss of one of his wings, Skylin."

I turn to see the owner of the voice. Sitting at the fountain, she has her long legs stretched out. Her boot-clad feet crossed at the ankles, she watches Skylin and me. Her violet eyes resemble Reign's reptilian ones, but far more devious. Her sleek, black wings are feathered, glimmering in the streaks of light coming through the trees. That same light touches her loosely braided, black hair. She adjusts her black-silk corset and then wiggles her bare shoulders back and forth teasingly. As she does so, she's not looking at Skylin; she's looking at me. Quite intently too.

Skylin scoffs at the older girl. "So now you want me to be thorough, Deamond, in spouting off our history?"

"How long have *you* been listening?" I ask.

Deamond purses her lips, in an amused sort of way. "To you and Skylin? Or you and that girl who went to get the others? Gem, as you call her."

My throat constricts. I resist the urge to grab one of my daggers. Instead, I ask, "Were you the one we heard singing?"

"Dea," Skylin scolds, "were you breaking RawZend's law, in wandering out into the Fleishyn Forest?"

"If you're never caught," Dea says, "how would anyone prove you broke a law? Hearsay isn't enough to condemn me. Besides, Crown Sentinels are allowed to wander out there. I'll be one next year, so long as King Aygor doesn't get in the way of it. What does it matter, in the end? I won't be breaking the law this time next year. Therefore, I'm not breaking any laws now."

"An interesting way of looking at it. Viewing the future as if it's the present." I make a mental note never to let Jed hear that standpoint. The havoc that could come of it sends a chill down my spine. Suddenly, I miss my two friends from back home. The Craven twins. *Will I ever see them again?* I wonder.

Dea eases up, fanning her wings out leisurely. "Would you like Gem, and the other thirteen mentioned between you, in your future?"

"Thirteen?" I ask, now alarmed at how long this Deamond may have been watching Gemma and me.

Dea gives a half-grin. "Don't be surprised, Tyler of Ravier. I was the one who led you to finding Skylin, after all. I made her singing travel farther than it would have, on its own. You've an aura, unfamiliar. Your species is mysterious to me, as well. I wanted a closer look at you. You're obviously part Withrasyn. But part something else. Something that I believe scares you. Do you know how it was that you made Skylin see her deceased mother?"

I shake my head, completely unnerved by this Deamond. Chills race through me. Their bite so deep, it hurts.

"I'll tell you, then," says Dea. "It's an old magic I've read about, in books, primarily."

Skylin scoffs again. "You read books, Dea? I've never witnessed such a thing."

"That's because you only see me, during the year's events. When reading books is a waste of time."

I ask, "What's this old magic you've read about?"

"Siveyra's Mark," Dea replies. "It's a class of magic few can perform. It's done mainly through emotions."

"That's impossible." Skylin rolls her eyes. "Magic through emotion? No one, not even my father, can do that."

Dea glares at her. "How do you know, Skylin? Do you follow Arsyn around all day long, every day?"

Skylin throws her knife at Deamond.

Though Dea dodges it, there's no escaping the wall of water that forms. Dea's slammed down, drenched, yet laughing. She flaps her wings hard, and lifts off from the ground to pelt Skylin with water droplets. A gust soon follows.

"Fine, Demon Dea!" Skylin shouts, shielding herself with her wings and arms. "You win!"

Dea stops flapping. Firmly, she plants herself down, her high-heeled boots clacking on the stones that surround the fountain.

Ignoring their antics, I ask "How do you learn that old magic?"

Dea purses her lips, looking jealous rather than amused this time. "I don't know," she says. "It was a myth. A legend to me, until today. It's what our storytellers talk of, on occasion, when some odd incident can't be explained by anything else. They'd start telling of Siveyra's Mark, claiming that the magic is rare, even rarer than a Sorsryn completing the Siveyra's Journey. Only one in one hundred Siveyras have this magic, they said."

"But he isn't a Siveyra," Skylin points out. "If that magic's real, how can *he* have it? Even worse! He doesn't know the histories. It's undignified.

He should at least know the histories."

"Ignore her, and her talk of the histories," says Dea. "Aside from winning duels and debates, nothing matters more to Skylin of the Jhire than being a *living* history book."

"You're lucky he's not a Lyre, Dea," Skylin fumes. "Or I'd be reporting your grievances to your guardian, King Aygor, himself. Though this Tyler was spying on me, I don't really want to see him executed. It's too severe a punishment."

I think to myself, *That's true.*

Dea turns to me. "Seems how you're *not* a Darklyre, you'd best be leaving soon. Crown Sentinels are out on patrol. Gem and your other friends are going in circles, at the moment. But, as I'm a resident of RawZend, I can shift the Fleishyn Forest, and have it lead them right to us."

"Then make it shift." I indicate to the patch of forest, where Gemma disappeared through. I'm furious at this woman, toying with us. We're not a game. I can only hope she's right in my magic activating with emotions. She should be thoroughly convinced to do what I want, with how angry I am.

She grins. "I will, after you answer this. You told Skylin you're looking for someone. Is that someone worth risking all your lives for, here in RawZend? Answer quickly. The Crown Sentinels will be finding your friends very soon, otherwise."

I flash through everything that counts on finding Lemawr. *Translate the journal. Hope that it leads to saving Talok and Paragon. Then we can rescue Droediin, imprison Merlynite, defeat Zymarc, and execute Caleiso. None of it can be done, until Talok's life isn't like a thread about to be snipped.*

It's now that Aysivak's words come to me: *By all means rush, but think about what comes after.*

I cross my arms again, musing, *How to know what comes after? And how can I be sure these two are trustworthy?*

Smiling inside, I get an idea. "Answer me. Then I will tell you." In one deep breath, I clear my mind. I envision Soren before me. The crazed one. The younger one. The feelings I had, while fighting him. Courage rises in my heart, and I recall when I made Zymarc tell of dragon hearts. It is then that I know this Deamond is right. My emotions make me stronger, not weaker. "What do you see, Dea of RawZend, when you look at me?" I ask.

She goes rigid. Her wings stiffen too. She takes three forced steps toward me. Her mouth opens, to speak. I see the desperation in her violet eyes. She's fighting my magic.

"Answer me," I command, in a soothing whisper.

"An aura, unknown," she says, squeezing her eyes shut. "Older than both Von and dyn, alike."

I press harder with my mind, letting anger well up. "What else?" I whisper, sounding so kind I wonder if it's even me speaking.

Dea cries out then, falling to her knees. "A creature, unknown. Not Sorsryn, nor Tamer. Not anything, yet everything."

"If you've told me all you see," I speak, sensing her heightened panic, "then why are you still resisting? Tell me the rest. Why are you afraid?"

Her eyes still shut, she shakes her head. "I fear you are a legend made flesh, before my eyes."

I hear the snapping of a whip, and know she's been released of my hold.

She coughs, and gasps for breath.

Skylin's mouth has dropped open in shock, and her wings are slumped, seeming defeated.

I look down, ashamed of the fear I've caused. "To answer you, I would give everything, to find the one we're looking for. His name's Lemawr. He's an Onyx Siveyra. He was raised by a Laykonian, King Lemara. His mother was a Sorsryn, Vayohl. That's all I know about him. Is it possible he's been through here?" I lift my head, to look.

Dea eases up. She steps closer to me. Her neck tenses, and her eyes appear hungry, yet she's focused on something past me.

A deep voice asks, from behind, "Friend or foe, Ravier?"

I spin around, and nearly faint in a fit of happiness bursting from within.

Ryco's right there, glaring at Deamond, his readied arrow aimed at her.

23

Hidden in Plain Sight

Ryco glances at me, whilst still aiming the arrow at Deamond.

I shrug at him, replying. "She's neither, yet."

He lowers his bow.

I comment, through a grin, "They're Darklyres, apparently."

Ryco grips my arm briefly. "Apparently, indeed," he replies, as his intensity fades somewhat. He beckons for someone to come out into view.

Talok rushes forth to grab hold of me. He hugs me so tightly, hardly can I take in a full breath.

"Cousin Tyler!" he exclaims, stepping back. "Forgive my words of earlier. I didn't mean them. You were right. It was the device talking. Ryco also told me what you and Khyra did for our people." Talok's chin quivers. He fights for composure. "I can't tell you how proud I am that you're here with us. It's just this wretched temper I have all of a sudden. I can't control it."

"I know how you feel," Skylin mumbles, shyly squirming on her feet. "Well, not me, personally. Deamond, here, has quite the temper. One of the king's other wards too. Keturah. She's rage, in possession of two wings. A full year younger than me. I avoid her when I can, at the events."

Deamond flashes a less-than-friendly look her way. "They don't care about that, Skylin."

315

Talok manages a grin. "I caught their names, but *who* are they?"

I reply, "Deamond's the one responsible for the forest shifting like a maze."

"Not the entire time," she corrects. "But I was responsible for keeping those two separated from you, for longer."

"For what reason?" Ryco questions, in seriousness.

"You've put quite a damper on our journey," Kent comments, wandering into view.

Warren adds, "Could have caused us quite a lot of inconvenience."

Eli states, "Barely did we escape a cluster of other Darklyres armed up to their necks."

"And for what?" queries Ryco. "To satisfy your curiosity? Or was it to prove your ability to us, before we even met you?"

Pursing her lips, Dea glances at all those emerging into the clearing.

"Well," Talok presses, "answer him. Unless you are too cowardly to answer."

Dea's stance goes rigid again. "I am no coward."

Quall comes in front of Talok, and pushes gently on my cousin's chest. "Calm down. We are on their land. Not ours." Quall looks over his shoulder. "Siege, you are most versed in foreign etiquette. I leave it to you, to keep our cultural ignorance from incurring too many insults toward them."

Sheathing his weapons, Siege answers, "Of course, Master Quall. But we should focus on our safety first."

"Those armed Darklyres," Musgrae points out, "weren't too far behind us."

"Do we have time to head farther north?" Quall looks in that direction.

Dea steps forward, declaring, "You do not. More Crown Sentinels will be patrolling that section of the Fleishyn Forest. Your best chance is to remain here. Let Skylin and myself help shield you from their notice. We can later lead you around the city, when it's safer. Skylin, you are adept in cloaking magic, correct?"

Skylin sucks in a gulp of air. "Yes, but I don't see how cloaking their auras will be helpful, Dea. We need to make them invisible. And invisibility spells are too hard for me, on my own. Plus, you and I don't match well with each other's magical signatures. Remember last year—"

Dea digs her fingernails into her palms, and cuts Skylin off. "If you wouldn't prattle on, all in one breath, Skylin, I could tell you . . . They have a Sylvadyn Parasogyn with them."

Those in our group can't help but cringe at the word's utterance. Even me. She said it so effortlessly, as if she uses the word daily.

"We don't call him that." I'm suddenly protective of Ryco. Every day, he's closer to being a friend, and I wouldn't let someone talk to my friends that way.

Skylin's forehead creases. She strides over to Ryco, to study him. "Oh?" she queries. "What do you call him, then? It's what he is: a child, and descendant, of a dragon's mistress. It's what Dea and I are too. Parasogyns!" She smiles. "All Darklyres are Parasogyns. But not Sylvadyn ones. I'd be honored to practice magic with you, Sylvadyn." Skylin lowers her wings, and they drape gracefully behind her. She then bows her head.

Ryco blinks rapidly. "You should not be saying that word, girl. But we'll argue over it, another time." He sighs. "Have you used a shielding-wall spell before this day?"

"I have." Skylin lifts her head. "But only a small one, for myself and a few friends. Not for as many as you. I don't know if I can do it. Dea, maybe it should be you."

"Can't," she says, "I need to go distract the Crown Sentinels, about to end their daily shift. Give you time to finish the spell. And, not to be impolite, but you are not endowed with the gift to distract the sentinels yet, little girl. Give it a few years, and maybe. For now, have fun partnering your magic with one of the masters of Gendras. Sylvadyns. You should have an easy time of it."

With a quick adjustment to her corset, her bare chest is puffed up further. Dea winks at Skylin and then rushes off, southward.

Even as sounds of Dea's footfalls fade, Skylin huffs. She looks down in disapproval, at her own small, girlish chest. Her scowl deepens. She then looks up at Ryco, who seems to be gnawing on the inside of one of his cheeks.

"Endowed!" Skylin shouts, looking to the south. "I'll show her endowed."

Ryco holds out his relaxed hands, palms facing up. "I'm sure you will," he says. "For now, you need to focus. Though she's right that Sylvadyns have an easier time practicing master Gendras spells, I'm only a quarter Sylvadyn."

Skylin's temper eases, and she grips Ryco's hands. "Your aura says otherwise, Sylvadyn."

"Regardless," says Ryco, "master Gendras spells take time, even if you are proficient at them." He grins in his special way, and the air fills with the scent of pinesap.

Skylin's blue eyes brighten with excitement.

Ryco turns grim, as he strolls forward a couple of steps. He grows in stature. Smoke emits from his nostrils. His breath sounds as a beast. It's only when scales form on his exposed skin that Skylin truly seems in awe.

Kent ushers us closer together, and toward a chubby tree. Drawing out his Katana, he plunges its tip into the ground. Carefully, he starts the line by the tree, and draws a circle about us. On the other side of the tree, he ends and then steps inside the drawn circle with us.

Gemma presses against me. She even grips my hand.

I'm content to have her close, yet nervous for what's about to happen.

His voice deeper, Ryco says, "I'll Mensa-div the words to you. Accept them, and follow the motions of my hands. We'll be drawing the words' symbols. When they are drawn on both sides of a barrier, it's stronger."

Happy, Skylin clarifies, "Therefore harder for even the strongest to break, or see past?"

Ryco nods once, then they begin.

Skylin's slow, in drawing the first two symbols. Ryco starts to work faster. His breath appears as a thin fog. Skylin keeps up, but barely. By the twelfth symbol, they're a blur of motion, going round the group of us.

When they stop, Ryco shifts to his usual self. Breathing hard, he says, "You have to go especially slow, for this last one. It requires absolute control. Are you good at that?"

Skylin lifts her wings, in confidence. "Flawless at it. Although, I doubt Dea would believe it, with how much I talk."

"It doesn't matter what she believes of you," Ryco states. "What do you believe about yourself?"

Glancing down at Gemma's worried expression and then to Skylin, I div to her, *"I know someone else who talks a lot. And I've come to trust her more than myself. We're trusting you with our safety. Possibly even our lives. No pressure, but I certainly hope that you think you're flawless at practicing magic, in this moment."*

Skylin's demeanor changes. She raises her hands gracefully, signaling she's ready.

Ryco begins.

The two of them appear to be in slow motion. The symbol lines glow blue.

Chatter erupts from nearby. It's Dea, chatting up a snarky storm of comments. Though I can't tell what's being said, I know it's teasing in nature. Masculine laughter, mixed in with defensive gripes, gives it away.

Skylin clenches her jaw. She struggles to focus.

"Don't worry over it." Ryco reassures her, "You have all the time we need."

Skylin holds her breath; Ryco does the same.

Dea emerges into the clearing. She sees us, still all exposed. She spins around, and grabs the hilt of a blade that's fastened upon a belt of one of the five unsuspecting sentinels. "Shall we check the strength of your enchantments, should there be intruders?"

She yanks the blade out, and runs for the fountain.

The blade's owner chases after her, and tries to grab hold of one of her wings. The four follow in pursuit, though they laugh at their distraught comrade whilst doing so. All match each other, in their brown-and-black uniforms. They resemble Onyx Warriors, aside from their leathery wings. They're less formal too. Far more uninhibited in garb, and carefree in manners. Comparing their differences is like comparing militia drills, with modern dance. One is calculated; the other is fluid.

Dea smashes the blade edge down on the stone fountain. Flames erupt. Then sparks fly out, to sizzle upon the fountain water. "Look, Seqwhyett! Your enchantment held." Deamond laughs, then bolts away, before she's caught by one of the five sentinels.

Ryco and Skylin finish, while there's a fit of wings flapping, men shouting, and Dea just being her devious self in the foreground. She's disarmed two more of their main weapon of choice. She tosses one blade to Skylin, and playfully exclaims, "Help a girl out!"

Catching it, Skylin grins.

The Crown Sentinels now take notice of her, and slightly frown. One even blushes.

Skylin's wings slump. "Don't be like that!" she scolds. "Just because Arsyn, leading Sentinel of Jhire, is my father, doesn't mean I'm a complete killjoy. In fact, hardly a killjoy at all."

"It's not that," says Seqwhyett. "We're simply nervous you're going to give us a history lesson on my named blade that Dea tossed to you."

"You have a named blade?" Skylin's wings flap some, and kick up loose dirt from the ground. "I'm jealous. Father says I can't have one, until I've beaten him in a duel." Enviously, she looks over the long, silver-black blade in her grasp.

"Good luck with that." One of the unnamed sentinels snickers.

The other three join in. Seqwhyett does not.

"I've already figured out a plan," Skylin chatters. "Since it's unlikely I could ever best him in a duel, I'll best him with bets. He's nowhere near as guarded, when making bets. When I feel I have earned the right to a named weapon or two, Dea's promised to help me win a few bets. See, I've already started recruiting a team to help me."

"Really?" queries the sentinel who blushed earlier. He crosses his arms, and his leathery, black wings fold up tight against each other.

Seqwhyett swallows nervously, before asking, "You're not planning on recruiting us, are you?"

"No," Skylin replies. "He would get too suspicious if, suddenly, a bunch of Crown Sentinels started making bets with him."

Dea perks up, glancing eastward, where the forest thins out. "Someone's coming," she says. "Seqwhyett, are your shift replacements supposed to meet you here?"

"They were already coming for patrol, when you found us. They should've begun, already."

Dea asks, "The usual route?"

"Yep!" says the snickering sentinel.

Dea sweeps a glance over where we're hidden. The tightness of her features relaxes. She seems satisfied that they can't sense us.

Skylin's wings slump again, though. "Vards!" she shouts. "I was supposed to meet my father for lunch. Doubtless, he's coming to check on me."

"You know," says the snickering sentinel, fanning out his brown, bat-like wings. "For being as smart as you are, Skylin, you certainly forget quite a lot of the simple things in life."

A tall Darklyre silently approaches. His blond, feathered wings wrap around his slender shoulders. Amused, he comes to a standstill by the fountain. "It's how you know someone has high intelligence in one or two aspects, while possibly lacking in others," he says.

In response to his voice, the sentinels turn and then lower their heads.

Skylin huffs. "I don't usually forget about the times I'm supposed to meet with you, Father."

"Which worries me," he says, strolling around in the foreground. "Did something happen?"

Dea replies, "She was busy enchanting a knife, at the fountain. And then testing it on me."

Seqwhyett breaks out a wide grin. "Is that why you appeared as a drenched bird, when you found us?"

"Did you think I went for swim on purpose, in this thing?" Dea leers, adjusting her corset again—less puffed up is her chest now, in appearance.

Focusing away from the sentinels and Dea, who's engaged with them, Arsyn does sweep his gaze over the forest. He slows the turning of his head, when making eye contact with me.

My heart starts to pound. But it's not fear that I feel. It's excitement. Joy at seeing his blue eyes light in recognition. It only lasts for seconds, before he moves his notice elsewhere. My blood turns cold. My heart gets sad. I desperately want to speak with him, though I've no idea why.

Southward of us, something crashes through the forest. The Darklyre group startles, except for Arsyn. They pull weapons from sheaths.

"Fall!" someone shouts from a short distance away. "Get down!"

Immediately, the five sentinels obey, covering themselves with their wings. Arsyn rushes for his daughter. But Dea's already shielding Skylin like a protective big sister.

Within our barrier of invisibility, we crowd even closer together. Talok shelters Gemma's other side. The King's Guard draw out weapons.

"Stay silent," Ryco whispers. "And don't move. Whatever's coming may not notice the barrier."

Ryco's barely finished with his instructions, when a massive, hairless beast crashes onto the scene. Its six limbs carry it quickly to wherever it pleases to go. Barely staying ahead of this black beast are two Darklyre girls, both smaller than Skylin.

Sounds of their screams are choked out by roaring screeches of the four-eyed creature. Filling its mouth are needlelike teeth, and four fangs, which resemble curved knives. It reaches a clawed hand out, and grabs hold of the blonde girl's ankle. She doesn't scream. Instead, she drops the bag she was clutching to, and fights to get away. Flapping her wings, she smacks the beast with them. But it bites into one of her wings. Her pale-yellow feathers end up getting shredded, but she manages to get away.

It all happens so fast.

Arsyn yanks the blonde girl to safety, immediately setting up a barrier shield.

The beast, along with the darker-colored girl, slams against it. This girl scrambles on the soggy ground. The creature's quicker to find its footing, using its four legs. Then, with its talon-like hands, it claws at the barrier. Giving up, it eyes the brown-winged girl hungrily. She stands, bravely lifting her head, readying herself to run away.

The five sentinels stay flattened on the ground. They're waiting for some signal.

Someone glides over them, and lands softly behind the beast. It's the biggest Darklyre we've seen yet. He's almost as large as the hideous beast, which reaches for the girl scrambling back and forth, dodging being caught.

This great Darklyre has one blade brandished. In his grasp, it resembles a massive, pointed butcher's knife. He digs his hand into the beast's back, and appears to grab hold of its spine. He flicks his wrist.

Sounds of bones breaking sicken me.

The beast screams in pain, and collapses. But it's not dead yet. Not until the Darklyre has carved its body in half, across the midsection.

I nearly vomit right there.

Talok—even with Ryco's warning glance at him—steps in front of Gemma and me. He blocks our view of what happens next. Still, we can hear its blood gushing out, as it takes the last of its gurgling breaths.

The darker-colored Lyre girl sits on the ground, covered in the maroon-red blood of the beast. She attempts to wipe some off from her face and neck.

Seqwhyett and the other sentinels start to ease up.

But the Darklyre points at them. "Stay down," he commands. "There are a few more of *those* coming. One has even managed to cloak himself. I need you to wait. Strike, when you know you can down them with one blow. Otherwise, don't move. They're night creatures, remember? Excellent sense of smell, but horrid eyesight in the daytime. You may as well be rocks on the ground to them."

Arsyn queries, "Why are they even out, King Aygor? Have they adapted themselves for day-hunting, here in RawZend?"

"Not exactly," replies King Aygor. "Keturah and Sonya woke them. Wandered too near to their cave."

"It was Ketty's idea," proclaims the girl with shredded feathers.

The girl drenched in blood bolts up. "It was not!" she shouts. "I simply wanted to pick different herbs and flowers, for our chefs to use in tonight's Opening Supper for the Events. Our choices were too limited, where—"

"Quiet!" King Aygor shouts. "Do you not understand? These creatures are dangerous."

Keturah cracks her knuckles. "They can't be too bad, being the prey of Greyvons."

"What would you know?" Sonya sneers. "Have you ever seen Greyvons, Ketty?"

"Just in pictures." Keturah bobbles her head, in mockery.

"Enough, girls!" Deamond commands. "They can hear us from a good distance away."

Rocks scatter from a several feet away. Growling sounds from the south, behind where the sentinels wait patiently to get their strikes in.

King Aygor asks, "Can your shield hold against three, and yourself, Arsyn?"

Arsyn nods.

"What about four?" King Aygor asks.

"Depends on how many attack it at once," replies Arsyn.

"Best not to risk it, then," says King Aygor, grabbing Keturah. He tosses her down into the mess of the dead beast's mangled body. "Stay there, Ketty, and they won't be able to sniff you out."

"I hate today," Keturah whines.

Skylin rolls her eyes, then divs to me, *"Maybe if she didn't waken the Gatroes, in their caves, she wouldn't be covered in the blood of one."*

"Is this the Keturah you're always trying to avoid?" I ask, in div.

Skylin puts her hand to her mouth, hiding a smile.

I div, *"I see why. First, reckless. Then whines about the consequences for it."*

"Precisely," Skylin divs back, before turning serious.

One beast walks out among the waiting sentinels. Then another comes up behind that one.

I div to Ryco, *"Should we help them?"*

"Gemma already asked that," he divs, *"Told her, only if it's absolutely necessary. For now, we wait, and hope they've got a handle on it. That aside, I want to get a look at their battle style, in case we end up in a struggle against them."*

King Aygor steps away from the dead beast, as I hear the invisible Gatro scuffling around in Arsyn's direction. It's sniffing and grunting too.

Dea looks that way, and senses it as well. "King Aygor," she whispers, "what do you want us to do?"

"Stay there," he replies. "You'll only get in the way."

Seqwhyett gives a hand signal, and two other sentinels confirm; they're about to make a move.

King Aygor studies the space surrounding Arsyn, trying to determine where the hidden Gatro is.

Seqwhyett and the two sentinels jolt up, and thrust their weapons into the unsuspecting Gatroes. Then the other two sentinels join in. The five hack into the two beasts repeatedly. It's over in seconds.

The while, King Aygor doesn't flinch at all. He searches, listening for the cloaked enemy.

Keturah sniffles some, and rubs at her nose. "How much longer?" she whispers. "Its blood is really starting to stink."

King Aygor lifts a hand to silence her.

The sentinels stand up, to wait for their king's instruction.

Something squashes the top half of the fallen Gatro that's beside Keturah. Her wings start quivering. She holds her hands to her mouth, trying to quiet her sporadic breaths.

Arsyn motions toward Keturah.

King Aygor nods and then studies the space around the frightened girl. He lifts his hand, beckoning the sentinels forward.

They aim weapons toward Keturah. She gradually looks over her shoulder, to see them.

King Aygor shouts, "Don't!"

The Crown Sentinels hesitate.

Something grabs Keturah by the throat, and yanks her up off her feet.

She thrashes and coughs, then claws at the invisible hand wrapped around her neck.

King Aygor breathes heavily, asking, "How long ago was your last scheduled fatality, Keturah?"

She tries to answer, but she's being choked too hard.

Even though she's scared, Sonya exclaims, "Two days ago."

"Death type?" queries Aygor, assessing where to strike in the air, to hit the invisible Gatro.

"Blood loss," replies Sonya, clinging tight to Skylin's arm.

Aygor grumbles, "I don't like it, Keturah, but I think you'll be fine. Especially with Arsyn here. I'm going to snap your neck. But, first, you need to stop breathing. Ready?"

Keturah shuts her eyes. Her body goes limp.

Aygor aims his open hand toward Keturah. He starts closing it into a tight fist. Shutting his eyes, he twists his fist in the air. Keturah's neck snaps. The beast reveals itself, standing on the body of the first dispatched Gatro. It screeches. Then it throws Keturah's body away like garbage. The sentinels rush to catch her; they blunt her descent.

Arsyn lets his barrier down, to help King Aygor fight the beast. Seqwhyett sets Keturah down gently, while the other sentinels surround the battling three.

"Keep it cornered," King Aygor commands his sentinels. "Narrow the battle zone. Do not let it escape. Deamond, watch and learn."

This Gatro's a good fighter. Fast, even though he's rather large. His six limbs might have something to do with it. Two are obviously arms, and two are legs. But the middle set shift to being whatever the Gatro needs. More speed? Four legs. More power? Four arms. This one takes on the two male Lyres as if they are his playthings. He disarms King Aygor, and growls out metallic laughter.

Arsyn shoves the king away, and takes a blow to the chest. He's ripped open.

I shudder. My chest hurts too. I can't breathe. Then I div to Ryco, *"Please, can't we help them?"*

"No, don't!" Skylin interrupts. *"My father's survived worse. Dea or I will tell you when to make a move."*

Ryco gives a nod, then glances to the others. They remain still. But they don't look a bit happy about it.

Arsyn gets up, and continues to let the creature strike. He keeps up his advancement.

The Gatro's starting to succumb to fatigue. Forlornly, he screeches. I even think he's about to turn, and run away.

Excitement permeates my body. My fingertips feel as if they're buzzing with sparks. For a moment, it's as if I'm connected to Arsyn; even more so, when his wings begin to glow like hot metal. His eyes turn brilliant white. Bright fire bursts from his hands, to engulf the creature in white flames. The Gatro's body vibrates fiercely, then bursts into fine dust. The cries of him fade to silence.

Arsyn collapses on his hands and knees, the glow of his eyes and wings now gone.

King Aygor brushes at one of Arsyn's wings, asking him, "Where did you learn a spell, such as that? You've made it into less than ash." Whirling around, Aygor instructs, "If you would, Deamond, help replenish Arsyn's magic. I fear that took quite a lot out of him."

"I'll be fine," says Arsyn, easing up unsteadily.

Skylin dashes to him, and he hugs her close.

"I am fine, my dearest daughter," he says. "It doesn't prey on full-grown Lyres. Only our young. It relishes the hunt. Then the fresh kill."

"Which is why"—King Aygor addresses Sonya—"I specifically told you and Ketty to stay within certain parameters."

"I told you," Sonya defends, "it was Ketty's idea."

Aygor shouts, "And why do you think I make the two of you go together?"

Wrapping her torn-up wings round her small frame, Sonya answers, "To make us bond more, because we're always fighting?"

In fury, Aygor says, "So that you can talk Ketty out of her stupid—" Aygor clamps his mouth shut. More calmly, he continues, "What I mean is, Sonya, you are more apt to obedience than Ketty is. I want you to influence her. Help her make better decisions, so she doesn't end up like that." He points to Keturah.

With her neck still snapped, she rests on the ground unmoving. If I thought Gemma's pose in her sleep was bad, Keturah's is at least three times worse in this moment. She's actually dead. Flashes of Khyra dying creep into my mind. My throat burns. I start getting choked up. The image is sickening. I look down at Gemma. She, too, is staring at Keturah.

Something warm presses between my shoulder blades, and I take deep breaths again. I didn't even realize I was starting to panic.

Kent Mensa-divs, *"It's all right. We're safe, for the moment. And, judging by their behavior, that girl will be fine too."*

Gemma glances back at Kent, grateful for the reassurance. But I'm skeptical. 'Safe now,' could easily turn into our nightmare: running for our lives. I wonder, too, *Where are Jasper, and the other three? Mekka, Merlynite, and Zeekryn?* In div, I ask Quall about them.

Quall divs back, *"Zeekryn got a letter from Paydinn, asked him to travel to Paragon. It seems a majority of Paydinn's family are traveling there, to meet with the advisers about an agreement. Possibly, an alliance."*

I smile inside, finding comfort in knowing that Paragon will have more protection, at least, for a little longer. I div, saying, *"Let's hope Zepharre's cooperative."*

"After what happened with the food stores," Ryco divs, *"he should be a little more bearable."*

Musgrae and Warren share a look, then they shake their heads.

"And the Greyvons?" I div.

Musgrae answers, *"Forest kept shifting too much. Despite my excellent sense of smell, we lost track of them. That was hours ago. Ryco and Siege sent out letters. Even sent one to Rorka, in Vondurheil. It'll be a bit, before we hear from them."*

His answer leaves so much to worry about. But what can be done? We're at the mercy of the Darklyres, and their Fleishyn Forest. All we can do is wait.

The silence and milling about of the Darklyres grows restless, in the foreground.

Finally, Deamond states, "She should be waking, by now."

King Aygor rubs the side of his face. "She's not had two moderate fatalities so close together, before. Since she turned eleven, it's been three days apart or more. But I am getting nervous, as well. Arsyn, have you any suggestions on waking her?"

"You won't like it," says Arsyn.

"Tell me anyway," states King Aygor.

Arsyn sits at the fountain edge, staring into the still water. After a time, he says, "A spell of Nekrosis might work."

King Aygor huffs out a breath. "You're right. I don't like that. Let's give her a little more time, to overpower her own death."

Minutes turn into near an hour.

The sentinels have thoroughly cleaned their weapons and uniforms.

Dea and Skylin try to appear calm. But it's easy to spot their worry over whether the barrier will hold for much longer. They won't stay in one place. Dea keeps fidgeting with her corset. And Skylin furiously wrings her hands.

Now as pale as Quall, Ryco has started to sweat. He rests both hands on the barrier. Even still, the symbols are starting to show on our side.

Skylin's showing signs of exhaustion, as well, with her tired eyes and lifeless, drooping wings.

Arsyn looks away from the fountain, to meet my gaze again. He holds eye contact for longer, this time.

My head pounds, as I div to him, *"Please don't give us away. You've no idea what we've had to go through, to get here."*

"Why shouldn't I reveal your presence?" he asks. *"You are intruders, after all. Breaking laws of RawZend."*

"Because Dea claims I have Siveyra's Mark," I reply. *"And I would bet you're curious now, to know if it's true."*

Arsyn grins some. "Not even a Darklyre, and you're making bets already? What of this? I continue to keep the others from noticing all of you, long enough that you can explain yourselves to me. If I don't like you, or your answers are unsatisfactory, I'll turn you over to King Aygorinaith, to do with you whatever pleases him."

I shrug in reply.

"What sort of answer is that?" asks Arsyn. *"I need words. You could also bribe me, to save your own necks. You've weapons on you that I'm rather interested in. Give them to me, and I promise safe passage to the north or south. Your choice."*

I'm reluctant to trust him, until Dea proclaims, "For Vards' sake, King Aygor! Let Master Arsyn revive her with a spell of Nekrosis. Hasn't he proved himself powerful and trustworthy, a thousand times over to the Lyres throughout the years?"

Sonya collapses in a fit of sobs. "Ketty's really going to stay dead, isn't she? Oh, I'm so horrible! It's all my fault!" she wails.

King Aygor clamps his lips tight together, refraining from his own outburst.

Arsyn divs to me, asking, *"Shall I let the girl wake up, do you think? She's been ready, for a little while."*

"Do all Lyres treat everything as if it's a game?" I ask, in div.

"Not everything," Arsyn replies. *"But everything to do with death? Now that is our game. Toying with it. Taunting it. Testing it. Then overcoming it. It's what Darklyres do. Overcome all the different levels of death. With each fatality, we gain resistance to it. The end goal is to be strong enough to overcome spells of the Dei-Athos-Kree. That is the strongest inflicted means of death. The kind meant to torment your soul, forever."*

"Maybe you can help us, then?" I div, sounding hopeful. *"Do you know much about Geldryn devices?"*

Arsyn doesn't answer me. Instead, he glances to Keturah, and says, "There's no need for me to revive her. She's waking up."

24

A Pretense of Wings

King Aygor rushes to Keturah and kneels down.

She eases up, rubbing at her neck. She rasps out, "I told you to run faster, Sonya. We wouldn't have needed rescuing, if you weren't so slow."

Sonya's joy is wiped away. She starts crying. "Shut up, Ketty! It isn't my fault I have shorter legs, and big fat wings that always get in my way." Sonya storms off, eastward.

Aygor jolts up. Trying to calm himself, he ambles away from Keturah. He's about to say something, but Keturah interrupts him with her coughing and gagging.

"Vards!" she exclaims. "Did no one think to wash me off a little, while waiting for me to wake up? I smell like death. And look at my dress. It's ruined!" Keturah stomps toward the fountain.

Aygor whirls around, shouting, "You dare wash yourself, Ketty, with that sacred water, and I'll toss you into a stream, in the middle of winter!"

Keturah stops in her tracks, utter shock on her face.

Cringing, Aygor calmly states, "What I mean is: that fountain's water is meant for enchanting weapons. Or washing yourself off, if, and *only* if, your enchantment process went awry and made a bit of a mess. That is all. And I've been studying around this fountain for a while, now. Did someone use it for an enchantment, recently? The foreground is more saturated than usual."

Skylin raises her hand. "That was me. I was enchanting a knife." She rushes to show King Aygor. "I did the wind enchantment at home. Saved the water enchantment to do here. I plan on using it in the Minor Gauntlet, tomorrow."

Aygor grips one of his wrists, standing tall. "Looks to be a stable enchantment. Care to test it out?"

Skylin starts to say, "Oh, but I already—"

Aygor lifts a silencing hand, then whispers. "Ketty needs a good washing, before she goes back to Grevagg's city limits. If you catch my drift?"

Ketty has her arms crossed, while the sentinels recount how Arsyn vaporized the big Gatro that had intended on eating her. She's completely oblivious to King Aygor's plotting.

He motions for Skylin to proceed. And she does. She throws the knife in Ketty's direction.

The sentinels scatter.

Ketty's thrown down by the wave crashing against her. She gets up, sputtering out water. She turns around, and glares at Skylin.

Skylin summons her knife back.

Ketty screams, "Don't you dare throw that again!"

Skylin does anyway; and again, a fourth time, then a fifth. The other Darklyres cackle. King Aygor simply glares at the girl fighting the weapon's enchantment. Skylin's about to throw her knife, for the sixth time. But her father goes and grabs hold of her wrist.

"Just one more time," Skylin pleads. "She's almost clean."

"She's almost drowned too," states Arsyn, keeping his laughter at bay.

Seqwhyett adds, "Most assuredly wounded by a bruised ego, as well."

King Aygor abruptly asks, "May I observe that marvelous knife closer, Skylin?"

She gives it to him.

He looks it over.

Deamond helps Keturah up, as King Aygor throws the knife at them. They're both drenched by a wall of water that's twice the width of the ones from Skylin's throws.

King Aygor nods. "Yes, I think they're adequately clean now. Sentinels, you may go."

Dea starts to follow them.

"Not you, Deamond." Aygor's voice deepens. "I have some things I wish to talk over with you."

"Now?" she asks.

Aygor snaps his fingers at Ketty, commanding, "Go with the sentinels. Head straight for the palace. They will wait outside your room, until supper is ready. No arguing."

Ketty marches off, making enough racket for three persons.

Arsyn glances from our direction, to King Aygor scowling at Deamond. "Perhaps," he says, "you should talk to your oldest ward, later, King Aygor. We are all still reeling from a nearly missed tragedy, aren't we? Keturah could've been that Gatro's last meal. He was about to bite into her, as you snapped her neck, you know?"

"I know," he replies. "That doesn't change the fact that Dea was supposed to keep an eye on them. It could've been prevented, altogether."

Looking down, Dea mumbles, "I don't recall agreeing to be their constant watcher, Sire."

"I'm not your sire, Deamond," Aygor says, a little too calmly. "Arsyn is right. We'll talk of this later."

Dea confidently strides forward. "I'd rather talk now, and get it over with. What is my punishment?"

"Punishment?" Aygor sounds surprised. "It's not so much as that, as it is an obligation, Dea. As my oldest ward—who will not be my ward, by this time next year—you will be expected to accept each and every request for a dance, this night, after supper. And I do so know how much you *adore* dancing." Aygor narrows his gaze on Dea. "I was going to let you out of it. But now? Not a chance." He starts heading back to the city, calling over his shoulder, "When she's done sulking, Arsyn, will you and Skylin be kind enough to escort Dea to the palace?"

"Of course," Arsyn calls back.

As soon as King Aygor's out of earshot, Dea bustles to Arsyn. "I can explain, you know."

Arsyn stretches out his fingers upon the fountain's water, commenting, "As can all Lyre women, plotting the course of their future. But there's no need. That barrier broke a while ago." He snaps his fingers, and the barrier makes a shattering sound.

There's no hiding now. We're completely out in the open.

Skylin's head dips down, as she whispers, "What are you going to do, Father?"

Dea asks, "You've been keeping it up, for nigh this entire time? Why?"

Ryco hunches over, and breathes heavily. Yet he never looks away from Arsyn.

"Curiosity," Arsyn proclaims. "And I made a bet with SynKievas this morning, claiming that I'm better at hiding things in plain sight than he is. The challenge is a thrill."

"Does that mean," Talok queries, "that you'll help us traverse to the north, safely?"

"I could do that," Arsyn agrees, before pointing at Talok's wrist. "But don't you want to learn more of that Geldryn bangle? They've an excellent library, here in Grevagg. Lots of Geldryn texts. Withrasyn ones too. Even the personal spell-book of Gaula: our Withrasyn Ancestor." Arsyn motions to me. "That one tells me, you've all suffered enormous hardship to get here. Since you're here, why not have a look around?"

"It seems too easy," Gemma divs.

I ask, "How do you plan for us to have a 'look around,' when we look nothing like you?"

"Give you wings." Arsyn grins. "Not real ones, of course. You won't be able to use them. But you'll feel the weight of them, and they'll look real to all other Lyres you meet. Unless, perhaps, you're that thieving SynKievas. He's stolen a whole armory from me, throughout these past five years, and I want my weapons back. Winning this bet should do the trick. Hiding a whole cluster of foreigners, right in plain sight? Believe me, I have plenty of motivation to keep you hidden. I have my two witnesses, as well. Skylin and Deamond. I'll reveal my deed to him, when all of you are long gone, safe and sound."

Quall queries, "Ryco, you're more versed in spotting deception. What do you think?"

"He could've given us away," Ryco replies, now standing alert. "But he didn't. That counts for something. I do think, however, that some of us should stay behind. I don't like us all being in one place. Too vulnerable for being caught, with no hope of aid coming our way."

"I will stay behind," says Musgrae. "I've dealt with Gatroes before, and I know their weak points."

Quall says, "I, too, will stay behind. Replenish our food and medicine stores. But I expect you to collect some food, while in there. Understood?"

"Yes, Master Quall," Siege replies.

"Two more to stay behind," Ryco states.

Warren strides over to Musgrae. "I'll be too noticeable, with this Kyanite skin. Plus, I need to up my skills, regarding this forest. It's similar to one I got caught in when I was a boy, training with the Kyanite Konverts. There are a few patterns, and I've almost got two of them memorized."

"Very good," says Ryco. "The other to stay behind will be Eli."

"What!" Eli exclaims. "But I want to see a new city."

"Don't care," Ryco replies. "I've enough to worry over, without you testing my patience. Or making a fool of yourself."

Gemma says, "I'll bring a good book back for you."

"At least somebody cares about me." Eli fakes a grin at Ryco. "Thanks, Gem. Don't have too much fun without me." He kisses her forehead, then goes to lean against the chubby tree, and sulk.

"More like," she says, "don't die of fright."

Musgrae adds, "And don't let Tyler do anything crazy."

"Too late," I div, to Gemma.

She chuckles. "That's a losing battle, Grae."

"He'll be in good company," says Arsyn. "All Lyres are some kind of crazy. Have to be, with all the fatalities we suffer throughout the year. Shall we get to the matter of wings?"

Talok volunteers, "I'll go first."

The process is a blur. I hardly know what to think of it. We're given long, spacious cloaks, which Dea and Skylin help to make. We're told that this kind of cloak is what Darklyres of the Ayzagaun Clan will be wearing, since they don't wish to flaunt their wings as much as residents of Clans RawZend and Jhire do.

After we're given our cloaks, Arsyn works to give us the appearance of having functional wings. What I feel is more and more weight being distributed across my back. It's not too terrible. But I do wonder how I'm going to sleep tonight.

"All done," Arsyn proclaims. "They'll move with you, looking and feeling natural. Depending on your movements, you might even have ghost sensations of them brushing up against your body. Just act normal. And don't try to fly. They won't work for that."

Dea states, "That's quite a lot of magic, Arsyn. Sure you can sustain it?"

"Positive. It has its basis in a Geldryn spell. As you know, Geldryn spells—"

Dea interrupts, stating, "Don't need further magic, to sustain them. Yes, I'm aware. But you do it with such ease."

Arsyn replies, "That's because I'm older than you think, Deamond of RawZend. I've traveled around my fair share of Muraine. I'll be fine. And so will they."

We wave goodbye to the four staying behind, then start for the city of Grevagg.

Kent calls back, "Don't let the Gatroes eat Eli, Grae."

"Nah!" Musgrae says. "We'll just let it gnaw on him a bit, then save his skinny hide."

"Ya never cared at all," says Eli. "Both of you. You've just admitted it."

Kent waves him off, shaking his head.

The sound of Eli and Musgrae's bickering fades away.

For a ways, we traverse down a steep hill. The trees of the forest get sparser, the farther we go.

Gemma whispers, "It's like having a fully loaded backpack on. I keep wanting to adjust the straps of it. Even take it . . . or, rather, them off, and carry them in front for a while."

"Vards," Skylin says, "that would be nice to do, on occasion. My back gets sore, after an entire day of practice and flight."

"I meant to ask, earlier," queries Siege, strolling beside Deamond, "what is: vards?"

"Vardiyas," Dea clarifies. "Only 'Vards' is an accepted cry of frustration or agreement, depending on the context."

The two start talking of etiquette and such. So absorbed is Siege by the conversation, he's oblivious to the city, once it's within view.

Sandstone structures, reminiscent of old Arabian cities, dot the entire area for miles. There's a towering structure, at least thirty stories high, a ways off to the left. Like a dull, rectangular mirror, it glimmers. Frontward, atop a hill in the distance, an elegant black structure finds respite. Its appearance is soft to look at. Four pillars are at the structure's corners. And its roofs are domed, with steeples stretching up like lightning rods.

We're at the base of the hill now, where the dirt is likened to reddish sand. It looks as if it's stained by blood, and I consider it fitting given how these Darklyres are obsessed with death. *Do they truly fear anything,* I wonder, *aside from night creatures feeding on their children?*

Treading upon a light-colored stone path, we pass by loads of shops selling food, and vendors offering weapon services.

They start to talk to us, but see Arsyn and Skylin.

"Oh, Master Arsyn!" one of the shop girls exclaims. "We didn't know you had friends from Ayzaga comin' this year. We'll leave ya be. Let us know whatcha need, lovely. Lookin' forward to the dancing, songs, and such tonight. Might you be there?"

"Wouldn't miss it," Arsyn replies, smiling tensely.

We continue on.

Skylin says, "I hate it when they call you 'lovely.' I swear, all the vultures want is to be called: Wife of Arsyn, or Skylin's Stepma."

"Put on a good face," says Arsyn. "We only have to tolerate it a few times a year, no?"

"I suppose," Skylin agrees.

Deamond pauses her conversation with Siege. "I could help with that, you know."

"I'm open to suggestions," says Arsyn.

Gemma tenses beside me, right then. She digs her nails into my forearm. A look of shock tightens her features. "Tyler," she whispers, "that Lyre up ahead. He looks like . . . Ben? It can't be."

I look to where Gemma's focusing. She's right. A black-cloaked Lyre, who's standing on the gray-stone steps that lead up to the black palace, looks very much like Ben. He's talking with two others: a man about the same height, but with a slightly larger frame, and a woman possessing long, raven-black tresses.

Arsyn turns enough to playfully study Gemma. "Oh, did I forget to mention? Some other strangers managed to get stuck in the Fleishyn Forest. I had to save them, in the middle of the night, because, well . . . they decided to take to a Gatro cave, for their place of slumber. That was a very long night, three days ago."

Gemma stifles laughter, then calls out, "Ben!" She raises her hand high, in greeting, waving slightly.

He breaks his conversation, to glance in our direction. Spotting Gemma, he waves back, still wearing the gloves I gave him. Then he practically gallops down the stairs.

Even the weight of Gemma's fake wings doesn't stop her, during her frantic rush through the crowd to get to Ben. Arsyn's handiwork holds up, and her wings sway naturally, whilst covered mostly by the dark-green cloak she wears.

Ryco sighs in relief. "Now I know why Rozeth hasn't been answering my letters. Nor Nyrim. Both were here with Ben, or lost in that maniacal forest."

Gemma plows into Ben, embracing him hard.

He laughs, as he steadies his footing.

I'm relieved to see him. Ecstatic, actually! Until he pulls away from Gemma, and kisses her full on the mouth.

My chest erupts with sensations of fire. I'm mad and jealous and happy, all at the same time. This is going to be long day . . .

25

Welcome to Grevagg!

Glancing at me, Talok comments, "Suddenly, all her questioning about Ben makes sense." He presses his lips together, looking amused.

But I'm not amused. It seems, neither is Ryco, as he gnaws on the inside of his cheek. I swear he even grinds his teeth.

I muse, *Maybe Ben's broken some guard code of Paragon, by kissing Gemma? Who knows, with Ryco? It could be all this unpredictability surrounding us. Too many variables to plan for. It's making me nervous too. Among other things.*

When Gemma pulls away from Ben, then smiles up at him, the fire in my chest subsides, only to be replaced by a sickening ache in my stomach. I don't know what to do with myself. So, I simply shrug at my cousin.

Talok nods. That knowing spark's in his gaze. He focuses on Nyrim and Rozeth ahead, who are walking past the young pair to greet us. They greet Ryco first.

"Are you surprised that we've beaten you here, Ryco?" Rozeth asks, giving a quick curtsy.

Nyrim adds, "If it hadn't been for Ben, we'd still be nearer to home. He—and I, as well—have quite the story to share. But we'll discuss it later."

Rozeth queries, "How was the journey? Thirteen days, since last we saw you, was it not?"

"Has it been that long?" I ask.

"It has," Kent replies, while poking at Ryco's fake wings.

Ryco ignores him.

Siege says, "But you were out for part of it. Then enraptured with that book, for another good portion of time."

"You're a reader, then?" Dea asks.

"When I'm motivated enough," I reply.

Dea closes her wings tighter together, not to shield her body, but rather, to force them into creating pleasing curves. In confidence, she walks forward, commenting, "Well, those three have certainly been *motivated* in exploring the city, and making fast friends with several other Lyres. Arsyn, however, gave no hint of knowing them prior to now." She studies him.

Arsyn studies her, in return, replying, "I would tell you my affairs are no business of yours, but, then, your offer for tonight changes that slightly, doesn't it?"

Gulping, Dea avoids Skylin's scrutiny.

"Offer?" Skylin queries. "What's he talking about, Deamond?"

Dea's wings stir, while she bites down on her lower lip.

Arsyn stands gallant, as he glances from his daughter to Deamond. "You will know soon enough," he says, "unless Dea can't work up the courage to ask for King Aygor's permission."

"Me?" Dea asks. "It's supposed to be you."

With head held high, Arsyn states, "You've already broken protocol, in asking rather than waiting to be asked. Therefore, you will ask Aygor. Not I. If he needs to hear it in person, I will confirm my answer to you in front of him. Do you deem it fair?"

"Yes." Dea sighs.

Skylin whispers to me, "Did you hear what she asked him?"

I shake my head. "I wasn't listening to them."

Ben and Gemma approach.

I don't know what to say.

Ben greets us, but the humor in his eyes fades. "Where are the others?" he asks.

"A ways behind," Ryco replies, before slapping Siege's hand away, the one poised to pet one of Ryco's wings.

Talok adds, "They wanted to get in a good hunt."

Crossing his arms over his chest, Kent asks, "How did *your* hunting go?"

"Better than could have been expected." Ben does his shy handclasp.

At the prodding of Arsyn and Dea, we continue for the palace stairs. With Arsyn near one side of Dea, Siege takes to her left, and resumes the conversation of etiquette. Arsyn, however, glances about pleasantly at the Darklyres we pass by. He nods, or sometimes lifts a hand, in greeting the ones who welcome us.

Rozeth, spotting me ambling beside Talok, comes and hooks her arm with mine. "I knew we would soon see all of you, Tyler. And I must tell you, you are close to getting some answers."

Behind me, Nyrim whispers, "If we can get a moment alone, Ben and I have news to share in regards to your aunt."

Talok trips a bit. He's about to ask Nyrim for more.

But Nyrim whispers, "Not here. Too crowded. Arsyn will do his best to get us new quarters, for the lot of us to have privacy."

Ben breaks his conversation with Gemma, to add, "King Aygor had to put us with other Ayzagaun Lyres, while the RawZend builders finished the last of the renovations to the palace."

"They're done, now," Dea proclaims. "Finished early this morning."

Arsyn starts up the flight of thirteen gray-stone steps first. There's a wide landing at the top of them, where many Lyres have gathered. Most are preoccupied with their discussions, or eating their lunch of cooked meats and flatbread. Others have taken to sitting near still pools of water, while reading various texts or letters.

Eight more stairs lead to the grand landing of the black-stone palace.

Once at the top, we're able to truly get a feel for the splendor of King Aygor's Palace. Made of matte-black and dark-gray marble, it softly glimmers in the afternoon sunlight. This close to it, we cannot see the top of it. It's a black wall, reaching for the bright, blue sky.

Dea glances at me, asking, "Does it please you?"

"Depends," I reply. "Can it talk? Mensa-div, I mean."

Skylin giggles. "It isn't sentient."

Dea states, "But you imply that you've encountered a sentient structure. You haven't really, have you?"

"My cousin couldn't say for sure," Talok interrupts. "Could you, Tyler?"

I reply, shrugging, "Not really. But the palace is impressive, whether it can div or not."

About to pass beyond the outer palace wall, I turn to gaze back at the city. It shimmers as would dust-covered, golden blocks, stacked no more than three stories high. The domed roofs of colored-glass, on various structures around, paint a mosaic of color in an otherwise two-toned cityscape. There's so much to explore. So many places where Lemawr could easily pass us by, and we'd never know it.

I wonder, *How are we ever going to find him here, if he's even here at all?*

We pass through the courtyard's open, wrought-iron gate, then traverse over groomed, green grass. Black trees with red vines, which line the inside of the pale walls, are like the ones in the Eye of Paragon, only smaller. Now past a wide, limestone archway, we enter the palace's grand hall. Our unit's footsteps echo on the floors of flaxen-colored marble. There's no hope of crossing through here, without being heard.

Let's hope, I muse, *that we don't have to slip out, during the night.*

Sixteen pillars of white are wrapped with indigo cloth. And, assigned to each pillar's side, are sentinels dressed in tans and browns standing still as statues. They face each other, separated by a distance of at least twenty steps. In front of the pillars, surveying all who enter, are sixteen golden statues. Creatures on the left are presumably of all the auras: Von, dyn, stag, eagle, horse, snake, a hooded-figure, and a Vardiya. The pillars to the right are kept by golden statues of people. The first is a one-winged Darklyre. Then it goes another Darklyre male. Two women. Two men. Then two more women. All pillars are guarded by one statue, and one sentinel, each.

Skylin asks, "Have you seen the Statue of Jhire, before? It used to be at the center of Ayzaga." She indicates the one-winged statue, then divs, *"I know you haven't, but I'm trying to be myself. And I ask lots of questions, always looking for opportunities to share Darklyre history."*

Dea interrupts, divving, *"More like you look for ignorant victims, to spout off facts to."*

Skylin's wings slump, and she lets them drag on the marble, while Ben leads Gemma and us over to the Jhire Statue.

"I haven't seen it, before," I reply. "Was it always in Ayzaga?"

Skylin's lackluster in answering, until I div, *"You've got a willing victim right here. I've got a lot to learn. So get talking."*

Skylin's demeanor brightens. I halfway expect her to burst out with a barrage of words. But she doesn't. She's calm, in replying, "Jhire's Statue was the first, among these, to be crafted; which was done in a Rubidyn's cavern."

Arsyn adds, "It stayed there, until King Rentwar gave it to Jhire, himself, as a gift. It was a sign of goodwill that Darklyres need never fear being attacked by the Rubidyns."

"Then they are allies of ours?" queries Siege, crowding closer to Nyrim.

"Not allies," says King Aygor, striding from up behind us. "If we are ever in need, they would give us shelter. At least, that was the promise made to Jhire. Haven't a clue if it extends to his descendants, and the many offspring of his seven siblings." At the front of our group is King Aygor standing nobly, appearing proud of his palace, until he spots Ryco in the middle of a yawn. His eyebrows draw together, and he quickly steps toward Ryco. "Forgive my manners. You must've made the trek in three days, and are utterly exhausted."

Talok agrees, "It's true."

Gemma raises her hand sheepishly, about to add something. But Ben says, through a smile, "And hungry, as well. At least, this one is."

Blushing, Gemma puts her hand down.

King Aygor relaxes. "You are Gem, then? Ben has mentioned you. And a Tyler and Talok too. Are they among you?"

Talok and I step forward, politely dipping our heads down.

"That'd be us," Talok replies.

"And sporting an old Geldryn bangle too," says Aygor. "Is it an heirloom passed down? You don't see those old devices too often."

Aygor motions for us to follow him farther into his palace, and we do.

"Something like that," replies Talok, repositioning the bangle on his wrist.

"Do you know much about it?" queries Kent.

Excitement rises in my chest, as I wonder: *Does King Aygor know how to get the device off Talok?*

Footsteps pound through the courtyard. Then someone's darting into the grand hall.

Aygor takes a closer look at the Geldryn device. His head sways side to side. "I would have to refer to the Geldryn texts in the Library of—"

"King Aygor!" someone shouts. "Is it true?"

A male Darklyre comes to a screeching halt at Aygor's side. Breathless, he grabs the king's arm.

King Aygor gawks at the fair-skinned Lyre, who's clinging to him. "SynKievas of Ayzaga," he scolds. "Whatever has gotten into you? You don't go running about, in such a grand place as this."

"Is it true?" SynKievas asks again, folding up his black, bat wings. "True that you gave Veldakryn to your newest Crown Sentinel? What's his name? I don't even know his name. The name of the one I am now forced to bet with." SynKievas's pleading, green eyes are transfixed on King Aygor.

Arsyn of Jhire chuckles a bit, and replies for the king, "It's true. You should now release the King of RawZend, before his Palace Sentinels dispatch you here and now."

SynKievas lets go of Aygor, and glances about at the sixteen sentinels no longer standing as statues. Fury on their faces, they've bows, blades, daggers, and spears aimed at SynKievas.

"They're no matter," says SynKievas. "I could take 'em. And *I* can take that young sentinel too. Where is he?"

"Seqwhyett, you mean?" Dea asks. "He's round here, somewhere. Probably tending to a few of the King's Wards, in his off-duty time. He was one of us, until earlier this year, when he turned twenty and was sworn in as a Crown Sentinel."

SynKievas's face darkens. "Is that why you've given it to him? He was practically a child of yours? And now you're showing him special favor? Well, that won't do."

SynKievas bursts up from the ground, flapping his big wings hard. His forest-green cloak whips about, but, somehow, doesn't get in the way of his flying up high above us, toward the many floors of the palace and domed roof.

King Aygor balls his hands into fists, then rests them on his hips. He glances to Arsyn, asking, "Shall I bring him down, or do you wish for that honor? I am aware of the weapon armory he's stolen from you, over the years, Arsyn."

Arsyn turns playful, extending his hand out to the nearest sentinel. "Your bow, sentinel, if you would?"

Gleeful, that sentinel gives it to him.

Feeling ambitious myself, I step toward Arsyn. "Would you show me, instead? Bet it'll be more injurious to his image, to have a fellow Ayzagaun shoot him down, don't you think, King Aygorinaith?" I glance at the king.

He laughs. "Ben was right about you. No hesitation, whatsoever, for being bold."

I grin wickedly. "So long as I'm not dumb about it, boldness seems to get me what I want. In this case, it's to learn how to improve my aim from Master Arsyn, himself."

Skylin divs, *"Good way to score points with my father."*

King Aygor relaxes his hands, while stating, "He *is* a fine teacher. Proceed."

Assisting me with the bow, Arsyn instructs, "Wait for his wings to draw in toward his body. Aim a hair below the top joint of one of his wings, then release the arrow. By the time it reaches him, his wings will be fully open. Yank the bow down, and a rope will reveal itself. Be quick, in grabbing hold of that rope. And brace yourself. SynKievas is strong. Even with an arrow lodged in one wing, he could still easily carry you up."

Ryco adds, "And then your grasp could slip, and you'd fall and break your neck. Remember how you broke one of your wings, yesterday? You got dispatched, and we had to help revive you."

Quickly, Kent clarifies, "What Ryco means is, it's unwise to risk another death the very next day."

I hesitate to take the shot.

Ryco grinds his teeth, for real this time, while divving, *"You're going to give us away, Ravier. These wings won't actually work, remember?"*

Disappointed, I heed the warning, and say, "Maybe it *should* be Skylin." I give her the bow.

Talok blows out a held breath. "A good idea, Cousin."

Above us, SynKievas is about out of sight.

Skylin takes quick aim. Yet it's someone else releasing an arrow.

A Darklyre, beside Aygor, reveals himself. "Too slow, Sky," he gloats.

"Grawllik!" Skylin shouts, in anger. "Must you always be the center of attention?"

He clicks his tongue, replying, "If winning a bet is the reward, always." Grawllik has hold of the arrow's tail of light-rope. He jerks down, and coils the slack.

Soon, SynKievas is pulled down. Once the snared Lyre spots his captor, he dives for him. SynKievas lands upon Grawllik, to wrestle the rope away from the much larger Lyre.

Blood's smeared on the palace floor, and Aygor's face turns furious.

Unfazed, Grawllik eases up, and adjusts his tattered, brown coat. "You can have it now, SynKievas. The bet was that I merely snag you mid-flight. Which I did, in front of witnesses."

SynKievas clenches his jaw, as he yanks the arrow out. It burns to ashes. Yelling in pain, he punches Arsyn of Jhire on the shoulder.

Arsyn hardly moves. But he rubs at his shoulder. "What are you abusing me for? I'm not the one who shot you."

"Better I punch you," says SynKievas, "than one of King Aygor's precious pillars or statues. I'm liable to be detached from my head permanently."

"True," agrees King Aygor, beginning to saunter forward. "Did you find it, Grawllik?" he queries.

Grawllik pulls out a worn, white journal, from his jacket. It's not overly big. But it must be at least six hundred pages long, since it's quite thick.

"Not his spell-book," Grawllik replies. "But his older twin's."

Aygor's breaths become shallow. "After so many centuries of Darklyres searching. Hundreds getting killed, during the hunt for one of them. And *you* found it, GreyLyre? You must tell me the story. But later. I must see the new arrivals to one of the renovated rooms."

"I'll wait, then, in the alcove near his library," says Grawllik, heading for a wide hallway beyond the eight creatures' pillars.

Skylin gives the Palace Sentinel his bow back. Arsyn starts healing SynKievas of his wound. But Deamond just stares off after Grawllik.

"Whose spell-book has he found, King Aygor?" Dea queries.

Aygor replies, "Monel, first Withrasyn King. Twin brother to Soren."

My heart nearly explodes. I get lightheaded, ready to faint. Talok tries to steady me, but he doesn't seem to be fairing any better. Rozeth grips my arm, and keeps me upright.

The air in the room suddenly feels heavier.

King Aygor continues, "I had hoped to get my hands on Soren's personal spell-book, but perhaps his brother's will be just as useful."

I want to ask, "Useful for what?" but I keep my mouth shut.

The rest of the trek is tedious. First, we go to a rail-less elevator platform. It takes us up. Then we traverse through countless corridors. Up never-ending stairs, we hike. The whole time, I'm dreading an interaction with Soren. What if something in his brother's spell-book helps him with his ultimate goal? Trading places with me. In this unfamiliar place, anything can happen. And that scares me into being on high alert.

III

Waken a Statue

"You've witnessed horrific wars,
but the greatest to be seen
lies within yourself."

<h1 style="text-align:center">26</h1>

<h1 style="text-align:center">A King's Past Deed</h1>

King Aygor pulls open a black-and-bronze door, motioning that we enter. "This one has the best view. And it's near to the channel that goes down to the kitchen, should you require midnight sustenance." He smiles at Gemma. "I'll have food delivered here, within the hour."

"Thank you," she says, glancing around the room of tan and ivory.

It's a total of three levels, not stacked directly on top of one another. The main floor contains tables, chairs, and couches. Otherwise, it's open. The second level is offset, to the side. A sizable, porcelain tub, recessed in the floor, is obviously there for washing in or relaxing. Four cloth panels fastened to the ceiling—as well as draped over an oval, metal ring, high above that tub—are currently twisted and tied round four pillars. If one desires privacy, one merely has to untie each cloth, and let them loose from the pillars. An alcove is found on the upper floor, with a bay window that covers the expanse of an entire wall. This level is also where six spotless-white beds, freshly made, wait for occupants such as us.

King Aygor states, "I'll leave the lot of you to get settled in. This first day of the Grand Clan Gathering is informal. Therefore, attendance at today's festivities is optional. You needn't even fear being absent at the Opening Supper, and later getting reprimanded for it."

The king is about to leave.

Dea stops him, with a statement of: "Wait, King Aygor. I've been meaning to ask you, but thought it might be inappropriate within the palace hallways."

"Get on with it," Aygor states. "I need to check on Ketty and Sonya. Make sure their emotional well-being is intact. There are the other wards, as well, that I've not seen all day."

Dea draws her wings up, until they no longer touch the pale, wooden floor. She starts, by saying, "I had wondered if I might forego accepting every invitation to dance this evening, if I have a partner for the night?"

Aygor stiffens his neck, not like he's angry. Rather, surprised. He comes farther into the room. "Has someone asked you for exclusivity?"

"I was the one asking, and he agreed," replies Dea, trying to ignore Skylin's look of distress.

"Father!" Skylin shouts. "You agreed to be Dea's dance partner, for the night? With . . . without consulting me?" she stutters. "Dea, how could you do this? Do you know the rumors this could start, back home in Jhire?"

King Aygor taps one of his forefingers to his lips. "You've agreed to be an exclusive partner of my oldest ward?"

"Only if it's agreeable to you," replies Arsyn, seeming untroubled by anything. He takes to sitting at one of the four small tables. "I admit . . . a night of being able to refuse several title-hungry women will be quite enjoyable. Look at the positive aspects of it, Skylin."

Skylin seethes, "That had better be your *only* reason for asking him, Dea." She storms up the steps to the second, then the third level. We hear her flop onto one of the beds dramatically.

Dea rolls her eyes.

King Aygor, after some thoughtful silence, says, "The both of you have my consent. But I must tell you, Dea. This only delays your obligation to dance with any whom ask, by one day."

Dea nods, then looks to the floor. Her wings slump, as well.

"Unless," he adds, "you share the same bed as Arsyn, this very night. And are seen sharing the same bed as him. I can arrange for private quarters, if that makes you more likely to find the 'said' scenario feasible."

Now Arsyn's distraught. Sweat forms above his brow. "That's a little far, for me, I'm afraid. Besides. This lot"—he motions to us—"they're descendants of some old friends of mine, now deceased. It would be unforgivably rude, to leave them the first night of the gathering."

We hear Skylin muffle her screams with a pillow. Seconds later, she shouts, "You dare *bed* my father, Demon Dea, and I won't *ever* forgive you!"

From the doorway, SynKievas says, "There's a loophole, in that scenario of Aygor's, you know?"

Dea scowls at him. "Oh really?" she queries. "All I foresee in it is letting Arsyn make me an official dragon's mistress. And I'm not ready for that."

Arsyn cringes, closing his eyes, as if pained. "Always have to make the conversation awkward, don't you, SynKievas?"

"It's what he does best," says King Aygor. "Although, he *is* right. There's a loophole, in what I've said. But I bet it will take you near all night, Dea, to figure it out. I'll now leave you to stew over it, and how much you wish to inflict bodily harm on me, this very day." Aygor turns on his heel, and exits the room.

SynKievas lingers, however, eyeing the lot of us. "You all hail from Ayzaga, by the looks of your attire. But I've not ever seen a single one of you. How have you managed that?"

Arsyn states, "They hail from the north of Ayzaga, not far from the Rubidyns' Main Lair."

SynKievas's posture relaxes, as he says, "Ah! That makes sense. You don't actually *live* within the city. Being so close to the Rubidyns' primary home, though, surely some of you have seen one?"

Rozeth nods. "Ryco and I have. I, at a distance; Ryco, from much closer."

SynKievas approaches Ryco. "Your parents even named you after a Rubidyn. They must be admirers."

"Actually," Ryco states, "my name has its roots, in both Rubidyn and Sylvadyn."

Dea queries, "Then 'Ryco' is the shortened version of your name?"

"Short for Ryco'Eldeis," he says.

"Eldeis!" SynKievas beams. "Of two dyns. Does your name mean: power of two dragons?"

"Close enough," Ryco replies, before he sits at the same table as Arsyn.

"I like it," SynKievas says, taking the seat opposite of Ryco. "My name isn't nearly as grand as that. And it took my parents a year, to name me. The Kievas, as I'm sure you know—"

Skylin interrupts, to state, "Means 'Black Heaven,' or 'place of death.'" From over the third-level railing, she glares harshly at Dea, adding in, "Where you will be going this night, Demon Dea, if you dare bed him."

"Weren't you listening, Skylin?" Dea fumes. "I'm not ready for anything like that."

Flying up to the third level, Dea starts a wrestling match with Skylin. There's squealing and screeching and wings flapping. Arsyn taps his foot on the hard floor, squirming a bit in his chair.

Ben grabs Gemma's hand in excitement, and pulls her along with him to the third level. Laughter erupts. Then playful shouts.

Talok smiles. "I'm glad some of us are fitting in quite well."

He and I take to another table; Nyrim and Rozeth join us, before glancing at SynKievas. They appear to want him to leave. Though he's likable enough, I want him gone too. The anticipation of what news waits to be told is strangling me.

Siege stands by, swaying back and forth on his feet. He keeps swallowing nervously every few seconds, while fidgeting with his hands.

Ryco pauses in conversing with the two Lyre men. "Go join in, Siege."

Siege doesn't need a second invitation. He bolts toward the supporting wall of the third level. Jumping, he catches the rail, and clambers over.

"Quite silent, isn't he?" SynKievas watches as Siege joins the fun above, then continues, "As I was saying, after I was eight days old, I started dying in my sleep, then reviving myself every morning. It frightened my parents to no end, the first month. They claimed that it stopped, after I was a year old. So, they named me SynKievas: Cheater of Black Heaven."

Arsyn adds, "Some say it means Marauder of Death."

In unison, Ryco and SynKievas say, "That's the Sylvadyn meaning."

Dea suddenly slams up against the railing. Before Siege is able to kick her in the chest, she jumps down over that section of railing. But her wing's feathers are jumbled, as she flaps. She flails wildly, then splats upon the floor, laughing in hysterics.

SynKievas chortles. "You and I, Ryco, are of the same signature, I think. As such, do you mind if I ask about your roots? Your eyes give way to your having Sylvadyn in your blood, somewhere down the line. One of your ancestors must've been an especially wayward dragon's mistress."

Dea quiets down, interested in what they're discussing.

"It's true," Ryco replies sullenly, clasping his hands under the table.

Dea queries, "What do you mean a wayward mistress, SynKievas? There are different levels of being a dragon's mistress?"

SynKievas lifts his shoulders. "Well, there's a dragon's mistress. Then there's a *dragon's* mistress."

"What he means," says Kent, sitting beside Ryco, "is that, while all Parasogyns have one mother and one father—"

SynKievas interjects with, "Unless you're Metimoran. Not really sure how that works for them. And I'd rather not ask Grawllik about it. Nasty GreyLyre mutt. I hate him."

Arsyn states, "*Hate* is a strong word."

"Yeah?" SynKievas says. "So's his name. Conqueror of Souls. Grawllik. That's what it means. It couldn't be something more humble like: Warrior of the Battlefield, or Master of the Blades. No! It had to be something unbeatable. Then there's the added injury of him being the piercer of my wing. It just healed from the last snagging too."

"Someone's not a sore loser at all," states Arsyn dryly.

SynKievas scoffs. "Actually, that's literally what I am. Sore. And someone else won a bet at *my* expense. There was no winning involved, for me. I'm tired of being arrow-fodder, that's for sure."

Dea looks to Kent. "Ignore him. He loves drama. You were saying something about Sylvadyn Parasogyns?"

Kent crosses his leg over the other leisurely, while replying, "Yes. Haven't you ever wondered how it is that Sylvadyns are so much better at Gendras than other races?"

"Of course," Dea says. "But I've never been bold enough to ask."

Continuing, Kent states, "Sylvadyn mistresses conceive, by way of one partner. Prior to that, however, they are bedded by many . . . others."

Talok's gaze sinks to staring at our table's mosaic of tiny, triangular tiles. His eyes trace along the scrolling, floral pattern.

Dea rapidly blinks several times. "I was unaware," she says, barely above a whisper.

Ryco stares at her, his expression unreadable. He's not angry, nor sad; perhaps, just pondering her reaction.

SynKievas ends the sudden silence, stating, "You seem to wear the shame of it, as if it happened within your lifespan, Ryco. Please. You've nothing to be ashamed of, in your ancestry. Here, among fellow Pairos, we all have a dirty history. I mean, only Jhire and one other of his siblings partnered with outsiders. The rest, well, you know." SynKievas lets the statement hang in the air.

Arsyn states, "Gaula and Ayzareel's grandchildren broadened the genetic pool, though. Mostly with BlacKaidyn Pairos. A few Emerald Sorsryns snuck in, here and there, to have families with Darklyres too. It's where the green eyes, such as SynKievas's, come from, isn't it?"

"I will neither confirm, nor deny it," replies SynKievas, before pointing at me. "And neither should you, boy. Let them ache to know our ancestry."

I straighten in my seat, replying, "What if you don't know it?"

"Don't know it!" SynKievas hollers. "I tell you, Arsyn, what is becoming of this next generation? They don't know their own lineage. Disgraceful! I'm leaving, before I hear something else that nearly makes my heart stop."

Arsyn nods. "Even if it did stop, you'd wake in the morning, wouldn't you?"

SynKievas smirks. "Funny, Arsyn. Before my heart has a chance to stop, this night, do you want me as the witness to you bedding down with the demon?"

Shrieking, Dea makes a move to claw at SynKievas.

He rushes for the door. Snickering a bit, he makes his escape.

Dea slams her fist on the closed door. "The nerve of him!" she yells.

"With you, there," says Skylin, peering over the railing again.

"Now that he's gone"—I look to Nyrim, who's trying not to laugh—"you and Ben were going to share some news?"

Turning serious, Nyrim stands up. "Ben and I visited the Arkivara, in Yharss-Rawshuen, shortly after arriving to the city, and, well . . . I'll let Ben show you."

We follow Nyrim and Rozeth up to the third level.

Ben's clearing the war zone made of feathers and wrecked bedding, while Gemma's collapsed on the floor by the bay window. Finishing her fit of giggles, she sits up, and wipes away tears of laughter. Once she sees the tension on Ryco's face, she quietly goes to help Ben remake beds.

"That can wait," Ryco states. "What did the three of you find in Yharss?"

Ben finishes pulling a set of blankets taut, then rubs his gloved palms together. "We didn't find items, per se. Rather, a message from LanSoren."

Nyrim adds, "Those gloves are enchanted, right? So, when Ben helped me open the Arkivara's door, it drew us in."

"And violently," Ben states, "like how the castle did with Tyler and Talok, after the city was attacked."

"She wouldn't let us out," says Nyrim.

Rozeth adds, "I tried every Gendras trick Siveyra Dezarin taught us, Ryco. She wouldn't budge."

Nyrim continues, "Finally, I had Ben attempt to go into the Heart of the Arkivara with me. He said something about how she was calling for him in Mensa-div."

"What did she sound like?" queries Gemma, sitting down on a bed.

"Sad," Ben replies. "But glad for company. Even with all the loss of life in her city, she is strong."

Kent asks, "What happened?"

"We saw LanSoren." Nyrim grins. "Quick, Tyler, give Ben your daggers. Those were LanSoren's instructions. You should then be able to see what we saw."

With trembling hands, I unclasp the sheaths from my belt and then give the daggers to Ben.

"We're glad too," says Rozeth, strolling about the room, "that you've kept those daggers with you, this whole time, Tyler. It's how we knew you were close. The gloves and daggers have a bond."

Ben grips RotaSyn first, saying, "If you're aware of it, and have one of them with you, you can track the other."

Rozeth continues, "They're as beacons to each other, always communicating. Ben sensed you were in trouble. But the gloves led us here, ahead of you. Then Ben asked Arsyn to keep an eye out for you, this day."

Arsyn looks to the bay window, and snaps his fingers. Black curtains are released from the ceiling, to cover the whole wall of windows. "Now you may," says Arsyn to Ben.

The room is in practical darkness, as Ben grips NeiSator. Bluish fire explodes out from the gloves and daggers, to create webs of light. Expanding, they fill the whole room.

Skylin's in awe. She slowly reaches up, to run her hand through several strands of light. "What is this?" she asks.

Kent's eyes glass over with tears, as he sits on one of the rumpled beds. "The Heart of Yharss-Rawshuen. I forgot what it felt like, to carry out the highest duty of an Arkivy. It's as if you are timeless. No beginning, no present, no future. But all of them at once." Kent buries his face in his hands.

Siege sits with him, but doesn't say a word.

Particles of light gradually break off from numerous strands around the room. They draw together. A figure starts to form. A flash of white blinds us. When our vision comes back, my father is standing in the center of the third level.

"Rueisvben'el Yharss-Rawshuen," he says, to the empty space in front of him. "I had hoped for it to be you that my son would bestow the gloves to. Since it is you, and not a foreigner to Yharss, I can impart a longer message to Tyler. I've recorded a lot of these messages, calculating, with Paydinn's help, whom he could possibly give the gloves to."

"Siveyra Paydinn?" Talok's mouth twitches in anger. "He's known all this, the entire time?"

Nyrim lifts a quieting hand. "It's a matter to do with being bound not to say. LanSoren's bindings were always unbreakable. Eishal and Quall have confirmed it, in the past."

My father continues, "At any rate, I'll get right to it. Eyo'el has been attacked, in your timeline, and quite brutally. I know." He sighs. "There wasn't anything I could do to prevent it, without worse things happening in its place. In one scenario, Tyler and Talok died together. Burned alive on a Blackwood Spike. If you're unaware of what those are, ask the Darklyres. Siveyra Gyron, as well, knows much of them. He was always a good friend, through it all."

Talok and I share a look.

But it's me who says, "At least it was together."

Talok grins. "Always together, Cousin."

My father paces around the room. He passes right through Rozeth, and she gives a little shiver, as he continues his message. "I feel it's important to tell you what I *had* planned. Something Quall said gave me the idea. I was going to tell your mother and you, Tyler. But I wanted an actionable plan, an escape route set in place. That's where . . ." He pauses, letting his slight smile show through, then continues, "Your *aunt* comes in. She goes by Miriam. But that's not really her name."

Gemma comes over, and whispers to me, "I bet she's the woman in that poem. Despairing Marion."

"It's true that she lives in England, and has a painting on the wall of her closet. Its twin is in Vondurheil. On one of the many trees, in their thick forest. Jasper hasn't a clue." He laughs. "But Mekka, Nebukahn, and Droediin know where it is. Naughty Vons even used it to scare Wayeland, one summer. Poor man! I watched the whole thing. It gave Wayeland nightmares for weeks. He started sleeping with a knife under his pillow. Remember to tell Eli that. Maybe even let Tadashi know, don't wake Wayeland in his sleep."

Those in the room savvy to the story laugh with my father a bit.

I div, to the confused Skylin and Dea: *"Tell you later."*

My father says, "I gave the painting to your aunt, after that. The plan was to fly to England, and escape to Muraine with her, you, and your mother. In case you're wondering, both paintings were done by Adair Galloway, while he was on Muraine. At least two centuries ago, in Muraine's time, he was apprenticed to Soren. That's why there's a likeness of him together with Soren; the very picture hidden away in my office. They became as close as brothers. Soren even disguised Adair as an Amethyst Sorsryn. Everyone was none the wiser. Except Zymarc. He spots deception faster than even King Rentwar. But he has a few holes in his armor."

Ben starts taking shallow breaths.

Nyrim approaches him, in concern. "You can let go, Ben. The fresh, residual magic in the daggers should be enough to continue the message to the end."

Ben wobbles his head. "No, there's more. We didn't see the whole of it."

Nyrim grabs Ben's wrist. Color seeps from his palm, and Ben's body absorbs it.

I go to Ben, and hold out my hand, "Give me the darker one."

As soon as NeiSator's in my left grasp, the strands of light around the room turn white.

My father whirls around, to look right at me. "Took you long enough. Now, stay right there. Is Awngeleik with you?"

"No," I reply.

"Good," he says. "That's how it should be, for now. What about Jokryns? Are they headed for Paragon?"

"Headed there, now," I state.

"Khyra was left there?" he asks.

I nod. "After we lifted the poison."

"Excellent! What about a Darklyre named Arsyn? Is he there with you?"

I glance over to Arsyn. He's leaning against a wall. His head is bowed. His eyes look deadened. And his face is blank too.

Confused, I reply, "He's here."

"Then you have all the pieces, which lead to crushing Zymarc," my father states.

"What about Talok, and the device?" I ask.

"Arsyn has the answer to that," he replies. "None of you will like it. But he has the answer. Good luck getting it from him. Seven out of ten conversations Paydinn and I viewed, he was stingy about giving it up."

"And Soren outsmarting time?" I ask. "Something's not right. I can feel it."

My father's happiness fades. "If you are in Aygor's City of Grevagg, you do have reason to worry. But I can't tell you why. Trust yourself, Tyler. And try to trust the ones surrounding you, in this moment."

"That's what I've been doing," I complain.

My father crosses his arms, then lifts a quizzical eyebrow. "Really? That's not what Paydinn showed me."

"Are you lecturing me from the grave?" I ask. "I don't even know how to take that. So, tell me this. Where did you instruct Eishal to bury you? Not even The Black Flame knows."

"Oo!" My father exclaims, stepping toward me excitedly. "An excellent question. You've been talking to Vak, haven't you? And The Flame too? That means you're in one of two possible timelines." My father looks off, in deep thought. At last, he says, "This is all I can say. My body lies where it belongs. At rest, in the place of reflection."

To clarify, I ask, "Not on Muraine?"

He agrees, "Not on Muraine. Now, there isn't much time left for more questions. I wish I could tell you Zymarc's weaknesses that I've learned over the years, but I think you already know of one. Use it to your advantage. Also, I must tell you of Soren. His history was legendary, on Muraine. You've no idea the trouble I went to, to erase him from Paragon's archives. It lessened the chances of him using time to *his* advantage. Aside from that fluke on the day of the attack, he shouldn't be able to appear in Paragon. Although, he could travel there, if summoned to somewhere else."

Gemma tugs on my arm. "Tyler, ask him if Soren uses memories of himself, to outwit time."

Swallowing hard, I feel sick. But I ask anyway. "Does Soren use memories, to transcend time?"

"Memories of himself, yes," replies my father. "He can persuade some, in their present time, to summon him from the past. But if they don't know who he is, they can't invite him. Summoned Sorshrynaks are also more powerful than typical Sorsryns invited to the present. Therefore, the summoner has to be of equal or greater strength, to keep their Sorshrynak in check."

Ryco states, "That explains more about why Gyron lost complete control over him, during the festival."

I shake my head, asking, "But who summoned him, on the day of the attack?"

"That is not for me to say. Nor is it necessary to reveal it," my father replies. "Tell me what you think you need to know, Tyler, and I will do my best to answer."

I get lightheaded. I've no idea what I *need* to know, in this moment. Then Dea reminds me, saying, "You're looking for a certain Sorsryn, remember? Ask him."

"Lemawr," I state. "Where do we search for Lemawr?"

"When the time's right," my father replies, "he'll find you. You won't be expecting him, either. You'll be distracted over other things. But, I will say, your time in Deivahl has helped a few things along. Be sure to pester Warren about what gift he claimed from Lemara's armory."

"Ask about the spirits," Ryco suggests. "The elements. How Zymarc could even hope to hurt them. Control them."

I talk faster, saying, "Zymarc's trying to control the six spirits. He's even injured The Flame. How, and why?"

"I'm not sure how," my father replies. "But he would only attempt that, to complete Vitiosus. Complete the breaking of the laws. Of order. And if it's true that he's injured death, itself, he's close to completing the Hex of Vitiosus. Deezalo was never able to complete it fully. He always had to have intervals in his rule of terror. Time to redo the hex, for a recharge. If Zymarc succeeds in completing an enduring hex, there's nothing he won't be able to do. On Muraine, at least. Earth would be safe. Now, you've one more question, then I'll end this with a memory sequence I recovered of

Queen Awleesia's."

"So you're a genie now?" I tease. "Instead of three wishes, I get three answers."

He smiles. "It's better than owing you three favors, as Gemma did."

"Which I've repaid," states Gemma proudly.

"Fair enough. One last question," I state. "I feel as though Soren and I are connected. But how?"

"He's bound me, Tyler." My father sighs. "And I am bound by others, not to say. But part of the answer waits for you downstairs, in the library. The Library of Soren. You *must* go there, before departing Grevagg. Every step you take, on the way there, will be agony. You must keep going forward. Part of the truth of who you are, waits down there. Especially now that Monel's spell-book has been delivered to King Aygorinaith."

I ask, "Going there can't really be worse than everything that's happened, can it?"

My father looks down. "I couldn't say, since I'm not you."

I chew on my lower lip, then say, "Go ahead with the memory sequence. We're ready for it."

"Until we meet again, Tyler." He speaks softly, "Thirteen, done."

I give a two-fingered wave, while pushing back all the confusion that's inside.

The daggers glow with wisping fire. Then my father's figure turns to energy and explodes out, shifting into strands of light again. They draw together, then form into two figures, as well as several objects: a desk and chair, a bed, pale curtains, one window, and various art pieces.

King ReNovak becomes one of those figures; a much younger, thinner ReNovak. He reminds me of the gangly Onyx Warrior, Zenzar. He's with a woman. Her fair skin seems to glow, in the soft torchlight surrounding them, as does her light-blonde hair.

The woman peers out the window, which faces a bustling city cloaked by night. When she shivers, she pulls her thin, layered robe of white tighter round her hourglass figure.

ReNovak comes up behind the woman, and wraps his arms around her.

"Send word, if a child takes root," he says. "I very much want an Onyx heir, Awleesia."

"Patience, ReNovak," Awleesia says, looking over her shoulder. "Fate will decide when you are ready for an heir."

ReNovak gives a wry smile, but remains silent, as he tugs Awleesia closer, to kiss her on the neck.

The scene turns to smoke. It then shifts into a different memory. It's Awleesia, wearing the same white robe, but in a different room. She inspects herself in a large mirror, while sweeping her delicate hands over her somewhat plump midsection. She tries not to smile.

A knock sounds on her bedroom door.

The joy fades from her face, as she says, "Come in, Soren."

He enters, striding directly toward Awleesia. He stops when there's five steps between them. "What do you think you're doing, Queen Awleesia?"

"About to ready myself for the festival, Soren," she replies. "What are you doing?"

"I've come to inform you of your foolishness." He points at her midsection. "I know what you and that Onyx King have done. It won't work the way both of you hope it will. He's using you. He's also lied to you."

"In what way?" Awleesia asks. "Perhaps I wish to be used. It's better than being turned away by fellow Sorsryns. We were deemed a plague. All shunned us, save for the Vaegons." Awleesia holds her head high.

"Deathasyns didn't turn you away," Soren remarks, while adjusting his black-and-white gloves. "And I know that to be a fact, because I asked King Vit'Dod, himself. Withrasyns never came knocking on their gates."

"Deathasyns," Awleesia hisses the word. She glances at Soren's reflection in the mirror. "The Geldryn hate them. It would've been an automatic declaration of war, to side with them. And I know that to be a fact, because I've read copies of the Geldryn bylaws, held within the archives of the Onyx city of Oniva."

"Very well," Soren says, as he lowers his hands. "But you can't keep that child, Awleesia."

"I don't intend to. Whether boy or girl, the child will be given to ReNovak at its birth. He means to break the Onyx free of the old Laws of Neutrality, through this child's dual citizenship."

Soren laughs. "So, naming Lemawr as his Onyx Prince didn't work, did it? I told him it wouldn't. Magic's too smart for that. And it will come with a cost, if you go through with bearing his child."

Awleesia's stance goes rigid. She stops looking in the mirror, and it cracks down the middle as she whirls around. "Are you saying I should kill it? Soren, how can you ask that of me?"

He takes a few steps forward, actually looking sorry for what he's about to say next. "Not kill, Awleesia. Rather, undo. To unmake the child. There can be others. I promise you, there *will* be others. But not this one. Please, listen."

Tears roll down Awleesia's face. All color has drained from her, and she looks like a ghost.

"Let me explain," Soren says, folding his hands protectively over his lower quadrant. "The Kyanites can make it so that the child never was. Never existed. Therefore, it's not killing, in the true sense of the word. Time will revert. As it's being done, you will feel the pain of death. The Kyanite performing the series of spells will feel the pain, as well. But the child will feel nothing. It will be at peace, until it is no more."

Awleesia's bent over, as she digs her fingertips into her midsection, and screams, "No, Soren! I will not agree to it. Never will I agree to it!"

"You have to!" Soren shouts back, now making a move to grab Awleesia by the arms and force her to stand up straight. "ReNovak's already broken laws, in placing this burden on you. He's cheated. He wasn't old enough to have Setharyn. He's not old enough now, to have another heir. I helped him cheat the first time. I tied the chance of death to him and his wife. If fate demanded a death in place of Setharyn's birth, it would be one of the parents. They willingly accepted the risk."

Awleesia quiets herself, to ask, "That's why Setharyn's mother died in childbirth?"

Soren nods, before asking, "Who was there, prior to you and ReNovak being with each other? Which essences of life were tied to this child? Who should die, in place of it being born?"

"I don't know," Awleesia replies, in hysterics. "I thought he had reached a Sorsryn's Fifty."

"He has not," Soren confirms. "A life most innocent may have to die, in order for ReNovak to have this heir he so craves. And that life may be claimed hundreds of years from now. Fate is patient, and it keeps track. It never forgets the lives owed to it."

"The Flame, you mean?" queries Awleesia.

"Yes," Soren replies. "He is one of six. Death. The Spirit of the Black Dyn: dyn-syn-Sivondel-lek-kai. He is waiting to strike. He craves a massacre. And he will get it, if summoned by the right soul. I fear someone will learn how to wield him as a weapon. Who's to say this child isn't the first step, in breaking laws that keep The Flame in check?"

Awleesia's deadened, gray eyes now darken over with rage. "I will never forgive him, and I will never forgive you," she seethes.

The scene turns to smoke. That smoke fades. The room's now in total darkness.

Skylin's first to say anything, asking, "Do you think she went through with it? Poor Awleesia. What a choice to make."

Someone snaps their fingers. The black curtains roll themselves back up to the ceiling, then stay that way.

My eyes adjust to the sudden brightness.

Arsyn lowers his hand. "Someone's bringing us dinner." Glancing at Nyrim, he adds, "I asked a sentinel to transfer your things to this room, as well. I suggest you talk of all you've witnessed, after they leave."

<h1 style="text-align:center">27</h1>

<h1 style="text-align:center">Anguish of an Answer</h1>

Hardly did I taste what we had for dinner. I know we were served some kind of fish and grain. Aside from that, I have no memory of what passed my lips. The entire time, I was thinking many things. Things to do with the memory sequence. One was this: *What was ReNovak up to, then? And what does he hope to do now?*

"Bet I can't guess your thoughts," says Dea, pulling her chair closer to me. She rests her elbows on our table, and cups her face. She waits for my answer.

"When can you take us to Soren's Library?" I ask.

"I can't," she says.

That answer is dissatisfying. Infuriating, even. I slide my plate closer to the center of the table, then wrap my left hand over the diver's watch on my right wrist. The tiles of the table are cold against my skin at first. But they quickly warm up.

Several in the room, previously occupied with their own thoughts or conversations, now come to listen in.

"Why not?" I ask Dea.

She sits back in her chair, and rests her hands in her lap. "King Aygor's worried that there isn't a proper amount of security spread around the city, for the Grand Clan Gathering. He normally has twelve Palace Sentinels guarding the hallway, leading to the library. Then another eight stationed within the library, itself. So, he set up a security barrier for the library, and assigned those sentinels elsewhere. Only he, and those he invites, may enter the library."

Talok queries, "He can't be convinced to invite us?"

"He may," replies Arsyn, still seated where he was during dinner.

Dea states, "Best to wait until tomorrow, though. The events of earlier have him on edge."

Arsyn suggests, "Or try making a bet with him tonight, during the Opening Dance. Then lose on purpose. Darklyres love winning bets, in case you hadn't noticed."

"Can you guarantee he will give us a tour," queries Ryco, "if one of us loses to him?"

Dea shakes her head. "Nothing is certain, when it comes to King Aygor."

I ask, "What about if one of us wins a bet with him? Will he honor letting us explore the library?"

"If the bet stakes are that you tour the library," Skylin replies, seated at a different table, "absolutely, he will uphold the agreement. If you lose, though, good luck stepping foot where King Aygor doesn't want you."

Dea chortles. "I warned you about the armory, those years ago. Should've listened."

Skylin leers at Dea.

I raise my hand, saying, "I vote that Gem makes a winning bet with him. If any one of us can win against him, I think she can do it."

Gemma blushes. "Thanks, Ty. But I'm out of my league, here."

I still say, "Make a winning bet with him, anyway. I'll attempt to lose. The rest, draw for it?"

They agree.

Gemma's team ends up consisting of Ben, Arsyn, Ryco, Dea, and Siege. Meanwhile, the others are my "losing" team: Rozeth, Skylin, Talok, Kent, and Nyrim.

Dea and Skylin head out, to go fetch clothes for us all to wear at the dance tonight. For assistance with carrying it all back, Rozeth and Kent leave with them.

Kent has almost closed the door, but stops to peek back in at me. "Let me guess. Tyler wants it all black?" He winks at me.

I shrug. "Why not?"

Skylin bolts back inside the room, her mouth agape. "No, no!" she exclaims. "You must have some color, at the dance. Sure, a lot of us will have a little black. But there must be color."

I try not to laugh, while replying, "I'll leave it to you, then."

Skylin's wings flap a bit, and she gives a happy nod. "I'll pick something SynKievas would be jealous of. Back in a bit."

Kent motions for Gemma, and she heads out too.

They all leave, in a storm of chatter. Eventually, the sound of them fades.

Talok's attention is now on the large tub that's recessed in the floor. He looks up at the ceiling. "How do you fill this with water? We all desperately need a good washing."

Ben wrinkles his nose, nodding his agreement.

Ryco, clicking his tongue, comments, "That Aura Etch on Ben's back needs finishing, as well."

Ben goes pale, and sputters, "But . . . I've already washed today."

"There's no rule against washing twice," Ryco states. "Undress from the waist up, if that suits you better."

Ben gulps, then starts the task of undoing his cloak and coat.

Nyrim sits upon one of the steps, which leads to the second level.

Arsyn deeply sighs, and the weight of our fake wings drops away. They've vanished.

I fall forward, and barely land on my hands and knees.

Talok tumbles into the porcelain tub, letting out a shriek.

Even Ryco's caught off guard. He stumbles forward, and slams into Siege. The two fall down in a tangled mass of weapons, cloaks, and buckles. They attempt to stand, but they're latched together, and laughing.

I go help Talok, as he slides around in the slippery tub.

Ryco, now frustrated with their clothes and weapons hooked together, starts undressing right where he is.

Siege is mortified, and stammering, "Ryke . . . Ryco! I can get it untangled, if you'll hold still."

Ryco worms his way out of his cloak and coat. His shirt is easily peeled off, after that. He stands up, and says, "It's your problem, now."

Siege puffs out air, his face reddening in anger. "Impatient Sylvadyn."

"Quiet Dragon's Voice," states Ryco, "never demanding your way."

Siege just blinks at Ryco, then looks down and starts untangling their stuff.

Ryco taps two of his fingers on his opposite arm, his face unreadable, before he comes to join Talok and me.

Arsyn undoes the tied-back cloth panels of the wash area. They unwind from around the pillars, then rapidly untwist. Instantly, the tub starts filling up with water.

Talok takes off his garb, starting with his boots. Ryco too. Arsyn, however, sheds it all, while covered by his wings. He sinks down in the swirling, hot water first. He looks me up and down, then narrows his gaze on my face.

I'm not even undressed yet, and I already feel naked under his scrutiny. *What's he thinking?* I wonder.

Siege slinks his way into the water, completely stripped, while somehow appearing to be stoic about it.

The water stops its flow.

The room is quiet.

"Ben!" Ryco shouts. "Get in here. You too, Nyrim."

Nyrim—covered by a towel, until the very last second—slips in. Once in the water, he throws his dry towel at Ben.

Pants still on, Ben enters the tub barefoot. He turns his back to Ryco, and huffs.

Ryco smiles wickedly, before saying, "At least Musgrae and Eli aren't here to patronize you. I'd say that it's the perfect time to finish this."

"Just get on with it." Ben props his arms on the tile floor, while he kneels in the tub.

Ryco says to Siege, "Keep his blood from running down into the water."

Siege queries, "You're sure this is a good idea, with the way Talok has been recently?"

Assessing the tattooed outline upon Ben's back, Ryco replies, "He's not pale, nor does he look hungry. So long as Ben holds still, this should go quickly. Therefore, there isn't any need to worry over Talok taking a bite out of Ben's neck."

Ben flinches. "Bite out of my what?" He looks back frantically at me, then Talok. "What's happened?"

Talok holds his wrist up to view. "It's this device. Seems to have given me a blood craving."

I state, "Eli will tell you all about it, when you see him."

Talok's look is one of embarrassed amusement as he says, "More like Musgrae will tell all. Eli's sore over it."

Siege grabs hold of Nyrim's discarded towel, then patiently waits.

Reaching for his pants, Ryco takes out a thin needle from one of the pouches, along with many jars containing liquid pigment. He dips the needle in black pigment, first, then runs it along the tattoo outline, scratching and tapping.

Ben winces.

When Ryco lifts his hand away from Ben's back, Siege wipes off the dots of blood mixed with pigment, before they can drip down Ben's back.

I undress, while they're all occupied with watching Ryco do his needle-work. Then I place my wet clothes on the tile floor, and sink into the water again, covering my vulnerability by crossing my legs together and then drawing my knees toward my chest.

Nyrim spots me, and mimics the pose. Talok does the same.

Arsyn's eyes turn playful, and he reaches out to flick one of the curtains.

Ice-cold water rains down on us.

Ben inhales sharply, gasping, as he bursts out of the bath.

Ryco's needle scratches one long, black line down Ben's back, in the process, and the Yharss-Rawshuen screams.

Arsyn laughs low. "I told you, Nyrim. At the first sign of trouble, I knew he would fly out like that. I was right. Pay up, when you have clothes back on."

"That's not amusing," Ben seethes, while hesitantly coming back to the bath. "How bad is it?" he asks Ryco.

Ryco clenches his jaw, before saying, "It'll take a little longer. Now, no moving. And *no* more startling him." Ryco makes a point to glance at Arsyn.

Arsyn nods, but still looks proud of his work.

The tightness in my chest eases. After a while, I brave the question, "Arsyn, what do you know about that device on my cousin? My father said you hold the answer."

He lets one of his wings stretch out of the water, and into an empty portion of the wash area. Then he studies me a few minutes more. "Ben told me of the device," he says. "Described it rather well, I might add. There are three, of similar build, that I know of. Now that I've seen this one in person, I know which it is. And your father is right. You won't like the answer."

"Tell us, anyway," Talok mutters.

Arsyn is forlorn, in saying, "One here, among us now, will have to die, in place of saving you. There is only one life to be given, with the guarantee of it working. It's a Deathasyn ritual. A Hex of Dei-Athos-Kree. I came across it, once, in a book contained in the Library of Soren. I took it, for fear of anyone practicing its powerful magic and curses. I carry it with me, at all times."

I ask, "Does the ritual have anything to do with the Blackwood Spikes my dad mentioned?"

"No," Arsyn replies. "And I'll not tell you of those, here, in the room where I will slumber this night."

Nyrim queries, "Which of us can save Talok?"

Arsyn looks down in shame, and draws his wings tightly against his body. He stands up, and leaves the bath. "Give me time to think of another way," he says.

I snatch up the Sleeping Dragon coat from the clothing pile, slip it on, and then clamber out of the water. In my haste, I stumble toward Arsyn, while shouting, "We don't have time. Seven days! That's all we have left, to save him."

Arsyn yanks his pants on, then turns around in fury. "Unless you took to the skies on the fastest dragon, enhanced by every hastening spell there is, you wouldn't make it there in time. To the Monel."

"Home of the Withrasyns?" queries Ben, now standing behind me. "Why would the ritual need to be completed there?"

Arsyn replies, "Because that is where it all began. The Plateau of MarcKand. Birthplace of the Sorshrynaks. Before the eight clans even existed, they were one race."

The door swings open suddenly. Rozeth and Kent enter first, followed by Deamond, Skylin, and Gemma. All are carrying various-sized bundles of clothes.

Gemma spots Ben, who's still shirtless and dripping wet. She loses hold of her bundle, and it all unwinds and thuds to the floor.

She cringes.

Skylin smiles.

Ben hunches his shoulders, before crossing his arms.

Wide-eyed, Rozeth looks past Ben and me. Whatever sight's visible behind us, makes her lift her eyebrows up curiously.

I glance over my shoulder to Talok, Siege, and Nyrim, standing in front of Ryco, all partially hidden by one of the cloth panels that they hold in place.

Ryco remarks dryly, "Rozeth, since this curtain may as well be translucent to *your* eyes, will you be kind enough to bring us our new clothes?"

Nyrim squirms behind the curtain; Siege blushes bright-red, and turns around; Talok just folds his arms, and rolls his eyes; then there's Ryco, looking utterly bored.

Rozeth laughs tensely, glancing away. "I had wondered why the four of you were standing in full view of the room, nude. That curtain's modesty enchantment is rather weak. Would you like for me to improve it?"

Arsyn's brow furrows together. "Weak? Your eyes must be like Vons, if you think that enchantment is weak."

"Well," she says, "I am of Von aura." Collecting various clothing from the bundles brought in, Rozeth takes them to Ryco and the distraught three.

As Ryco takes his clothes from Rozeth's outstretched hands, he queries, "Does this remind you of our younger days, Rozeth?"

"A little," she replies quietly.

"As I recall," Ryco states, "it had been a long day, on that *particular* day."

Rozeth scolds, "Evie would slap you for that."

"But you wouldn't," Ryco comments.

Rozeth says, with a sharp tone, "In Evie's words, 'put your clothes on, Ryco of Paragon. We're going out, and we don't need no Sylvadyn skin taunting the forest, and visible for all Emerald eyes to see.'" Fearlessly, Rozeth stares Ryco down.

Ryco grins wickedly. "Whatcha natterin' about, Rozeth? I am the forest. At least, a quarter of it."

Rozeth presses her red lips together, before sheepishly saying, "Just put these on."

"As you wish," he replies, then snaps his fingers. Instantly, he's dressed, and walking out from behind the privacy of the curtain panel.

Gemma states, "We thought the brown, black, and yellow would look best on you."

Ryco adjusts the long-sleeved cloak, replying, "It'll do fine, Gem."

She grins. "Since you and Ben are to be posing as brothers, his is patterned opposite of that one. Just a little touch of yellow, like yours, though." Gemma offers Ben his bundle, helping him make sense of how it all goes on: five different pieces that buckle or tie together, to make the fake wings less obvious.

Kent divvies out the bundles to the other three.

Ryco states, "Rozeth, you are banished to the corner, while the young chaps get changed behind the curtain."

"How 'bout a game of cards, instead?" she asks.

He agrees, and joins her at a table, as Skylin gives me my new clothes.

"Gem said you would want to keep that coat on," Skylin states. "So, I picked a black, green, and gray mosaic cloak that can easily be reworked to fit with what you have." She holds it up, unsure of her choice.

It's a scaled fabric, resembling a lizard's skin. A black dragon pattern has been branded on it, about where the shoulder-level would be. From there, three blades point down from the dragon. The center one of gray stretches all the way to the cloak hemline. The other two end at knee-level. The left is black, the other is white.

Feeling the sinuous strength of it, I ask, "I won't stand out too much?"

Skylin replies, "With other *Ayzagauns* in green and gray walking about, not a lot. But SynKievas will be absolutely envious. Mosaic scales are hard to come by. Then to find one etched with the original Darklyre emblem? He'll be wanting this from you."

Interrupting, Dea clarifies, "In other words, no bets with SynKievas."

Arsyn states, "Prepare yourself for all the compliments about to come your way. Few Ayzagauns wear their ancestral garb to the Clan Gatherings, for fear of losing them in bets."

Skylin cringes. "Maybe I should've picked something else."

"Don't be ridiculous," says Dea. "It'll draw King Aygor right to him, give him more chances to make losing bets."

"How so?" I ask.

Dea replies, "Because that cloak was his, in his youth. It's been passed down, for many generations. Possibly, it belonged to one of the eight forebearers to Darklyres. He thought he misplaced it. He doesn't know that one of his wards stole it, years ago. And, now, he's quite forgotten about it. But he'll recognize it on sight. If he should make inquiries, tell him someone gifted you with it. It's not a lie, right?" Dea puts a hand on her hip, and wiggles her shoulders back and forth a couple of times.

I state, "Remind me never to introduce you to a friend of mine back home."

"Who?" Gemma asks.

"Jed," I reply, as I take the rest of my clothes from Skylin, and head for the wash area's privacy. I pull the curtains closed.

Siege, Talok, and Nyrim have already made their escape, their egos barely intact.

"Want help, Tyler?" Ben queries.

I move the curtain back enough for him to enter. It's just the two of us, as Ben hands me the pieces of clothing one at a time. After I have on pants, I take off my coat. Ben takes it, to start cleaning it with water seeping from his palms.

I ask him, "How's Brash? Did he help you make good time, on the way to Yharss?"

"Most definitely." Ben glances up from his work of cleaning, to look at me. "He hasn't lived up to the name yet, though. I left him with my former guardian, Symovi. Asked him to take care of Yharss-Rawshuen and its City Warrior, while I'm away."

"Then the three of you came here, with other horses?" I ask.

Ben simply nods.

Several moments of silence pass.

Finally, he says something. "I had hoped to tell you of my deeds with Gemma, before I left. No time was right, though. But I wish to know . . . do you care? I know how she's your friend. And Musgrae mentioned the way you look at her, when you think no one's paying you mind."

That sick feeling creeps into my chest, and sinks on down, settling in the pit of my stomach.

"We're just friends," I reply. "Days before coming to Muraine, we were enemies. So, why would I care? She's a friend. A very good friend. But nothing more." With each word, I talk faster. I sound desperate, even to myself.

Will he believe me? I wonder.

Ben asks, "So, you don't mind that I kiss her?"

I swallow spit, rather than spitting upon the floor. Even more, I force myself to shake my head. "Not at all," I reply. "But I'm not going to watch the two of you, on purpose, or anything."

Slowly, Ben nods and then he hands me my coat. "I was worried of what you would say. But you've made this conversation easy. I thank you, Tyler."

I swallow again, though there's no spit to swallow now. I just end up with this strangling sort of feeling stuck in my throat. But, at least I didn't shrug. I think, *That's an improvement, right?*

With my coat in place, Ben helps me into the cloak.

"I admit," he says, "I've given up with Khyra. She'll never see me as more than one of the King's Guard. But with Gemma, she asks me of my life, my opinions. And she shares things of herself, in return. It's rather nice to be noticed. To converse with someone not so distracted by everything that can grow in the dirt, or be reshaped."

Though I still feel sick, I smile at Ben. "I know what you mean." Pausing, I add, "Just remember that we're from another world."

Ben looks me in the eye, with those wise, brown eyes. "But will you ever be going back, do you think?"

His question hits me hard, and that's when I shrug. I'm speechless, and scared. I don't know the answer. *Will I ever make it back?* I wonder.

The rest of the time is a haze.

Before I know it, it's dark outside, and the event's Opening Dance is soon to start.

28

Tastes of Sweetness

On a stone balcony, King Aygorinaith stands. Proudly, he looks out over the vast arena composed of five main levels, and various sublevels—all levels constructed of the same marble as his palace.

The Opening Dance started a few hours ago. Darklyres trickled in, at first. Some dispersed throughout the arena's structure, whilst others chose to go to the center. An open space of hardened, reddish dirt, dotted with a mosaic of patterned, copper-colored stones. The arena, lighted by torchlight, is now filled with thousands of Darklyres. That's not including the Darklyres dancing together, upon the arena's open center. It's easy to spot the Ayzagauns, among the other Lyres. All have their wings tucked away under fabric and cloaks, much like those of us trying to remain unnoticed.

From my spot on the second level, I watch King Aygor again. He announced the start of the dance from there. And that's where he's remained since.

I think, *How are we going to get a bet in, and increase our chances of seeing Soren's Library, if the king's in his guarded balcony all night?*

Ben stands beside me, eyeing the situation too. At least, that's what I assume, until he's asking, "Mind if Gem and I go dancing, Tyler?"

Stunned, I look at him. "What? No. It's fine. Go ahead. I'll stay, and watch King Aygor." I wave him off.

Ben playfully taps his fist on my shoulder, then walks off with a slight bounce in his step.

How can he be thinking about dancing, right now? I wonder. Then I see Gemma, and know.

Rozeth and the girls stayed behind. Dea said something about showing up when the real dancing begins; when she, Arsyn, and other *night* couples are to be announced by King Aygor.

I hope, *Maybe* that's *when Aygor will leave his balcony?*

Gemma has her long hair done-up, the loose little tresses curled and pinned back in place. There's no hair strand for her to twirl. Even from here, I can tell it's what she wants to do. Instead, she plays with a delicate necklace resting on her porcelain-soft skin. I want to take it off, and kiss her neck. The thought excites me. Then her turquoise-and-gray dress stirs in the slight breeze emitting from the arena's outer walls, and the excitement grows.

My heart beats faster.

The dress hem whips around enough to lend me several glimpses of her small feet barely covered by sandals. Their skinny straps go all the way up on her calves, and her olive-toned skin shows through the crisscrossed, leather lacing. All the Darklyre women wear similar ones. Though they're quite attractive in their garb, I don't have the urge to keep staring at them. Only Gemma. Her legs are strong, and slender. Most likely, she won't tire out from dancing any time soon.

Once she spots Ben headed her way, she holds her head all high and confident-like. As soon as Ben's within reach of her, he doesn't even wait for a greeting. He kisses her right on the mouth. It lasts longer than seven seconds. I look away.

While gritting my teeth, I lose track of time. I'm just brooding, when Skylin seems to magically appear beside me.

She asks, "What do you think of the dancing, Tyler?"

"Looks complicated," I reply.

"Want to have a go with me?" Skylin asks. "I give good instruction."

I gnaw on the inside of my cheek, flattered that she would ask. But it's not fair to her. I've fallen for Gemma, and no one else will do.

I think to myself, *Besides, I don't even know—*

Stopping my thoughts, I whisper to Skylin, "I don't know how."

"To dance?" Skylin asks.

I nod.

"Oh," she says.

I rest my elbows on the second level's railing, and cup my face in defeat.

Skylin perks up. "How 'bout we just wander around? Look for the others on our team. Let's see. Rozeth, Talok, Kent, and Nyrim, right?"

"Yep," says Talok, coming to join us. "Go on, Cousin. I'll keep track of him, for us."

I watch the graceful couples, who are midair, flying round each other. Then, down, at the ones dancing up a storm on the reddened dirt. They're all so joyous and playful. I'm jealous. Slightly more so, when I see Ryco and Rozeth, among the current couples on the ground-level, dancing in harmony. But I'm sickly envious, when spotting Ben and Gemma moving in near perfection together.

I state, "A walkabout sounds nice." I grab Skylin by the hand, and leave Talok to watch it all without us. Without me. For I cannot keep watching that.

Finding the nearest refreshments area, I release Skylin, to grab two stemmed glasses off a sculpted ice-table. "Water, or Farivoo?" I ask her, while eyeing the drink fountains.

"You're getting my drink for me?" queries Skylin.

I comment, "Why else would I ask?"

"It's not typical is all," she replies. "Water, please."

I fill one, and give it to her.

She takes a tiny sip, about to say something, as I fill mine to brimming with Farivoo.

I gulp it down. It tastes sweeter than I remember. But I don't care. I start refilling my glass.

Skylin's mouth drops open. "Tyler, stop," she orders. "Someone might've spiked the drink fountains. You always should start with a sip. No need to be a victim of a bet." She sets her glass down, and takes mine away, doing the same. "We should get out of here, before you start acting weird. You could give everything away, otherwise."

"Weird?" I ask. "Act weird, how? Are you sure it's been spiked?"

"No," she says. "But, to be on the safe side, we should leave."

"What about bets with King Aygor?" I ask.

"Shouldn't you be trusting your comrades more?"

"Yeah," I reply halfheartedly.

"Good. Your cousin would be proud of your progress. And, besides, *your* bets won't matter, if your Mazhrein's become intoxicated."

I brave the question, "What if it has? I don't feel any different." I'm not lying to her, either. I still feel sick with longing for a dance with Gemma. A shared kiss with her too.

Skylin states, "We can check, by having you perform a few spells. We'll bleed the intoxication out. You'll feel horrid tomorrow. But at least you won't go berserk, or anything."

I laugh tensely, asking, "Berserk? Care to enlighten me about that?"

Skylin presses her lips together.

I huff. "Well, I'm not leaving until I've made a bet with Aygor." I start heading back to Talok.

The music for the current dance ends.

Everyone claps or cheers.

The sound is thunderous.

My ears ring. I lose my footing. I can't make sense of up or down. I stumble around. Everything's spinning, much the way it did when Ryco transported me to the barn, back home. I grimace, and ball up my fists. The weight of my fake wings is like a boulder crushing me from behind.

I must not black out, I tell myself. *Not again. Not now. What if I wake after the seven days are up, and Talok is dead?*

King Aygor's voice is far away, announcing various Darklyres by name. Then he pauses in the long list, before continuing. "But this Grand Clan Gathering is of especial import to me," says the Darklyrian King. "This night, my oldest ward—a daughter of Clan RawZend—shall be the night partner to one, Arsyn of Jhire."

Skylin stifles an angry squeal. "Ooh! We're missing it."

Cold hands cup my face. A wave of nausea shoots down.

"Vards!" Skylin exclaims. "You're burning up."

Something soft sweeps across my forehead, and the sickness and spinning subside.

Skylin asks, "Better?"

I stand up, rubbing my face. "Yeah," I reply.

She tugs me back to full view of the dance center.

Arsyn, Dea, and several others are out in view, beginning a dance. The playfulness is gone, replaced by intensity. It's reminiscent to Caleiso slowing her pace to study me, while looking for an opening to jab with those crimped and cruel daggers.

"Can we just go?" I ask.

Skylin doesn't answer. She's transfixed on her father and Dea dancing. They look as if they want to tear into each other. At last, Dea unsheathes Arsyn's main blade. He takes hers, from her, at the same time. She kicks him back, and he lets her. Flying up, Arsyn then rushes down at her. His flight and steps are controlled. But Dea is without reserve. When their weapons clash together, the sound is powerful. It echoes, even over the drumming music. The other couples engage in similar behavior. It looks like a mass of duels, not couples dancing.

I ask, "Teach me to dance like that?"

Skylin's eyes brighten. "Really?"

"Would I ask, if I didn't want you to? Besides, it might bleed out the 'intoxication,' at the same time."

Skylin takes one look around us. The Darklyrian women watch the dancers with hatred. If they could, I swear, they'd jump off the second level, and run after Deamond to dispatch her right there, ripping her limbs off, so she could never dance with Arsyn again.

Clutching my abdomen, I tell Skylin, "I don't feel so great."

"Ha! We can go. I'm now satisfied that the vultures got a knife to their greed."

I roll my eyes, and say, "Whatever that means."

Skylin leads us out of the arena. We take to a hedge-bush maze, not far from there. It's halfway between the arena and the palace. Trickling streams of shimmering water run through it. Lots of sculpted ice-fountains are there too. Mostly of birds and dyns.

Skylin sits me down on a stone bench, and smiles.

"What now?" I ask, while looking up at her.

She slaps me hard across the face.

I fall off the bench, unsure of what's just happened. I press a hand to where she slapped me. "Dragon Spike!" I shout. "That hurt."

"But you're not angry?" she asks, fluttering her eyes innocently at me.

"Of course I'm angry!" I shout again.

"So, you want to hit me back?"

"Yes," I seethe, calming some. "But I won't."

After I've gotten up, and brushed myself off, I watch Skylin.

"That's good," she says, starting a stroll around the area. "It means the intoxication hasn't affected your aggression reactiveness. Unless you would typically strike out, right away."

"Not right away. No. But when your guard's down, Skylin, you better have Dea there to watch your back."

She stops her strolling. "I can take care of myself. And, since you seem to be feeling better, shall we begin?"

Crossing my arms, I ask, "Where do we start?"

She approaches shyly, glancing away as she gets closer. Her wings slump, then drag on the ground. Those big, blue eyes of hers disarm me.

Awngeleik's pout doesn't compare. Skylin's is irresistibly cute. She's far more docile too. Kind, even. In fact, she's very pretty. I start to wonder what it would feel like to have her close. I sigh, giving in. After stepping toward her, I take the usual dance position: one hand on her waist, the other gripping one of her hands.

The lessons are frustrating to no end. Yet, Skylin's patient and determined through it all. She won't let me get upset over my two left feet.

"You're getting it," she encourages. "Let's start at the beginning again."

Over and over, we restart the dance steps, keeping our time with the faint music playing in the distance. I get a little farther, each time, before I step on her foot; or smack into one of her wings; or bump my head against hers, while in a turn. After some time, I'm relaxed, and having fun. We dance until we're out of breath, and then we collapse on the ground, laughing hard. Both of us quiet down, and I stare up at the stars. There are so many. I look for the constellations of Earth, but then remember where I am. Muraine. It isn't the same. Far from it. And that's fine by me, except for the fact that a Vitiosyn King wants my cousin dead; and, me, for his next apprentice.

Skylin sits up, to look at me. "You got quiet."

"Does Muraine have constellations?" I ask. "Star patterns?"

"Oh yes!" She grins. "Can't you guess them?"

"The Auratic Creatures?" I confirm.

She points them out to me. Above Grevagg is one of the dyn constellations. In the Fleishyn Forest's direction is the Vardiya's Constell. Skylin lists off a total of six dragon ones, and many others. She starts talking so fast, I don't take it all in. I can't. She sounds too far away.

When faint voices get closer to us, my senses come back.

Alarmed, I ease up and go approach where the sounds are coming from. Skylin follows silently behind me. We take a turn in the hedge maze, and my heart sinks.

It's Gemma and Ben. Happily talking, at first. Then kissing again.

I turn on my heel, and start tramping out of the maze, to make my way to the palace.

Skylin trots behind, whispering, "We didn't get into the Duo's War Dance, yet. Are you done?"

"Yes," I state. "I'm done with this night."

"If you're jealous of them," she says, still keeping pace with me, "why not do what they're doing?"

I stop in my tracks. "Why do you think I'm jealous?"

Skylin looks at her wings, while stroking them. "No reason. But why not end the night like them? Looks exciting."

Impulsively, I turn to Skylin, and capture her waist with both my hands. I yank her to being as close to me as possible, and she gasps.

She studies my face, unsure, yet longing. I rest my forehead against hers, and wait. I want to feel something. Anything. But I feel nothing. She's not Gemma, though I want her to be in this moment.

Skylin grips the front of my coat, and then pulls me down enough to kiss me gently on the lips. It tickles, until she presses harder. Her lips are smooth, and quivering. She's nervous, and I think it's adorable. But not entirely fair.

I pull away. "Goodnight, Skylin." I turn to leave.

"Am I that bad?" Her voice trembles.

Guilt tugging at me, I turn back. "It's not that. It's not you. We don't know each other. And it's not kind, to use you. To continue to kiss you, when I feel nothing."

Angry, Skylin lifts one of her hands, and water shoots toward me. I'm thrown to the ground, drenched.

"That was Oonda." She clarifies, "Water. And this is wind." She presses her wrists together, and cups her hands, shouting, "Ventus!"

I'm blasted with a warm wind.

When Skylin repositions her hands a bit, and shouts, "Pru-eina," the wind turns ice-cold.

"Okay, okay!" I shout, holding up surrendering hands. "I get it."

Skylin puts her hands down.

The wind stops.

I struggle up, barely able to feel my numbed legs. "I deserved that. Want to start over?"

"With the dance?" she asks, sounding resentful.

"The kiss," I reply.

She lifts her head defiantly, before saying, "It depends."

"On what?" I ask.

"If you do it right," she replies.

"Is that a challenge?" I grin wickedly.

"If you make me *feel* something, I'll let you have that enchanted knife I planned on using tomorrow, in the Minor Gauntlet."

I state, "Sounds like a bet to me, and I accept."

As my legs warm back up, I approach Skylin with more shyness. I've hurt her feelings, and I don't like it. This time, I start. Gripping the sides of her neck, I brush my thumbs along her jawline. After she licks her lips, I bend down to kiss them. I tease her, kissing and then pulling away. She claws into my coat, to keep me from pulling away a third time. When I run my tongue over her bottom lip, she kisses me back. I wrap my arms around her waist, and let myself get lost in kissing her. My body tingles. Not just my lips. I ache to kiss her harder, as if she's Gemma. But I know she's not. My chest hurts. I start to feel that boiling sensation in my blood.

This time, Skylin's the one to pull away.

I'm left panting for air, nearly out of breath.

But she's not. She continues kissing my face, then down toward my neck.

When white-hot pain surges into my neck, I want to scream. Instead, I can't breathe.

The pain quickly turns euphoric. I can barely keep from falling. I realize that Skylin's bitten into my neck, not even warning me. She drinks my blood. I feel some of the hot liquid trickling down. I smile. I want to laugh. My heart has a sudden lightness. A feeling of strength. A closeness to Skylin that I can't make sense of. I don't understand why Rorka thought it hurt, when Gyron bit into her. It's a pain so temporary, and worth enduring.

A deep voice says, "A little young for that, aren't you, Skylin?"

She suddenly pulls away, but holds her hand to my neck. "Grawllik! Can't you ever mind your own business?" she seethes.

"Until blood is spilled, yes," replies Grawllik. "Wouldn't have said anything at all, if you were older."

Skylin scoffs. "But now?"

"Now you owe me a favor." Grawllik cracks his knuckles. "Refuse, and I might let talk of this incident slip out to your father, over morning breakfast."

When Skylin lifts her bloodied hand off me, I reach for my neck. It's healed enough that scabs are left behind.

"Well," she says, "you had better ask for that favor now. Or I will have thought of a way to discredit your accusation, by morning."

Grawllik replies, "First, I wish to know this. How serious are things between Deamond and Arsyn? Are they exclusive partners, for the whole gathering? Or is it merely for tonight?"

"Why do you care?" Skylin asks.

"Because I had wished to be formally introduced to her," Grawllik admits. "I hear she's a bit of a wild thing, right after she wakes from being dispatched, whether she wakes by herself or with assistance. It doesn't matter. I desire to know if it's true. I want to duel with her. I want to win. I want to kill her, and watch her come to life again."

I swallow hard, getting sicker with each passing moment. This GreyLyre disturbs me with his dark talk.

Skylin's wings protectively wrap around her small frame. "I don't know if it's true," she confesses. "Ask my father of it. He's witnessed it. So he says."

Grawllik nods. "Very well. In the morning, I shall. I bid a good night, to you."

"You're turning in, for the night?" Skylin queries. "But Darklyres prefer to be nocturnal."

"You will recall"—Grawllik taps his temple—"that I am a GreyLyre. And I'm tired. I arrived here, after a lengthy travel from MarcKand."

"MarcKand?" I burst out, asking, "You've been there?"

He replies, "King Aygor asked me to find Soren's spell-book. So, where else would I start? I failed to find it, but I was fairly certain he would be equally as excited to obtain Monel's. I've been away for ten months, first making my way to The Monel, then exploring it. Every hole and wall. Barely made it here, in time for the Clan Gathering."

I ask, "How long's the journey there?"

"Twelve days, from here," Grawllik replies, "if on a mighty fast dragon.

My initial trek to The Monel took me a hundred and forty days. Or, rather, five months. But I had a lot of stops, and delays, along the way. A forest legion of Sylvadyns being one of those delays. Nasty creatures. I detest them, and what the Sivos line does to their own young."

"What do they do?" Skylin queries.

Grawllik smirks. "That is not for someone of your young age to know."

"Well, then," Skylin states, "goodnight, Grawllik. Don't let a rock fall on your head, in the night, and smash your memories into oblivion." She pivots on her heel, then starts inspecting my neck. But she turns back to face Grawllik. "Oh, and Grawllik? You should know, before you ask Dea to a duel, she *is* partner to my father for the entirety of the Clan Gathering. And, though it *would* be weird, if my father wishes to make her my Stepma, I wouldn't be entirely against it. Just thought you should know, before you go making a fool of yourself with Deamond." Skylin inspects my neck once more.

Grawllik's smirk evaporates. He leaves, not uttering another word.

When he's out of earshot, I state, "That guy's creepy."

"Mm-hmm," Skylin mumbles, "and hungry to have offspring of his own."

"Is that why you lied?" I ask. "About Dea and your dad, I mean."

She nods. "Just looking out for a friend. My dad would never harm anyone he's decided to bed down with. But Grawllik has a cruel glint in his gaze. I don't like him. I don't trust him. Dea deserves better."

"Spoken like a true friend." I smile. "But he has the right idea. Sleep. I'm exhausted."

She chortles. "I bet you are."

As Skylin leads us back to our palace room, everything's unlit. It's total blackness.

"Do you have night vision, or something?" I ask, after a while.

"Don't you? Didn't even think to ask. Want a light?"

"Nah!" I proclaim, "You're a good leader. Haven't tripped on a thing, yet."

"Hold on to me, then," she says. "We're on the lift."

Forgetting myself, I do more than that. I feel for her face, in the dark.

When I find one of her bony shoulders, I trace my fingers along to her wet lips, then I kiss her more firmly than before. She presses against me, and cups my face. The lift takes off, and Skylin keeps us steady.

When the lift stops, the hallway torches light themselves.

Skylin pulls away, and giggles. "I think you've lost some of your shyness."

"Gotta be the spiked Farivoo," I state.

We get to the room, and Skylin silently closes the door.

I start peeling off all the layers. The clothes, the weight, I can't stand them anymore. My back aches. My shoulders. Everything, I decide, just aches for freedom. And I feel as if my body's boiling from the inside out.

"What are you doing?" she asks, sounding horrified. "If Dea's not ready for that, I certainly am not."

"Relax!" I exclaim. "I just need to cool down."

Before I know it, I've stripped down to my pants. I then proceed to collapse on one of the beds, annoyed at the fake wings' weight still lingering. What happens after that, I have no idea.

29

Don't Open Curtains!

Background chatter bleeds through to my senses. I make out Arsyn indignant over something.

Very groggy, I still manage to think, *Did Skylin confess to what we did?*

Water splashes, nearby. Then heavy footsteps pound toward my bed, and continue on past it.

Arsyn proclaims, "There, SynKievas! You've seen us in the same bed, together. Now get out, so I can finish my bath in peace. I'm tired."

Kent adds, "What he means is, we're all weary of you, the bets, the noise. We want sleep. Just look at Tyler. Out cold. I'm jealous."

SynKievas chuckles. "Very well. But I'll be back, to ask him of that cloak. Everyone was talking 'bout it. And, now? He's not even wearing it. I wonder where it went off to."

A weight lifts away.

All goes quiet again.

Sometime later, sunlight streams into the room. Not all the curtains have been drawn tight. I sit up, and look around. Ben's in the same bed as me. And, like me, he's only wearing pants. Gemma's splatted beside him, still in her turquoise-and-gray dress. Her hair has been let loose, now a black nest of tangles. Our wings are gone, and I'm relieved to be free of them.

Skylin's alone, shivering in the bed adjacent to ours. Most likely, Gemma abandoned it, to be by Ben. The bed closest to my side has the biggest surprise of all, though. Arsyn, who's sleeping on his side, holds Dea in his arms. It's like seeing my father in bed, holding my mother close. I only saw them like that a few times, when they left their bedroom door open all night.

Tears well up in my eyes, but I fight them off, and lie back down. The memories sting severely, and I wonder, *If she knew the truth of LanSoren of Trauvo, what would she do? How would she react? Would she still love him? Resent him? Would she even care at all?*

I roll onto my side, and glance at them again. They look content.

Someone rustles in a nearby bed. Soft footsteps pad on the floor. It's Skylin, wandering past my bed, to throw herself down beside Deamond.

Arsyn jolts awake, reaching for his blade, which rests on the floor. When he sees that it's Skylin, he relaxes back to a slumbering position. "Skylin," he whispers, "it's not appropriate for you to be in bed with me, anymore. You're far too old for that." He pulls Dea close to his bare chest again.

"But I'm cold," she complains, huddling closer to Deamond. "Gem abandoned her assigned post, partway through the night. I think she got hungry."

Arsyn groans. "Girl, I don't care. Get out of my bed," he orders, before gripping Dea's limp hand to kiss the back of it. "Three," he counts.

"Father," Skylin moans quietly, "I just want a little warmth, without starting the day using magic."

Dea stirs, mumbling, "Is it time for breakfast, already?"

"Almost," says Arsyn, kissing Dea gently on the forehead. "Two," he says.

Skylin flutters her wings. "Don't you *dare* kiss her for real."

"Then get out of my bed," he commands.

Dea yawns, glancing over her shoulder at Skylin.

Skylin's livid, as she rolls off the bed to thud to the floor.

"What's wrong?" queries Dea, still sleepy.

Arsyn replies, "Skylin's being a morning pest is all. Go back to sleep."

Yet again, he pulls her close.

Dea sighs, in contentment.

My chest aches. I miss my parents. I even miss my mom's nagging about putting a shirt on. *What would she say, to all this? I wonder. And who was it she saw that night, a few days before I left for Muraine? Droediin? It had to be. Will I ever see him again? Will I get a chance to see her again, and tell her the truth my dad never could?*

I start wondering what's happened to Jasper, Mekka, and Merlynite too, but Skylin interrupts that by coming to my bedside, still shivering.

"Move over," she orders, in a whisper.

"No way," I say, under my breath. "There isn't room."

"There is, if we cuddle." She shoves me over, and plops down in the fetal position, her wings hugging close to her body.

I start to pity her. But then I remember how we kissed last night, and how out of character that sort of thing is for me. Sure, maybe I would've contemplated doing what we did. But to actually act on it, like I'm Jed? My face flushes. I can't help but feel my shame. That's when Skylin puts her ice-cold hands on my face, and I fight them off.

"Skylin," her father chastises her. "What are you doing?"

"I told you," she whispers. "I'm cold, because Gem left her post."

Arsyn growls low, sounding a little like a beast. Then he ignores Skylin, as he starts softly stroking Deamond's wings.

Skylin huffs, divving to me, *"What are they doing, behind my back?"*

"Cuddling," I div. *"Although, both are consenting to it. Unlike us."* I pinch her arm.

She gawks at me. *"Uncalled for! I wasn't the one who spiked your Farivoo."*

"But you took advantage of the situation, didn't you?"

"Perhaps," she divs back. *"You looked upset, watching your two friends. I wanted to cheer you. Then I had a chance to get my first kiss. So, I did both. Oh! And I finished bleeding out the intoxication in your Mazhrein, with that bite on your neck. It's why you were so"*—she rolls her eyes—*"lovey, afterwards."*

"Fine," I div, in the middle of a sigh. *"I forgive you. But I'm not going to thank you. That was my first real kiss too, and I had wanted it to be with someone I've known for a while."*

Skylin sits up, divving, *"Sorry I ruined it."*

She starts getting off the bed, but I stop her with a pet at her wings. *"It was still nice,"* I div. *"Just not what I had planned."* Moving my hand to reposition my pillow, I then tuck both hands under it.

She forces a grin, and stays sitting on the bed.

Distant racket sounds outside our room, from somewhere in one of the palace's hallways.

Dea jolts upright.

Arsyn growls low again.

"Someone's coming," Dea whispers, shaking Arsyn on the shoulder.

"Why's that matter?" he asks.

Dea points at us. "They don't have their wings, Arsyn."

Unamused, Arsyn snaps his fingers; the weight of our wings returns.

Many around the room start stirring out of their slumber.

But, as soon as someone begins turning the doorknob, the King's Guard are alert.

Ben leaps off the bed, then dives over the railing, scaring Gemma awake. She scrambles to the floor.

By the railing is Ryco, already aiming a readied arrow at the door.

Kent, beside him, has flames wisping in his grasp.

Then there's Siege, who's leapt down, and silently positioned himself in front of the door's hinged side, ready to attack with a pair of tiny daggers if need be.

The door flings open. Keturah hurries in, tears streaming down her face. She flies up, over the third-level railing. As soon as she's spotted Deamond, she bursts out sobbing.

Arsyn sits up, grumbling. "Everything good in Rentwar's Light, what *is* wrong?"

Ketty ignores Arsyn, but runs toward his bed. She throws herself between him and Dea.

"So much for a relaxing morning," he says, while flopping back down.

The King's Guard calm down slightly, and head for their things stored on the third floor.

Dea consoles Ketty, who's sobbing on her chest. "What's happened, Keturah?"

Quiet footsteps climb the stairs, up to the third level. Sonya emerges into view, timidly making her way for Deamond.

Dea sees her. "Sonya, do you know what's happened?"

Sonya exclaims, "It's your own fault, Ketty! If you had knocked on his door—"

Ketty screams, in anger, "I did knock!"

"But you didn't even wait for an answer!" Sonya yells back. "Before you burst in there, and . . . and saw . . . s-saw him . . ." Sonya stutters to a stop, blushing a deep red.

"Saw whom?" Dea asks.

"King Aygor," Sonya replies, in distress.

This triggers a new wave of angry tears from Keturah. She clings to Dea again.

Continuing, Sonya says, "Ketty got up real early, this morning. Made breakfast for King Aygor, his top five Annual Sentinels, and us. The King's Wards. She went to get him, to invite him to dine with us. But he was . . . busy." Sonya blushes again.

Dea asks sharply, "Busy doing what?"

Ketty screams it out, "Bedding my trainer! Litreez. I hate her!"

"Hate is a strong word," says SynKievas, from the third level's top step.

Arsyn grumbles, "SynKievas, go away. It's just barely light out."

"I would," he replies, "but King Aygor's rather distraught, this morning. Saw me in the courtyard, and asked that I help him find one of his female wards. About thirteen, dark and brooding. Would that be you, Keturah?" SynKievas grins awkwardly. "King Aygor was so upset that he forgot to tell me the ward's name."

"I'm not dark and brooding," Keturah defends, now wiping her tears away.

The King's Guard begin dressing for the day, but I refuse to get out of bed. My body still aches. And I want no part of this dialogue. Better to just watch, and listen in.

Grawllik comes up behind SynKievas, stating, "But you're clearly upset. Let us take you to King Aygor. He'll be relieved to see you."

"No!" Ketty says firmly.

Ryco interrupts, asking, "How much food did you prepare, Keturah?"

Ketty startles, gawking at Ryco, as he slips his coat, cloak, and weapons on.

He continues, "Do you think you've made enough, for this lot to dine with you?"

Ketty curls her wings over her shoulders, asking, "An Ayzagaun wants to dine with children?"

"Children don't bother me," replies Ryco. "But that's not the notion I was thinking. Dining with the King's Wards isn't dining with children. But, rather, the fearless, don't you think? Many talked, last night, about what happened to you yesterday. That a Gatro got a hold of you. Almost ate you. But you were brave, in letting King Aygor dispatch you to distract the Gatro. A fearless act of trust, on your part."

"Was that you, Keturah?" SynKievas queries. "Why then, Grawllik and I would be honored to dine with the fearless, as well."

A wide grin spreads on Keturah's face; Sonya presses her mouth together, trying not to smile.

Ryco glances at me, then Skylin, then back to Ketty. Drumming his fingers on one of his arm bracers, he adds, "I would say that I think you're reckless, as well. But you're more likely to remember the first word. So why bother with the second? You will have forgotten that one, by lunchtime."

Dea nods her agreement, pushing Ketty off the bed. "Now that *two* Ayzagauns have deemed you fearless, Ketty, will you sit quietly and wait for us?"

Ketty's head bobs. She then makes her way to the first floor, to wait at one of the tables. Sonya follows.

SynKievas and Grawllik watch the two girls pass them by on the stairs.

Then SynKievas is asking, "Now that that's settled, I had wondered if Tyler is up for talking of that cloak he had on last night."

Sighing deeply, I sit up, saying to SynKievas, "I don't know where it is, and the room's a little dim for finding it. But what did you want to know about it?"

SynKievas hesitates.

Grawllik then treads toward the curtains.

Skylin shouts, "No, Grawllik, don't open those yet!"

Grawllik doesn't listen. He grips two curtains by the edges, and yanks them apart.

Morning's light streams in, as Skylin dives under my bed. Gemma joins her.

Arsyn growls and hisses, then lunges from his bed in a rage. Steam comes off him, as the light hits him. Dragon scales form on his chest, arms, and face. He's clawing at Grawllik. Gripping fistfuls of Grawllik's clothing, Arsyn throws him over the railing, down to the first level. He flies after him.

The two girls shriek, running up the stairs and into the safety of Dea's outstretched wings.

The King's Guard draw weapons again; Rozeth and Nyrim join in, this time.

Talok, however, is still fast asleep.

As Arsyn roars at Grawllik, SynKievas creeps his way to the curtains. With quivering hands, he yanks the curtains back to being closed. "There, Arsyn. They're closed. It's all right." He flies over to Arsyn and Grawllik. "No need to continue this. Grawllik's learned his lesson, haven't you?"

Arsyn gives a deep, beastly snarl.

Ryco shifts into his Parasogyn form, and jumps down to where Arsyn has Grawllik pressed against a wall. His breaths are deep and reptilian in sound. In this moment, Ryco seems more dragon than the Darklyres could ever hope to be.

Arsyn starts a drawn-out snarl at him. But Ryco growls out sounds. They seem to be words. It's hard to tell. The sound's so low in pitch that it vibrates the room. The tremors catch in my chest, making me feel oddly calm. I don't particularly want to be calm, yet I am.

Arsyn releases his hold on Grawllik, then flies back toward his bed. He shakes out his wings, and the scales shed off him like shimmering dust. They're gone, and Arsyn's back to being himself.

Ryco, as well, is in his usual form, but with the added fake wings. "Talok!" he shouts. "Wake up! We're going to breakfast."

Talok stretches beneath the blankets, in no hurry to leave the bed's comfort.

Ryco, on his way past my bed, tickles my bare feet, and I jerk them away, out of his reach.

"You two are definitely related," says Siege, in good humor. "Both the last ones out of bed."

As Grawllik comes back up the stairs, Arsyn's buttoning up his sleeveless shirt.

Grawllik utters, "I was unaware of how old you are, Arsyn. Therefore, how could I have known that dawn's light hurts you?"

Skylin crawls out from under my bed, saying, "If you had listened to me, I could've told you."

Arsyn finishes getting his coat into position, then reaches out to cup Dea's face. She relaxes, and the two girls give them space.

"Sorry for startling you," says Arsyn, eyeing Dea in her pale nightgown that reaches to her knees. "You're beautiful, this morning."

Turning playful, Dea asks, "But not for the rest of the day?"

Taking his hand off her face, he replies, "You're a Sentinel's Tease, most of the time, from what I hear."

"It's true," Ketty confirms.

Dea swipes her on the arm.

That's when Grawllik says, "I had wished to ask you to an afternoon duel, Deamond. But now doesn't look to be a proper time for asking. Perhaps, later this year." He turns to leave.

Dea states, "You can't ask me to a duel. We haven't been formally introduced. Although, I'd love to accept."

SynKievas raises his hand. "It's what I came to do. Introduce the two of you. Then, it just so happened, I found the distraught ward King Aygor's been looking for. We'll go find him. Tell him to meet us in his personal banquet room. That *is* where the food is, yes, Ketty?"

She nods.

They exit the room.

Gemma crawls into view, brushing off her dress as she stands up. She hands me the cloak of interest, saying, "Pack this away, if you want to keep it. Aygor was looking everywhere for you, last night, in the arena. SynKievas and several other Lyres were too."

While getting dressed, I ask, "Did anyone make bets with him, last night? I wasn't feeling well. So I never had a chance to."

Gemma replies, "We all did. None of them really worked out the way we had hoped for. And, when Nyrim's went awry, it put Aygor in a bad mood."

Ben says, "Possibly Gemma's bet with Arsyn will impress King Aygor. We'll see, at breakfast."

Fully dressed, Talok yawns out the words, "Shall we go down, then? I'm about as starving as Gemma was last night."

Kent states, "Glad someone's gotten an appetite back."

Sonya asks, "Have you been sick, Talok?"

"Can't keep food down all the time," he replies.

"This meal should be perfect, then," Ketty declares, rocking back on her heels. "I put several curse-countering spices in the food, and anti-sickness tonics in the Farivoo."

I ask, "Ketty, you wouldn't happen to have spiked the Farivoo, last night, by chance?"

Ketty's eyes widen. "No! King Aygor has forbidden his wards to do anything like that."

Gemma gives me that witchy-look

Then I think, *She knows who it was. Devil-witch. I'll get it out of her, in div, over breakfast.*

30

Dine with the Fearless

Surrounding us are warm colors, seemingly touched by a faint light that emits from within. We all sit round a large banquet table that's covered by white cloth. Above that table, a simple, glass chandelier further lights the area. The wait isn't long, for when SynKievas leads King Aygor and Grawllik into the spacious, simplistic room.

King Aygor's frantic, until he sees Keturah. She patiently stands beside the table's stately, carved chair. She timidly smiles at him, and pulls the chair out, gesturing that he should sit.

His eyes glisten, as would a proud father's hiding his sheer joy. He takes his seat with honor, and Keturah helps him position his wings so he's more comfortable. She then sits to his left; Sonya, across from her.

Seven other wards (four boys, three girls), all younger than Keturah, have joined us. Everyone serves themselves, starting with Keturah. We pass the food to our left, until everyone's been served. There are plentiful grains and fruits, flavorful in appearance, along with many different meats ranging in color from almost white to salmon-pink to jerky-red then to squid-ink black. Everything's been crafted to bite-sized portions, like little pieces of edible artwork.

King Aygor looks it all over, serving himself last. But he takes the first bite. It's a little square of pink meat, topped with white, yellow, and green bits to resemble a flower. "It's perfect," he says.

Keturah's face lights up, and she looks genuinely happy.

All ten of the wards begin their meal; the rest of us too. There's lots of table talk, discussing various bets that were going around. Throughout the meal, many compliment Ketty on her cooking skills. Then Rozeth praises the exquisite array of dancing and magic seen last night.

"It's one of the best times I've ever had," she says.

King Aygor finishes off his first glass of Farivoo, asking Sonya for more. "I'm merely glad," he says, as his glass is refilled, "that I didn't get threats, over letting Dea be the night partner of Arsyn. You should've seen the looks of displeasure among my clergy and sentinels, when they found out. Seqwhyett seemed most disappointed, as well. Then you, SynKievas, but I imagine it was over that cloak." Aygor looks at me. "Where ever did you get it, Tyler?"

"It was a gift from a friend," I reply.

"Friend, indeed!" SynKievas pauses the consumption of his meal. "And tell us who this friend is. They should be ashamed. Whom would dare give away their ancestral garb?"

Grawllik adds more food to his plate, replying, "Probably some stupid soul, with no care for family and tradition whatsoever."

"Family isn't everything, Grawllik," says Dea, readjusting her corset. "You can make family ties with those whom you have zero blood relations to, you know?"

Grawllik clears his throat. "Yes, that's what marriages do."

Dea drops her fork, and the delicate fruit, carved to resemble a butterfly, splats on her plate.

Ketty squirms in her seat.

Grawllik leisurely continues his meal, adding, "It also can happen, when you're not careful. When you get lost in a moment, caring a little too much. You know, King Aygor? You should be careful whom you let yourself love. She might use you for her own gain."

Ketty bobs her head. "Yes. My trainer, Litreez. You shouldn't trust her, King Aygor. She only wants position. To start a family with you. And then where would that leave us, your wards? Litreez doesn't want us. Doesn't love us. She's just mean, always driving me to the point of hating her."

King Aygor looks down at his half-empty plate, clasping his hands on the table. "Is that what you feel for Litreez? Hate? I have raised you, to only hate the bad things in this world. So, why is it that you believe Litreez is bad?"

"She wants to take you away from us, to have children of her own," says Ketty, getting choked up.

King Aygor wipes his mouth with a napkin, then says, "I see. That does make her horrible, indeed, doesn't it?" Aygor pushes his chair away from the table. "Thank you, Keturah, for this most excellent meal. If it was your way of apologizing for your disobedience of yesterday, I accept your apology. Now, I've a very busy day ahead. I had better get started."

The room's heavy, as Aygor leaves. But Gemma perks up, saying, "King Aygor?"

He stops to look at her with a sad gaze.

"I had wondered, before you go," says Gemma, "do you mind helping me with a bet I made against Arsyn last night?"

"Of course not," he replies. "What is it?"

Arsyn dumps the contents of one of the food bowls onto Talok's empty plate. Then he fills that bowl with Farivoo, poured out from a canteen that he unhooks from his belt.

Gemma takes a bit of bluish powder from Ben, and sprinkles it in the Farivoo. It swirls around, then fizzles. The red drink's left bubbling with carbonation.

"Place your hand in it," Gemma instructs.

Hesitantly, King Aygor complies, and when he does, the bubbles in the liquid draw together into small, violet dots. At least a dozen of them.

Gemma's triumphant, as she says, "Take your hand out."

Aygor does, and his fingernails are left with a deep purple tinge to them. "That's new," he says. "What's it mean?"

Gemma stands up, and offers him a napkin to dry his hand with. "First, tell me which refreshment table you visited last night, then I will tell you why you made that choice."

Excitement fills Aygor's dark-brown eyes, as he replies, "The third farthest table, from my personal balcony at the arena."

"I thought as much." She glances at the Farivoo in the bowl. "And this confirms it. See, here's my reasoning. If you're the King of RawZend, you'll be suspicious—at every turn—of being a bet's victim, whether you're the targeted one or not. You know some bets will involve yourself. Others will target your sentinels. You're one hundred percent certain the water and Farivoo closest to your balcony are spiked with various effects."

Aygor nods. "So I would avoid those, altogether. Yes, go on."

"The second closest table," Gemma states. "You're fairly certain one of them has been altered there. You take a small sip of each."

King Aygor adds, "But one tastes sour. The Farivoo, if I recall right."

"Yes," Gemma replies. "You're suspicious of that. So, you move on. The third table you're less leery of. It's not on the first floor, where thousands are entering and more likely to be a victim. It's farther from your balcony, but not too close to your clergy's ledge to warrant concern. And, in fact, you realize that it's in a quiet, tucked-away spot. Only two glasses have been taken. You're not the first one to have been there. But no one's lingering around, acting strange. You deem it a safe bet, then take a drink of Farivoo."

His expression confused, Aygor states, "And it tastes sweeter than I recall."

Gemma points at him. "But you blame that on the sour Farivoo you just tasted. After all, Farivoo is reserved for special occasions. Perhaps it was always that sweet. You're not sure. You drink a whole glass of it. Then another. A third one. You've missed it all year. As you know, the last event's batch spoiled."

Aygor barely holds back laughter. "Girl, I like the way your mind works. So, what was your bet with Arsyn?"

Gemma replies, "That twenty-one would drink from my spiked Farivoo, before the end of the duo's dances, and that Arsyn would only have fifteen infected from his."

"I bet twenty-two for me, and eleven for her," says Arsyn.

"So, how close were we?" Gemma asks.

Dea replies, "I checked Arsyn's count last night. Talok was gracious enough to drink some, in order for us to get a total. His hand revealed Arsyn's number to be seventeen."

Arsyn leans forward, looking into the Farivoo bowl. "Looks like yours, Gem, is eighteen. Your total was only off by five, whereas mine was twelve away. Plus, you caught the king. The highest position of mine was Crown Sentinel."

Gemma raises her glass of Farivoo, and says, "Cheers!"

Everyone claps, or gives nods of acknowledgment to a bet well done.

The joy then fades from Aygor, as he glances at Ketty. "What exact effect did you spike yours with, Gem?"

Gemma swallows a sip, replying, "Nothing too drastic. Just lower inhibitions. More courage to act on how you feel in the moment."

Arsyn adds, "Mine was increased fatigue and hunger. Sorry, Talok."

Everyone's happy, teasing Talok, and congratulating Gemma.

But my stomach churns. I kissed Skylin, because of Gemma's spiked drink. The irony sends my pulse soaring. I glance at Skylin. She won't meet my gaze. She knew. When the group of them were getting the clothes, or readying for the dance, they planned something like this. And Skylin didn't say a word. Just that you never know when the drinks have been spiked.

I'm suddenly impulsive, and standing up. Needing to know for sure, I dunk both hands into the Farivoo bowl.

The teasing and talking cease.

I take my hands out, and shake them off. Like King Aygor's, my fingernails are stained a deep purple.

Gemma's eyes grow wide. "Tyler, you drank the spiked Farivoo? Skylin was supposed to keep an eye on you."

Skylin bursts out of her seat. "He downed a whole glass, before I could stop him. You didn't tell me which one you were going to pick. It's not my fault."

I claw at my face, desperately wanting to scream at Skylin. She used me.

Then she lied, not owning up to the truth, afterwards.

King Aygor eyes me, in pity. "I take it, you were her first victim of the night?"

"Last night, sure." I shrug (it's the fail-safe). "But Gem's had loads of victims, in the past. I told all of you, she'd be our best bet in besting King Aygor."

"Besting me?" queries Aygor. "Any particular reason why you should want to *best* me?"

I state, "To get an invitation, to visit Soren's Library."

Siege adds, "We didn't want to be too bold, in asking outright."

"Ah, I see," replies Aygor, clasping his hands together. "Well, with how things played out, I wish you had made the simple request. But then, that wouldn't really be the Darklyre way, would it?" Glancing to Ketty, Aygor asks, "Will you excuse us, in ending the breakfast dining early, Keturah?"

She replies, "Sonya and the others will help me clear everything away."

"Good!" Aygor says. He turns to the group of us. "Follow me."

We head out with him, then through the palace's main entrance. Suddenly, the statues of the original Darklyre siblings, along with the creatures of aura, seem to be watching me. I don't feel that usual cold-heat creeping through my veins. It's something different. I don't know what. But I don't like it. I want to turn, and run. Yet, when someone brushes their hand along the back of my shoulder, I'm filled with the briefest confidence. I don't know who it is, and I refuse to look. I just keep my eyes fixed on Aygor's wings, as they sway with each of his footsteps.

We go down a long, winding hallway, getting closer to Soren's Library.

Closer to the answers I desperately seek.

31

Soren's Library

The bustling about of Darklyres within King Aygor's palace fades. Only the footsteps of our group echoes down the long path. I'm incredibly nervous, the deeper we go into the hallway that leads to Soren's Library.

Grand arches carved of black granite soar up to forty feet high above us, with an empty space of twenty feet, for us to pass through. Farther along, the arches begin to narrow in: first, at thirty feet high, with a space of fifteen; then twenty and ten; lastly, ten and five. The vanishing point they create is somewhat disorienting. It appears to go on forever, never-ending.

I fight to keep my breath steady. Then I struggle to simply breathe. My lungs feel filled up with powdered sugar. A cough tries to escape, but can't. I sense that I'm choking, yet not a sound comes out. I can't show *any* sign of my distress. I'm panicking. But, to all, I must appear just fine. When trying to hold my breath, I find that I can't do that either. My feet are steady. My hands are still. My breaths become calm. *But how?* I wonder.

Someone Mensa-divs then, saying, *"Your father said your steps to the library would be agony. Thought you might get too overwhelmed, and run."* I realize it's Ryco. *"Now you can't. Without a fight, that is. By the time you might be able to resist the control, we'll be at the library. You're welcome, Ravier."*

I want to claw his face. Instead, a little smile's able to break through. No shrugging, just a smile. I attempt to tense every muscle. It doesn't work.

Imagery is next. Peaceful days at the lake with my dad; saving Nyrim from the overwhelming of memories; being witness to the violence in Paragon; but the strongest visual is of Caleiso. The duel we had, while I wanted to rip her apart for betraying my feelings. Screams fill my head, but I'm still forced along the Darklyrian hallway.

Ryco, beside me, sighs out a contented sort of sound.

I manage to div one word to him: *"Sadist."*

He divs back, *"I thought we were long past the name-calling, Ravier. No? Sleeping Dragon? It is rather fitting. You certainly sleep a lot. If you were a dragon, you'd put dragons to shame."*

I try divving another name for him: Parasogyn. I don't know what's gotten into me. I feel such violence rising up. It's as if I'm a prisoner, being dragged down the hall to be locked up at the end of it. I'm livid, aggressive, but scared.

Grawllik asks, "Do you have Monel's book with you, King Aygor?"

Aygor holds it up into view, wiggling it back and forth, before tucking it in the hidden pocket of his coat. "Won't ever let it from my sight, now that I have it. Was going to put it in the statue's hands, yesterday. But I lost the courage. The wait's been long. Many generations in my family, yet I will be the one to carry out the task. The honor is heavy."

When Aygor stops at the last archway, I feel Ryco's control break away. Consumed now by fear, I start sweating up a storm. I'm exhausted, and the day's only started. I miss what Aygor does to bring the shield down, before he leads the way through the last archway, and into the library. Ryco strides to the front of our group. Only Aygorinaith, Grawllik, and Arsyn are ahead of him.

As I step into the large room, I haven't any idea of what to expect. But what greets us certainly wasn't it—simplicity awaits.

Sure, its ceiling is over a hundred feet high. But there aren't any grand tapestries, on the walls of this cylindrical, hollowed-out room. No pictures or paintings at all. The pale floor's covered by tattered rugs. They must've been dark-red, at one point. They're now a rouge-pink and dusty, worn through in places to show the marble floor beneath. Sparse pieces of furniture—some tables, as well as a few chairs with desks—are yellowed whitewood. Antiqued, with lots of scratches scuffed into their surfaces. The bookshelves have fared slightly better. They're more ivory-colored than yellowed-white, and not so fragile in appearance.

Books fill the shelves in an orderly fashion, and those shelves go on, all the way to ceiling. It could take a Murainian's lifetime, to read everything contained in here.

Siege whispers, in awe, "All the books in the world. I've never seen so many, in one place."

"How many rows deep are the books?" queries Kent.

"Nine or ten," Aygorinaith answers. "Depends on the section you're searching through."

"How much of it have you read?" I ask.

He replies, "I've read nearly all the myths and legends. It's helped me over the years, in dealing with errant young wards, refusing to go bed; or to stay in bed, once there. Dea was the worst night walker imaginable, guilty of adamant refusal."

"I remember," Dea says, whilst she brushes dust off a desk with her palm. "I also recall you telling me the more frightful myths, rituals, and curses, to do with the early-morning hours. It's a wonder I didn't have nightmares, as a little girl. Especially of that Soren statue."

Skylin gets giddy, asking, "Where is it, King Aygor?"

"Yes, the Soren statue." I feign familiarity of it. "Wasn't it supposed to be in here?"

Talok grins nervously, saying, "My cousin's anxious about seeing it, King Aygor."

"Is he, now?" Aygor turns to me. "Whatever for? It's not actually able to take on life of its own accord, as I told Dea when she was little."

"But aren't you hoping to bring it to life with that?" Arsyn points to Monel's spell-book, as RawZend's King pages through it.

"Not exactly. I'm unsure what will happen, when I place it in his hands. Shall we find out, together?" King Aygor closes the book suddenly, then walks farther into the room, toward the crumbling, dried-up stone fountain. He makes his way for the library's center. Once at the far side of that fountain, he motions for us to come have a look.

Siege states, "And there he is . . . in a golden likeness, no less."

Ben adds, "It's rather chilling."

"You get used it," says Aygor. "I spend much time in here. And he's never spoken a word. Nor has he Mensa-divved instructions, contrary to how our storytellers have told; able to break laws of time. It's ludicrous!" Aygor bellows out a laugh.

We attempt to smile, to show amusement. But we know the truth. Soren can. And his statue may yet come to life, when Aygor gives over Monel's spell-book. I stare at the golden likeness, carved to be in a pose of ease. Soren neither looks down, nor holds his head high. He gazes frontward, seemingly to a far-off object. His expression is one of wanting, longing, perhaps even concern. He reminds me of the younger Soren we encountered, and that comforts me a little.

Still, I div to Ryco: *"Should we try to stop him?"*

Ryco gnaws on the inside of his cheek, as Aygor cautiously approaches the statue.

At the last second, Ryco says, "Shouldn't we draw out weapons, in case it does come to life, King Aygor? While he may have had goodwill, at one point, who can say he won't wake up with violence in his heart?"

Aygorinaith jerks the book away from Soren's expectant grasp. "A good point," he says, drawing out his own blade one-handed.

At near the same time, Arsyn and Grawllik draw their short-blades. The others follow suit, except for Gemma and me; Skylin too. She, instead, finds safety behind Dea and Arsyn. While all gazes are transfixed on the statue, Aygorinaith opens the book and then places it in Soren's hands. Quickly lifting his wings, he flies back away from the statue. Never once does his gaze leave Soren's still likeness.

Minutes tick by.

Nothing happens.

King Aygor grinds his teeth. "Come, now. What's it going to take?"

Gemma suggests, "Maybe you didn't pick the right page for him to see."

"Are you sure," queries Arsyn, while sheathing his blade, "that this statue was meant to be woken up, King Aygor?"

"I'm positive that, given the right book, *something* will happen. I know not what, however. In one of the books held within these walls, I read of the statue's origin."

Nyrim says, "Perhaps you should recheck the facts. Ensure you've got the details right."

"Not a bad idea," says Aygorinaith. "While I search for it, Arsyn, please be kind enough to collect several of the Geldryn volumes, for young Talok to read through. See if he can't learn more about that family heirloom on his wrist."

Arsyn's shoulders tense. He hesitates briefly, as he looks to the device slowly transforming my cousin. Oddly enough, something has changed about Talok's progression. He hasn't had a blood craving, or been nearly as pale, since we arrived in Grevagg.

I wonder, *Does it have to do with being near this library? Certain enchantments, on various things around the city? Or is it the calm, before something worse happens?*

I assume it's the latter, and I dread what's coming.

Arsyn's about halfway up the many bookshelves. He must've found the Geldryn section, because, next, he's grabbing volume after tome and tossing them over his shoulder. They start to fall, but shift into beige-colored birds of varied size. The mismatched flock makes for the square table twenty feet across from Soren's statue. They all hop about. Then they turn back into tomes, forming six stacks, books askew.

Ryco puts away his weapons. Then the group follows his example.

Talok blows out a breath. "Well, Siege, Rozeth, shall we get started on those?"

The three sit, and begin the lengthy process of reading.

When King Aygor takes longer in finding the storybook, the rest of us assist in perusing the tomes. Siege writes down words and symbols to search for. Then we get busy.

Hours pass.

None of us discover anything useful.

But it seems that Aygorinaith has, as he's flying down, all excited. "Found it," he proclaims. "I'll go ahead and read it, if you're at a good stopping place in your research."

We give him our attention.

"Very good," he says. "I'll start at the interesting part. I haven't a clue as to whom the author of this work could be. Whoever it was, though, writes as if they were there with Soren." He flips through the large-covered, thin volume, reading aloud, "Soren had received word, days prior, to come before Rentwar, the Rubidyn. He felt it was a trap, of sorts. Many had hunted him, since the Era of Withrasyn Kings had ended. Suspicion plagued him, with every step he took on down into the cavern under the white mountain."

Skylin asks, "The white mountain? What's its actual name, King Aygor?"

He glances up, replying, "Dyns'hyn, or Ignic'Krawva. Depends on who you ask."

Skylin smiles. "Home to Dragons, or Spark of Prophecy. Why's it have two names?"

"It was originally called Spark of Prophecy," replies Grawllik.

Dea adds, "But, during the War of Ichors Von, the other races started calling it Home to Dragons. No other dragons, except for Rubidyns, have a designated home. They move about, with the times or seasons. Rubidyns do not. In doing so, they silently declare they are greatest among dragons, unafraid of having their lasting home invaded."

Skylin crosses her arms. "Vards, Dea! You *do* read the histories, *and* remember them."

Dea sits adjacent to Siege, while he handles one of the Geldryn books. "It has helped," she says, "having access to Soren's Library year-round. I've read half of the lower sections. Plus, a quarter of the upper cases' books."

"Stop it!" Skylin exclaims. "You're making me quite envious."

Dea wiggles her shoulders back and forth, teasing Skylin without uttering a word.

King Aygor grimaces. "We'll talk of your reading of the upper sections, later, Dea. You know it's not permitted, before you're twenty. How did you even get up there?"

"It was three years ago," Dea replies, "before you put the barrier in place."

The Darklyrian King grumbles something inaudible, but then continues with the story. "When he finally arrived, before the king of dragons—greater than all, save for The Flame—Soren knew something was different.

"Rentwar was in the upright, two-legged form. He stood taller than a Geldryn of full height. Taller than a Parasogyn, of Ayzareel and Gaula's bloodline. Mightier, still, than a GreyLyre, with a gaze more piercing than that of Jasper of the Greyvons. Soren almost didn't recognize the Rubidyn King. If he hadn't been occupying that golden throne, meant to seat a mighty dyn, Soren would've been none the wiser as to his identity. He bowed low to Rentwar, as that is proper etiquette in dealing with one of equal or greater status than yourself."

Aygorinaith starts reading their dialogue:

Still kneeling, Soren asked, "Have you summoned me here, to kill me?"

"If that was my intent, Sorshrynak," replied Rentwar, "you'd have been dead, on the first step into my home. No. I have want for other things. I'm preparing you, for the future."

Soren couldn't imagine what these preparations were. Rubidyns aren't Metimoras, with books of time. But he knew of their prophecies. Has Rentwar seen a vision to do with me? he wondered. What could it be?

Rentwar continued, saying, "As you can see, magic is growing. Becoming stronger. Dyns shouldn't be able to take this form similar to Sorsryns. Greyvons can, because they're highly adaptive. Their Crae-Shand makes it achievable. Although, I think you knew that, already. But Red Magic, Rubidyn Magic, wasn't meant to alter appearance."

"What of Dosce-meina?" Soren asked, "The spell to make dual-blooded Rubidyns?"

"That is not what that spell is for," said Rentwar. "It is to allow species, other than Rubidyn, to practice Red Magic without breaking the Laws of Magic. It's a loophole, if you will."

"Are you going to offer to use that spell on me?" asked Soren.

Rentwar replied, "Your mind's too broken, for that."

"Then tell me why I was asked here," said Soren.

"How's Awleesia these days?" Rentwar asked, in return.

"I've not seen her for a while," replied Soren. That fear was creeping back. Rentwar had a glint of knowing something rather important. It was maddening to Soren, waiting for Rentwar to out what was actually on his mind.

Rentwar continued, "Then you're unaware? Ignorant of the fact that she's been spending a significant amount of time with King ReNovak?"

"Why ever would I care of that?" queried Soren. "If she becomes the next Onyx Queen, all the better."

"No." Rentwar's voice deepened. "It won't be better. Aren't you aware, Soren, of the great lengths ReNovak will go to, for bringing his Setharyn back to life?"

"The Onyx Prince?" Soren asked, now alarmed. "ReNovak can't bring him back. He's gone. I should know. I helped make it possible for him to exist, before it was his time. Bringing him back is impossible."

Rentwar replied, "By the normal means, yes, but ReNovak's cheated. This time, without your help. Awleesia doesn't know what's happening. You must fix this."

"And why is that?" asked Soren. "You're fully capable of doing it, yourself."

In sadness, Rentwar replied, "You, dear Sorshrynak, are the only one bold enough to do what needs to be done. To convince Queen Awleesia to do what is right, and restore the Laws of Magic."

In anger, Soren asked, "Are you not an upholder, to the laws?"

"It's true," Rentwar agreed. "But I'm limited, in how I may uphold them. That aside, I couldn't ask Awleesia to do what I know you will have the bravery to ask. Jasper couldn't, either. And the Vardiyas are too benevolent."

"What has that Onyx King done to Awleesia?" asked Soren, in spiteful grief.

"You will know," replied Rentwar, "by the end of today. And what you will have to do will finish breaking your mind. I lied, earlier. I could give you the ability to practice Red Magic. But a broken mind, with the ability to practice such a powerful class of magic, is a dangerous thing. It will make Deezalo's Regime appear like a young BlacKaidyn napping under warm coals. Think of

how the twin Geldryn brothers laid waste, to the heirs of Vosh-Vendei and the relatives of his mother. He was their half-brother, so you've told me. Did they care of that? No! They cursed him. Vosh-Vendei. Everywhere he went, a trail of death remained. It will be like that, everywhere."

Soren replied, "But the magic could fix me. Heal me. Couldn't it?"

"That isn't for certain," said Rentwar. "What is certain is this: The Black Flame revels in life, and new growth. He is promised a plentiful bounty, when those life sources have reached their time of death, and must be laid to rest."

Soren stated, "Yes, he knows he will always have a supply, to quench his hunger for decay."

Rentwar continued, "Therefore, he is patient. Not overly greedy. Certainly, he likes wars. But too many? Too much death? He doesn't like that at all."

Soren asked, "Because it creates a time of famine for him?"

"Precisely," Rentwar replied. "He's warned me of you. Not to give you too much power, in case your mind should be finished off. He said you've been dying for thousands of years, a death most painful. The sense of who you are? Lost. What you were born to do? Taken. You've witnessed horrific wars, but the greatest to be seen lies within yourself."

Soren's eyes filled with tears. It was so long ago that the creature of darkness pierced him in the night, within Vosh-Perida, all while the Vardiyas watched and wept for the loss of their friend.

"I cannot help you," said Rentwar quietly, "any more than pointing you in the right direction now, and bestowing this golden statue forged in your younger likeness. May it be a reminder of better days, Soren, when your life's purpose was of goodwill. When you were brother to Monel. Esteemed savior of one. Instead of portrayed murderer of many."

"What am I to do, with a statue of myself?" Soren asked.

Rentwar replied, "It's enchanted to guard your mind. When you are near to it, it will fend off your insanity. Slow its progression. What else you plan to use it for, is up to you. But I will offer some ideas."

Soren asked, "Why are its hands open, waiting to be filled? Why not forge weapons for me to hold, if all I'll ever be from now on is a killer?"

"You always loved to read," replied Rentwar. "Even now, you love it. I thought

you might want to enchant certain pages, for your likeness to hold, to bring it to life. See. Even after you're gone, you won't be gone completely. You can choose any books you wish, but only up to three sets can be made to breathe a type of life back into it. Only three beginnings of new spells can be rendered from your statue. And only three entities may be summoned to it, from the past. But nine will free you."

"Nine?" Soren asked. "Those three sets of three, being done, will free me?"

Rentwar replied, "I'm bound not to say."

Soren approached Rentwar, accusing him with this: "Rubidyns cannot be bound, as can the other species. Tell the truth, King Rentwar. What are the nine?"

"You'll know, prior to your appointed day of death," replied the Rubidyn King. "You could also look to your brother, Monel. It's a story he told you long ago. You didn't want to believe him, then. Perhaps, you will now."

King Aygorinaith utters that last syllable with finality, then shuts the book.

Talok asks, "Have you ever figured out any of the three sets?"

Aygorinaith replies, "Many have tried numerous summons; all failures. Although a Jhire summon—performed by my older brother, Khrendawll, before he abdicated—made the statue take on a dark-blue hue, it returned to normal. Therefore, it was more of a half-failure."

Arsyn adds, "No one's discovered the books. Many believe them to be one, each, amongst Monel, Soren, and Nyxane's collection of books."

Skylin comments, "I didn't know you had a brother, King Aygor. Does he ever come to visit you?"

"No," he replies. "He and Grawllik's father set off eleven years ago, perhaps ten, to seek out the items for this statue. Last I heard from them was eight years ago, right before the last Sodon. I had hoped to attend it, this year. But the Grand Clan Gathering is understandably more important for me to be present at."

Excitedly, Ben asks, "The Sorsryn's Onyx Day of Neutrality is this year?"

Ryco states, "Even if we wished to go, the dragon's flight is six days. It would take us double. There's no time for that."

A clawing chill runs down my spine. In misery, I think: *We're running out of time to save Talok. Only six days left.*

King Aygor sighs. "I would have loved to get my hands on Nyxane's spell-book. The Sodon presented the perfect opportunity. Masses flocked to one place, creating chaos within Nyxane's capital of Oniva? It would've been perfect." Looking at the book in his grasp a last time, he tosses it up.

It shifts into a beige-colored bird. When it finds its place on a shelf, back it turns into a book and wiggles its way into alignment with the other tomes.

I ask, "Do all the books have an enchantment on them, so that they do that?"

"No," replies King Aygor. "That's too much of a hassle. Soren, when he started this library, placed an enchantment on the room. All books thrown within here will take on some form of a bird, or dyn. The ones Soren brought to this library are the sand-colored creatures."

Before I know it, I've emptied the contents of one of my pouches on a table, and am now digging through to find my father's journals. *This is why we're here,* I think, *to learn something from these journals.*

"Cousin, what are you doing?" queries Talok, as sweat glistens on his forehead.

King Aygor comes to view the contents strewn on the table amongst the Geldryn books.

But I give him a look. "These are ancestral things," I state, as the contents enlarge to full-size.

Aygor startles, saying, "Of course. I let curiosity overcome manners. I'll watch from over here." He goes to Soren's statue, and starts flipping to different pages of Monel's spell-book.

I, on the other hand, grab hold of the jade-colored journal (the one that has the coat of arms upon its cover). I weigh it in my hands. Then I look to Ben, and offer it to him (he takes it). To Nyrim, I give the golden-bronze one with pages edged in black. The Murainian one, I keep.

Nyrim goes first, tossing his high. It lights up, bursting into round grains colored like gold. They draw together, forming a miniature dragon. Its body is long, with six wings upon it. It shifts to the color of black and then takes a different form. A type of human form, kneeling. Cloaked, it stands up, wearing fabric of black and white. The pattern is akin to the scrollwork on the door that led into the Arkivara.

A feminine voice speaks out of it, one word: "Izhead'Razodiak." Once taking its prior form of a dragon, it bursts back into the golden grain, and becomes a book again, resting in Nyrim's hands.

Aygorinaith pauses in his task, to look back in confusion. Then he returns to worrying over Monel's book.

Ben motions that I throw next, and I do.

The black journal folds in on itself, like origami paper. Then it ignites, shifting into something else. Something bright and red. A miniature version of a Rubidyn, most likely. It flies around once, in a triangular pattern, then the same voice as before, whispers the name: "Rubiletta." The dragon crumples up like tissue paper. Smoothing out, it unfolds, transforming into its original form (the Von-dyn journal). It floats back to being within my grasp.

Ben's next up to throw a journal. White flames set fire to it. Those flames then turn even greener than the journal, itself. The coat of arms pulls away from the cover, growing larger than the pages. It wraps around the book, and shape-shifts into another type of dragon. A striped, black-and-white one.

A tormented screech rings out, then that dragon takes on the look of a Sorsryn. Tall, masculine as well, his features quickly become too blurred to make out. "One will end his fate," he says. "Heir to Neftelliim. A Galloway. Thirteen of them, but nine will best them all." Holding out his hand, a scene emits from him, whilst he fades to nothing.

Soren's voice echoes in the room, asking, "Little girl, why does she cry?"

"You startled me is all," says a young girl. "What were you doing?"

"Practicing magic," replies Soren. "Would you like to learn?"

"Why not," says the girl, sounding happy.

The scene that plays in front of us is not of Soren and the girl, but Soren with someone else. Adair. I recognize him from the painting.

He waves goodbye to Soren, and passes through the portal back to Earth. Once he's gone, tears stream down Soren's face. "One," he says. "The first one of Galloway. We will see each other again, my dear apprentice, Adair."

Quickly, it shifts through Soren counting the Galloways. Adair's two sons. Soren walks forward, motioning to them, saying, "Two, three."

Then Tadashi, a woman, and young boy appear. They're much younger than they would be, in the present day. "Four, five, then six," says Soren, sounding desperate. "It must not stop there."

Sounds of shattering glass echo in the room. Chaotic shouting ensues. Soren weeps. Sinking to the floor, he says, "Five, six, and seven—dead."

A woman screams in pain. A newborn cries. The shouting stops.

"Take care of her, Tadashi," says a woman weakly. "Life will be hard, without a mother. We should know."

Soren stands up, proclaiming, "But eight will rise. And nine will be better. I do not need any of the rest. At thirteen, it will be done. The end. It can't come soon enough."

The scene fades.

The journal morphs to its normal form. Once in Ben's grasp, he places it among my things.

Tears brimming, Gemma glances at me. Then she presses her hands to her face, and starts crying.

I don't know how to comfort her, without giving us away. I feel badly for her, though. She's just had her Galloway history recited to her. By Soren, no less. If there was any doubt before, there isn't now. Gemma's number nine. On two accounts. Ninth 'item.' Ninth Galloway.

I look down at my things, as Talok starts resizing them to fit back into the pouch. I stop him from resizing The Dark Prince storybook. So far, it's been useless, except to convince me of Gemma's importance. *Soren wants her to free him. But how?* I wonder. *He's dead. Gone. It doesn't make any sense.*

Aygorinaith, who's nearest to Gemma, helps her along to a chair. "I never knew how important Adair was to Soren. It is tragic, Gem, isn't it?" he asks rhetorically.

Ryco, motioning for me to throw the tiny storybook, divs, *"That one has a personal note from Soren. Maybe it will do more, here, than the other books."*

Gripping it, I throw it like it's a disc. The small book whirs, resonating as metal would. It changes into a metallic circle, with fire crackling on the edges. The disc fizzles out, then implodes in on itself.

A scene emerges from lingering smoke, to show a sorrowful King ReNovak holding a small, squirming child. On this child's forehead is an eight-pointed star mark. It looks as if it had been tattooed on the child. "Prince Setharyn," he whispers. "The Onyx have waited forever, for you. And now I will see the end of our curse. The curse of Onyx Neutrality."

Smoke blurs them out.

The scene transitions into another one.

ReNovak calls, "Hurry up, Setharyn. You'll be late for your meeting with the clans."

A boy enters the scene. He can't be more than twelve; fair-skinned, and with coal-black hair, like ReNovak. But his eyes are green, akin to mine.

Setharyn asks, while buttoning up his black coat, "Am I really giving a speech, today, and in the citadel of the Gedosawk, no less? How did you convince the Geldryn to allow it, Father?"

"Soren persuaded them," replies ReNovak, leading the way out of a grand cathedral made of black brick. "Since there's no longer any Withrasyn King, Soren's become a figurehead. But with no king's authority. Also, you know how the Geldryn and Silverians are, in regards to women leading. They've not considered Awleesia a queen, since King Morseif died, succumbing to the curse."

Setharyn lowers his voice, to ask, "Does anyone know who cast *that* curse on their men? Such a horrible thing to do."

"I suspect who it was," ReNovak replies.

"Can't you punish them for it?" Setharyn asks. "We are Onyx, after all. Meant to keep the balance of things. Wiping out an entire Sorsryn clan, isn't that genocide?"

ReNovak forces a smile away, saying, "Whoever it was played by the Rules of Engagement very well. The curse took the men so slowly, spanning over centuries, that there was never a mass of death all at once. Therefore, Onyx couldn't investigate the situation."

"Weren't some of them your friends?" queries Setharyn.

"No, no," replies ReNovak. "I hadn't come about, yet. My father was king, when the curse was enacted. My brother, Jzorrdawv, was ruler, when Awleesia sought a new home for herself and the women. He had to turn them away. He was kind enough, however, to at least meet them at the Gate of Oniva, and tell it to their faces. The other clans shunned them entirely, not accepting anything more than letters, out of fear that the curse would be brought upon them as well." ReNovak pauses, to look at his son. "But now we know they are not cursed. Already, Withrasyns have had families with the Vaegons. Their boys have become men. Girls became women. They have no signs of the curse, whatsoever."

"If they are happy, Father," Setharyn asks, "why do you wish for them to leave the Vaegons, and come here to Oniva?"

ReNovak replies, "Withrasyns and Onyx were always meant to be together, Setharyn. We were driven apart. First, by Geldryn. Even more so, by a curse. But *our* curse cannot be undone, until Onyx and Withrasyn are united. And that unity must begin with the Onyx Prince, chosen by the Vardiyas. He'll have their mark upon him, to prove its truth."

Setharyn adds, "That the Onyx will one day be free."

The scene shifts again.

Setharyn's older. And near the time of his death, by the looks of him. Still too young to die, he's pale and sickly thin.

ReNovak's yelling at Soren, unaware that his son watches from a doorway. "Soren, you promised me a son. What good is he to the Onyx, if he dies of a curse? Can't you take me, instead? Casseil is already gone. Why not take me too?"

Soren's cold, in his reply, "I'm not The Black Flame, ReNovak. Death claims whom it will."

"This isn't his doing," ReNovak argues. "This is Vitiosus. It's killing my son. He can barely walk. Hardly any strength left to talk to me. It's worse than any spell of Dei-Athos-Kree. It takes him to the edge of death, then holds him there. He's in too much pain, to even cry out during an episode."

Soren states, "We've all tried to ease his pain, ReNovak. There's nothing more to be done, other than to cut him down. Ask him how he wishes for his end to be. Death, by way of Vitiosus? Which is already happening. Or to have his people send him off, with honor? A Wounded Warrior's End. Ask him."

"I will not!" ReNovak shouts.

Setharyn, using a staff for balance, hobbles into the room with the two Sorsryns. "Thank you, Master Soren. And, you, Father. But I'll take the third way. I will end myself."

"I forbid you, Setharyn." ReNovak begs, "Please! Give me more time to figure something out."

"We're out of time," Setharyn declares, while hobbling his way to stand in front of his father. "And there's no law against ending your own life. So, that is what I shall do. I shall not become a pawn. Whomever this new Vitiosyn is, who has replaced Deezalo, won't have won."

"What of ReNovamen?" ReNovak nearly sobs. "Will that work to save—?"

Setharyn cuts him off with, "Soren and I already discussed it. It will fail to save me. But don't worry, Father. We will see each other again. For I have found favor with the Vardiyas. They rather like me. When they are able, they'll find a way to send me back to you. It's not goodbye, forever; it's goodbye, for now."

The scene of them disappears.

32

Legends of Two Sorsryns

The storybook reforms, and throws itself onto the table. As if not wanting to share space, it knocks every single item off—pouch, tiny journals, resized items, Geldryn tomes—all of it, onto the floor. Whichever items are books, shift to creatures of flight. The tomes fly up high to their place, on the middle bookcases. The tiny journal dragons flap about, and collect all resized items that have scattered, before crowding everything into the pouch. During the flurry of things, the storybook has set itself nicely upon the table's center. It's now motionless. If it could, it would be laughing.

Gemma wipes at her lingering tears. Ignoring the flurry of things, her gaze is instead fixed on Soren's statue. She rushes to it, saying frantically, "Maybe this book will tell us more. What if you're supposed to only give him a certain number of pages? That passage did say 'set.'"

Aygorinaith's attention jerks to Gemma. "Girl, you can't possibly be suggesting I rip pages out, can you?"

"What else are you planning on using them for?" queries Gemma, as she twirls her hair strand.

"I understand that you're distraught," Aygorinaith states, "but we're not ripping up Monel's spell-book."

"It's fitting with how Soren is, though," I comment.

"What he means," Kent says, "is that Soren was bold."

Siege rubs at his neck. "Surely, all the legends of him prove that to be true."

"And it's a bold thing," Rozeth adds, "to devalue a book, by ripping some of its pages out."

Ryco agrees, "It sounds like a Soren-thing to do, if you ask me."

The Darklyrian King stares at us. "You Ayzagauns are all at the level of insanity. You don't rip up, such a book as this." He points to Monel's spell-book, still resting in Soren's hands.

Arsyn strolls over to King Aygor, then pats him on the shoulder. "Hypothetically, if you did have to rip pages out, what would you do? Which ones would you pick?"

When the king hesitates, Grawllik says, "Naturally, you'd have to pick three physical pages."

Finding his voice, Aygorinaith adds, "Yes, and they would have to be in numerical order. I would want the first to start with a sum of eight. I've chosen pages one hundred thirty-four through thirty-five, as that adds to eight and nine. Add those, together, and you get seventeen, then eight. One of the completions to magic. But, if Grawllik is right, that set doesn't work at all. One thirty-four to one thirty-seven. Three physical pages, yes, but the numbers are all wrong for Soren."

I suggest, "If it needs to include thirteen, change the starting page to one thirty-five. That way, it'd end with one thirty-nine. Or, rather, thirteen."

Aygorinaith adjusts his sleeves violently, a look of dissatisfaction creeping onto his face. "Nine is an unusual choice for Soren. In fact, an unusual choice entirely."

Arsyn comes to my rescue, saying, "But even Rentwar said nine would free him. And one of those scenes showed the importance of nine, to Soren. Take it as a hint, King Aygor. We don't have all day." Arsyn flies over to Soren's statue, and takes the spell-book in his hands. He rips out three pages, and gives the violated book to the distraught king.

Dea's quick to stop her king, right as he's about to claw Arsyn. "Highness!" she shouts. "He's right. Nine works. You end up getting a triangle of nine, thirteen, and twenty-two."

Pausing, Aygorinaith mulls it over. At last, he gives Dea the spell-book, and takes the three pages from Arsyn. "This had better work, Arsyn, or you'll owe a year of servitude to me. Don't you *ever* again tear up a book belonging to me."

Arsyn lowers his head. Staring at the marble floor, he acknowledges the potential consequence.

Aygorinaith then places a single page within each of Soren's hands, before holding one vertical between them.

Soren's eyes flash green; at the same time, the pages glow a brilliant white.

Those in proximity rush away, adding distance between them and the statue.

A metallic droning sound comes from Soren's likeness.

The three pages burst into crackling flames.

Soren's eyes stop glowing.

Reduced to ashes are the pages, now soot upon Soren's feet. Swirling smoke dissipates. Nothing else happens, and nothing's different. Except for the demeanor of Aygorinaith, that is. His neck's tensed so hard it's making his head start to shake in anger. "If you don't leave this minute, Arsyn," he says, "I will tear your head off, right here, right now. Please. Leave."

Trying to remain calm, Arsyn gradually goes for the doorway. He's about to step out, but a whispering voice makes him hesitate.

We all hear it.

It's similar to chilling, demonic chants. I liken it to the chants of the Vitiosyns demonstrating the Dance of Death. Rather than loud, it's whispering, and far worse. Pain pricks at my nerve endings. It seems to start from within and radiate out.

We then hear one word familiar, among the chant.

"Galloway," it whispers, like a ghost envious of the living.

We all hold our breath. But nothing more does it whisper. It is silent in the room.

"Do you still wish for me to leave?" queries Arsyn, looking apprehensive.

Grawllik asks, "Why would he be speaking about a Galloway?"

Aygorinaith replies, "I've only read of one. Adair Tomatsu Galloway. He was apprenticed to Soren, centuries ago. Soren mentioned him, in an entry dated not long before his death. Said something to do with Adair being the biggest disappointment of his life. His last chance to save face, or redeem himself. To my knowledge, Adair never had family here. He went back through some portal, and was never seen again."

Arsyn suggests, "Why not ask Tyler if you can place that green book into Soren's hands? Who's to know what might happen."

Aygorinaith stretches his wings out, looking taller. "Those are ancestral belongings. I already feel disquieted over witnessing something I probably shouldn't have."

"Why not leave the library, then, Your Highness," Arsyn mutters.

"I am King to Clan RawZend. I'm not going to leave this place unattended."

While they argue, I div to Gemma, *"I think it has to be you, Gem. The one to awaken the statue. Do something with the ashes. Rub them on Soren's eyes, possibly, since that's what changed on the statue."*

The two older Lyres keep up their argument, while Gemma makes her way for the statue. Part of me wonders if Arsyn is distracting the king for us, on purpose. In any case, Gemma has to climb up onto the statue with my help. Once the deed of smearing ashes on Soren's statue eyes is done, Ben's there to catch Gemma, now jumping down.

Ryco indicates that we take cover quickly, then shouts, "Aygor, Arsyn, move it! The statue's waking up."

They flap their wings, flying away from Soren's likeness, as light bursts out of it. Several books around the room fall off their shelves, before transforming into beige-colored birds that flutter about the room.

Soren's chilling laughter echoes around us.

The room turns ice-cold. Something's not right. I'm about to run for the way out, but Ryco catches hold of my wrist. I'm able to calm down enough to stay put, and watch.

A ghostly, bluish light-figure steps out of the Soren statue.

"Let me tell you a story, Brother," says this ghostly figure. He's tall, with a straight stance. All confidence, he continues, "My time is near, nearer than either of us would wish for."

The Soren statue takes on color, coming to life. The gold cracks away. Soren reaches up to pull a white hood over his head. He steps off the pedestal, and approaches the light-figure. When he touches that figure on the shoulder, it takes on lifelike color too. "Don't talk like that, Monel," says Soren, sounding like the younger one.

I hold back a gasp, when Monel turns around to face all of us. He's my father's lookalike. They're near identical. Only variance I can tell is the sound of their voices. But age, alone, could explain that difference.

Aygorinaith snaps his fingers, as if trying to get their attention. Then he paces about a bit, before stating, "Seems we can't interact with them."

Dea queries, "Are you relieved, or disappointed, by that?"

"I don't know," he replies.

Monel continues, saying, "My time is up, Soren. It will be for another, to take my part. But, you, my brother. You have a chance to steal back the future. You will be known, then feared, then hated. Long into the future, you'll almost be forgotten too. But Sorshrynaks find a way to remain, especially you and me. Withrasyns."

Soren asks, "Withrasyns? What are those, Monel?"

"It's what you and I will become. But our little brother, Nyxane, will become something different. Onyx. He'll uphold the Laws of Magic. Even against their will, he and others like him will be used as peacekeepers, then weapons of war, won through a series of accomplishments. They will be the mightiest of Sorsryns, only able to use half their strength, until they announce their victor. Then they shall render their ally's enemies to ashes on the battlefield. The power of Vardiyas, the cunning of Vons, and the malice of dyns shall be with them. None can stand against them, but one. He sleeps. The Onyx Prince, with a Vardiya's Mark upon him."

Soren undoes his cloak. "Monel, you're not making any sense!" he shouts, while yanking his hood off. He lets his cloak slide to the floor. Their voices lower to inaudible. It's as if the sequence has been damaged.

It keeps cutting in and out.

I've seen enough, though, to make my skin grow hot. I lean on the table. I want to run so badly, and hide from King Aygor's scrutiny. But it's far too late for that. He's already seen it. Seen the truth. That Soren and I are identical. Darker skin, green eyes, jet-black hair. He looks barely older than me too.

King Aygor narrows his gaze on Soren, but he points to me. "Remarkable resemblance. You and this young Soren. Is that why SynKievas and you are so hesitant to talk of lineage? You're related to Soren? How's that possible? If Soren had descendants, all of Muraine would've known."

I shrug, answering, "I told you, I don't know my lineage."

King Aygor growls low, then says, "But I think SynKievas does. Grawllik, go get him. I have some questions that need answering."

After Grawllik bows in respect, he exits the library, taking long strides.

As soon as Grawllik's steps have diminished, King Aygor takes the stance of a readied warrior. He glares at me. My skin feels on the verge of blistering. Though terrified, I know I must stay here, in the library. There's only one exit. Possibly a hidden one too. Either way, I think Arsyn will detain the King of RawZend, if things don't turn out well. I don't know why it is that I trust him to protect me. I think, *Maybe it has to do with my dad mentioning him.*

"You're not really Darklyres, are you?" queries King Aygor, drawing out his weapon.

Everyone draws their weapons or magic, as well. But they wait for King Aygor to act first.

"Please, Highness!" Dea begs, coming to shield me.

King Aygor yells at her, and she drops to her knees. He takes his Parasogyn form. In an instant, he grows to twice the size of what he was before. "You led them here, Deamond!" he shouts. "Knowing they are outsiders. Knowing that they must be cut down."

"I brought him here," says Dea, through tears, "for you, King Aygor. Tyler has Siveyra's Mark. And, Gem? She's a Galloway. I heard him call her that. If any could awaken the statue, I thought it might be them."

Though his face is stone cold, tears roll down. King Aygor rasps out, "You don't know what you've done, Dea."

Suddenly, Monel and Soren's dialogue comes back to full volume. King Aygor strides for the entrance. There he stands, guarding it, while watching the memory play out.

"Stop it, Monel!" Soren shouts. "You're not going to die!"

"I can't live forever," says Monel. "But will you ensure that none forget the name? My name. Monel. Make a spell of it, if you wish."

Soren shakes his head, confused. "A spell from a name? That's impossible, Brother."

"Not for you," Monel proclaims. "You were always talented with magic. And you will continue to be, esteemed savior of one. After me, will be one to take my place. He will do what we never could. You'll see him. He'll come from afar. And you will hate him, for how he's fashioned like me. Better than both of us, put together, he shall be. LanSoren eldes Trauvo-Rawshuen."

"I will not let this come to pass," says Soren, in sorrow. "We will defeat the creature of darkness. Not this LanSoren."

Monel replies, "No. It will be for them. LanSoren and his Savakaidyn."

Their following argument fades out. Monel vanishes. Soren puts his cloak back on, then slowly becomes the golden likeness. He trails back to the pedestal, to take his former position.

The room goes quiet.

Positioned to fight, Arsyn asks, "What are you going to do, King Aygor? Grawllik won't be long."

"I know," replies the king, glancing to us Paragonians.

Rozeth steps forward, boldly saying, "We're not without friends. They wait, where it is safe. My Mensa-div can reach them, in an instant. In fact, it already has. You know not how many we are. Do you wish for a war, King Aygorinaith? It's not why we're here."

A voice near the dried-up fountain says, "But it's why I'm here."

Ryco fires off an arrow at the speaker.

Once unseen, but now noticeable, is the King of Vitiosus sitting on the edge of the fountain. He bats Ryco's arrow away, and it deflects to the floor, rolling to a stop on a faded rug.

Zymarc wears a different Geldryn mask, a darker one. Yet, it still obscures the lower half of his face. Consequently, it's hard to judge his mood. But then his amused eyes of crimson-red signal his delight. He's here for something, or someone. Not just a war.

Is it me, I wonder. *And if it's me, do I have the strength to resist him, as I am now? Or is it Soren's statue? Could be Monel's spell-book too.*

The horror of what he could do, with either one, sickens me.

Easing up nonchalantly, Zymarc stands up straight. "Hello, Ravier," he says.

My racing heart plummets. *It's me he wants.*

Zymarc takes a few steps toward us, saying to me, "I was wondering, the other day, how you're feeling these days, Ravier. The stress of it all must be wearing on you. Especially that day, in Eyo'el. The horror of thinking you're Soren. That you see him, in yourself. It must be disheartening. Do you still believe it, I wonder. Now that you've seen him, as he was before the change, do you trust it as truth even more? And if you do believe it, will you lose your sanity, as he did? Is it only a matter of time? Do I hold the answer, to saving you from yourself . . . I wonder."

I suddenly can't breathe. *Do I still believe I'm Soren? He and I* did *look identical, at one point. What if Zymarc's right?*

Talok comes to stand in front of me. "You address me, Vitiosyn. Not him."

Zymarc draws out Winter's Vondaen, and points its tip at Talok. "Then convince me you are the true King of Paragon. Take up your steel, and fight me, young Talok. Fight for your life, your country, that dyn, your cousin. All will be mine, if you don't."

Talok tenses his hands into fists. He's actually thinking of falling for the ploy. I grab my cousin by the arm, as he starts reaching for his weapon. "Please, Talok, not here," I beg.

Aygorinaith already has two blades in his grasp. He looks at Talok, then Zymarc. "This is my city," he proclaims. "You will state your business,

Vitiosyn, or suffer the consequences."

Zymarc lowers Winter's Vondaen, replying, "I had hoped to gain an alliance with the Darklyres, starting with Clan RawZend. But I see the Paragonians have captured your heart. Can't say I blame you. They have the Son of LanSoren, and a Galloway, with them, after all. Interesting how Caleiso failed to mention her surname. Not that she really matters. She's no Adair. Therefore, no threat to me."

Gemma stands behind me. I feel that soft grip of hers, on my left shoulder. *"The word for fire is* Oostrina," she divs. *"Burn him, Tyler. It won't stop him, but it'll get his attention. We don't have to worry about him retaliating too much, either, because he admires how brash you are. Kent suggests using your darker dagger to channel the magic. It'll help you stop the spell too, so you don't get too drained."*

I quickly grip NeiSator, and rip it off my belt. Automatically, it unsheathes itself. Instinct then takes over. "Oostrina!" I shout, as I slash the air separating Zymarc and me.

A short burst of fire discharges from the dagger, and hits Zymarc right on the chest. The flames wisp over the fabric of his coat, then extinguish to smoke.

"Boy!" he yells, slapping at the singed fabric. "I've about had enough of you breaking the rules."

I stride forward in confidence, asking him, "Isn't that what Vitiosyns do all day long? Break the rules. The Laws of Magic."

"Is that what you want?" Zymarc asks, in return. "To break the rules? Because if it is, you're entirely on the wrong side. You want to learn how to break the rules properly? I'll teach you."

"I didn't know there was a proper way," I state, in sarcasm. "Techniques for cheating? What *else* will you teach me?"

The tension behind me is fierce. Lots of movement, and whispered tones of complaint. I know the Paragonians must be panicking. Yet they're trusting me. At least, that's what I hope is happening.

Arsyn and Aygorinaith take the opening of Zymarc's distraction to attack him. I halfway expect him not to be able to engage them in their rapid flight very well, but it's clearly no trouble at all. The Darklyrian King gets entangled in sticky vines of magic. Trapped in Zymarc's web, he lights it on fire, then begins clawing his way out.

Arsyn fares better, dodging most of Zymarc's elemental attacks.

Then Grawllik and SynKievas show up.

"King Aygor?" queries SynKievas, knocking on the invisible barrier. "Everything all right? We feel the room being tossed about, a bit, in there. Are you having a war of books? That's mighty fun, you know."

Aygorinaith shouts, "A little help!"

"Busy!" Arsyn shouts back, clashing blades with Zymarc.

Dea traverses the room with ease, dodging the dueling pair. She gets to King Aygor, and helps him remove the sticky vines.

Behind me, Rozeth and the Paragonians have spread out in partners. Only Gemma is right by me, while Talok stays near Skylin, to shield her.

I hear SynKievas say to Grawllik, "I think something's going on in there. Go get some sentinels, and hurry. I'll wait here."

Grawllik strides out of sight, even as Arsyn and Zymarc are dueling directly in front of the open doorway.

Looking over my shoulder to Gemma, I whisper, "What other words of magic do you know?"

Gemma quickly goes through some, "*Oonda*, for water; *Ignicuel*, for spark."

I interrupt, saying, "Sparks will do."

I'm about to cast it, but Gemma stops me.

"Wait, wait!" She says, "Try the plural. *Ignicuellos*. Start saying *Ignicuel*, then hold tight to the hilt. You're charging up the spell. When you're ready to cast, loosen two of your fingers' grip on the hilt, and finish saying *los*. Make sure your aim's right, as you say the last part."

I ask, "How long can I charge it, before it backfires?"

"Twenty-two seconds," replies Gemma, "but Ryco recommends eight. Though, he thinks you can handle thirteen seconds." She squeezes my arm, and says, "You'll need some space. Good luck, Ty."

She rushes away, leaving me a nervous mess.

Why do I need space? I wonder.

I follow Gemma's instructions. Now I'm simply focused on Zymarc's every move, and counting.

One-two-three. I take a deep breath, and glimpse Aygorinaith letting SynKievas in.

Four-five-six. Chaos ensues. SynKievas isn't the only one to enter. Immediately after him, Azabahk and several other Vitiosyns bustle in. They have some of King Aygor's Wards held at knifepoint; Keturah and Sonya are among them. They're all trying to hold still, while not crying.

Seven-eight-nine. *Should I strike Zymarc?* I wonder. *What good will it do, now?*

Ten-eleven. Seqwhyett with numerous other sentinels chase the Vitiosyns into the library. It's unclear who is more intimidated. Watching the lot of them is SynKievas, looking curious.

Twelve. My veins burn. I can't hold the charge much longer.

When King Aygor notices his wards in danger, he shouts, "Arsyn, stop fighting him. Lay down your weapons."

The Darklyres obey. But SynKievas slinks his way out of sight, into the shadows of the room.

At thirteen, Zymarc relaxes, looking on in victory at the distraught Darklyres. That's when I smile, and finish speaking the word. I fling the bolting sparks at Zymarc. It's ear-shattering, akin to a crack of thunder directly overhead. Hitting his right side, the sparks tear through his coat. He cries out, collapsing to his knees.

Blood drips from the fingertips of my casting hand. Though bearable, it stings.

Those behind me, rush to protect me. But I'm not done. I hold up my right hand, and run forward, loudly speaking out, "Ventus!"

The Vitiosyns race to guard their wounded king. But they are flung aside. SynKievas is quick in cutting down several of them, before slinking back to the darkest shadows of the room.

I get to Zymarc, as he struggles to take in full breaths. Without thinking, I press the dagger tip to his neck, and stare into his eyes. I want fear to be in them, but there isn't. Merely admiration.

"Well done, Ravier," he says weakly. "Never thought you could do it. Break through my coat's enchantment. Do what you've earned. Slit my throat, and be done. That dagger can do it, you know?"

"Not until you've freed my cousin," I state, while hatred burns within. In this moment, I feel a power only felt that day I met Aysivak. Power borrowed from my future self. It's a mere fraction. Still, it emboldens me.

Zymarc sighs. "You've no worry for that. With my death, comes a new leader of the Vitiosyns. King ReNovak. He is next in line for my throne. As I am next for his, should he perish before me."

Hesitating, I pull the dagger away ever so slightly. "Is that written in magic?" I ask.

Zymarc nods, as his gaze softens on me. There's not an ounce of hate about him. It confuses me.

Why isn't he commanding his Vitiosyns to attack? I wonder. *It's as if Zymarc wishes to die. In death, does he win? Seeking to control the elements might end with needing to die.*

I remember those whispered phrases of Caleiso's. *Fire of the Soul. Wake of the Water. How to break their laws?* Then the other ones: *Prison of the Air. Blood of the Land. Who can truly wield the keys?* How she managed to mimic my father's voice, I may never know. Regardless, I think now, *He's trying to defeat the elements, and I'm giving him what he wants. Zymarc's death must come, by some other means.*

I pull the dagger away from his neck, then stand up straight.

Talok divs, *"Don't stop, Tyler. You have him at your mercy. Kill him!"*

I take a step back, and the wounds on my casting hand heal.

Zymarc shuts his eyes, in disappointment. As he sighs heavily, his own wound heals too. Then the coat's singed fabric weaves itself together. It's made like new.

"I ask this, instead," I demand, while Zymarc eases up to face me.

"I'm listening," he says, stuffing his hands in his pockets.

Winter's Vondaen has fallen from Zymarc's grasp. I now stoop down, to pick it up, and give it back to Zymarc, before making my request of: "Add thirteen days to the device."

Azabahk chortles out a scoff-like sound. "You could've ended King Zymarc, yet days of thirteen are all you ask, devil-born tyke."

Zymarc counteroffers with, "Eleven days."

I div to Ryco, asking, *"Is that enough?"*

He subtly shakes his head.

"No," I reply, to Zymarc. "Thirteen days. Or we're done." Just to make him understand the seriousness of my request, I aim the dagger tip to my own throat, and add, "You'll be giving my cousin those thirteen days, or you'll be watching me shove this dagger into my throat. Your choice."

I know the bet that I'm the hole in Zymarc's armor is risky. But, for whatever reason, he doesn't seem to want me dead. Quite the opposite. Very much alive, and apprenticed to him. To what end, I've no idea.

Zymarc scratches at his throat. Then he sheathes Winter's Vondaen. "Done," he says. "Bring him here."

I lower the dagger.

Ryco and Rozeth drag a resisting Talok toward Zymarc. He's almost to him, when a ruckus sounds within the wide hall outside.

Unconcerned with the approaching noise, Zymarc steps forward. "Did I mention," he says, in innocence, "that I brought a certain old Von-dog with me? Turns out, he couldn't stay away. He had to try to save his son. I confess, I've starved him for nearly two days, to work up his appetite. And he's *very* hungry."

The space surrounding Talok's wrist darkens, and Zymarc manipulates the device. But we can't tell what he does. Zymarc concludes his work. The shadow fades, and as it does, Quall, Musgrae, and Eli are chased into the room by Merlynite. He's in that vicious, metal-beast form. Behind him are Mekka and Jasper, in Von form, trying to corner their turned comrade. All of them are beaten down, or bloodied up, save for Mekka and Merlynite. The two Vons go at each other. Darklyres and Vitiosyns flee to their own spaces of safety in the library.

Jasper roars, and the room shakes. Books fall off shelves, and turn into birds. They head right for Jasper. As they pelt against him, he takes on his metal fur, and eyes likened to hot coals. He's bigger than Mekka now, yet nowhere near as quick.

Frightened by this form of Jasper's, the birds fly off. When they land on various surfaces, they change back into books.

"Jasper," I call out, "there's a Soren statue. Monel's spell-book too."

Jasper rushes that way, taking giant leaps; Zymarc goes to cut him off. He manages to dive over a desk, and kick Jasper down.

Jasper rolls, shifting into human form. He's bruised and bleeding. His chest hammers out each breath, as he weakly calls to Mekka, "You have to kill Merlynite. He's born of the same generation as me. He seeks to claim the title. He seeks to drain me till I'm dead."

"Please, Alpha!" Mekka growls, in sorrow. "I can't kill him!"

"Then Musgrae," says Jasper desperately. "Musgrae, you do it."

Jasper closes his eyes. His hair starts turning white. His breaths get even shorter. Zymarc watches, in fascination. He seems honored to be here, witnessing the death of a great Von.

Musgrae's crouched down, hiding from Merlynite, as are most within the room. A few Vitiosyns and Darklyres have been made fodder for Merlynite, and their blood has splattered all over, staining Soren's library.

Hiding up on the rafters are King Aygor, and the surviving Darklyres. They shoot magic and arrows down, ensuring that the wards—still held at knifepoint—are safe from the Greyvons. Yet, they do not hit a single Vitiosyn.

I go crouch down by Musgrae, and give him an encouraging nod. "Go on," I whisper. "Merlynite doesn't know what he's doing. He's a pawn, slowly killing his alpha. He would want someone to take him down. And he couldn't have a more noble death, than by your hand, Mooz. Restore his honor, back to a Von."

"What of those answers you want from him?" queries Musgrae, sounding gruff. "Gemma told us about who you think he is. You may never get answers for why he was there, hunting you near your home."

"It's all right," I reply, "I can live with that. Save Jasper."

Musgrae nudges my shoulder, as he stands up. He grips his blade tightly, before making the rush frontward. He and Mekka move as partners. Musgrae lines up his blade. He's ready.

Mekka senses this. The hair on his spine stands up slightly. He heightens the severity of the dog fight with Merlynite. It takes a while of maneuvering, but Mekka gets an opening, and Musgrae takes it, cutting deeply into Merlynite's chest. Almost the entire blade is swallowed up by Von flesh. And that Von yelps from the sharp pain. His metal fur changes back to that scruffy coat of Vons.

Unexpected tears stream down my face. Then more flow, as Mekka bites into Merlynite's throat, and holds him down. He suffocates his former comrade, till the old Von-dog stops his struggling. He lies still.

Musgrae pulls the bloodied blade out.

Mekka lets go, his snout covered in blood too.

They appear more defeated than Merlynite does now, even as he bleeds out upon one of the old, pink rugs, staining it back to red. He's gone.

Hardly do I believe it. The beast that hunted Gemma and me, back on Earth, is dead. Yet I've no answers, for why he hunted us in the first place. Did he have a master, who wasn't Jasper? Was Zymarc already his master? Or was it something else, driving him? I may never know. And, now, I must let go. For what is coming, will call for every measure of strength within me. It's time to discover what aura I am.

Do I hold the strength of dyns? Or the cunning of Vons? Is it arrogance to think that I could be an aura of both, the way the Onyx Prince, Setharyn, was? Unlike him, I've no mark of Vardiyas upon my forehead. Therefore, I must choose an aura, and I choose the dragon aura. I decide to hunt the dragon within. But I quickly realize that I already have. I've already been bold and strong, in the way a dragon would be. Further, I must cultivate, what has begun. I must become bolder and stronger. For the only way to defeat Zymarc may be to overpower him. Outsmarting him seems unlikely. In fact? Near impossible. He has set his pieces down perfectly, for whatever goal he seeks. So, what good would Von aura do, for me? I am not a Von, though some say I am equal to them.

Zymarc moves his focus off Merlynite, lying lifeless in the middle of

Soren's Library. The Vitiosyn's gaze stops searching, when he spots me. He divs, *"This day, I shall never forget, Ravier. The day I gave you a false sense of hope, then broke your spirit. For, while you were asking for what you thought you wanted, secretly, I had already planned to take away what you needed. Answers. And now? Certain ones you shall never have. Yet, I will let you live. But the others, with you? Only the spirits know their fate."*

Brokenly, I reply, in Mensa-div, *"Come what may, I'll not let you succeed. I'll learn the truth of what you're really planning. And I will stop you."*

His div echoes, *"Yes! Stop me! I want to be stopped, by the Son of LanSoren."*

For the briefest of moments, his appearance flickers to resemble Soren of the Monel. Then he's back to being the King of Vitiosyns. Zymarc . . .

The one I must now find a way to break, in order to defeat Vitiosus forever.

Afterword

Dear Reader:

Can you believe you've read my second book? I barely believe what started out as a rough draft of 126,000 words, in 2015, is now going to be three books. Even more unbelievable is that I started the first idea for this series back in 2005, as a writing prompt. The prompt? Ask a question, then write a story answering that question. Follow where the imaginings take you. My question was: 'what if horses had wings, and could fly?' Simple, I know. Too simple. It started in a forest. Tyler found Awngeleik, who was originally named Angel. No Paragonians delivered her to him. That came much later. About four years later, give or take.

As for the landscape of Muraine . . . I wanted something unique. See, I grew up in a place with few trees around. Always took twice as long for them to grow to a "normal" size. It was a place at risk of droughts, well, quite a lot. Very dry. Unbelievably windy. Lots of snow, in the winter (usually). As you can imagine, I wanted a place vastly different to escape to. A place with lots of trees. Hence, Paragon was born. A model of excellence. The ideal sort of place I'd love to escape to. I later realized it needed a foreign name. Therefore, Pawv'Ragaen it became. I think that was in 2014.

Around the time Hurricanes Katrina then Rita hit, in 2005, is when I made the start. It was such a sad year. Yet a good year. Lovely Texans opening their hearts to their Louisiana neighbors . . . that was a beautiful thing. Recently home from a lengthy visit to Texas, my heart was bursting with so many emotions. Through it, I found a love for writing. And here I am, more than fourteen years later. In short, if you want a dream badly enough, chase it. Don't give up. Just know that it takes time. Persevere.

I wish all the best for you,
   Julie

Appendix I: Cast of Characters

<< >>

Earth

<< >>

The Raviers

Alec Ravier – supposedly Miriam's son. Tyler's eight year old cousin he's never met.

Amira Hajjar Ravier – Tyler's mother. Married to Lance for seventeen years. Her family moved to the U.S. from Iraq, in the 1980s.

Lance Oren Ravier – Tyler's father, died one year prior to the start of Volume I.

Miriam Ravier – Tyler's aunt whom he has never met. Lance's little sister. Supposedly lives in London, England.

Tyler Malik Ravier – only child of Lance and Amira's. Fourteen years old, at the start of Volume I. Thirteen, when his dad died.

Galloway Household

Gemma Elizabeth Galloway – Tyler's classmate and neighbor. The rich girl. Ends up proving to Tyler that she's changed, in Volume I.

Ginger Jones Galloway – Gemma's mother. Lance's girlfriend, during one of his years in college. Jack Wayeland's girlfriend, in high school.

Haru Maki – assists with security at the Galloway mansion, and does odd jobs for Tadashi.

Kaida Galloway – Gemma's older sister.

Kane Himura – oversees Tadashi's home security. Is also protective of Gemma.

Molly Smith – went to school with Tadashi. Longtime friend of the Galloway family. Now, she's their fulltime cook.

Tadashi Galloway – Gemma's father. Met Lance Ravier, when they were teenagers.

Other Mentionables

Bruce Parson – founder and CEO of Aviridian Corp, a company dealing mostly in technology.

Ginger Snap – Lance's horse. The only one Tyler convinced his mother not to sell, after his dad died.

Goliath & Cosmo – two of the Ravier's horses they sold to Tadashi Galloway.

Hunter Mason – Kaida's former boyfriend. Accused of stealing one of the Galloways' paintings.

Jack Wayeland – friends with the Galloway family, and the Raviers. Allegedly saw the "Bear-Wolf," while out on a hunting trip.

Jed & Jaxson Craven – two of Tyler's closest friends. Jed is the older of the twins, and has an attitude. Jaxson is quieter, and more easygoing.

The Phantom of Muraine – mysterious being, who wrote notes to Tyler in Volume I. Also protected Tyler and Gemma from the lurking beast, near Mirror Lake.

»–«

Muraine

»–«

Paragonians

Callie of Dysarda – was there in the Eye of Paragon (Eyo'el), for the yearly festival's celebration. Befriended Tyler and Gemma, during her stay.

King Kailon (Kailon of Dysarda) – was king during the time of the Withrasyns' curse. Took in the Withrasyn women, and gave them a new home.

King Sosha – Talok's father. Brother-in-law to LanSoren. Married LanSoren's little sister, Miriam.

Kristos of Dysarda – younger brother of King Kailon.

LanSoren of Trauvo – Lance Ravier's real name. Full name: LanSoren eldes Trauvo-Rawshuen. Mysterious cause of death. Odd relationship with Zymarc of Vitiosus. No one really knows how well the two knew each other, or the nature of their interactions.

Leira of Dysarda – Kent's mother. Lokasi's wife. After Kent's little sister died, she and Lokasi separated. She has been away from Dysarda for eleven years. In Volume I, Kent mentioned that she's with some Sorsryn bent on exploring Muraine.

Madeleine of Dysarda – a friend to LanSoren. One of Paragon's finest tailors. She and LanSoren designed the Sleeping Dragon coat for Tyler. Knows all of the King's Guard quite well, as she is the one fitting them with new uniforms every year. Lost a third of her memory, during the attack on Eyo'el.

Marion of Trauvo – Lance and Miriam's mother.

Miriam of Trauvo – Talok's mother. LanSoren's little sister. Has a different father than LanSoren. Allegedly died when Talok was five.

Yigoshi – one of the top Blacksmiths of Paragon. Well acquainted with many in Paragon's government: the Paragonian Sovereignty.

Zima – owner of and head cook at LanSoren's favorite tavern: Zima's Kitchen. It's where Tyler and Gemma had their first meal, in Paragon. It's also where Tyler was served Farivoo for the first time.

Paragonian Sovereignty, in order of rank

King & King's Guard:

King Talok of Paragon (Pawv'Ragaen) – Tyler's cousin. Lance's nephew. Miriam and King Sosha's only child. Age 16. Became the Paragonian King, when he was barely thirteen. His uncle helped to bridge the gap in his nephew's lack of experience and wisdom.

Quall of Trauvo – First of the King's Guard. Age 47. Full name: Quallendeis'el Trauvo-Rawshuen. Grew up with LanSoren, in the Paragonian city of Trauvo.

Ryco of Paragon – Second of the Guard. Age 28. Full name: Ryco'Eldeis de Pawv'Ragaen. Born and raised in the Eye of Paragon, or rather Eyo'el de Pawv'Ragaen. He and Tyler had an instant dislike for one another, in Volume I.

Kent of Dysarda – Third of the Guard. Age 25. Full name: Kentel le Dysarda-Reine. The only King's Guard who is pure Vaegon—a Keeper of Memories.

Musgrae of Bethsaide – Fourth of the Guard. Age 24. Full name: Musgrae'es de Bethsaide-Reine. Has a "pinprick" of Greyvon in his lineage.

Warren of Veldar – Fifth of the Guard. Age 23. Full name: Warren'Eisawv es Veldar-Ruedawn. If Tyler had been born and raised on Muraine, he and Warren would be the same age.

Siege of Gayza – Sixth of the Guard. Age 20. Full name: Siegel le Gayza'Ragaen.

Eli of Kirja – Seventh of the Guard. Age 17. Full name: Eliyek le Kirja-Ruedawn.

Ben of Yharss – Eighth of the Guard. Age 15.5. Full name: Rueisvben'el Yharss-Rawshuen.

The Arkiveis: Keepers of Memories

Grover of Paragon – was once the Arkivy of Trauvo. When the Arkivy position opened up in Eyo'el, he got it. Now, he's considered the Prime Arkivy.

Eishal of Trauvo – is actually the oldest of the Arkiveis, even though Grover considers himself to be the oldest. Knew LanSoren quite well.

Lokasi of Dysarda – the current Arkivy, for the city of Dysarda. Kent's father. Has tended all active Arkivaras, except for the one in Eyo'el.

Drauggen of Veldar – descendant of the first Arkivy.

Ragaz of Kirja – the Arkivy of Kirja. The shortest and stoutest of the Arkiveis. He's also the Keeper to Gayza. The Arkivara there is thought to be dormant. That's why there are only seven Arkiveis.

Yevolta of Bethsaide – tends the youngest Arkivara. Calmest of the Arkiveis. Well acquainted with Musgrae.

Nyrim of Yharss – the youngest Arkivy. Age 20. He and Ben were raised as brothers, even though they are not blood brothers.

The King's Advisers:

Zepharre of Paragon – head adviser to Talok. Grew up with Ryco and EmiKal, in The Eye of Paragon.

EmiKal of Trauvo – secondary King's Adviser. Though he grew up in Eyo'el, he moved to Trauvo after finishing Guard School.

City Warriors:

Zepharre of Paragon – also the City Warrior of Eyo'el.

Symovi of Yharss – both the Warrior & Medic of Yharss. Raised Nyrim and Ben as his own sons.

City Architects:

Khyra of Paragon – the Head City Architect. Oversees the cities' innovations, primarily in Eyo'el. Once she turns sixteen, she gains her full authority as the Head Architect.

Eva & Dhavin of Paragon – Khyra's parents, who are often traveling. Architects to both Yharss & Dysarda.

Greyvons, in order of age

Matriarch Shena – deceased. Died in the War of Ichors Von.

Merlynite of Vondurheil – born in the same generation as Jasper.

Oldest member of Jasper's personal Von pack of Thedaesiim. Droediin is the last of his living offspring.

Jasper of Vondurheil – the current Alpha of the Greyvons. Was well acquainted with LanSoren.

Mekka of the Vons – one of the last alpha candidates still competing for the title.

Rorka of Pariah – one of the few matriarch candidates to have existed, since the death of Shena. Has her own pack called Theocktras.

Droediin, Son of Merlynite – Mekka's last competitor for the title. Eighth son of an eighth son.

Taeso – one of the newest members of Jasper's Thedaesiim. Gemma's favorite Vonsai.

Dragons (dyns)

BlacKaidyns:

Reign – was the dragon of the former king, Sosha. Now he calls himself Talok's Dragon.

Scepter – Zymarc's head dragon. Also Reign's older brother. Leads the Vitasadyns and their Vitiosyn riders.

Mystadyns:

Claudys – a Mystadyn who frequents Paragon often. Well acquainted with Siege.

Rubidyns:

Matriarch Fayel – deceased. Died in the War of Ichors Von. Farivoo Eldyn was named after her: Fayel's River Food for the Dragons.

Rentwar – King of the Rubidyns.

Rentwar's Recruit – previously under Rentwar's pupilage. Has been promoted for doing Rentwar's bidding.

Other Species:

AshCrawft – ancestor of the GreyLyres, of Grawllik.

Ayzareel – younger brother to AshCrawft. Ancestor of the Darklyres.

Grawllik – a GreyLyre. Technically a distant cousin to the present-day Darklyres.

Horses (EquiNeins) & Hybrids

Awngeleik – the dragon-horse (Equidyn). Was given to LanSoren, as a sign of goodwill from Zymarc of Vitiosus. Since LanSoren's death, King Zymarc has been demanding that she be returned to him.

Brash – the horse with broken wings. Was the first of the horses Tyler healed. Ended up being Ben's companion horse, for the journey to Yharss.

Nebukahn – half Greyvon, half nein. Mekka's cousin. Often travels with the youngest Jokryn brother.

Sorsryns

Withrasyns:

Avilon of Paragon – last living Withrasyn. No one's seen her for quite some time.

Awleesia of Waykron – former queen to the Withrasyns. Negotiated with King Kailon, to secure a new home for her women. Knew Gyronawv and King Jzorrdawv. Was also well acquainted with Soren.

Gaula – Withrasyn Ancestor of the Darklyres. Partner to Ayzareel. Considered the first official Dragon's Mistress.

King Morseif – last Withrasyn King. Married to Awleesia of Waykron. Had many children. Only his daughters lived on, to have families in Paragon and elsewhere.

Monel – first Withrasyn King. Brother to Soren and Nyxane.

Soren of the Monel – a Sorsryn of Old (a Sorshrynak). Able to meddle with time. Revealed his identity to Gemma, when she was a little girl. Able to interact with LanSoren. When summoned from the past, he's able to interact with what's around him. Knew Adair Galloway.

Onyx Sorsryns:

Casseil – Setharyn's mother, who died in childbirth. ReNovak's one and only wife.

King ReNovak – current Onyx King, when Tyler and Gemma visit Muraine.

Prince Lemawr – Gyron's nephew. Adopted son of the Laykonian King, Lemara.

Prince Setharyn – King ReNovak's only child. Died from a Vitiosus spell. Had the Vardiya's Mark on his forehead, at birth.

Siveyra Gyronawv (Gyron) – Warrior of the Nyxane. Bound to serve the current Onyx King.

Zenzar – a young Onyx Warrior.

The House of Dovak: line of succession, ending with ReNovak

Nyxane – first Onyx King.

Dovak – daughter of Nyxane.

Siveyra-lord Novak – only child of Dovak's. Father of Divoldane.

Divoldane – daughter to Novak. Mother to RethnoBane.

RethnoBane – second son of Divoldane. Father of Aygawnax.

Aygawnax – only son to RethnoBane. Father of Jzorrdawv and ReNovak. Was the Onyx King, when Gyron became the Warrior of the Nyxane.

Jzorrdawv – ReNovak's older brother. Married to **Ayna**. Never had children. Died on the battlefield. **ReNovak** inherited his throne.

Other Sorsryns:

Dezarin of the Aeown – a Siveyra thrice over (Diveyra). Clan: Emerald.

Evie – Rozeth's cousin. Deceased.

Rozeth of the Aeown – a former apprentice of Dezarin's. Was a twin apprentice, partnered with Ryco. Clan: Emerald.

Vayohl – Lemawr's mother. Former lover to Gyron's younger brother. Mother of Princess Krina. King Lemara claims that she's been missing for ten years.

Vit'Dod – last Deathasyn King. Knew RayVora and Soren well. Was executed by Zymarc.

Vosh-Vendei – a Sorshrynak. Half-brother to the Geldryn twins. Clan: Deathasyn.

Vitiosyns, in order of rank

King Deezalo – deceased. Born as a Geldryn Sorsryn, he became the first Vitiosyn.

King Zymarc of Vitiosus – leads the Vitiosyn Clan. In a former century, he killed King Vit'Dod and the rest of the royal family of Deathasyns. As such, he was able to take over most of the Deathasyn Clan.

Prince-General Azabahk – Zymarc's right-hand man. Underwent ReNovamen. His knowledge spans far back into the past.

Belzara – a Prime-Warrior. Also underwent ReNovamen. In a former life, she served King Deezalo himself. She was once favored by Zymarc. Something she did turned him against her, but not enough for Zymarc to have her executed.

Caleiso – former Apprentice to Vitiosus. Now promoted to the rank of Prime-Warrior. Perhaps Tyler's most hated enemy.

Belzara's Beloved – a small Vitiosyn woman who was dispatched by the Onyx Warriors under Gyron's command. Rather than leave her in the forest near Eyo'el, Gyron and the warriors take her to the Onyx territory of the Nyxane.

Jokryns, in order of age – all are Siveyras (older than 1,000 years)

RayVora – Queen Mother to the Jokryns. Was partner to a Metimoran named GrawVadian. She is primarily Amethyst and Deathasyn, but has bits of all the Sorsryn clans in her lineage.

Paydinn – Keeper to the Watchman's Log—a Book of Time. RayVora and GrawVadian's firstborn son. He's considered to be the Father of the

Jokryn, for the many children he has helped to produce. His eyes change color, with his mood.

YaeVorkk – the second of RayVora's sons. Has taken up the trade of being a mentor. He has had many apprentices over the centuries. Currently, he's under a sleep curse. No one is sure where he is, but it's suspected that he's in a Vitiosyn prison.

Zeekryn – the third of RayVora's sons. He has been a warrior. Now, he's a scholar. Very knowledgeable in many things. But he has no interest in getting involved in the war, and no interest in starting a family like his brother Paydinn. However, he's willing to travel with the Paragonians, and guide them through the Metsundai (Forest Lake).

Craesha – the youngest of RayVora's sons. Very mischievous, but also powerful. Most of his magic is used for toying with those around him, especially his older brothers. Often goes out on adventures with Nebukahn. Doesn't take much seriously.

Metimoras, in order of age

GrawVadian – former King of the Metimorans. Abdicated the throne, around the time Deezalo's Regime reached its height. Was keeper to the most powerful of the six Books of Time he helped to create: The Grandmaster Journal. No one has seen it, since he died. His family believes that his killer holds that first created Book of Time.

Queen Iissa – current Monarch of the Metimorans. She was blessed by GrawVadian, to the lead the Metimoras. She knows the Jokryn family quite well, as they come to pay homage to GrawVadian's former status as king.

Illveidra – Paydinn's first wife, now deceased, or rather in the process of a transformation.

Giveidra – Paydinn's second wife, who's now his first wife.

Laykonians, in order of rank

Liffa-Aroh – Lemara's father. Originally from the world of Jextoran.

King Lemara – Ruler of the Deep. King of the Laykons (Laepurians). Lives in the underwater city of Deivahl. Father of Princess Krina. Married to Vayohl.

Princess Krina – King Lemara's firstborn.

Brinkorr (Brink) – a teacher to the young Laykonians. Was the former bodyguard of Prince Lemawr, before Lemawr left Deivahl. He's also the only one who cooks King Lemara's dinner. When necessary, he's head warrior to the Laykonians.

Broena – in charge of Princess Krina's intellectual education, and training in warfare.

Dae'loog Dauger – a Water Dragon (Legharian). The official greeter to those on the surface looking to visit the city of Deivahl. During harvest time, Laykonians do not accept visitors.

LeiHymurs – one of the races that came with Liffa-Aroh from Jextoran. Larger and more animalistic than Laepurians. They visit Deivahl often, and are especially fond of playing games with the Laepurians, in the Drivvell Den.

LeiHymids – mutated LeiHymurs, adapted to live in deeper waters for long periods of time. They never visit the surface. They merely travel up to Deivahl, when necessary. Otherwise, they live deep in Muraine's ocean.

Notes about Laykonians:

Lemara, Krina, Brink, Broena, and other Laykonians like them in appearance are considered to be Laepurians. Legharians are the dragons. LeiHymurs are a six-limbed species adapted to prefer water, even though they can survive on the surface for a time. They are the defense of Deivahl's waters. In times of the harvest, they are the gatherers. LeiHymids are a subspecies of LeiHymurs that evolved over time to be able to live deeper in the ocean. The closest they can get to the surface is the city of Deivahl.

Spirits, Vardiyas, & Such

Spirits:

Aeowneis – Tree Stag. Holds the essence of light, and memories of life.

Sivondel – The Black Flame. Spirit of the Black Dragon. Holds the keys of death. Life essence is given to him, through the flesh and bones of the deceased.

Vardiya(s):

Aysivak – a Vardiya. Able to wield time. Introduced in Chapter 3 of Volume I. Named, in Chapter 2 of Volume II.

Others:

Gatroes (Gatro) – six-limbed, hairless beasts. They prey on Darklyre offspring, primarily. Night creatures (nocturnal). The preferred food source of the Greyvons.

The Phantom – mentioned by LanSoren, in entry 233 of the English journal. LanSoren felt he had to find the truth of what and whom the phantom is, to escape his fate of death.

Darklyres, in order by clan then rank

Clan Ayzaga (Ayzagauns):

SynKievas of Ayzaga – name means Cheater of Black Heaven, or Marauder of Death (Sylvadyn meaning). He has stolen a whole armory from Arsyn, over the past five years. Also has an obsession over knowing a person's lineage, and the meanings of names.

Clan Jhire (Jhiresons):

Jhire – the firstborn son of Gaula and Ayzareel. Deceased. At some point, he lost one of his wings. He was the founder of a city named in his honor. The term Parasogyn was re-coined to Pairos, by Jhire. A golden likeness of him and his seven siblings reside within the Palace of RawZend.

Arsyn of the Jhire Clan – Leading Sentinel of Jhire. A well sought after widower, among all Darklyres. Older than he looks. As such, he has a sensitivity to dawn's light that younger, more evolved Darklyres do not.

Skylin of the Jhire Clan – Arsyn's only child. The same age as Tyler and Gemma: 14. Loves history, enchanting weapons, and winning bets. Talks a lot.

Clan RawZend (RawZendians):

Khrendawll – Aygor's older brother, who abdicated the throne. He and Grawllik's father set off ten to eleven years ago to hunt down certain items. Aygor hasn't heard from either of them, in eight years.

King Aygorinaith of RawZend (Aygor) – the current King of Clan RawZend. Resides in the city of Grevagg. Is considered the head of the three Darklyrian kings. As such, it is his responsibility to oversee all clan events and various gatherings. Though he is not partnered to anyone, he takes in orphans and troubled children. In Volume II, he has a total of 10 wards. He assigns trainers, to oversee the wards' daily care. Past age 16, they no longer have trainers.

Seqwhyett of RawZend – newest Crown Sentinel. Age 20. Used to be one of the King's Wards. As such, he knows all of them rather well. King Aygor gave him the named blade: Veldakryn.

Deamond of RawZend (Dea) – the oldest of the wards. Age 19. Nicknames include: Demon Dea, the demon, Sentinel's Tease, etc. Is said to be fierce, after waking from death. Highly intelligent and well-read. Also very devious. Aspires to be a Crown Sentinel.

Keturah of RawZend (Ketty) – second oldest ward. Age 13. Constantly disobeying King Aygor. Generally combative with others.

Sonya of RawZend – third oldest ward. Age 12. Easily frightened. More levelheaded than Ketty. Genuinely cares for others, even if she's just met them.

Litreez of Grevagg – Keturah's trainer. Instructs a handful of Darklyre girls, but oversees the education of many residing within the city of Grevagg.

About the Author

J.R. Vaineo is a self-published indie author, residing in Salt Lake City, UT. In 2018, she published her first book: Kings of Muraine. When she's not writing, she and her husband, Jessie, have many adventures together. Mostly in cooking, hiking, photography, analytical talks, and fawning over their two adorable fur-babies.

While J.R. Vaineo writes mostly fantasy fiction—combining elements of epic, portal, paranormal, and dark fantasy—she enjoys reading all genres; except, perhaps, for horror stories. After finishing a creative writing program, through the Institute of Children's Literature, she continued to improve her craft of writing. In 2013, she graduated with her AA degree in psychology. During that time, she expanded on many things, especially focusing on what would prove invaluable for fleshing out characters and plot twists. What started out as a writing prompt, in 2005, has now become a nine book series she is currently working on: The Journals of Ravier. Sometimes, she is quite jealous of the characters' abilities, found within her own writing. If that is a sign of anything, it is this: Obsession.

You can connect with me on:

- https://www.jrvaineo.com
- https://twitter.com/JRVaineo
- https://www.facebook.com/j.r.vaineo
- https://www.instagram.com/j.r.vaineo
- https://www.goodreads.com/JRVaineo
- https://www.bookbub.com/authors/j-r-vaineo

Subscribe to my newsletter:

- https://www.jrvaineo.com/newsletter

Also by J.R. Vaineo

The Journals of Ravier books are about finding yourself amidst the losses, victories, and journeys in life. You begin to discover, through personal trials, who you are at your core. Come join Tyler Ravier on his winding path to an important truth: Why did his father have to die?

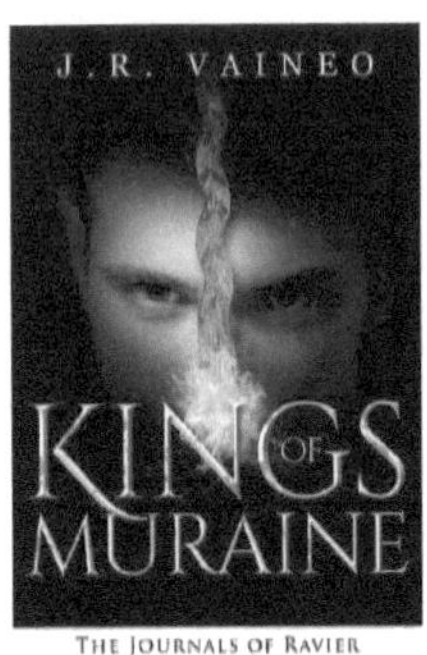

Kings of Muraine – Special Edition
https://www.jrvaineo.com/where-to-purchase
That night changed my life, forever. I saw them. Two strangers from another world. The one with fangs claimed to be a king. But he was a young king, at best. The King of Paragon. He broke the news to me. My dad wasn't from Earth. Instead, he was from a world filled with magic: Muraine. His other home.

The Special Edition for Volume I has the Murainian Calendar, as well as tables that list off the members of the Paragonian Sovereignty.